"Felicity?" Jake murmured sleepily. "Is that you, sweetheart? What's the matter, are you sick?"

She stood, riveted, staring in awe at the Adonis sitting in the bed. The dim glow of the waning fire cast giant shadows across the chiseled planes of his bronzed chest. His thick, chestnut hair was tousled, his eyes limpid with sleep. It was several moments before she could find her voice. "No, Jake," she whispered. "I'm fine. I came in here to—anyway, I just wanted to thank you, and . . ."

"And what, Felicity?" he asked quietly.

"Well, in my family, we had a tradition that a person must receive at least one kiss on their birthday to ensure a year of good health and prosperity."

He looked at her, his hazel eyes fathomless. "Are you goin' to kiss me, Felicity?"

"Yes," she breathed . . .

Silver Caress

CHARLOTTE SIMMS

AVON BOOKS ◆ NEW YORK

AVON BOOKS
A division of
The Hearst Corporation
105 Madison Avenue
New York, New York 10016

Copyright © 1990 by Jane Kidder and Charla Chin
Inside cover author photograph copyright © 1990 by Michel Karin Tritt
Published by arrangement with the authors
Library of Congress Catalog Card Number: 90-92983
ISBN: 0-380-76179-3

First Avon Books Printing: August 1990

AVON TRADEMARK REG. U.S. PAT. OFF. AND IN OTHER COUNTRIES, MARCA REGISTRADA, HECHO EN U.S.A.

Printed in the U.S.A.

RA 10 9 8 7 6 5 4 3 2 1

To Allen

Chapter 1

"Please, please don't let anyone know I'm here!"

Sister Fidelis gaped at the young man hiding under her bed. Bending down to get a closer look at her uninvited guest, she gasped, "Who are you? How did you get in . . ." The door to her cubicle swung open and the novice whirled around to face the steely-eyed gaze of the Reverend Mother.

"Sister Fidelis, do you have a *man* in your room?" Mother's voice was incredulous, accusing.

"A man?" Fidelis squeaked. "Of course not, Reverend Mother! Whatever would make you think that?"

"I distinctly heard a man's voice through your door." Reverend Mother's tone was icy as she walked further into the room, her eyes sweeping the small chamber. Marching up to the bed, the old nun sat down hard on the thin mattress, eliciting a startled grunt from the man beneath.

Sister Fidelis exhaled a tiny, distressed moan as Reverend Mother unceremoniously hauled the tall, lanky figure from under the cot.

"Sister Fidelis! What is the meaning of this?"

"I . . . I don't know, Mother. I never saw this man before in my life!"

The nun's gaze riveted the novice. "I am grievously disappointed. Of all the women in this convent, you are the last one from whom I would have

suspected this type of behavior. I will see you in my
office at eight o'clock tomorrow morning."

Turning on her heel, Reverend Mother grabbed
the hapless man's arm and marched him out of the
cubicle, closing the door behind her with a resounding slam.

Felicity Howard sat on a hard wooden bench in the
Philadelphia train station and tried, for the hundredth
time, to make sense of the shambles of her life. Sister
Fidelis was no more. Dismissed, disgraced, removed
from the rolls of the holy sisterhood.

Ever since the age of ten, when she had gone to live
at the Convent of St. Margaret's, all she had dreamed
of was becoming a nun. The older sisters always assured her she had great promise. Pious, compassion-
ate, modest, resolute—all the qualities the church
hoped to find in a novice were inborn in Felicity.

So how had this happened? Why was she sitting on
this bench waiting to board a train for Colorado and
an unknown future as a miner's housekeeper? The
past few weeks were hardly more than a nightmarish
blur in her mind. The strange young man in her room,
her tearful confrontation with the disbelieving and un-
forgiving Reverend Mother, the desperation of knowing she had only three months to find a new situation
for herself, and this morning's final, devastating departure from the convent. Oh, why didn't she wake
up to discover this whole fiasco was only a bad dream?
But the reality of the small bag by her side, the train
ticket clutched in her icy hand, and the frayed and
crumpled letter inside her reticule made it painfully
clear that she was wide awake . . . and facing the most
frightening moment of her life.

The letter. Her entire future hinged on one sheet
of paper. Although she had memorized every word
Joseph McCullough had written since then, she
pulled that first well-worn epistle out of her bag and
read it again:

Dear Miss Howard,

Thank you for replying to my advertisement with the Hand and Heart Lovelorn Agency. I was surprised and pleased to hear from you.

I would be delighted to have you come work for me as a housekeeper. Although I registered with the agency to find a wife, all I'm really looking for is someone who can cook, clean, and help me keep my business records in order.

I wouldn't be honest if I didn't warn you that I live in a very rough and lawless area. I am a miner in Silverton, Colorado, and live a good distance from any real civilization.

I have a small cabin between Silverton and Howardsville. My mine promises to pay well and I devote most of my time to working it. I also like to garden and have a large vegetable patch that I tend in my spare time.

To set your mind at ease, I want you to know that you will have my protection and utmost respect. The fact that you have left the holy order of the sisterhood is your business and you do not need to worry that I will press you for explanations. I am a God-fearing man, past my middle years, don't drink much, and am respected in the community. I hope you will decide to come to work for me. If you do, send me a telegram and I'll send a train ticket and some traveling money. The only thing I ask is that you promise to stay for at least one year. Train fares are expensive and your promise will assure me that you will be here long enough for my investment to be worthwhile. If I don't hear from you in the next month, I'll assume you've had a change of heart.

Sincerely,
Joseph McCullough
Silver Lady Mine
Silverton, Colorado

Felicity drew a ragged breath as she returned the letter to her bag. The possible drawbacks to this situation were endless and terrifying. Mr. McCullough *sounded* like a nice man, but what could one really tell from a few letters? The man could turn out to be a monster. He could work her like a slave and refuse to pay her. She could end up trapped in the middle of nowhere with no way to get back to civilization. He could make demands on her, insist that she be intimate with him. He said the town was lawless; perhaps it was a veritable pit of corruption. What if—

She bit her lower lip to control her rising panic. Maybe she shouldn't go. It wasn't too late to change her mind. She still had a small portion of her inheritance from her parents in the First National Bank of Philadelphia. Would it be enough to allow her to find a room in a boardinghouse in Philadelphia and continue to look for work? No. She had been over this before. There were almost no opportunities for a young, inexperienced woman in the big city. The only places willing to hire her were the textile mills, and anything was better than the slavelike conditions the mills imposed on their female employees. Joseph McCullough was her only chance for a decent future. Besides, she had given her word. She had to go.

"All aboard!"

The conductor's voice boomed like a tolling bell. It was time. Get on the train, Felicity, she commanded herself. Reverend Mother always said your only failing was impetuosity. Come on, girl. This is a great adventure, so brace up and be impetuous!

She picked up her small bag and marched across the huge train station. With determination, she boarded the westbound express for Chicago and settled herself in a seat. A twinge of unexpected anticipation coursed through her as the train pulled away from the station, and raising her chin, she cast her eyes toward the West—and her destiny.

Chapter 2

$\sim\!\!\infty\!\!\sim$

Five weary days later, Felicity boarded the narrow-gauge train in Durango, Colorado, for the final three-hour trip into Silverton. Except for one night spent in a Chicago hotel and another in Pueblo, Colorado, where she got off the Santa Fe Railway, she had spent the entire five-day journey sitting up on the train. Exhausted as she was, her nervous excitement at finally reaching Silverton and meeting Mr. McCullough made the idea of catching a nap impossible.

She squeezed into the crowded passenger car and quietly took a seat. Looking around at her fellow passengers, she was dismayed to see that she was the only woman on board. She stared out the window and tried to be inconspicuous.

As the various trains had moved west, more women had departed and fewer had boarded. Although she had admired the stylishly clad women who had ridden through Pennsylvania and Ohio, she was now grateful for the obscurity that her wardrobe of gray, brown, and black afforded her. It hadn't been easy to find a dressmaker in Philadelphia willing to make clothing to her rigid specifications, but Felicity had been adamant in her demands. She was appalled to see how the new, low-waisted suit jackets hugged the body, accentuating the bust and waist, and demanded that the jackets of all her new traveling suits be made at least two sizes too large.

Unaware of how outlandish the baggy clothes looked on her, she was delighted with her new wardrobe. She wanted to make a good impression on Joseph McCullough and used the layover time in Durango to change into a fresh, dove-gray velvet suit. The velvet was much too warm for the July weather, but she thought she looked very fashionable. The outfit was severely plain except for the white, stand-up collar of her blouse which showed above the collar of her jacket. Of necessity, the skirt fit perfectly. The front was tiered in a pretty, apron-like drapery and the material gathered in the back to form a small bustle.

She looked up as a few more men pushed their way onto the train, some taking seats, some just wandering around, slapping backs and passing a liquor bottle to friends. After riding all the way across the United States, she knew this was not normal behavior aboard a train and she became increasingly apprehensive.

Just then, the conductor stepped into the car to collect tickets and proudly announced, "Welcome to this grand, historical event. This here is the first-ever passenger train into Silverton!"

"Whooee!" guffawed a bearded old man up front. "Of course it is! Why, me and Willie came all the way down from Silverton just so's we could ride this here new contraption back up!"

A thundering cheer went up among the jubilant men and more whiskey bottles were passed.

This is no place for me, thought Felicity with dismay. I've got to get off. These men are all intoxicated! As she hurriedly rose from her seat, a brightly clad woman sat down beside her, effectively blocking her way to the aisle. Felicity sank back down, feeling slightly better now that there was another woman on board, even though her outfit did seem rather . . . garish.

"Hi there, sweetie!" the woman sang out cheerfully. Felicity's gaze swept over the woman and she stifled the gasp that rose to her lips. She realized she was staring, but she had never in her life seen hair quite that shade of red. With a radiant smile, the woman grabbed her hand and pumped it in a vigorous handshake. "My name's Roxie, honey, and who might you be?"

Despite all the heavy rouge and eye makeup, the woman's gaze was friendly and sincere. "Sis . . . uh, Felicity Howard, ma'am," she answered politely.

"Felicity!" hooted Roxie. "Well, ain't that sweet and proper. What's a little schoolmarm like you doin' with this rowdy bunch?" She flung her arm wide to gesture at the boisterous crowd of men.

"Why, I'm going to Silverton."

"Sure picked some time to go, honey." Roxie chortled. "And what would you be doin' in Silverton? We already got us a teacher. You gonna marry the preacher?"

Felicity blushed. "No, ma'am." Despite the woman's bizarre appearance, her friendliness was somehow comforting and Felicity found herself relaxing. She studied Roxie's outrageous scarlet and purple ruffled dress and decided it must be some kind of costume for the celebration. Felicity couldn't take her eyes off the bodice; it was cut so low that the woman's ample bosom looked like it would tumble out if she took a deep breath. "I'm going to Silverton to meet Mr. Joseph McCullough," she ventured shyly. "He has hired me to be his housekeeper. Do you know him?"

"Well, I'll be. Sure, I know Joe, but I've been out of town for a while so I'm behind on the gossip. Didn't know he'd sent for a housekeeper." Felicity watched, amazed, as Roxie took a long puff on a thin, brown cigarette and gave the bodice an impatient tug. She turned her head from Felicity to politely blow the smoke in the opposite direction. The purple plume in her upswept curls tickled Felicity's nose and to her mortification, she sneezed.

"Oh, excuse me, Miss Roxie." Felicity turned an embarrassed pink.

"Damn thing!" Roxie reached up and yanked the offending feather from her hair. "Sorry 'bout that, honey. By the way, it ain't Miss Roxie, just Roxie."

What a wonderfully strange woman, Felicity mused. "Roxie, forgive me for being so forward, but what is that costume you're wearing?"

The train gave a sudden lurch and the noisy crowd burst into renewed cheers, making it necessary for Roxie to yell to be heard. "Costume? This ain't no costume. These are my workin' clothes." At Felicity's blank look, Roxie continued, "Come on, honey, you know, workin' clothes! I entertain the men. These here miners get mighty lonesome."

Felicity's brows drew together in perplexity. "Entertain the men?"

"Yeah, you know . . . *entertain* them!" Roxie wiggled her eyebrows meaningfully and looked at Felicity for a glimmer of understanding. Seeing none, she frowned and said, "Look, sweetie, how can I put this? I sing at the Last Chance Saloon and serve drinks, and . . . entertain the men who have some money to spend."

Felicity's emerald eyes widened and she gasped as the woman's meaning finally sank in.

"Now you got it, honey." Roxie laughed, nodding her head vigorously. "If you ain't the most innocent little thing I've ever met. Where do you come from anyway, Felicity?"

She hesitated for a moment and then admitted, "St. Margaret's Convent in Philadelphia."

It was Roxie's turn to be wide-eyed. "You're kiddin'! I've never met *anybody* from an honest-to-God convent! You're not some kind of nun or missionary or somethin', are you?"

Felicity blanched. Here it was. All the way across the country, she had pondered how she would answer this question. Unable to come to any decision, she had finally decided to wait until the situation presented itself. Now the moment had arrived. In a barely audible voice, she responded, "Not anymore. I . . . I was a nun, but something happened that made me leave my order."

Roxie's eyebrows rose with interest. "I didn't know nuns *could* leave," she remarked. "I thought bein' a nun was sort of like a life sentence in prison. Once you were there, you were there."

Felicity couldn't help but smile. "I assure you, a convent isn't a prison. And being a nun can be a wonderful, fulfilling life."

Roxie's curiosity was now thoroughly aroused. "Honey, it sounds like you didn't want to leave. What happened? Did you get tossed out for somethin'?"

Roxie instantly regretted her bold words when she heard Felicity's sudden, sharp intake of breath. "I'm sorry, sweetie," she said. "It ain't none of my business and I shouldn't pry."

Felicity's next words were spoken so softly that Roxie had to lean toward her to hear. "I did get thrown out."

"You did? What did you do?"

"Reverend Mother caught me with a man in my room."

"What?" Roxie asked in astonishment. "Who was he? Did you have a beau on the side?"

Felicity's head snapped up. "Certainly not! I just came into my cubicle one night and he was hiding under my bed. I had never seen him before in my life!"

Roxie looked at her in bewilderment. "I don't understand. If you didn't know him, why did you get tossed out?"

"You don't know Reverend Mother, Roxie. She said that since I couldn't prove I didn't know him, and since he refused to admit who he was really there to see, that she had to make an example of me. I don't really think she believed that he and I were involved, but she said that if she allowed me to go unpunished, then all the novices might think they could get away with the same thing.''

"Well, it sounds mighty unfair to me," declared Roxie. "I thought in America you're innocent till you're proved guilty."

"Unfortunately, that's not the way it is in a convent." Felicity sighed. "The ironic thing is, there were novices who had been forced into the convent against their will and maintained relationships with old suitors. But I certainly wasn't one of them. Look at me, Roxie. Do I look like the type of woman a man would risk arrest to see?"

Roxie studied Felicity closely. The girl was right. There was nothing remarkable about her looks. Her height was average and her figure appeared to be slim, but who could tell under that baggy suit she was wearing? Her tawny hair was pulled tightly back into a prim chignon, effectively subduing its luxurious abundance. The only thing that distinguished Felicity were her large, green eyes. They sparkled like emeralds and were fringed with lush, sandy lashes.

"Well," said Roxie pragmatically, "life ain't always fair, that's for sure. But who knows? Maybe you'll be happy out here in the wilds. Joe's a real nice man and I'm sure he'll treat you fine. But you better brace yourself, Felicity, 'cause compared to what you're used to, Silverton's gonna be a real shock!"

Impulsively, Felicity reached over and touched Roxie's hand. "I can't tell you how nice it is to have someone to talk to," she confided. "I hope you and I will become good friends."

Roxie's face broke into a delighted grin. "You know somethin', honey? I have a feelin' we just might!"

A moment passed as the women sat watching the chaos around them. "Tell me about Silverton," Felicity suggested. "I have no idea what to expect, and after seeing this crowd of men, I'm feeling a little nervous."

"Oh, don't worry about them none," Roxie reassured her. "They're just celebratin' the train's maiden run. They get a little loud and some of 'em drink too much, but they won't hurt you." Roxie laughed. "Wait till you see how quiet the town will be tomorrow, what with all of 'em nursin' their headaches. Why, you'll think you're back in that convent!"

The rest of the trip passed amicably as Roxie described Silverton and some of the town's more colorful inhabitants. The train finally pulled into the station and as the two girls disembarked, Felicity glanced nervously around the crowded platform.

"Is Joe McCullough meetin' you here, sweetie?" Roxie asked.

"Yes, that's what he said in his letter."

"Well then, don't worry. I'm sure he's here somewhere." Roxie scanned the large crowd of men. "I don't see him nowhere, though. You want to wait over at the Last Chance with me?"

The conductor handed Felicity her bag and she set it next to her on the station platform. "Thank you, but no. He might just be a little late and I wouldn't want to miss him. There's such a big crowd here that he may be having trouble getting up to the platform."

"You're probably right," Roxie agreed. "Listen, Felicity, I gotta go, but if he don't show up, you just walk down to that corner over there and turn down Greene Street." Roxie pointed the way. "The Last Chance is in the middle of the block. You can't miss it."

"Thank you very much, Roxie. I hope I'll see you again soon," said Felicity sincerely. The other woman smiled and waved as she disappeared into the crowd.

An hour went by with no sign of Mr. Mc-

Cullough. Felicity paced the now-empty platform and, finally, walked up to the ticket window. "Has there been a Mr. McCullough inquiring about a Miss Felicity Howard?"

The man behind the grille looked up with a bored expression. "Nope."

"Do you know Joseph McCullough?"

"Lady, I don't know nobody here. This is my first day on the job and my second day in town."

"Oh, I see. Well, thank you anyway." Feeling lonely, she picked up her bag and headed down the platform, trying to decide if she should go over to the saloon and find Roxie or continue to wait. What if he's changed his mind about wanting a housekeeper? she thought despairingly. What if he's not coming at all? *Then* what am I going to do?

Willing herself to remain calm, she took a deep breath. No, Mr. McCullough was much too nice in his letters to do something like that. Maybe he got confused about what day I was arriving. Maybe he thinks I'm coming tomorrow. That thought made her feel slightly better, and she looked down the street to see if there was anywhere she might go to send him a message: a hotel, perhaps.

She didn't see a hotel. What she did see was a small platform not far down the street with a crowd gathered around it, listening to a speaker.

Suddenly a group of about ten young boys streaked helter-skelter through the gathering, shouting and chasing a squealing, greased pig. Men laughed uproariously and moved aside for the rowdy children. A gun exploded and Felicity jumped, closing her eyes as her hand flew to her heart. Two men riding burros came racing down the center of the street right into the middle of the throng of people and the pig-chasing boys. A couple of drunks joined the melee and ran after the burros, yelling and shooting their pistols. Complete pandemonium broke out as the crowd tried to disperse to avoid being shot or run down.

Felicity flattened her body against the wall of the train station and crossed herself. "Saints preserve me, what kind of place *is* this?" She was so preoccupied with the bedlam in the street that she failed to notice a disheveled drunk who shuffled up behind her. A sudden sharp pain made her flinch and grab for the back of her skirt. Rubbing her abused bottom, she turned around to face her assailant and found herself nose to nose with a sour-breathed miner.

"Now, where did you co . . . come from?" he slurred.

Felicity quickly moved back from the reeking creature and stepped down onto a well-dressed stranger's foot.

Whirling around, she cried, "Oh, I'm sorry, sir!" Her drunken admirer lunged forward to give her another pinch and Felicity nearly toppled forward in her effort to escape his grasping fingers.

The other man's hand shot out to steady her. "Whoa there, miss. Are you all right?"

At that moment, Felicity wished the boardwalk would simply open and swallow her up. Finally catching her breath, she looked up and answered weakly, "I'm fine, sir, thank you."

The miner stumbled forward, a stupid grin on his face. "Wanna go to a . . . a party, lady?"

"Amos, get on with you," the dark-clad gentleman chastised roughly. "Go home now, you're drunk. Can't you see this is a real lady?"

The miner gave Felicity a befuddled look and wove off down the platform.

Felicity turned frightened eyes to her rescuer. He was of medium height and slim, with coal-black hair which was slicked back from his forehead. His eyes were as dark as his hair and sparkled with an almost diabolical mischief. A small, neatly trimmed mustache graced his thin-lipped, hard mouth. She noticed that one of his teeth was capped with gold. He was dressed in a black frock coat and trousers, and, except for the gleaming tooth, he looked blessedly respectable. Flashing her a charming smile, he inquired, "Ma'am, might you be Miss Felicity Howard?"

This can't be Joseph McCullough, Felicity thought. He's much too young.

As if reading her thoughts, the man said, "No, miss, I'm not Joe McCullough."

"I'm sorry, sir. I'm being rude. Yes, I am Felicity Howard. Did Mr. McCullough send you to meet me?"

"No, not exactly, ma'am." The man hesitated and Felicity thought he looked uncomfortable. "My name is Yancy Parnell. I own the Last Chance Saloon."

"Oh, I see," she responded lamely, not really understanding at all.

"When Roxie came in saying she'd met a lady on the train who was coming to Silverton to meet Joe McCullough, I thought I'd better come down here and get you."

"But whatever for, Mr. Parnell? Isn't Mr. McCullough coming?" Felicity was tired, confused, and fast giving way to panic. What was going on in this crazy place?

"Ma'am, I don't know how to tell you this, but Joe McCullough died two days ago."

She swayed and Parnell reached for her arm, as if thinking she was about to faint. She leaned against him weakly and clutched her throat. "Dear heavens," she murmured to herself. "I've come all this way. *Now* what am I going to do?"

Although he was a professional gambler, used to stifling his kinder impulses, Yancy Parnell felt a stab of pity for the young woman. He cleared his throat and continued, "Ah, ma'am, I know all about your arrangement with Joe. I reckon the whole town does." Felicity blushed to the roots of her hair. "Now, don't you worry," he continued. "Joe told us all about you leaving a convent and wanting to get a fresh start out here in Colorado. The whole town sympathizes with your situation. That's why I came down here when I heard you had arrived." Felicity stared at him blankly. "I figured I'd escort you over to the hotel."

She nodded and allowed him to take her arm. As they made their way along the crowded street, he explained that Joe McCullough had died in a mine explosion. Parnell stopped briefly and looked into Felicity's distraught face. "Now, ma'am," he said soothingly, "I know you feel like you're all alone here, but don't you worry. I'll get you settled at the hotel for the night and tomorrow we'll see about getting you back East."

Again, she gave a distracted nod. The thought of reboarding the train and facing the endless trip back to Philadelphia was almost more than she could bear. Not only that, but what was she going to do when she got there? She was so lost in her troubled thoughts that she didn't even notice when they entered the hotel.

"Sorry, Parnell, we're full up 'cause of the celebration. You're not gonna find a room anywhere tonight."

Felicity looked up and saw that they were standing before the hotel clerk. No rooms? she thought wearily. What next?

Yancy Parnell gave a disgruntled snort. "Come on, Henry, you've got to have something for the lady."

"I'm tellin' you, Parnell, we're full up."

"Wait a minute, Mr. Parnell," Felicity interrupted. "Mr. McCullough said he had a cabin. Could I perhaps go there to spend the night?"

Yancy looked into her beautiful, exhausted green eyes. The girl was far from pretty, but those eyes . . . a man could lose himself in those eyes. He seemed to contemplate her suggestion for a moment and then answered, "Joe's cabin is off by itself up in the mountains, ma'am. It's a good hour's drive over a rough road."

Felicity sighed. "Mr. Parnell, it can't be any worse up there than it is here in town."

As if to prove her point, a man stumbled through the hotel door and fell flat on his face. He grunted and then passed out where he lay.

"Well, you may have something there," Yancy said with a chuckle. He picked up her bag. "Come on, Miss Howard. My wagon is parked behind the Last Chance."

It was late afternoon when Felicity finally spotted a small cabin nestled back amidst the trees off the wagon trail. "Is that it, Mr. Parnell?"

"Yes, ma'am. We're here."

She looked up into his coal-black eyes and smiled. "I can't thank you enough for everything you've done for me today. You've been very kind."

"I was happy to oblige. Joe was a friend of mine." Parnell pulled the wagon off the trail and stopped in front of the tiny cabin. Walking around to where she sat, he reached up to help her down, and was amazed at how small her waist was beneath the camouflage of her voluminous jacket. He studied her intently for a moment before removing his hands, but she was too overwrought to notice his speculative expression.

She hurried up the path to the cabin door as Yancy swung her bag over the wagon's side. Reaching for the latch, she gasped in surprise as the door was abruptly opened from the other side. "Oh!" she gasped. "Who are you?"

Felicity found herself staring at the most handsome man she had ever seen. Heavily lashed hazel eyes gazed at her expectantly. Thick, chestnut-colored hair waved back from the man's wide brow. His nose was narrow, the nostrils slightly flaring, and his questioning smile bore a crescent-shaped dimple at one corner of his mouth. Felicity's eyes involuntarily swept downward past the square, lean jaw, and suddenly widened as she realized that his densely furred chest was bare. She felt herself blushing but couldn't seem to pull her eyes away from that broad expanse. The man was huge; what the romance novels that the students used to sneak into the convent described as brawny: tall, with bulging muscles. The thought struck her that she was standing before an Adonis, one far more handsome than any hero she had ever heard the girls whispering about. Her heart pounded in her ears and her chest felt tight when she tried to draw a breath. He was so . . . so male!

Her eyes continued their downward path, but suddenly came to an abrupt halt at the line where the man's dark, curling body hair disappeared into his slim-waisted Levi's. She flicked her gaze back up to his face, and, struggling to regain her composure, stammered, "I beg your pardon. I didn't know there was anyone here." She knew he must have noticed her reaction to him and turned an even deeper shade of crimson, feeling like a complete fool.

Jake McCullough grinned. He was well aware of the effect his looks had on women, especially the plain, nondescript type like the one before him. He looked over her shoulder and watched a dandified man walk up the path, carrying a suitcase. Jake frowned, wondering what was going on. Looking back at Felicity, he suddenly remembered that she had spoken to him. "Sorry, miss. I wasn't expectin' company. I'm Jake McCullough. Is there somethin' I can help you with? You folks lost?"

"Did you say Jake McCullough, mister?" Parnell asked.

"Yeah, that's what I said. Who are you?"

Yancy looked suspiciously at the larger man and said, "I've never heard of any Jake McCullough."

"Well, you have now," McCullough answered flatly.

"How come I've never seen you in town?" Yancy asked belligerently.

"I've been out of the country for about six months. Guess you weren't here when I left."

At Yancy's doubtful look, Jake's eyes narrowed and he demanded, "Just who the hell are you to question me? Joe McCullough was my pa. I just rode in yesterday and found out he'd been killed. Anythin' else you want to know?"

Felicity noticed that Yancy looked extremely unhappy about something. "How do we know you're not just some lousy claim jumper?" Parnell continued aggressively. "Joe never mentioned having a son, far as I know."

Jake McCullough's expression was stony. "Looks like you'll just have to take my word for it, don't it? Now suppose you tell me what you two want and then move on out of here. I'm not feelin' much like entertainin'."

Felicity finally found her voice and said, "We're sorry to disturb you, Mr. McCullough. My name is Felicity Howard and your father sent for me to be his housekeeper. I just arrived from Philadelphia today and found out about the accident. There were no rooms available at the hotel so I asked Mr. Parnell to bring me up here for the night."

"Pa hired a housekeeper?" Jake exclaimed. Then he burst into laughter. "That's a good one. Now, who are you really?"

"But, I told you, I . . ."

"Look, lady, I wasn't born yesterday."

"Now, wait a minute, McCullough," interrupted Yancy, "the lady's story is true. Everybody in town knew that Joe advertised for a wife with that Lovelorn Agency."

"Wife!" Jake bellowed. "She just said housekeeper!"

"Well, you see," began Felicity, "he and I had a special agreement that I would come here in the ca-

pacity of housekeeper. But he did originally adver-
tise for a bride.''

Jake snorted contemptuously. ''You expect me to
believe that? Pa was at least fifty-five. How old are
you? Sixteen? Seventeen?''

''Eighteen,'' she replied indignantly. Reaching
into her reticule, she pulled out a copy of the Hand
and Heart advertisement and Joe's first letter to her.
''Here, read these. They explain everything.''

Jake took the papers and quickly scanned them.
''I can't believe this, but it does look like Pa's writ-
in'. He must have been goin' daft to send for a
woman he'd never even met.''

''Your father was a lonely man, McCullough,''
Yancy countered.

Jake's glance flicked over Felicity insultingly and
he muttered, ''Yeah, he must've been *real* lonely.''

Felicity gasped at the affront as Jake shoved the
papers back into her hands. ''These make no difference. I don't want a wife *or* a housekeeper, so you
can go right back into town.''

''But, Mr. McCullough, there are no rooms in
town!'' she protested.

''That's not my problem, lady.'' Jake could see
the woman was near tears, but he remained un-
moved. ''Let's face it, you thought you could come
out here, cozy up to an old man, and end up with
a silver mine when he kicked the bucket. Looks to
me like you might be what we call a gold digger.''

Felicity sucked in her breath. She was angrier than
she'd ever been in her life. ''Look at me, Mr. Mc-
Cullough. Do I look like that kind of woman? How
dare you insult me like this? You're . . .'' She
plunged desperately into her limited vocabulary for
a word adequate to describe him. ''You're despicable!''

Jake's laugh was laced with scorn. ''I *am* lookin'
at you, lady, and it looks to me like this scheme of
yours is probably the only way you could ever hope
to get a man.'' The stricken look in the girl's large,

green eyes was so pathetic that Jake almost regretted his words. It wasn't his nature to be cruel. And why hadn't he noticed those eyes before? Oh, hell, he thought, it doesn't matter. She's just a little money-grubber come to prey on a poor old man's affections. She deserves whatever she gets.

"I ought to push your face in, McCullough," snarled Yancy.

"You can try it, mister, but if I was you, I wouldn't get myself all dirtied up for the likes of her."

Yancy took a threatening step forward, but Felicity grabbed his arm. "Please, Mr. Parnell, let's just go. It's been a long, terrible day."

As the couple retreated down the path, the girl looked back over her shoulder and Jake saw tears sparkling on her cheeks. He cursed loudly and slammed the cabin door.

Chapter 3

The slam of that door was like the swift demise of all the hopes Felicity had planned on this venture West. Now what am I going to do? she agonized. Go back East? And what if I do? What is there for me in Philadelphia? She sighed, her shoulders slumped in abject disappointment.

Yancy Parnell slapped the reins across the horse's rump and peered at Felicity out of the corner of his eye. He truly felt sorry for her, but he had problems of his own to deal with. Damn! Why hadn't he heard anything about Joe McCullough having a son? The mine, as Yancy had made it his business to find out, was registered solely in Joseph McCullough's name.

Hell! Just when I thought my way was finally clear to take over the Silver Lady, a prodigal son turns up, he thought in frustration. Yancy knew he hadn't made much of a first impression on Jake McCullough, but there was still a chance that Jake's interests might run elsewhere and that he'd be willing to sell out cheap. Despite old Joe's unwavering resistance to Yancy's offers to buy him out, it was doubtful that he had really known the Silver Lady's true value. Yancy also felt safe in assuming that Jake McCullough was as ignorant as his father.

Three months before, when he'd won the Dead Horse mine in a poker game, that had been exactly

21

what Yancy thought he'd won . . . a dead horse. Then, Jed Croft, his mine foreman, had come into the Last Chance one night and excitedly told Yancy he'd unearthed a huge, rich vein. Unfortunately, it was soon discovered that the vein's major lode emptied into the mine that Joe McCullough had set claim to on the other side of the slope. Swearing Jed to silence, Yancy had begun his crusade to purchase the Silver Lady, but Joe McCullough had been stubborn in his refusal to sell. Now Yancy knew why—the old goat had a son.

But he, Yancy Parnell, had dreams—big dreams—that he intended to make into reality. All he had to do was get his hands on the Silver Lady. There was Jake McCullough to be dealt with, but there were ways of convincing a man to sell if he was uncooperative. Cave-ins were easy to rig, and the time and cost of rebuilding after one of these catastrophes often dissuaded even the most optimistic, unless a man knew for sure that large quantities of silver lay beneath the tons of rubble.

More than one miner had shrugged his shoulders, cursed the fates, and disappeared, leaving the remains of his claim to be seized by the next challenger with a strong back and a hopeful spirit. Yes, McCullough could be taken care of. Yancy's worst enemy now was time. Any day now, the Silver Lady crew could uncover the vein. It would be a major strike, and if McCullough found it, Yancy could kiss his dreams of riches good-bye.

Lost in his brooding, Yancy was taken off guard when, without warning, the wagon suddenly heaved sideways and one wheel rolled off the track and into a deep rut. The jolt catapulted Felicity from her seat and landed her across Parnell's lap. When she looked up from where she lay sprawled across Yancy's legs, the dizzying view of the steep drop-off just inches away made her stomach lurch sickeningly. She shrieked, scrambling away from the wagon's edge and burying her face in Parnell's coat.

Yancy frowned at the hysterical woman and turned his attention to the potentially dangerous position of the wagon. "Get up, there," he shouted to the horse. The animal lunged forward several times and finally managed to haul them out of the rut. When they were pulled clear and on level ground again, Yancy stopped the wagon.

"Are you all right, Miss Howard?"

Embarrassed, Felicity slid back to her side of the seat. "Yes, thank you, I'm fine." Self-consciously, she tucked a stray curl behind her ear and looked down at her lap. "I'm sorry I acted like such a ninny back there. I've always been afraid of heights, and then, too, I was so preoccupied with my problems that I was taken by surprise."

His smile was grim. "I'm afraid I was doing some woolgathering myself or I would have seen that pothole and avoided it. It's getting pretty dark and these roads can be treacherous even at midday. I apologize for frightening you, Miss Howard. Guess I better pay attention to business."

"Mr. Parnell, I . . ."

"Please, just call me Yancy."

"Oh, well, all right," she said, smiling. "If you will call me Felicity."

"I'd be honored," he agreed genially. He clucked to the horse and they started on their way again.

"Yancy, I hate to impose on you, you've been so kind already, but do you have any more ideas of where I might find a place to stay tonight?"

He contemplated her tired, drawn face for a moment, "I do have an idea, Miss How . . . Felicity, but I don't know how you'll take to it."

"Yancy," she returned, "right now, I'm so tired and hungry that I'd settle for a piece of dried beef and a horse stall lined with fresh straw."

He chuckled. "I think I can do a sight better than that. You remember Roxie from the train today, don't you?"

"Of course."

"Well, she has a double bed in her room above the saloon, and the way she was talking about you when she came in, I just know she wouldn't mind putting you up for the night."

"The *saloon!*" she gasped, shocked at the idea. However, after giving the matter another moment's thought, she realized she didn't have any other alternative. She wasn't exactly in a position to be picky.

Yancy smiled reassuringly. "There's a back stairs to all the rooms, Felicity. No one need ever know that you spent the night over a saloon."

"I'm sorry," she said, "I didn't mean to sound ungrateful. Thank you for helping me out. I think I will make use of those back stairs, though," she added. They both laughed and rode on in companionable silence as the sun made a spectacular descent behind the snowcapped mountains.

Roxie was delighted to share her room with Felicity and called down the stairs to the brothel's maid, ordering her to prepare a tub for Felicity's use. Yancy left the two women chatting amicably and sent over to the hotel restaurant for a huge platter of food. Within an hour, Felicity was bathed, fed, and ready for bed. Roxie tucked her in as if she were a child, bid her good night, and hurried downstairs to work the faro table in the saloon.

Despite the tinny piano music and the drunken laughter of the customers, Felicity slept soundly, waking only when the bright morning sun streamed across the bed. She was surprised to find Roxie already up and dressed.

" 'Mornin', Felicity." Roxie smiled.

"I thought you'd still be asleep, Roxie. I never even heard you come in last night."

"Normally, I'd still be in bed, but Yancy told me 'bout what happened to you and I figured you might need some help decidin' what to do about the fix you're in. That Jake McCullough should be horsewhipped for treatin' you so bad. I don't know him very well 'cause he took off about six months ago for England. That was just shortly after I got here. He always seemed kinda nice though, in a quiet sort of way, and he sure is good-lookin'! The first time he came into the saloon, why, he about took my breath away!''

Felicity sincerely hoped her face did not reveal that her reaction to Jake McCullough had been much the same. Quickly, she asked, ''Why was he over in England?''

''Well, his pa said he went to study their methods of hard-rock minin'. I guess they've been doin' it over there for a long time.''

Felicity frowned in confusion. ''How is it that you know Jake McCullough but Yancy doesn't?''

''Oh, Yancy just blew into town a couple of months back and won the Last Chance off the original owner. Jake was already gone by then, and I guess Joe just never mentioned to Yancy that he had a son. I don't think Joe agreed with Jake about buyin' all this expensive new equipment and tryin' these newfangled ways of minin'. I know there's plenty of men doin' it, though. Some have even brought in miners from somewhere called Cornwall to teach 'em how.''

''It must have been a terrible shock for Jake to come back and find out his father had been killed,'' Felicity mused.

''I reckon it was,'' Roxie agreed. ''But he still had no right to treat a sweet little thing like you the way he did.''

''At first he seemed really nice. Then, when I explained who I was and why I was there, he became very nasty and even called me a gold digger. I was so angry and insulted that I lost my temper and called him a name.''

''Oh?'' said Roxie in surprise. ''What did you call him?''

''I'm embarrassed to tell you,'' Felicity answered.

"I told him I thought he was despicable. I've never said anything like that to anyone before."

"Despicable? Well, don't worry about it, honey." Roxie chuckled. "I reckon he'll live through it. He probably doesn't even know what it means. I'm sure I don't."

Felicity gaped at Roxie in amazement and then, recovering herself, said, "Well, it means horrible, terrible, awful, and now that I've had time to reflect on the whole situation, I'm ashamed that I said it. I should have realized that he was mourning his father and probably wasn't thinking clearly."

"Bah! He's lucky I didn't hear him talkin' that way to you," Roxie huffed. "I'd have cut him clear through, and with words he could understand! Yancy says I've got the sharpest tongue in the whole state."

It wasn't hard for Felicity to imagine the verbose Roxie loosing a barrage of colorful insults. "You know, Roxie," she said, laughing, "I bet you could send the meanest gunslinger hightailing it right out of town just by giving him a piece of your mind!"

Roxie nodded her head. "You might just be right, sweetie," she agreed. "Now, come on over here and have some breakfast. We gotta discuss what you're gonna do."

Felicity donned a wrapper and joined Roxie at a small round table in front of the fireplace. Her piquant face was framed by thick, tawny hair and her emerald eyes were clear and sparkling after her night's sleep. Roxie studied the other girl covertly. Imagine, she thought in amusement, a nun in *my* room! She bit her lip to squelch the giggle that threatened. Her gaze continued to roam over Felicity, assessing the other girl's looks. Actually, she's real pretty, and that figure! Why would she hide those breasts and that tiny waist under those awful, dowdy clothes? Roxie again smiled to herself as she realized that, with Felicity's background, it was probably a good idea that the woman-hungry min-

ers in town didn't realize what she really looked like.
The poor little thing had enough to cope with right
now.

Seeing only one plate of food on the table, Felicity
asked, "Aren't you eating?"

"Lord, no! I'm usually not up till at least eleven
and I can't even look at food until noon. Coffee is
all I want at this ungodly hour." At Felicity's reproving glance, Roxie looked shamefaced and murmured, "Sorry, I didn't mean to take the Lord's
name in vain." Felicity nodded primly and settled
herself on the other side of the table.

"Now, sweetie," Roxie said, "tell me, have you
thought about what you're goin' to do now that the
bottom has fallen out?"

Felicity sighed. "Well, I don't have enough money
to get home. I was afraid to carry too much cash
with me. I guess I'll have to send a wire to the bank
in Philadelphia and arrange for some to be sent here.
Do you know how I might go about doing that here
in Silverton?"

"Sure, honey, you can do it, but why go back
East? Do you have folks there?" Felicity looked
down at her lap and shook her head. "I figured as
much," said Roxie matter-of-factly. "So why go
back? Why not stay here in Silverton and settle
down?"

"But, Roxie," Felicity protested, "how would I
support myself?"

"The same as you would back East, of course. Get
a job! This town is growin' like crazy, Felicity. We
got a population near a thousand what with all the
miners hereabouts. We got hotels, restaurants, dress
shops, a school, and a couple churches. Why, we
even have a Catholic church—St. Patrick's."

"Really? A Catholic church?" Felicity was astonished.

"Really." Roxie smiled. "You know, I bet you
could get a job at the new Grand Hotel. It's the biggest and fanciest place in Silverton."

"I don't know, Roxie," Felicity said doubtfully. "I'd have to give that some thought." She daintily spread butter on a piece of toast and popped it into her mouth. "I admit there's not much for me in Philadelphia. About the only thing I can do really well is bake and clean. That's why I thought I'd make someone a good housekeeper."

"Sounds to me like you'd make someone a good wife," Roxie noted wryly. "What you need, girl, is a faithful man and a houseful of kids." At Felicity's quick, negative shake of her head, Roxie laughed. "Come on! You ain't a nun anymore and marriage can be fun. I was married once. He up and died of a fever before we had any little ones, but I was real happy while it lasted." Roxie reached for her coffee cup and drained it. "Well, I guess you're the only one that can make that decision. But, no matter what you do, I think you're gonna need that money from back East. Yancy said he'd be available if you needed anythin' today, so I'll go tell him to be ready to take you over to the bank."

"Thank you, Roxie. I feel terrible putting the two of you to so much trouble on my account. You and Yancy have been so kind to me, a perfect stranger. I don't know what I would have done without you. How can I ever repay either of you?"

"Now, honey, we ain't strangers!" Roxie protested with a wave of her hand. "We settled that on the train yesterday, remember? Besides, friends don't expect to be paid back for helpin' each other out. I thought you good Christians always preach that that's what friendship is all about. And don't you worry none about Yancy, neither. The saloon will be dead until tonight anyway. He'll enjoy escortin' a pretty woman 'round town."

"Roxie, you may be good at cutting someone up with that sharp tongue of yours, but you're even better at making someone feel better."

It was Roxie's turn to look embarrassed. "Go on

with you." She laughed. "Get dressed and I'll go find Yancy."

An hour later, Yancy Parnell handed Felicity into his wagon and headed down Greene Street. He didn't mention the ugly confrontation with Jake McCullough the day before, and not wanting to spoil the lovely day, she didn't bring it up either. In truth, the experience had so humiliated her that she just wanted to forget the whole thing.

She listened attentively as the handsome gambler indicated various points of interest, including the homes of some of Silverton's permanent citizens. The small frame buildings looked primitive compared to Philadelphia, but Yancy told her that just five years before, Silverton hadn't been much more than a tent city.

They turned a corner and Yancy pulled the wagon up in front of the San Juan County Bank. "This is where Joe McCullough did all his business," he announced. "I thought it would be best to bring you here. I have some business to see to as well." She nodded and accepted his help down. Several passersby curiously eyed the strange woman with Parnell. Anyone who knew Yancy knew that the lady at his side did not resemble his usual paramours. Hurrying her along, Parnell tossed the onlookers a scowl and ushered her into the bank.

Yancy introduced Felicity to the bank's manager, Jonathan Werkheiser, who escorted them to his office at the back of the building.

"And now, how can I help you two?" Werkheiser inquired.

"Jonathan, Miss Howard is the lady who Joe McCullough was expecting. Unfortunately, due to Joe's recent passing, she now finds herself stranded here with very little in the way of funds."

"I do have money at the First National Bank of Philadelphia," she quickly put in. She didn't want this man getting the wrong idea the way Jake McCullough had. "I just need your assistance to contact my bank there so that the funds can be transferred here to Silverton.''

''That's no problem at all, Miss Howard. I'll wire Philadelphia right away. I should have verification later this afternoon. In the meantime, you need to go see Joe McCullough's lawyer, Benjamin Ford.''

''Why is that necessary?'' asked Yancy.

The banker puffed up indignantly. ''Not that it's any of your concern, Mr. Parnell, but I met with Mr. Ford just this morning over the matter of how I was to handle Mr. McCullough's account. He mentioned that it was imperative that he locate Miss Howard before anything could be settled. He knew she was expected at any time and it seems that Mr. Mc-Cullough's will cannot be read until she is present.''

''Me?'' Felicity gasped in surprise. ''What have I got to do with the reading of Mr. McCullough's will?''

Mr. Werkheiser smiled. ''It would appear, Miss Howard, that you have been named as one of the beneficiaries.''

Felicity threw a look of astonishment at Yancy and then gazed back at the banker in perplexity. ''But why would that be?''

''I don't know, miss, but I think you should go and find out,'' Mr. Werkheiser urged.

''Well, yes, of course I should. I'll go right now.'' As Felicity stood to leave, she remembered that Yancy had said he had business at the bank. ''Yancy, I'm sorry. Perhaps you'd like me to wait in the lobby while you conduct your business with Mr. Werk-heiser.''

''No, I can take care of that matter later,'' Yancy assured her. ''This is much more important.''

''Well, if you're sure, but I really don't mind wait-ing.''

Parnell stood and took Felicity's arm. ''I'm quite sure. Besides, aren't your curious to know what old Joe left you? I know I am.'' And *that* is an understatement, he thought to himself. Earlier that morning, he had almost changed his mind and asked Roxie to escort Felicity on her errands. He was now very glad that he hadn't.

Felicity offered her hand to the banker. "Thank you for your help, Mr. Werkheiser. I'll return later to see if you've received that verification."

Werkheiser shook her hand and walked her to the door to point out the exact location of Ford's office. "Thanks, Jonathan, but I know where Ben's office is," Parnell assured him. "I'll make sure she gets there directly."

Jonathan Werkheiser gave Yancy Parnell a speculative look before softly closing the door of the bank.

The couple proceeded down the street until Yancy stopped in front of a small office building. Large lettering across the window proclaimed BENJAMIN FORD, ATTORNEY AT LAW. Felicity was still astonished that she had been included in Joe McCullough's will. "Why, we only wrote to each other a few times. I never even got to meet the man," she mused. "Why would he have done such a thing?"

"You!" came an outraged bark from behind her. Felicity's heart jumped into her throat as she whirled around to confront the broad-shouldered form striding toward her. She apprehensively raised her eyes and her worst fears were confirmed. It was *him*, bigger than life, and even more handsome than she remembered—and every bit as angry.

"Are you speaking to me?" she squeaked. One word from him and she was reduced to a state of near speechlessness, hardly the picture of intelligence and poise she wished to project. Oh, *why* did this man have to be as handsome as he was mean? If only he were ugly, it would be a whole lot easier to at least appear composed in his presence. But he was far from unattractive and her usually agile tongue was somehow tangled up in her teeth.

"What the hell are you doing here at Ben Ford's office?" Jake McCullough demanded.

Her dignity finally asserted itself and she drew herself up to face her adversary. "Not that it's any of your business, Mr. McCullough, but I have an appointment with Mr. Ford."

"You couldn't," Jake sneered, "because I do." As he moved forward to push rudely by her, the gentleman in question suddenly appeared in the doorway.

"Ah, Mr. McCullough, and you must be Miss Howard." Benjamin Ford extended his hand to Felicity in greeting. "How lucky that you have arrived at the same time. Now that you are both here, we can begin." Always a man of peace, Ben Ford thought it wise to ignore his clients' obvious hostility toward one another and graciously ushered them into his office, Yancy trailing behind.

"I thought you wanted to see me about Pa's will," Jake growled. "What's she doin' here?"

"Miss Howard is also a party to the reading of your father's will, Jake," responded Ford with a bland smile.

Jake's expression was thunderous and the lawyer held up a hand to stay the explosion he could sense was coming. "If you will both be seated so that we might proceed, everything will be explained."

As they sat down in the two chairs opposite Mr. Ford's desk, the attorney offered one last comment in an attempt to calm the fuming McCullough. "After the accident, when the rescue crew brought your father in to Doc Brown, Joe insisted they fetch me. He dictated the changes he wanted made to his will just before he died."

Jake scowled and jerked a thumb toward Yancy, who was standing behind Felicity's chair. "What's *he* got to do with this?"

Mr. Ford shrugged and looked at Felicity expectantly. "Mr. Parnell doesn't have anything to do with it," she blurted, "but I would like to have him stay here with me. Is that allowed?"

The lawyer looked back at Jake. "I have no objections to his being present during the reading, but if you do, it's your right to insist that he leave. This is a confidential matter."

Felicity threw a challenging look at Jake, daring him to deny her request.

"No," Jake finally conceded, "no objections. Let's just get this over with. I got work to do up at the mine."

Ben Ford breathed a sigh of relief and quickly read through the legal formalities of the will, pausing only when he came to the bequests. " 'To my son,' " he read, " 'I leave fifty percent ownership in the Silver Lady mine.' "

Jake jumped to his feet. "What?" he shouted. "Fifty percent? I'm his only livin' relative and he left me only half the mine? Why?"

"Jake, please!" Ford pleaded. "If you will just be patient, I can continue and you will hear the full terms of the will. You are making this very difficult!"

Jake sank back into his chair, a fierce glower marring his features. "Go on, Ben," he muttered.

Felicity kept her eyes on Ford, not daring the slightest glance at Jake.

Ford resumed his reading. " 'The remaining fifty percent of the mine is to go to Miss Felicity Howard, along with full ownership of my cabin. I very much regret that she has made the long and arduous trip from Philadelphia, only to find herself in Silverton with no protection. From our correspondence, I've come to hold Miss Howard in high esteem, and I know my son, Jake, will understand my feelings of responsibility to the lady, considering that she has recently left the holy order of the sisterhood and has no relatives or means of support.' "

Jake was again on his feet. His mouth gaping, he stared at Felicity as if she had just sprouted another head. "You're a nun? My father hired a goddamn *nun* for a housekeeper? He must have gone crazy!" Turning back toward the lawyer, he barked, "This will ain't valid, Ben! Pa turned into a ravin' lunatic while I was gone! He went and sent for a nun to move in with us. That alone should be proof enough that he'd lost his mind.''

''*Mr. McCullough!*'' Benjamin Ford's normally placid face was beet-red. ''I will not tolerate any further outbursts from you. Now, sit down so that we can finish with this reading!''

Jake promptly sat down.

''To continue,'' said Mr. Ford, clearing his throat, '' 'As to the matter of the funds I have on deposit at the San Juan County Bank, this money is to be shared equally by my son and Miss Howard for maintenance of the mine and winter supplies needed at the cabin.' '' The room was silent as Ford finished the will and removed his round spectacles.

''Is that all, Ben?'' asked Jake quietly.

''Yes,'' responded the attorney, ''that's it.''

Jake leaned back in his chair and stared at him in utter disbelief. Felicity's expression was one of stunned incredulity and Yancy Parnell just looked pleased. Benjamin Ford fidgeted nervously, apprehensive at Jake's sudden calm.

Finally, Jake stood and faced Felicity. Offering her a mocking bow, he said, ''Congratulations, Miss Howard. You now own just about everythin' my father worked his entire life to earn. And I thought nuns didn't care about material goods.''

Felicity flushed at this insult and the conclusions Mr. Ford must be drawing. Gathering her dignity about her, she stood and softly addressed Jake. ''Mr. McCullough, I would like to make it perfectly clear to you that I am no longer a nun. Due to a situation which I do not choose to discuss with you, I left the sisterhood. Your father was aware of this situation and extended me an offer of employment which I gratefully accepted. That was the only agreement your father and I ever had and I can assure you that this bequest is as much a surprise to me as it is to you. Now, despite your unforgivable rudeness toward me, I would like to take this opportunity to extend to you my sympathy and condolences. I will remember your father in my prayers and also pray that you will not suffer overlong in your grief."

With a slight nod in Ford's direction, she turned on her heel and, with great dignity, left the room. Yancy grinned smugly at Jake and followed Felicity's rigid back out the door.

As they exited the building, Felicity stopped and leaned weakly against the wall. At Yancy's puzzled expression, she said, "I must speak with Mr. McCullough when he comes out."

Before Yancy could question her motives for seeking another confrontation with the furious McCullough, Jake stormed out onto the street, slamming the door to the attorney's office behind him.

She immediately straightened and stepped toward Jake. "Mr. McCullough, may I have a moment?"

He cocked his head and eyed her warily. "What for? Seems like you just said everythin' that needed sayin'. I'm goin' up to the mine. I wasn't kiddin' when I said I have work to do."

"But that's just what I wanted to speak to you about. I would like to ride with you up to the cabin."

His jaw dropped. "I must have heard you wrong, lady."

"I don't think so, Mr. McCullough. It was a simple request. I said I need a ride to my cabin and since you're going up that way, anyway . . ." Her words trailed off.

He was aghast. "Yeah, that's what I thought you said, but I didn't think even you would have the nerve to ask me that. The answer is no, Miss Howard. I wouldn't give you a ride across the street."

"I'll take you to your cabin, Felicity," Yancy quickly volunteered. "We need to stop by the saloon and pick up your things anyway."

Jake eyed her derisively. "The saloon, Miss Howard? Better be careful about the company you keep or folks around here ain't gonna believe that prim and proper front of yours. Nice women don't stay in saloons—and I sure as hell ain't never seen no nuns in there! Remember that next time you're tryin' to convince some sucker that you're a lady."

"That's enough, McCullough," Yancy growled. "You know damn well that there were no rooms available at the hotel last night. The lady spent the night in Roxie's room and never set foot in the saloon."

Jake gazed at Yancy speculatively. "Why are you goin' to so much trouble for her, Parnell? Do you think she's gonna sell you her half of the mine?"

"That's ridiculous, McCullough!" Yancy blustered. "How could I have known that your father was going to leave anything to her?"

"I've been told you tried to buy the Silver Lady off Pa several times." Jake studied the gambler closely for a moment and seemed to come to a decision. "Tell you what, Parnell, you bring the *lady* and her belongin's over to the general store, and I'll make room for her in the supply wagon."

"There's no need," Yancy spit out angrily.

"You heard me, Parnell. I'll take her up to the cabin. I don't want the likes of you anywhere near my place. I don't want her there either, for that matter, but since it seems Pa went crazy before he died, I guess I ain't got much choice."

Felicity gasped aloud at this latest insult and Yancy advanced on Jake in a fury, the muscles of his arms bunching for a blow. Felicity leaped forward and grabbed Yancy's arm just as Jake raised his fist. Unable to block the punch, Yancy took a hearty cuff on the chin and stumbled backward out of Felicity's grasp. Felicity cried out in horror, but Yancy warned her off with an upraised hand and a curt shake of his head. "Stay out of this, Felicity."

"But, Yancy, I . . ."

Parnell launched himself toward Jake's midsection, his weight carrying both men out into the street. Benjamin Ford rushed out the door of his office just in time to see Jake dusting off his hands with a self-satisfied grin.

"Oh, dear," fretted the lawyer, "you've done it now, Jake."

"Yup, Ben." He chuckled. "I've sure done it now. Now I gotta take Sister Beneficiary here over to the Last Chance and get her bag myself." With that, he grabbed Felicity's arm and commandeered her past Parnell's inert form and down the street.

She stumbled and resisted the hand clamped on her arm, but Jake simply looked down at her and smiled tightly. "Mr. McCullough, you don't have to drag me off like some kind of caveman. Now—let—go—of—my—arm!" Jake ignored her as he continued to pull her toward the saloon. "Mr. McCullough!" Felicity shrieked. "Stop it this instant! I am not ready to get my bag yet. I have to go to the bank first!"

He halted abruptly, his expression menacing. "So," he sneered, "you just can't wait to dip into the treasure chest, can you?"

She had had about all she could take from this man, and to her horror, tears glazed her emerald eyes. "Mr. McCullough," she choked, "I asked Mr. Werkheiser over at the bank if he could wire my bank in Philadelphia and have some funds transferred to me here. I only want to go see if he was successful. That's all!"

Jake felt like a brute. He was aware that the girl was trying desperately not to cry, but despite her efforts, a single tear trickled down her cheek. Almost without realizing it, he tilted her chin back and wiped the tear away with a sweep of his thumb.

Jake silently conceded that he'd been wrong about her desire to immediately help herself to his father's money, but that didn't mean he had misjudged her basic motive for being in Silverton. Steeling himself against the poignant picture she presented, he asked, ''Are you all right?''

''It's a little late for your concern,'' she returned resentfully.

''Look, I apologize for what I said about the money. I'll take you over to the bank before we go to the saloon to get your things. Will that satisfy you?''

She realized that there was no sense in continuing to spar with the man and nodded her head. ''Yes, Mr. McCullough, that will be fine.'' She turned away and started down the street toward the bank, her shoulders rigid, her back ramrod-straight.

With a curse, he hurried after her, not catching up until she had already swept through the doors of the bank building.

Chapter 4

"So this is home," Felicity announced to the empty cabin. A tour of the rough interior revealed only two rooms: a large common room where she was standing, and a smaller room off to the side which was apparently a bedroom.

The afternoon sun beamed through a dirty, curtainless window at the front of the cabin, illuminating the sparse furnishings. She noted that although everything seemed to be neatly arranged, a fine layer of dust blanketed the furniture and there was evidence that the floor hadn't been swept for some time.

Beneath the large window, a rickety table sat perched next to a tattered old settee. She tossed her reticule onto the settee and a small cloud of dust puffed upward. Dirty stuffing frothed out of several slits in the faded cushions and she made a mental note, the first of many, to see to its repair. Well, she thought, sighing in resignation, at least it's a roof over my head. I just hope it doesn't leak! She giggled and turned her attention toward a small fireplace on the south wall. Several rifles were mounted above its crude, split-log mantel. On the floor in front of it lay a multicolored, braided rug and a small basket of wood.

Hearing one of the horses whinny, she glanced out the window and watched as Jake unharnessed the animals from the wagon. He hadn't said a word to her during the long trip up from town and when they finally reached the cabin, he merely nodded in the direction of the small dwelling and grunted something about bringing her bag in after seeing to the stock. Left to her own devices, she had jumped down from the wagon seat and gone directly into the cabin.

As she gazed at Jake McCullough's tall, muscular physique, she shook her head, wondering how she could make peace with the impossible man.

I'm not a schemer! she thought in frustration. Why does he have to be so quick to jump to the wrong conclusion? If he and I are going to be partners, I'm going to have to make him listen. He has to give me a chance! She knew that changing Jake's opinion wouldn't be easy, but she was determined to think of some way to convince him that she wasn't what he thought she was.

She turned away from the window and continued the inspection of her new home. A wood plank table sat in the middle of the room with several three-legged stools shoved carelessly beneath it.

Near the fireplace was a large iron cookstove. She wrinkled her nose at the pool of congealed bacon grease inside an iron skillet, and pushed it to the back of the stove. A crude counter had been built next to the stove and, above it, three shelves were attached to the log wall. The shelves were well above her reach and she made another mental note to speak to Jake about lowering them.

The shelves were well-stocked with sacks and tins of flour, sugar, rolled oats, beans, coffee, and other foodstuff. The lowest shelf also held an odd assortment of mismatched plates, bowls, cups, and cutlery. In a box below the counter she found a few onions and several potatoes. Good, she thought, nodding, if there's some meat around here, I can at least fix some supper. The very thought of food made her stomach growl and she glanced around guiltily, then chuckled as she realized there was no one to hear it. Audible body sounds were definitely frowned upon by the older nuns at St. Margaret's and any novice unfortunate enough to hiccough or have her stomach grumble within Reverend Mother's earshot was severely reprimanded.

A pitiful whining and scratching sound drew her attention to the back door. She hurried to investigate, almost tripping over a narrow cot sitting close to the door.

She pushed the portal open and stepped outside, but the sight that met her eye caused her to plaster herself to the cabin wall, There, not five feet away, stood the largest dog she'd beast had a rough brown coat with paws the size of dinner plates and a head as big as a small cow. His immense jaws where open, displaying teeth which Felicity felt sure rivaled an adult bear's.

Seeing a stranger, the dog danced around in a circle, barking noisily. Since there were no animals at the convent, she misunderstood the dog's friendly overtures. To her the animal looked ferocious . . . and hungry. The dog continued to play, gradually closing the distance between himself and the panic-stricken girl. Sure that this might be her last moment on earth, she swallowed her hysteria long enough to find her voice. "Mr. McCullough!" she shrieked. "Help me, please!" Just as Jake rounded the corner of the cabin, it occurred to her that he might decide to end his problems by simply letting this monster devour her. Why, he might even command the brute to do so!

Felicity's terrified scream sent gooseflesh racing down Jake's spine. Had a bear come out of the woods and cornered her? He dropped the bag he was carrying, grabbed his rifle, and ran like he was being pursued by all the demons in hell. He burst into the backyard to see Felicity cowering against the side of the cabin, as the huge dog leaped and barked in playful invitation. Throwing the gun aside, he planted his hands on his hips and shook his head in disgust. "For God's sake, girl, what the hell's the matter with you? That's just my dog! Boozer, cut that out!" he ordered angrily. "You stupid mutt," he scolded as he gave the huge beast an affectionate pat on the head. "Calm down, boy, she doesn't understand you want to play." The dog obediently sat down next to his master and nuzzled his hand.

Jake took a closer look at Felicity's ashen face and felt a pang of guilt. "Guess I should have warned you about Boozer. He gets a little rambunctious sometimes, but he's harmless."

She nodded, her terror-stiffened body beginning to relax. She suddenly felt very foolish. "I'm sorry if I alarmed you, Mr. McCullough. I thought it was some kind of wild animal that wandered in from the woods." She peeled herself away from the wall, but didn't move any closer to him or the dog.

"If you're gonna be around for a while, you better come over here and make friends." He bent down on one knee and rubbed the dog behind his ears. Boozer's eyelids drooped in ecstasy as he reveled in the attention.

"What should I do?" she asked hesitantly.

"Just walk over here slow and offer your hand for him to smell. You don't have to worry about Boozer, there ain't a mean bone in his body. In fact, there's been a few times when I wished he wasn't so friendly."

Reluctantly, she inched closer to the dog, her hand extended palm upward. Boozer opened his eyes and thumped his tail. Despite Jake's assurances, she remained wary. "Nice dog," she said coaxingly. Her voice cracked and she wondered if this monster could tell how scared she was. She bent slightly so that the dog could sniff at her hand. However, she misread his intentions and jumped backward when his long, pink tongue shot out and licked her knuckles.

Jake chuckled. "Don't worry, that's just a dog kiss."

"Does that mean we're friends now?" Felicity asked doubtfully.

"Yeah, but then Boozer's everybody's friend, especially if they'll share a whiskey with him once in a while."

She dropped to one knee to pet Boozer's head and rub his ears as she'd seen Jake do. "Well, dog, you won't find whiskey anywhere near me!" she said primly.

A sardonic grin lifted one side of Jake's mouth.

Oblivious of Jake's reaction, Felicity asked, "Does his taste for spirits have something to do with his name?"

"Yeah, you could say that. Boozer and I first met at a saloon in town about a year ago after he sneaked a drink of my whiskey. It's a good story but it'll have to wait. I dropped your bag by the wagon when I heard the commotion. I better go get it before the raccoons or bear cubs do."

"Bear cubs?" she gasped. "You mean there really are bears around here?"

Jake looked at her in amusement. "Miss Howard, this ain't Philadelphia. This is the country and we have a little bit of everythin' here. Bears, mountain lions, wolves, you name it. Even some horny miners. You gotta be real careful around here."

"What kind of miners?" she asked.

"Never mind." he chuckled. "You wouldn't understand. I'm goin' to get your bag." Still chuckling, he disappeared back around the corner of the house.

She stood up and stared after him in wonder. Had they just had a conversation without any arguments? Maybe there's hope yet for peace between us, she mused. But I still want to know what a horny miner is. I'll ask Roxie next time I see her. I bet she'll know.

Boozer interrupted her thoughts by jumping up on his hind legs and resting his front paws on her shoulders. His tongue stretched out and caught her beneath the chin before she could duck. "Oh, for heaven's sake, dog!" She laughed and shoved him off, but Boozer didn't appear to be the least bit offended. Instead, he wagged his tail enthusiastically and followed her back into the cabin. His large claws tapped against the wood floor as he trotted over to the rug in front of the fireplace and lay down.

She was headed for a look at the bedroom when the front door crashed open and her bag flew in, landing with a loud thunk at her feet. She looked up in surprise as she heard Jake's hobnail boots hit the floor. "Take one of these," he ordered, indicating the hefty supply sacks in his arms. She hurried to comply, staggering over to the table and setting the heavy bag down.

"What do you have in here? Rocks?"

"Nope, just potatoes," he replied as he set the other bag down. "And some oranges."

"Oranges!" she exclaimed. "Why, I haven't had an orange for . . . oh, I don't know how long!" She eagerly rummaged through the bag until she located the smaller bag filled with oranges. Pulling it out with childlike glee, she set it on the table. Then, suddenly remembering her manners, she paused and asked, "Do you mind if I have one?"

He looked up from the supplies he was unpacking and smiled at her excitement. For a moment he almost forgot their differences. "Of course not, that's what I bought 'em for. Help yourself."

"Oh, thank you!" she said enthusiastically. She quickly chose the largest orange and turned to look for a knife. She spotted one high on the top shelf, but knew she couldn't reach it. Undaunted, she grabbed one of the three-legged stools from beneath the table and set it down in front of the counter.

Just as she raised her skirt and placed a small foot on the seat, Jake's voice halted her. "What are you doin'? You could fall and break your . . . somethin'." She lowered her foot and looked at him like a guilty child. He moved behind her, taking her shoulders and gently setting her aside before reaching up and getting the knife. "Here. Is this what you want?"

"Yes, thank you." She took the knife and returned to the table. As she sat down and began to peel the orange, she said, "You know, you need to do something about lowering those shelves. They're much too high for me and it will be a real nuisance having to climb on a stool every time I need something."

He frowned and seated himself across the table from her. "Yeah, well, before we do any changin' around here, I think there's some things we need to talk about." He stopped, suddenly fascinated as Felicity slowly slid a wedge of orange into her mouth. A drop of juice glistened on her full lower lip, but before it dripped onto her chin the tip of her tongue darted out and retrieved it. He stared.

"Mmmm, this is so good! Would you like me to cut one for you?" She didn't wait for his response, but reached into the bag and deftly pared another orange into wedges. She ignored his look of surprise as she handed him the neatly cut piece of fruit. Still concentrating on her moist lips, Jake absently popped a wedge into his mouth. He merely nodded when she asked, "Isn't that the most delicious thing you've ever tasted?"

Her expectant expression snapped him out of his reverie. He finished his orange quickly, determined to broach the subject of their partnership before she got caught up in the idea of staying. For some reason, he found her method of eating oranges highly erotic and that realization rankled. He gave himself a mental shake and wondered what had come over him. The girl was a nun, for God's sake!

Disgusted with himself, his voice was sharper than he intended when he finally spoke again. "All right, Miss Howard, now do you suppose you can stop feedin' me oranges and interruptin' me so that we can have a serious discussion?''

Her momentary feelings of well-being vanished and she braced herself for a return of Jake's belligerence. She couldn't imagine what she had done to upset him this time, but she was determined to avoid another senseless argument. Sitting up taller and squaring her shoulders, she smiled amicably. ''But of course, Mr. McCullough. I'm sorry. Please continue. Now that we're partners, naturally I want to learn everything there is to know about our mine.''

''Yeah, well, it's the partnership I want to talk to you about.'' He noticed the barely perceptible stiffening of Felicity's shoulders and silently commended her on her control. It irritated him to hear her refer to the Silver Lady as ''our mine,'' but, since throwing his male superiority and strength around hadn't served him with this woman, he put a damper on his hostility and softened his voice. ''Runnin' a silver mine is dirty, rough, and dangerous, Miss Howard, and it sure ain't no place for a lady. Now, I'm not sayin' you wouldn't understand how things are done,'' he quickly added. ''I can tell you're an educated and intelligent woman, but that's not the point.'' He knew nothing about her intelligence or education, but it was always better to tell a woman something complimentary before trying to reason with her. He regarded her closely, trying to gauge her mood, but her expression betrayed nothing. ''I'm not doin' a very good job of this, but what I'm tryin' to say is that I'm prepared to buy back this cabin from you along with your share of the mine. Then you'd be free to take the money and go back East. If you don't want to be a nun anymore, there should be enough for you to start some kind of business.''

Felicity's teeth worried her lower lip and she stared down at her lap. When she finally looked up, he was surprised to see a look of pain in her green eyes, but he stubbornly steeled himself against her.

This woman had something that rightfully belonged to him and he was going to get it back. He couldn't afford to go soft over a pair of beautiful eyes.

"Mr. McCullough, I . . . I really don't want to go back East." He opened his mouth to object but she held up her hand. "No, please, let me explain. When I discovered that your father had died, I thought my only choice was to return to Philadelphia. Then Roxie told me how fast Silverton is growing, and when Mr. Parnell took me about this morning, I saw for myself that living here could be an exciting opportunity. You see, I have no real home in Philadelphia anymore, no family or friends who would be in a position to advise me. Why would I go back?"

He shrugged. "But what's out here for you? What made you decide to come all the way to Colorado in the first place?"

"As I told you earlier, Mr. McCullough, there were personal reasons for my leaving the order. I had to find employment and since I was the convent cook, I felt I was best suited to be a housekeeper. I answered an advertisement your father had placed for a mail-order bride and when the agency told me that he was really only looking for a housekeeper, I offered my services. Then, when I got here . . . well, you know the rest."

Yes, he thought bitterly, I know the rest. Now I'm left with a tight-mouthed little ex-nun livin' in my house and ownin' half of everythin' I thought was mine. With my luck, she'll have me lightin' candles and sayin' prayers at bedtime before the week's over!

She watched a myriad of emotions wash over his face as he stared out the front window. She knew he resented her intrusion into his life and felt she must somehow convince him that it was never her intention to take advantage of him or his father. "Mr. McCullough, I want you to know that I realize it probably wasn't right of me to accept the inheritance your father left me, but I truly did not have much of a choice. I have very little money and this bequest from him is like a gift from heaven.'' She blushed uncomfortably. ''What I was trying to say before we got off the subject, was that even if your father had not remembered me in his will, I probably would have stayed on in Silverton.''

''All right. So stay in Silverton. I'll pay you off and you can invest the money in a business here if that's what you want. I don't care where you go or what you do, just so long as you're out of my life.''

She shrank back in the face of his continued animosity. ''How can I explain this to you?'' she whispered. ''I need you!'' At his startled look, she rushed on. ''It's true, I am well-educated in some things. Reading, languages, and mathematics—but I know nothing about business. And, because I've lived in a convent since I was ten years old, I realize I'm also terribly naive about the world. I'd be an easy target for a swindler. With you as my partner, I have the chance to learn without risking my inheritance. On my own, there is every chance that some scoundrel would cheat me out of my money. Then what would I do?''

''What makes you think you can trust me, Miss Howard?'' He raised an eyebrow, then leaned forward, curious to hear her reply.

She didn't blink an eye. ''It's to your benefit, as well as mine, that the mine does well. If it fails, we both lose.''

''I could still cheat you out of a lot of money.''

''You won't.''

He laughed cynically. ''And just how can you be so sure of that? You know absolutely nothin' about me . . . what kind of man I am, how honest I am, nothin'.''

She locked her emerald gaze with his. ''I feel like I came to know your father, Mr. McCullough. His letters revealed a kindness and understanding that told me a lot about him. Then, too, the people in town have nothing but good things to say about him. I don't think a man like that would raise a son to be a liar and a cheat."

He looked at her in amazement. The woman was good. He had to give her that. She was damn good. Even if he was a thieving rat, he'd never be able to cheat her after such a glowing speech about his father.

Jake McCullough was scrupulously honest, and somehow this woman had delved beneath his cynicism and bitterness to ferret out that trait. So now what was he going to do with her?

For a long time, he studied Felicity through narrowed eyes, and was impressed when she looked right back at him. There were not many men who could stand up to one of Jake McCullough's penetrating stares, but this mousy little girl's gaze never wavered. "All right, Miss Howard, you win."

She grinned. "Does that mean you'll accept me as your partner and try to get along with me?"

"Do I have a choice?" he asked sarcastically.

"Perhaps not in being my partner," she responded, "but it's still your choice to be agreeable or disagreeable. I sincerely hope you'll choose to be agreeable."

He frowned. That he'd been unsuccessful in deterring her plans irritated him. "Maybe you better hear my terms, Miss Howard, and then you'll know exactly what it will take for me to be 'agreeable,' as you put it. There are a few details we've gotta get straight if this partnership is goin' to succeed and the mine is gonna run profitably."

"Very well," she said equably, "state your terms."

"I will have complete control over the mine. I say how it's run, how everythin' is done, and you will stay out of it. Also, you will never go to the mine without me. Not only are miners a rough bunch, but they hate a woman anywhere near a mine—some are real superstitious about it—and they'd never take orders from a woman. If you want to see the operation, I'll take you up there sometime when no one else is around." He stood up and crossed his arms over his chest, confident that she would argue. "Those are my terms. There will be no negotiations. Agreed?"

Felicity rose and faced him. She was well aware that he expected her to protest and it gave her enormous pleasure to disappoint him. She was surprised to find that she was actually enjoying this game of wills. Cocking her head, she played her part to the hilt, feigning deep consideration. "Very well. I accept your terms, provided, of course, that you accept mine." He arched a brow but didn't interrupt. "First, even though you will be running the mine, you will keep me abreast of everything that goes on there. Secondly, we will make all the major decisions together. Naturally, I will defer to your superior knowledge of the mining business, but you will consult me and you will listen to my opinions." Mimicking his stance, she crossed her arms over her chest and arched a brow. She knew very well that her terms were reasonable. He could not find them unacceptable. "Are we agreed?"

"Who said you were naive about business?" he snapped. "You can be sure I won't make the mistake of underestimatin' you again."

She held out her hand, even though he hadn't agreed yet. His face was hard, his eyes cold, and for a moment she doubted he was going to accept. He looked down at her proferred hand, then back up at her clear, frank eyes. His lips thinned as he finally took her small hand into his huge grasp. "Agreed, Miss Howard," he ground out. "Let's just hope you don't come to regret it."

She barely heard his reply. The heat of his touch sent shock waves reverberating through her arm and she hastily withdrew her hand.

Jake caught a glimpse of the fire that leaped into her eyes, but she turned away so quickly that he thought he must have imagined it. He shrugged mentally. The only passion that warmed Felicity Howard's heart was her desire for money.

She blushed and dropped her eyes. Had he read her thoughts? She must never let him know that his nearness made her head spin, that his touch caused strange yearnings she couldn't begin to understand. He'd just laugh and taunt her for being a lovesick, homely little fool. Was she being foolish? No, of course not, she silently convinced herself. It's just that I've never been around a man before. I'm not so addle-brained that I'm going to fall into a swoon just because a handsome man touches my hand. From beneath her heavy lashes, she detected his expectant expression as he waited for her to reply to his comment.

She lifted her chin with determination. "I'm sure I'll not regret our bargain, Mr. McCullough." She paused, then added, "Now then, if we've finished with that bit of business, I think I'll start preparations for my supper. You're welcome to stay if you like. By the way, do you keep any fresh meat around here?"

He could scarcely credit the woman's audacity. Where did she *think* he planned to eat? He laughed derisively and asked, "You sure you can cook?"

"As I told you earlier, I was the cook at my convent and oversaw the preparation of three meals a day for eighty people." Her eyes twinkled mischievously. "I might just be the best cook Silverton has ever seen." She had heard it said that the way to a man's heart was through his stomach. Though Jake McCullough's stomach was no doubt made of cast iron, it was certainly worth a try to reach his sensibilities through his taste buds. If it didn't improve his disposition, at least it would be a step toward proving to him just how wrong he was about her.

"That's a mighty brave brag, Miss Howard. I'm sick to death of my own cookin', though, so I guess I might as well give yours a try."

She ached to slap his arrogant face, but she continued to smile. The effort made her cheeks hurt.

"There's some beef in one of those sacks of supplies I bought today. I'll cut off a fair chunk for you and take the rest down to the river."

"The river?"

"Yeah, Pa sank a glass container into the river. The icy mountain runoff keeps meat fresh for several days."

"What a good idea! Well then, I'll make some egg noodles and we'll have roast beef. We do have eggs, don't we?"

Jake frowned. "Yeah, there's some old hens out in the lean-to. I was in a hurry this mornin' so I didn't check their nests, but there should be a couple of eggs out there. I'll get them on my way back from the creek." He went to the shelves and retrieved a large meat knife, then set about cutting off a piece of beef.

"Mr. McCullough?"

"Yeah?" He sliced through the meat deftly.

"Why did you scowl when you mentioned the hens?"

" 'Cause the damn things near peck a man's hands off when he's just tryin' to gather a couple of lousy eggs. I hate those hens."

She couldn't stop the giggle that slipped out. "Well, would you like me to give it a try? Maybe the hens would prefer a female."

He looked up from cutting the meat and shook his head. "You promised to cook tonight. You can't cook if your hands are all pecked, and you're not gettin' out of it that easy. No, Miss Howard, I'll gather the eggs. There's plenty of time for you to get to know those blasted hens."

He set the knife down and pushed the bulk of the meat back into a bag which he slung over his shoulder. "I'll be right back with the eggs. While you're gettin' supper ready, I'm gonna make a quick trip up to the mine and make sure everythin's all right."

She nodded, her hands already submersed in a pile of flour on the counter. Boozer jumped up and followed Jake out the door.

She didn't even realize that she had stopped mixing her dough and was gazing at Jake McCullough's broad back as he disappeared into the woods.

Two hours later, supper was ready. Jake appeared just as she was setting a huge bowl of beef and noodles on the table. His damp hair waved back off his forehead, evidence of a recent bath in the creek. She also noticed that he had changed into a clean, plaid shirt. Boozer followed Jake to the table and immediately sat down on his haunches next to him, his big eyes assuming an expression of utter deprivation.

Jake could certainly sympathize. His own mouth watered at the sight and smell of the meal in front of him. Large chunks of roasted beef swam in a thick, egg noodle gravy. She had found the ripened tomatoes he's purchased in town that morning and had sliced them onto a plate. Pouring a steaming cup of coffee for each of them, she took a seat across from him and bowed her head. He had been about to dig in, but stopped self-consciously and waited for her to finish her blessing. She crossed herself, then looked up and smiled. "Please eat!" He didn't need to be told twice, and heaped his plate with keen anticipation.

She watched anxiously as he took his first bite. He closed his eyes as if he were in heaven. Unaware that his appreciative reaction had given him away, he opened his eyes and said coolly, "Not bad, Miss Howard. The noodles are a little chewy, but with practice . . ."

Thrilled with his silent reaction, she had been about to thank him. However, as his derogatory words sank in, she caught herself and retorted icily, "Just a small contribution to the partnership, Mr. McCullough. I may not be able to swing a sledge-hammer, but I can stir up a pretty good meal. I'm sure you'll come to appreciate my cooking as soon as your palate becomes more educated.''

One for you, Miss Howard, Jake silently congratulated her. He knew he was acting like a bastard, but he still couldn't accept that his father had saddled him with this pious little pigeon. In truth, he'd never tasted anything as good as this supper. He smiled a little sheepishly and scooped up another helping.

Conversation was minimal during the rest of the meal until finally, after his fourth helping, Jake groaned in pleasurable misery. He caught himself and sat up straighter, scanning Felicity's features for signs that she'd noticed. She had. Amazingly enough, her smile was one of genuine pleasure and not the triumphant smirk he'd expected.

Jake hurriedly pushed back from the table, picked up his plate, and carried it over to the counter. ''You don't have to do that,'' Felicity protested. ''I'll take care of cleaning up.''

''Ah, another talent to add to the partnership,'' he quipped. ''How nice. I might begin to like this.'' He set his dish on the counter and headed for the door. ''Boozer needs a walk, and so do I. See you later.'' As he stepped out the door, he flung over his shoulder, ''The big water pail's under the counter.'' At her look of confusion, he continued, ''Pa dug a well out back, not far from the door. That way it's not so far to haul water. You can fetch some to wash the dishes.'' Then he whistled for Boozer and was gone.

She bounded from her chair and furiously grabbed the pail, muttering all the way to the well and back. ''Thank you for a lovely meal, Felicity. Why, you're welcome, Jake. So glad you enjoyed it. Come again soon. Next time I'll remember to put rat poison in your portion.''

Half an hour later, as she was putting the last dish away, Jake and Boozer returned. Boozer found his place on the rug as Jake lit a lantern and made himself comfortable on the settee. His long fingers searched his shirt pocket and pulled out his tobacco. He rolled a cigarette, struck a match to light it, and leaned back, staring at the ceiling.

By now she was over her anger and she was anxious to know more about her new home and the man who had built it. She sat down on the rug next to Boozer, tucking both of her legs to one side and making sure her ankles were well-concealed. She didn't know if he would talk to her, but decided it was worth a try. "Mr. McCullough, in your father's letters, he sounded like he intended this cabin to be his permanent home. Would he have stayed here if the silver had run out?"

Jake continued to stare at nothing, but he shrugged and answered, "Pa loved these mountains. He wasn't gettin' any younger and I reckon he figured this place was as good as any to live out his days. Then, too, he knew he could always get work with one of the bigger minin' outfits if ours didn't pay. No one knew explosives like Pa did." His face took on a pensive expression. When he spoke again, it was as if he were thinking aloud. "I just can't figure Pa makin' a careless mistake like that. Somebody else had to do it."

"What do you mean? Do you think someone deliberately caused his accident?" Just the thought of someone doing something so evil made her skin crawl.

"I don't know nothin' for sure. I checked the scene of the accident, though, and it didn't look to me like Pa's normal way of settin' a charge. I'll probably never know the truth. It's almost impossible to tell what happened." He lapsed into silence again and Felicity sensed that he didn't want to say any more on the subject.

"Mr. McCullough, I really meant it today when I said I was sorry about your father's death. From the little correspondence we shared, he seemed like a kind and caring man. I know you must miss him very much.''

Jake heard the honest sympathy in her voice, but he couldn't bring himself to talk any further about his father. The pain of his loss was still too raw.

She observed his troubled demeanor and decided her curiosity could be satisfied at another time. She watched him stub out his cigarette, and was reminded of the warm, tingly glow that his handshake had sent surging up her arm. Was this rush of feeling a natural occurrence between a man and a woman? And, if it was, why hadn't she felt it with Yancy Parnell? Yancy was handsome and yet . . . It was all so confusing. She had a better education than most men, and yet she was realizing, with every hour, how ignorant she was when it came to understanding anything about the real world. She sighed wistfully and scratched Boozer behind his ears.

His cigarette finished, Jake stood and stretched his arms high above his head. ''Time to turn in. I've been usin' the bedroom but I'll clean off the cot over there and use that. You'll have more privacy in the bedroom.''

She leaped to her feet. ''You can't mean that you're planning to sleep in here, in the cabin?''

Jake, who was halfway to the cot, stopped short and looked at her over his shoulder. ''Just where else did you think I'd sleep?'' At her continued look of astonishment, he added, ''Look, I just said you could have the bedroom.''

''I know, and I fully intend to use it, but you can't sleep in this cabin with me. Mr. McCullough, what would people say? I have a reputation to consider. It's not proper for an unmarried woman to stay in the same house with a bachelor. I'm truly distressed that you would even consider such a thing.''

His patience was burning on a short fuse. ''Look, lady, up here in the mountains, people make the best of things. Besides, who do you think would know or care where I was sleepin'? Why, I could climb into bed with you every night and no one would give a damn. Now, I'm tired and I'm gonna sleep on that blasted cot over there." He strode to the cot and, with one emphatic gesture, swept it clear of clutter.

Hands on hips, she pierced him with an icy glare. "Now see here, Mr. McCullough, this is *my* cabin now. I make the rules here. I don't mind cooking for you, but you're not going to sleep in here! Now, please remove yourself. Take whatever you need and leave. Right now."

His eyes raked over her with cool disdain, his gaze traveling from her concealed bustline to her invisible waist and on down to the bottom of her long skirt. Slowly and deliberately, he moved his eyes back up her body with mocking indifference. "Miss Howard, I assure you, your person and your precious reputation are *completely* safe with me."

Felicity felt as if she had been slapped in the face. She knew she was no beauty, but his repeated snide references to her physical shortcomings hurt. She thought they had reached a truce of sorts, but it was cruelly apparent that the truce would only be maintained as long as she worked like a slave and agreed to every one of Jake McCullough's whims. Once again, he had put her on the defensive just because she wanted to protect her reputation. She tried to tell herself that his remark didn't matter, that the important thing wasn't what a person looked like but who they were on the inside. Still, what he thought of her *did* matter. It mattered very much. Tears welled up in her eyes and threatened to reveal the pain he had inflicted. She blinked them back, refusing to give him that satisfaction.

Squaring her shoulders and lifting her chin, she said, "Mr. McCullough, since you seem to enjoy exchanging insults, you should know that you're no prize yourself. In fact, you're a boor and a bully." She stepped in front of him and grabbed hold of the canvas cot, tugging the back door open at the same time. Using her body to hold the door wide, she inched the cot toward it.

"Oh, for Christ's sake," he cursed, "give me that!" He lifted the cot out the door and yelled back over his shoulder. "I'll go sleep in the damn lean-to. Come on, Boozer, this is no-man's-land."

She couldn't resist one last small gibe and called after him, "In the lean-to, Mr. McCullough? With the hens?"

"Yes, Miss Howard," he thundered. "In the lean-to . . . with the hens!"

Chapter 5

Felicity's eyes fluttered open, only to close immediately as they were stabbed by bright, mid-morning sunlight. She snuggled further down into the cozy warmth of her blanket, reluctant to start the busy day ahead of her. Busy day! Bright sunlight! She bolted upright and sprang out of the large, comfortable bed. Assessing the angle of the sun, she groaned. How could I have slept half the morning away? she thought. There's so much I have to do today.

Then another thought struck her and she peered guiltily out the window toward the lean-to. Her worst fears were confirmed. The small structure was empty except for the wagon horses. Jake had evidently already gone up to the mine. Oh, no, she thought, now he's probably angrier than ever! In the heat of the previous night's argument, she had thrown the wood bars across both doors, locking him out. That meant he'd had to leave for the mine this morning without eating anything. She felt profound sympathy for the men who had to work with Jake today. She had little doubt he must be in a fine temper.

It was then that she noticed the much-maligned hens avidly scratching the yard for some tasty morsel. Their snaky little necks made quick, bobbing movements as their sharp beaks pecked between pebbles and pine needles. Perched on the overhang of the lean-to sat a large, proud rooster.

"Why didn't you wake me up?" she chastised the bird. "Some rooster you are!" As if he'd heard her reprimand, the chanticleer threw back his head and crowed arrogantly.

Still grumbling to herself, she shed her nightgown and put on a clean dress. She was pulling on her shoes when she finally noticed the state of the room around her. Seeing it by daylight was a shock. No wonder the front room was so neat, she thought, the men must have thrown everything they didn't know what to do with in here. The only surface that wasn't piled high with paraphernalia was the bed, and Felicity now noted that it was none too clean.

Having already wasted precious hours, she skipped breakfast and got right to work. She began by yanking the dingy gray sheets off the bed, wincing at the thought of having slept on them all night.

By mid-afternoon, the sheets were clean and dry and the bed was remade. She concluded that the bed must have been Joseph McCullough's one concession to luxury. The fine, cherry-wood frame, though plain in design, looked brand-new. Its tall, rectangular headboard was crowned by a center panel of disks, below which was a fretwork cornice. The footboard was a less ornate version of the headboard. The bed sat on plain, rectangular feet with protruding chamfered blocks on the sides of the legs. It was a lovely piece of furniture and Felicity decided that all it needed to complete its beauty was a colorful patchwork quilt to replace the worn blanket.

She worked most of the day clearing the room of debris. Everything she didn't know what to do with she tucked into a large box which she shoved into a corner for Jake's inspection. The floor was thoroughly swept, and lacked only a good waxing, though that would have to wait until she could get into town to buy the necessary supplies.

Her own clothes now filled the small, nonde-

script, and heavily marred chest of drawers, while
the men's clothes were neatly folded and placed into
another large box. Glancing about the room, Felicity
sighed in satisfaction. Her stomach growled, reminding her that it was well past lunchtime, but
there was so much she wanted to accomplish before
Jake returned for dinner that she merely peeled and
ate an orange and drank a quick cup of coffee.

It was late, almost seven o'clock, when she finally
spied Jake through the front window. He was crossing the yard and heading in the direction of the
creek. Not knowing when to expect him, she had
fixed a stew. The longer stew cooked, the better it
tasted, and this one had been simmering for hours.
She filled two bowls and set biscuits, butter, and a
pot of honey on the table. She then poured coffee
and sat down to nervously await his arrival. Several
times during the day, her thoughts had wandered
to Jake McCullough. Each time she'd scolded herself
and forced her concentration back to the task of
cleaning her new house. But now he was back, and
after last night's disastrous end and a long day at
the mine, she supposed good humor was too much
to hope for.

She scanned the room for the hundredth time. The
furniture was dusted, the floor swept, and the rag
rug had been beaten free of dirt. She wrinkled her
nose as she looked at the filthy settee, but she would
need help to drag it outside before it could be
cleaned and repaired. The iron stove was spotless
and the counter and shelves had been scrubbed and
neatly rearranged.

This last task had been accomplished despite her
nearly falling off one of the three-legged stools. Not
trusting her balance on the stool again, she had
yanked her skirts above her knees, and in a very
unladylike display, had thrown one leg up on the
countertop and hoisted herself onto it. With shaking
knees, she had slowly stood up and gone about her

task, thankful that no one had witnessed her awkward ascent.

Her overwhelming fear of heights had turned the simple task into a grueling ordeal. Even now she shuddered to think about it. Just being a few feet off the ground sent her head into a dizzy spin and her stomach into a nauseated roll. It was only through sheer determination that she had managed to complete the job.

The door opened and Jake sauntered in with Boozer trotting obediently at his heels. A lock of chestnut hair fell over his forehead and lines of fatigue etched his handsome face. His lack of expression gave Felicity no clue as to his mood. He silently took his place across the table from her while Boozer sat at Jake's feet. Felicity bowed her head to give thanks. When she looked up, her eyes met Jake's, but he quickly averted his gaze to the food before him. She might as well not even be in the same room for all the attention he paid her. Felicity sighed. It was going to be a very long evening.

After several silent minutes, he fished a chunk of beef out of his stew and dropped it into Boozer's mouth. The dog swallowed it in one gulp and licked his chops with relish. She saw her opportunity to break the unbearable tension and pounced on it.

"I saved a large bone for Boozer. Do you mind if he has it?"

He started at the sound of her voice and lifted his hazel eyes to meet hers. "No, of course not. I'm sure he'd love it, but you better give it to him outside. He'd really make a mess of your clean floor."

So, she thought with delight, he *did* notice that I cleaned! To Jake she only said, "Fine, I'll send him outdoors with it after supper." He nodded curtly, laid his spoon down, and walked over to the stove to get another helping of stew. Felicity smiled to herself. At least his sullen mood hadn't affected his appetite. From beneath her thick lashes, she watched him move back around the table and sit down. The little stool creaked with his weight and she wondered why he would furnish his home with these tiny, rickety stools. They seemed so impractical for a man his size.

His presence seemed to fill up the entire cabin. The man radiated raw, masculine strength, but rather than frightening her, she found it fascinating. What must it be like for a woman to rest her head against a man's broad chest, to run her fingers over muscular shoulders, or feel warm breath against her cheek? She blushed at her own wayward thoughts and turned her mind to the practicality of all that strength. She had read enough about hard-rock mining to learn that it was no occupation for the small and weak. Whether single jacking or double jacking with another miner, strength and stamina were essential to wield an eight-pound sledge all day.

Sensing Felicity's scrutiny, Jake looked up and caught her staring at him. She groaned silently in acute embarrassment. He'd caught her gaping at him again, and she could imagine what he must be thinking.

His knowing smile was instantaneous. She blushed and waited for a caustic remark, but he simply lowered his gaze and returned to devouring his bowl of stew. There was no question that he was aware of his appeal to women, and she was not about to help fuel his overblown ego. Ignoring him completely, she removed her dishes to the counter.

Although she had never given her looks much thought before coming to Silverton, she knew she wasn't pretty. She also knew with certainty that Jake McCullough did not find her even slightly appealing. He'd made that perfectly clear, and she was not about to give him any more opportunities to remind her. Their relationship was strictly business, and there was no reason for her to accept his mockery. She deserved the respect he'd give any other business partner. With this thought in mind, she wheeled to face him. ''Might I be let in on the joke, Mr. McCullough?''

The smile playing at the corners of his mouth vanished. ''Ah, it was nothin', Miss Howard.'' He sounded embarrassed and guilty. ''I was just thinkin' about somethin' funny that happened at the mine today. You wouldn't understand the humor of it.''

''I see.'' She wasn't fooled, but she shrugged and changed the subject. ''Do you think I could see the Silver Lady's accounts soon? I didn't find any ledgers while I was tidying up today, and I'd like to know exactly what our financial situation is.''

He cleared his throat and his voice matched her businesslike demeanor. ''The books are all in a shack at the mine. Pa used it for an office, but like I told you before, it wouldn't be a good idea for you to go up there. I'll bring them back with me tomorrow night.''

''Thank you, Mr. McCullough. I would appreciate it.'' Seeing his empty bowl, she inquired, ''Could I get you some more stew?''

He frowned. ''I'll get it myself.'' He got up and filled his bowl with the remainder of the stew. She washed her own dishes and rinsed out the soup kettle as Jake finished his stew and ate the last three biscuits. The man had certainly worked up a ferocious appetite. She'd never known anyone who could eat as much. She fervently hoped the mine was turning a healthy profit because it would take a king's ransom just to keep him fed.

Jake swallowed the last bit of a honey-drenched biscuit and sat watching her efficient movements as she cleaned up the counter. His gaze wandered above her head and fell to rest on the neatly arranged shelves. She had to have climbed up on a stool, and probably even onto the counter to reach the top shelf. It's a wonder she didn't break her fool little neck, he thought soberly. When she came back to the table to gather up his dishes, he remarked, "I see you've been climbin' again, Miss Howard."

"I had no choice, Mr. McCullough," she returned. "The shelves needed cleaning. Besides that, all the food I need to prepare meals is on those shelves. You wouldn't have had any supper tonight if I hadn't climbed up there." She wasn't about to ask him to lower the shelves again. Once was enough.

"Well, it's your neck," he countered, dismissing the subject. "Have you got Boozer's bone over there?"

She was tempted to throw the large, greasy bone in Jake's face, but instead, she plucked it off the counter and gingerly handed it to him, taking extreme care that their hands didn't touch.

Jake grinned down at Boozer. "Come on, boy, let's go out for a walk." He waved the bone toward the door and Boozer bounded after him, barking in eager anticipation.

"Mr. McCullough?"

"Yeah?" He turned to face her again.

"Will you be wanting breakfast in the mornings?"

He smiled wryly. "Why, yes, Miss Howard, I'd like breakfast, but I can't be hangin' around here all mornin' waitin' for it. I have to leave by six o'clock. Is gettin' up that early too much for you to handle?"

She choked back a sharp retort. "Oh, I think I can handle it, Mr. McCullough." He opened the door to leave, but hesitated again when she asked in a voice fairly dripping with sweetness, "One more thing. Do you think *you* can handle bringing the eggs in tomorrow morning or would you prefer I gather them for you?" The only response she heard was a disgusted snort followed by the slamming of the back door.

The rest of the week passed quickly. Felicity saw Jake only at breakfast and supper, and conversation was limited to what was absolutely necessary. By the end of the week, she was beginning to feel very lonely. While a student at St. Margaret's, she had shared a room with three other girls and privacy had been a rare and cherished state. Now she had all the privacy she wanted and ironically found herself homesick for the sound of smothered laughter and whispered confidences. She even missed cranky Sister Angelica's constant reprimands. It was imperative that she get out and meet some people. She'd go stir-crazy if she didn't. She promised herself that she'd rise early on Sunday and go to church.

On Saturday morning she was awakened by the sound of hammering. Her room was still dark and a quick glance out the window attested to the early hour. She slipped from her bed, eased open the bedroom door, and cautiously peered out. Seeing nothing, she leaned out the door a bit further, and a broad smile stole across her face. She quietly retreated back into her room and covered her mouth to stifle a giggle. Had he actually thought she wouldn't be awakened by all that racket? She sat on the edge of her bed, shaking her head. What a ridiculously proud, stubborn man. Still, she'd not antagonize him by putting in an appearance. After all, for the first time she was getting her own way. Jake McCullough was lowering her shelves.

She knew there was no way he could hear her, so she quickly made her bed, washed, and dressed. She smoothed her skirt down over her hips and sighed, wishing she had a full-length mirror. The small round mirror over the chest of drawers didn't allow her to check her appearance below her face, and since the mirror was losing its silvering, even this small image was blotchy and distorted.

Just as she put the last pin into her tightly wound chignon, the hammering came to an abrupt halt. She heard the clanking of tools being thrown into a box, and then all was quiet. Nudging her door open, she looked out again. The food and dishes which were normally kept on the shelves were strewn across the kitchen table. There was no sign of Jake. She hurried over to inspect the shelves. Imagine being so excited about three little shelves, she laughed to herself. But deep down, Felicity knew that it wasn't just the shelves that had so elevated her spirits. He had taken the time to do something nice for her and it made her feel inexplicably happy. She hummed a gay little tune as she put the supplies back.

Sunday morning found her spirits slightly dampened. Jake had not stayed for dinner Saturday night, but had merely stopped by the cabin to tell her that he was going into town with friends. Talking to herself as she prepared for church, she grumbled, ''Well, it's his loss. Here I go to all the trouble of traipsing through the woods at the risk of getting lost or eaten by a bear or who knows what else, just to find some stupid berries to bake him a pie. Well, he's not getting it now. I'll take it with me to church and give it to the priest!''

She shoved a hat pin into her wide-brimmed straw bonnet with a vengeful glint in her eyes. He hadn't returned to the lean-to until almost dawn. The peal of a bawdy song had preceded him up the mountain trail, nearly scaring her witless, until she realized it was just Jake—a very drunk Jake. Her innocent ears still burned as she recalled the gist of the lyrics in his final number.

She knew enough about the evils of alcohol to know that he would probably have a colossal headache when he woke up. Her steps were jaunty as she closed the cabin door and headed for the lean-to. The sight which met her made her laugh until tears streamed down her face. He had missed the cot completely and lay face-down, spread-eagled in the straw with one of the dreaded hens perched regally on his rump. At her approach, the hen hopped down and haughtily strutted away.

Jake roused and croaked a grumbling complaint. ''What . . . what's going on?'' He rolled over and attempted to sit up, but grabbed his head and fell back into his straw bed.

"Mr. McCullough," Felicity demanded loudly, "if you don't get up right now, you're going to make me late for mass."

"For Christ's sake, keep it down, will you?" he moaned. Shooting her a jaundiced look through bloodshot eyes, he finally managed to sit up. "Did you say mass? What time is it, anyway?" He opened his eyes a little wider. "What are you all dressed up for?"

Now that she had had her fun, she really was worried about missing the start of the service. "Mr. McCullough, you're going to make me late for church. And please watch your language! I really cannot tolerate you taking Christ's name in vain."

He grabbed a wood beam and pulled himself up. "What have I got to do with you bein' late for church?" He gave his head a shake as he tried to make sense of what this pesky woman was talking about.

"I can't ride a horse or drive a wagon, Mr. McCullough. You have to take me to church."

He ignored her command and asked, "What are you carryin'?"

"A pie." She sighed impatiently. "I made it for you to thank you for lowering the shelves, but now it's a gift for the priest."

She was so exasperated that she was about ready to throw the pie in his whisker-darkened face. "Damn it, woman, you ain't makin' a lick of sense this morning," he said irritably. He pointed a shaky index finger at her. "Now, let me get this straight." He pulled a wisp of straw out of his dusty chestnut hair, looked at it in surprise, and flicked it away. "You want me to take you to church so you can give my pie to the priest?"

"That's close enough," she agreed. "Now, will you please hurry up and get ready?"

"I don't go to church, lady. Hell, I'm not even Catholic!"

"Fine!" she exclaimed. "Then I'll walk!" She abruptly turned on her heel and strode off toward the road.

"Oh, for God's sake! Hold on a minute, will you?"

She stopped and watched in amusement as he laboriously harnessed the horses to the wagon. She handed him the pie so she could climb onto the seat, astutely guessing that he was probably incapable of helping her, even if he'd been gentleman enough to try. He lifted a corner of the linen towel from the top of the pie and peeked underneath. He inhaled the tantalizing aroma and sighed wistfully. Then he suddenly headed back toward the cabin, carrying the pie.

"Mr. McCullough, where are you going with my pie?" Felicity called in protest.

He looked over his shoulder with a crafty grin. "This is my 'thank you' pie for takin' you to church!"

She rolled her eyes. "Oh, all right. Just set it down inside and hurry! I'm going to be late."

On the way to town, she hinted that he wouldn't have to bother getting up to take her to church if he'd teach her how to ride a horse or drive the wagon. Jake only grunted.

Another week had almost passed before Felicity felt that her new home was clean enough. It was Friday, and she decided that today was going to be just for her. She had prepared a huge breakfast for Jake and he'd left for the mine soon afterward. Having to cook eggs, flapjacks, bacon, and biscuits every morning dirtied almost every pan and dish in the house. Now, as she put the last of the clean dishes away, the thought of playing hooky for a day was exhilarating. The best part was that there was no one to tell her that she couldn't. It was definitely one of the advantages to being on her own.

The first thing she wanted to do was take a real bath. Her sense of propriety didn't allow a swim in the creek, but a couple of days before, she'd found an old copper tub behind the lean-to. After hauling it back to the cabin and painstakingly scouring it, she had lugged it into her bedroom where it now sat beckoning from the corner. She could sit in it to soak if she didn't mind pulling her knees up to her chin, but she'd have to stand up to wash. Still, it was better than a sponge bath from the shallow basin that sat on top of the old chest.

She gathered all the buckets she could find, filled them with water, and carried them inside to heat on the stove. By the time her bath was finally ready, she was out of breath from her exertions, but still full of eager anticipation.

She stood by the side of the small tub and began to remove her clothing. A little French tune that she had learned long ago came to mind and she gaily sang the happy words.

Jake tied his horse's reins to the post in front of the lean-to. I don't know what's the matter with me lately, he chided himself. If I'm not droppin' somethin', I'm forgettin' it. I swear it's havin' to put up with a female partner. He headed toward the back of the cabin, but stopped short near Felicity's window when he heard her singing. He couldn't understand the French words and moved a little closer.

He didn't realize that he was gaping as he crept up to one side of her window, his eyes glued to the creamy-skinned goddess inside the cabin. He stared as Felicity pulled the narrow pink ribbon on her chemise and let it fall open. Drawing her arms out of it, she tossed it onto the end of her bed with the rest of her clothes. His jaw dropped. But what was that contraption she had wrapped around her chest?

She reached around and unhooked the breast binder. Sister Angelica had always told her that she was overly endowed, and had insisted, even before she joined the order, that she bind herself. With the binder released, she sucked in air and lifted her full breasts in her hands. It was always such a relief to remove the uncomfortable garment. She pushed the alabaster globes upward, massaging the ache caused by their restraint.

Jake was thunderstruck. Felicity Howard had the most beautiful breasts he'd ever seen, and he'd seen more than his share. He knew he should move away from the window, but he couldn't help but wonder what other wonders were hiding beneath all those ugly trappings the girl wore.

She slipped her pantalettes down over her slim hips, kicked them into the air, and tossed them on top of the growing heap on the bed. Now naked except for her stockings, she unwittingly treated Jake's hungry eyes to the stunning sight of her narrow waist and the feminine curve of her hips. He feasted on the sight of the curly blonde triangle at the juncture of her thighs. He could almost feel its softness between his fingers.

She reached up and pulled the pins out of her tawny hair, causing it to tumble down in thick, undulating waves that came to rest at the top of her hips. Jake knew he was acting like the worst kind of scoundrel by standing there peeping into her window, but he felt as if he were rooted to the spot. His view of her body was temporarily impaired until she turned and bent over to remove her stockings. Her loose hair framed her small face, softening her cheekbones and wiping away the look of severity her prim bun gave her.

His heart pounded in his chest as he realized that Felicity Howard was a classic beauty, the type of woman who would only get better as she matured.

She had her stockings off now, and was adding them to the pile. Her legs were long, slender, and tightly muscled. Not an ounce of extra flesh marred their perfection. Her little bottom was round as a plum. Two perfect handfuls, he thought irreverently. Why the hell does she disguise that gorgeous body with all those awful clothes? he wondered. She ain't a nun anymore and it just don't make sense to hide that kind of beauty. Images of gleefully setting fire to her breast binder raced through his besotted mind.

She stepped into the tub and sank to her knees. She dipped the washcloth into the water and reached for a small bar of rose-scented soap. The soap represented her one frivolous purchase before leaving Philadelphia and she smiled as she inhaled its heady fragrance.

His heated gaze enviously followed the path of the water as it sluiced a warm trail down the slopes of her breasts and dripped off the tips of her rose-hued nipples. The small buds instantly hardened to little pink pebbles.

A familiar tightening in his loins drew his attention away from Felicity. He looked down in amazement to see his denim jeans stretched tightly over his swollen manhood. Cursing himself, he wheeled around and left the window, feverishly striding down the path to the back of the cabin. What's wrong with me? he thought in disgust. I must be goin' crazy! He stopped in his tracks as realization dawned. Hell, McCullough, you're not crazy, you're just aroused as hell and you can't believe it's Felicity Howard who did it to you.

He grabbed the cable line that he'd forgotten that morning and stomped over to his horse. Throwing himself painfully into the saddle, he set a thundering pace up the path to the mine.

All afternoon, he contemplated the scene he had witnessed that morning. He'd had no idea what a desirable temptress his little church mouse really was. Every time he thought about how she'd looked, the familiar masculine ache returned to plague him. Damn, he cursed himself, get hold of yourself, man! Sure, she's got a great body, but there's only one way you'd ever get her in your bed, and that's to put a weddin' ring on her finger first.

He had seen enough of his parents' disastrous marriage to know that matrimony wasn't for him. When his father had left their farm in Ohio and gone to seek his fortune, Maryanne McCullough had dutifully followed. But, when the going got rough, she hadn't even tried to stick it out. After pleading—to no avail—with her obstinate husband to give up his crazy dream and return home, she'd packed her bags and left. She'd tried to take ten-year-old Jake with her, but Joe had put his foot down, telling her she'd never take his son away from him. Maryanne had returned to Ohio and they'd never heard from her again. Five years later Joe had received news that she'd died from a fever.

Despite her abandonment of him, Joe had never stopped loving his wife and it nearly killed him when he heard of her death. Jake, however, felt nothing but resentment toward his traitorous mother and couldn't understand his father's unrelenting defense of her actions. No woman was worth the kind of heartache that Joe had suffered over Maryanne.

There was no way he was going to saddle himself with a wife, especially just to get into some girl's drawers. He much preferred to simply enjoy a willing woman's body for a night and then go his own way. He had his work and he lived pretty well. That was enough for him. What made me think of a wife anyway? he asked himself irritably.

Then he remembered the little nun with the body of a goddess who was living in his cabin and sleeping in his bed. He knew that something had to be done about Felicity Howard. And it had to be done soon, or he'd end up in her bed, all right, but with a little gold ring on her finger and one through his nose.

"Hey, Jake," called Pete Brady. Jake looked up at one of his shoremen. "You hear about the dance over to Howardsville next Saturday night? It's gonna be a real big shindig. Only costs a quarter and there's bound to be some pretty girls there.''

"I heard somethin' about it last Saturday in Silverton,'' Jake called back. "You goin', Pete?''

"Hell, yes, I'm goin'! Wouldn't miss it for nothin'.''

As Jake returned to his work, he was struck by an idea so inspired that he laughed out loud. He'd take Felicity to the dance so she could meet some of the men. If he could marry her off to some poor sucker, the temptation of that sexy little body of hers would be somebody else's problem. Well, he thought, chuckling to himself, maybe *problem* isn't exactly the right word.

But finding a husband for Felicity would solve a multitude of difficulties. First and foremost, it would get her out of his cabin. Maybe he could even persuade her to sell him back her share of the mine, which would also get her out of his life. The more he thought about it, the more pleased he was. Yes, indeed, with a little bit of luck, by next week at this time, the little nun would at least be engaged!

Felicity had just finished her noon meal when she heard a horse gallop up to the front of the cabin. She glanced out the window to see Yancy Parnell dismounting. As usual, Yancy was dressed in a fine black frock coat, dark trousers, and an immaculately clean, ruffled shirt. He wore a horseshoe-shaped diamond pin in his lapel and matching cuff links at his wrists. She smiled as she saw him slick back his hair before approaching the cabin. If I didn't know better, she thought, I'd swear he's come courting. She opened the door with a welcoming smile. "Yancy, what a pleasant surprise,'' she said enthusiastically. ''Please come in and we'll have some coffee.'

Yancy returned her smile and stepped inside the cabin. He'd only been in the place once before when he'd come to try to talk Joe McCullough into selling out to him, but the changes were immediately noticeable. "Looks like you've been busy, Felicity."

"Yes, I have, but there's still so much to do. Before I can clean any more, though, I need to go into town and fetch some supplies."

She led Yancy over to the kitchen table since the settee was still so disreputable. "Have a seat, Yancy. The coffee is still hot." She poured two cups and set a plate of cookies on the table. "I'm so glad you came. I've been hoping to see you so I could apologize for what happened that day at the attorney's office. You'd been so kind to me, and then to have you hurt for your trouble . . . well, I just felt terrible about it."

"It wasn't your fault," he replied. "You mustn't blame yourself." He dunked a cookie into his coffee and took a bite. "I've been worried about you, though. Is Jake McCullough behaving himself?"

"Everything is fine now," she assured him. "We have reached an agreement of sorts. We just don't talk to each other unless it concerns the mine."

"You mean he's not living in the cabin anymore?" he asked curiously.

"Oh, my, no. That wouldn't be at all proper."

"I don't like the idea of you being up here all by yourself." He frowned. "A woman on her own in the wilderness is fair game for any drunken miner who might happen along. You really should take a house in town."

"Oh, I'm not really alone, Yancy. Jake comes for breakfast and dinner, and at night he sleeps in the lean-to. If someone was snooping about, he'd take care of them."

Yancy chuckled at this revelation. "I bet Jake doesn't like those sleeping arrangements much."

She blushed and took a sip of her coffee. "Well, no, he doesn't, but I wouldn't have it any other way."

Yancy tried to imagine the scene which must have taken place between Felicity and McCullough. He smiled in satisfaction. At least McCullough was being paid back for some of his arrogance that day at the lawyer's office. From the sound of things, he and Felicity were barely speaking. Yancy couldn't be happier. It made things a hell of a lot easier for him. "You must get kind of lonesome up here all by yourself," he said solicitously.

"Yes, I'm afraid I do," she admitted. "I'm used to being around a lot of people all the time. When I was at the convent, I dreamed of having more privacy and time to myself, but now I have too much. I'm hoping some of the church members might come calling."

"I'm sure they will, and so will the other folks from town once they meet you. In a way, that's why I came by today. There's a dance at Howardsville next Saturday night and I'd be honored if you'd attend with me. Even though it's at Howardsville, all of the Silverton folks will be there. It will be a good way for you to meet the ladies from town and start to get acquainted."

"How nice of you to think of me," she replied sincerely.

"Not at all." He smiled. "I assure you my motives are entirely selfish." He leaned over and took her hand in his. "What do you say, Felicity, will you go with me?"

The front door of the cabin flew open and both of them turned in surprise to see Jake standing in the doorway, scowling at them. "Jake, you're back early," exclaimed Felicity. She flung Yancy a warning look, but he just smiled reassuringly and nodded. She would have withdrawn her hand but his grip suddenly tightened.

Jake looked at her hand enclosed in Yancy's and lifted his eyes to stare with loathing at the other man. He didn't know why, but this tender little scene enraged him. "What are you doin' here, Parnell?" he snapped. "I thought I made it clear that you ain't

welcome around here." He walked aggressively into
the small room and stood glaring at Yancy.

But Parnell wasn't about to be intimidated. His
stool scraped the floor as he stood up to face Jake.
Felicity tried in vain to pull her hand out of Yancy's
grasp, but he merely pulled her up beside him and
held on tighter. She was a bit shocked at Yancy's
behavior, but was more concerned with the possibility of the men coming to blows in her house.

"I just came by to see how Felicity is doing and
ask her to attend the Howardsville dance with me
next Saturday."

"Well, then, it's too bad you rode all the way up
here for nothin'." Jake smiled smugly. "She's already promised to go to the dance with me."

Felicity gasped in outrage. "That's not true, Jake
McCullough, and you know it! Why, I didn't even
know there was a dance until Yancy asked me to go
with him. How dare you act in such a high-handed
fashion?"

Jake turned a furious scowl on her for exposing
his lie. "As concerned as you are about your reputation, Miss Howard, I figured you'd rather go with
me than with a two-bit gambler who owns a saloon
and a whorehouse." He wasn't sure if she knew
what the girls at the Last Chance did up in those
rooms, but if she hadn't known before, this new
knowledge would set her straight in a hurry.

Felicity turned a bright shade of crimson at his
crude words. However, she wasn't about to let him
get away with this show of arrogance. How dare he?
she thought resentfully. After all his insults about
how unattractive I am, now he has the audacity to
assume I'd choose him over Yancy. She felt a familiar twinge of impetuosity, but she didn't care. At
this moment, all she wanted was to show Jake
McCullough that he had a lot to learn about her.

For a moment, she thought of Jake holding her in
his arms for a whole evening. It would have been
heavenly! She quickly squelched that fantasy and

glared back at him. He'd probably never even intended to tell her about the dance, let alone ask her to go with him. He just wanted to antagonize Yancy.

Yancy knew by Felicity's outraged expression that he'd won the day. He offered her his most charming smile and gave the hand he still held a slight squeeze.

Felicity threw Jake a haughty look. "It just so happens that I've already consented to go to the dance with Mr. Parnell." She winced inwardly at her lie, but consoled herself that no one would be hurt by it. She did intend to accept Yancy's invitation.

Jake was furious, but knowing that venting his anger on Parnell would only encourage her sudden propensity toward the man, he simply answered, "Fine. So what's for supper? I'm hungry."

Yancy swung Felicity around and smiled down at her. "I was just about to ask you to join me for dinner in town tonight. It's still early and I could have you back before dark."

At that moment, she could have kissed Yancy Parnell. "Oh, Yancy, that sounds wonderful. I never get out of this cabin to do anything fun. I'll just get my shawl."

Yancy watched her disappear into the bedroom and then turned to give Jake a triumphant smile. Jake stormed out of the cabin, cursing silently. Calling Boozer, he grabbed his rifle from where he'd left it, mounted his horse, and headed for the mine. There was still enough daylight to get some more work done.

He was mad as hell about Felicity going to the dance with Parnell, but he told himself it wasn't because she wouldn't be going with him. It was just that he didn't like her getting cozy with Yancy Parnell. The gambler had been trying to buy the Silver Lady for some time now. He'd even approached Jake last Saturday night when he'd gotten so drunk in town. Why was the man so insistent about buying a mine that was barely breaking even? One thing he was almost sure of, Yancy was courting Felicity for her share of the Silver Lady. The man couldn't be aware of the beauty that lay hidden beneath her layers of clothing, and her naive, prudish ways certainly couldn't hold any allure for him.

He consoled himself with the fact that at least she would be attending the dance. That was the main idea to begin with, to introduce her to some decent men. Now, he thought, if I could just get her to leave off that damned breast crusher without her knowing I found out about it, maybe somebody might even be interested in her.

Two days later, Jake had to run another unexpected midday errand at the cabin. He'd previously seen the rope that Felicity had strung for her laundry, but he'd never seen any of her clothing hanging from it. Today, however, the line was full and the first items his eyes lit upon were two of her breast binders. He grinned and glanced around to see if she was nearby. Assured that she wasn't about, he swiftly grabbed the binders and stuffed them inside his shirt. Feeling like a mischievous boy, he hurried down to the creek and threw the blasted garments into the swiftly flowing water. For a few minutes they floated on top, but they were soon pulled under the surface and disappeared from view.

Jake retraced his steps and mounted his horse, forgetting his original reason for returning to the cabin. When he got back to the mine and his top driller, Jim Cranston, reminded him, he wasn't the least bit upset. He just shrugged his shoulders and smiled smugly. His shoreman, Pete, and Jim exchanged confused glances and went back to work. There was just no figuring Jake McCullough.

Chapter 6

❦

Saturday finally arrived and the day couldn't go fast enough to suit Felicity. Tonight, she was going to a real dance! Before she'd joined the order, she had been taught the rudiments of dancing in deportment class with the other girls from the convent school as partners. She had never been terribly fond of dance class, but she guessed that dancing with a male partner might be a very different experience.

She put the last breakfast dish away, wondering why Jake was still idling at the table. Twice in the past week he had shown her how to harness the horses up to the wagon and had let her drive it around the yard, but other than that, he'd remained coolly aloof. On those two occasions, however, she had caught him staring at her with an unreadable expression. When he'd realized she was returning his curious stare, he'd abruptly directed her attention to some aspect of driving the wagon.

She shrugged away her thoughts. She had a lot to do to get ready for the dance tonight and nothing was going to distract her. She wanted to look her best, not just for Yancy, but to make a favorable impression on the townspeople she hoped to meet. She could hardly bear the anticipation as she hurried to finish her morning chores.

Jake was bewildered by the secretive smile on her

face. Even dressed in her usual baggy garb, she somehow looked unusually pretty this morning. When she headed off toward her bedroom, he leaped up from the table and called, "Miss Howard?"

Felicity turned so quickly she almost bounced off his broad chest. He reached out and steadied her, then quickly dropped his hands from her arms and moved back a step. He noted that her figure still had the same boyish shape and surmised that he'd obviously failed to dispose of all of her breast binders. She hadn't mentioned the missing garments, but then he supposed that a lady didn't discuss her underwear, missing or otherwise, with a man. For that he was extremely thankful.

"What is it, Mr. McCullough?" she asked after righting herself. She hoped he wasn't going to start something that would spoil the day for her.

"I'd like to talk to you for a minute."

"Is something wrong at the mine?"

"No, of course not."

"You and I usually only talk about business. Couldn't this wait until tomorrow? I have a great deal to do today."

He frowned and shook his head. "No, we have to talk now. Tomorrow will be too late. Come on, let's sit on the settee for a minute."

Intrigued, she settled herself on the edge of the freshly cleaned and repaired settee and waited for him to speak.

Now that he had her undivided attention, he was unexpectedly nervous and unsure of how to begin. After shifting his position several times, he cleared his throat and began. "Miss Howard . . . do you know how to dance?"

She jerked her head up and glared at him. "Of course I know how to dance," she returned indignantly. "I learned at school." Why does he always have to treat me like a social misfit? she wondered irritably. "Do you know how, Mr. McCullough?

Perhaps you'd like a quick lesson this afternoon so you don't embarrass yourself tonight.''

He waved her angry question aside. ''Look, I didn't mean to offend you. I just wanted to give you some help if you needed it.''

''That's very kind of you, but what brought about this sudden concern? Surely it wouldn't bother you if I disgraced myself and embarrassed Yancy. We both know how you feel about him.''

''Forget Parnell for now,'' he responded in annoyance. ''I think it's important that you make a good impression on the men who will be at the dance tonight.''

''The men, Mr. McCullough? Why should I care about any other men? Yancy's escorting me to the dance. I'll be his partner for the evening.''

''Well, that's one of the things I thought we should discuss,'' he interjected hurriedly. ''You see, up here there's a big shortage of women—*good* women, that is. Whenever there's a dance like this, a lady is expected to dance with a few of the other men. It's sort of a polite rule in these parts.''

''All right.'' Felicity nodded. ''I see. I don't mind sharing a few dances with other men and I'm sure Yancy will understand. He's probably well aware of the customs here.''

Jake shrugged and continued hesitantly, ''Now, don't get me wrong, but there's a few other things we need to talk about. Not customs or nothin', just things about you.''

She raised her eyebrows. ''Oh? And what might those be?''

''Well, don't you think you should fix yourself up a little?'' At her gasp of outrage, Jake held up his hand. ''Now, don't get mad. Just shut up a minute and let me explain.''

Felicity could hardly believe her ears. The man's impudence was unbelievable! ''Mr. McCullough, I assure you that I am well aware that the occasion calls for a little extra primping on my part.'' Taking several deep breaths to control her anger and humiliation, she adjusted her position on the settee so that she was staring out the window.

Jake swallowed hard. "No, it's not exactly that. It's just, well . . . you're not in a convent anymore, Miss Howard." She continued to stare out the window as he rushed on with his lecture. "You have pretty hair. Why don't you loosen it up a little? You know, let some curl around your face or somethin'."

He was finding her complete lack of response unnerving, but, undaunted, he closed his eyes to gather his courage and continued, "Then there's that . . . that thing you wear." Her eyes darted to his with a look of confusion. Jake felt his face turn a bright shade of red. "Damn it, Miss Howard, you know what I mean! That *thing* you wear that makes you look like a boy!"

"*Mr. McCullough!*" Felicity gasped. She started to jump up, but he gently pushed her back down with a light hand on her shoulder.

Seeing that his face was as red as her own made her feel a little better. He obviously wasn't enjoying this any more than she was. So why was he doing it? Her curiosity now piqued, she flicked his hand away and sat back, waiting to see what he was leading up to.

He cleared his throat. "That thing might be all right for nuns, but I gotta tell you, a man likes a woman who's got a little shape to her. You know . . . curves."

Felicity looked at him, shocked. How *dare* he mention such things to her?

Interpreting her silence to be agreement, he plunged on eagerly. "Look, Miss Howard, I'm no expert on female trappin's but I do know that your clothes are all way too big. They hang on you like a burlap bag."

She stiffened and her mouth tightened into a thin line. Jake realized that maybe he'd gone too far and eyed her warily, waiting for the explosion he was sure was imminent. To his surprise, she remained silent. He knew that any other woman would have slapped his face. He had even braced himself for it, but all she did was sit there. Somehow, not knowing what she was thinking was worse than being slapped.

Long moments passed before she finally answered, a slight tremor in her voice revealing her agitation. "Why are you telling me all this, Mr. McCullough? I don't understand why you care how I look."

He looked away, angry with himself for feeling like a heel. Hell, he rationalized, I'm actually doin' her a favor here! His gaze returned to hers and he was shaken by her soft-eyed vulnerability. For a second he was almost tempted to give up on his plans to marry her off. Before he could change his mind, he blurted, "I care because I think it would be a good idea for you to consider gettin' married to somebody."

"Married?" she asked incredulously. "Why should you concern yourself with my getting married?"

Her question caught him off guard. He mentally scrambled for a plausible answer and finally stammered, "Well, I . . . that is . . . havin' you up here makes me feel responsible for you. And that's not fair to me. You should have a husband to take care of you. Why, I can't even go into town on Saturday night without havin' to worry if you'll be all right up here by yourself."

"That certainly hasn't seemed to stop you before," she responded wryly.

He ignored her barb, astutely realizing that some subjects were better left alone. "The fact remains, Miss Howard, that you can't protect yourself, and the way I figure it, that job should belong to a husband. You have to be careful in the choosin' though, because there's some men who'd marry you just for your share of the mine. That could be real bad for both of us. Fortunately for you, I know which men would make the best suitors.''

''Why am I not surprised?'' she asked cynically. She could not believe Jake's audacity. Although she'd always been taught that women should be subservient to men, she couldn't help resenting this man trying to manage her life.

He frowned at her sarcasm but he was determined to finish what he'd started. Reaching into his pocket, he pulled out a crumpled piece of paper and handed it to her. ''Here's a list of good prospects. You might want to spend some time memorizin' these names so that when you get to the dance and are introduced, you'll know who to be extra nice to.''

She stared at the paper in disbelief. How could he do this to me, she cried inwardly. It's humiliating, degrading! First he tells me that I look like a burlap bag and then tries to shove me into marriage because I'm a burden to him. And not only that, he even has the gall to tell me who's acceptable to him and who isn't!

She slowly rose. She looked down at her feet and took a deep breath. ''I thank you, Mr. McCullough, for your consideration. You have obviously given this quite a lot of thought.'' He smiled and nodded, relieved to see that she understood. ''I warn you though,'' she continued evenly, ''if and when I ever decide to get married, I'll do my own choosing and what you or anybody else has to say about my choice will be of no consequence.''

His smile disappeared.

She dropped the slip of paper into his lap and turned her back in dismissal. ''Now, if you don't mind, I have a lot to do before the dance, as you have so kindly pointed out. Please leave.''

He watched in bewilderment as she walked sedately into her bedroom and closed the door.

The discussion left him with mixed feelings. It was a relief to have it over with, and yet he wasn't sure if she would actually heed any of his advice. She had rejected the list he'd prepared, but he didn't consider that to be serious. At least she knew where he stood and what he expected of her. What was troubling him now was the moist shimmer in her eyes that he had seen before she turned her back to him. Hell, he thought irritably, I didn't mean to hurt her damn feelings. I'm just tryin' to tell her what's best for everybody!

Jake knew he wasn't good with words, especially when it came to discussing something most women knew without being told. That hurt expression of hers had almost tempted him to put a comforting arm around her shoulders. Lord! Didn't he know better than anyone what a mistake that would be! He could never allow himself to indulge in that kind of weakness. If he even so much as touched her, he knew he wouldn't be satisfied until that sexy little body of hers was snuggled up next to him in bed and he sure as hell couldn't let that happen!

He practically ran out the front door. If he didn't stop thinking about that body, he was going to need a cold dip in the creek!

At first Felicity cried, then she got mad. The harder the bone-jarring hiccoughs shook her, the madder she got. Oh, she'd been angry with Jake McCullough before, but this was the limit! The older nuns always preached that "pride goeth before the fall," but she decided it was time to assert hers.

With new determination, she pushed herself up from the tearstained bed cover and ran to the old chest, yanking open drawer after drawer. She tossed a crisp white blouse on the bed and followed it with a plain gray skirt and white petticoat. From the last drawer, she withdrew her small round sewing box. She stripped down to her underclothes and removed her chemise. The breast binder was discarded with a vengeance. She redonned the chemise, grabbed up the blouse, and pulled it on.

Smiling smugly, she opened the sewing box and began to pin the large blouse so that it hugged her trim figure.

At half past five Jake strode through the back door of the cabin, his heavy boots grinding to an immediate halt at the sight that met him. Felicity was just stepping out of her bedroom, but she hesitated a moment when she saw him staring at her.

He was so astounded at the vision she presented that he just stood and gaped. Her heavy hair was pulled back, but she had allowed it to puff around her head before wrapping the ends into a soft, shiny chignon. Her high-necked, white blouse was buttoned to the top as usual, but it now molded her full breasts and clung snugly to her small rib cage. A hint of white-laced petticoat peeped out from beneath the plain, tiny-waisted skirt. Over her arm was a small gray jacket. It, too, showed signs of being altered.

His gaze locked with her bright, emerald eyes and he swallowed hard. What have I done? he asked himself. Although she was still very proper, Felicity Howard was definitely going to turn every man's head in Howardsville tonight. She was the essence of feminine beauty and innocence. Innocence that begged to be corrupted. A sudden anger surged up within him at the thought of all those woman-hungry miners undressing her with their eyes. Well, this is what you wanted, isn't it? he argued with himself. You wanted her to attract the attention of some marriage prospects, didn't you? So why are you getting so damned riled up at the idea of all those men touchin' her tonight?

It was a mistake, a terrible mistake. The possibility that she could look this good had never occurred to him. There was no doubt that she'd attract men, but until she chose one, what was *he* going to do? If she made it a habit to look like this from now on, he'd be hard-pressed to keep his own hands off her until she was married. He nearly groaned in frustration. Self-denial had never been one of his strong points, especially where women were concerned. This damn woman had been nothing but trouble right from the start!

Felicity watched in bemusement as the expression on Jake's face went from astonishment to anger. Mistaking his reaction, she sighed dejectedly. Apparently, she still didn't measure up to his expectations. She had secretly hoped that he'd be jealous when he saw how nice she looked. Even she had been surprised when she'd studied her reflection in her bedroom window. For the first time in her life, she had taken a critical look at herself. She was pleased to realize that her figure could measure up to any of the fashionable beauties she'd seen in Philadelphia. Even if she hadn't liked what Jake had said to her, she had to admit that he'd been right about a few things. She did look better wearing clothes that fit.

She shut her bedroom door and walked over to the window to await Yancy's arrival. There was no sense in giving Jake the satisfaction of knowing how disappointed she was. But, blast it, she'd wanted him to eat his words! All that work this morning and she still couldn't win his approval. She stared glumly out the window, trying to concentrate on the scenic beauty surrounding the little cabin. Ponderosa pines, blue spruce, and aspen trees bathed the secluded clearing with cool, peaceful shade. She breathed deeply of the fresh, woodsy smell which permeated the lengthening shadows of the coming evening.

Jake came up behind her and halted just a step away. "Miss Howard?"

She noticed an odd light in his eyes that she'd never seen before. For a moment he looked like he might touch her, but he took a hasty step backward and smiled instead. "You look real nice."

"Nice? But I thought . . ." She stopped before she

gave herself away. "Thank you, Mr. McCullough, for saying so."

He mentally shook himself. Careful, man, he cautioned silently, or she'll be addin' your name to that list of prospects!

A more familiar facade settled over his features, astonishing her with the abrupt change. Grinning, he quipped, "The fact is, you look good enough to attract even Walter Beasley—and he's about the best-lookin' and richest miner in these parts."

Her eyes blazed. "Mr. McCullough, I assure you that it is not my intention to 'attract' anyone!" She turned back to the window, not wanting Jake to see how much his careless words hurt her. Resuming her watch, she murmured, "I do hope Yancy gets here soon. I don't want to be late. Shouldn't you be getting ready, Mr. McCullough?"

"Yeah, I should," he muttered. "Did you happen to find some dress clothes when you were cleanin' up the bedroom?"

"As a matter of fact, I did. I packed them away in a box. It's still sitting in the corner to the left of the window."

"Then, if you don't mind, I'll go in and get what I need." Not waiting for her answer, he strode off to the bedroom.

"Oh, here's Yancy," she called to the empty room. She glanced behind her, but Jake, if he'd heard, didn't bother to reply.

Yancy was delighted with the "new" Felicity Howard. His earlier suspicions were now confirmed. The girl had a beautiful body. As he escorted her into the Howardsville Community Building where the dance was being held, he stood a little taller and his shoulders were thrown back a fraction farther. He hadn't been looking forward to being seen with such a plain woman, but he had to admit, she sure looked good tonight!

It was apparent that the other men at the dance thought so too. She was whirled and twirled around the large room as several fiddlers and a piano player enthusiastically sawed and pounded on their instruments. When the band took a short break, Yancy finally reclaimed her and seated her near the refreshment table. She gazed admiringly at his handsomely attired figure as he waited for the stout man behind the table to fill their cups. People milled about chatting, and several ladies stopped and introduced themselves.

When Yancy returned with their drinks, he sat down close to her and smiled. "Be careful of that drink, Felicity. I think some of the boys added a little punch to it."

She looked confused. What was so unusual about punch at a party? She swept a few errant curls from her face and took a thirsty swallow. Immediately, she was seized by a fit of coughing. Her throat burned like fire and her eyes watered until tears streamed down her cheeks.

Yancy saw the problem right away and ran for some water. When he returned he handed her the cup. "Drink this," he ordered gently, "it's just water." She gulped the cool liquid and smiled her thanks. "I'm really sorry about that, Felicity," Yancy apologized. "I guess I'm so used to the liquor they pour in there that I didn't realize how strong it would seem to you."

Regaining her composure, she laughed. "I didn't know what you meant by punch. We always had punch at special functions at the convent but it wasn't anything like this, believe me!"

Yancy laughed loudly, then said, "I'm sorry, honey. I'm not really laughing at you. It's just that I've never met anyone quite like you."

She blushed at Yancy's endearment, but she was enjoying his friendly teasing. If felt good to be out among people and it felt very good to laugh. She hadn't done enough of that lately. She joined in Yancy's hilarity and laid her hand on his where it rested on his knee. "Oh, Yancy, I'm so glad you brought me tonight. I'm having such fun. You make me feel so happy and—well, like a woman instead of a nun.'' Her cheeks again bloomed with color at her last, rash statement.

As the band mounted the small platform at the front of the room and took their places, Yancy again led Felicity out onto the floor. ''Felicity, there's no need to blush. You *are* a woman . . . and a very pretty one at that.'' He was a little surprised to find that he meant it. When she smiled like she did now, her whole face lit up and her beautiful green eyes had the power to entrance a man. He'd asked her to the dance with only one thing in mind: to gain her trust and get her to sell her share of the mine to him. If she absolutely wouldn't sell, he'd even convinced himself that he'd go to such extreme measures as proposing marriage to her. Yancy was willing to do *anything* to get his hands on the Silver Lady.

Unbidden, another woman's face swam before his eyes, but he quickly shoved the vision aside. Affairs of the heart could not be considered when money was involved.

From across the room, Jake could see Felicity and Yancy as they moved to a slow waltz. He'd witnessed the tender little scene of them holding hands and had heard her happy laughter. Never had he seen a woman look so beautiful, and never had Felicity Howard laughed like that around him. Well, what does it matter, anyway? he asked himself angrily. He just wanted the little intruder out of his life.

With that thought, he sauntered over to an attractive, raven-haired woman and asked her to dance. The woman smiled invitingly and took his hand, tilting her head back to see his answering grin. Jake read the silent invitation and held her so close that her large breasts pressed indiscreetly against his white shirtfront. His muscular thighs brushed her skirts and he could tell by the sultry expression in her dark eyes that she could feel his heat even through her petticoats.

Ever since he had seen Felicity at her bath, his need for a woman had grown stronger and stronger till it had become a physical agony. He bent and whispered something in his seductive partner's ear. The woman smiled sensuously and nodded. But, as they turned to leave the dance floor, Jake was suddenly stopped by a heavy hand clamping down on his shoulder. "Mind if I have this dance with my *wife*, mister?" Jake's hand dropped from the woman's waist as if he'd been burned.

"Of course not. Thanks for the dance, ma'am." He beat a hasty retreat to the back of the room and blended in with the other unpartnered miners. "Women!" he cursed. "Can't trust any of 'em!"

Felicity watched Jake and the lovely, dark-haired woman. An unexpected pain shot through her at the sight, a pain so intense that she missed her step and nearly lost her balance. Yancy instinctively tightened his grip to keep her from falling. "Are you all right?" he asked with concern.

She swallowed the lump in her throat and looked up at him with a brilliant smile. "Of course. I'm just a little clumsy."

Yancy was shocked when she pressed closer and laced her fingers through the hair at the nape of his neck. He wondered what had come over her, but decided not to question his good luck. Felicity had noticed that another man had taken Jake's place with the woman and she hoped Jake was watching *her* now.

He was.

As the evening progressed, she danced with one partner after another, many of whom asked if they might call on her. They were all surprised to hear that she was part-owner of Jake McCullough's Silver Lady mine. One by one, her partners managed to find Jake where he now sulked in a shadowed corner.

"You mean that fine little filly is your partner and she's livin' up there in your cabin with you?" one envious miner asked. "Shit, you got it made, McCullough! What I wouldn't give to be in your shoes!"

John Randolph from the Three Aces mine chimed in, "Yeah, you can bet if it was me, I wouldn't be sharin' that pretty piece with no Yancy Parnell."

Jake pushed himself away from the wall and towered over the luckless miner. "She's a lady, Randolph, a real lady. I'm not livin' with her in the cabin and if I hear you say one more dirty thing about her, I'll smash that ugly face of yours till even your own mother won't recognize you. You got it?"

John Randolph knew when to shut up, and quietly slunk away. Only a fool would start a fight with Jake.

"Hello there, Mr. McCullough. How's everything up at the mine?" Jake looked down to see his lawyer, Benjamin Ford, grinning up at him.

"Everythin's fine, Ben. How 'bout you?"

"Oh, same as usual. Nothing very exciting." Ford glanced out over the dance floor and saw Yancy dancing with Felicity. "I'm surprised to see those two together after what happened in town that day."

Jake folded his arms across his chest and leaned back against the wall. "Yeah, well, Miss Howard is just full of surprises," he said belligerently. Ford cast him a curious glance.

Pete Brady and his constant companion, Jim Cranston, joined Jake and Ben Ford. "Hey, Jake? How come you never told us you was partners with that pretty little gal over there?" Pete pointed at Felicity.

Jake shrugged. "Subject just never came up, I guess. 'Sides, it didn't seem worth mentionin'."

Jim looked closely at him and frowned. "Well, I ain't seen you dance with her yet, Jake. Seems only right that you ask the gal to dance. After all, she is your partner and all."

Jake scowled. ''I didn't choose her for a partner, Jim, and I pick my friends real carefully.''

Pete and Jim exchanged sly smiles. ''Just the same, I wouldn't let no slick gambler get one up on me,'' Pete challenged. ''No sirree.''

''Pete's right, Jake,'' Jim interjected. ''Partner or no, she's still a good-lookin' woman and I think she deserves better than that sleazy sidewinder Parnell. Have you seen the way he's holdin' that sweet little thing?''

He saw, all right. And he didn't like it one bit. He remembered too vividly how indecently close he'd held the ebony-haired woman and what he'd planned to do with her. Was Parnell, at this very moment, pressing himself against Felicity with the same randy intent? Jake forgot all about his previous conclusions regarding Yancy's interest in Felicity. If that bastard tried anything . . .

''Good! There goes Corny.'' Pete looked pleased. ''He's gonna cut in on the gambler.'' Jake watched as the little Englishman took Yancy's place with Felicity. Some of his pent-up anger was released in a sigh of relief.

A half hour later, the last dance of the evening was announced. There was an excited murmur among the ladies as the men headed for their sweethearts. Jake had, by now, been joined by most of his mining crew, all of whom were egging him on to ask Felicity to dance. ''Bloody hell, McCullough!'' chided the Cornishman. ''This is your last chance and there goes that gambler heading right for her. Hurry, man!''

''Go get her, boy!'' encouraged Pete.

Yancy stepped up next to Felicity and held out his hand in invitation.

''Well, Jake, ol' boy, looks like you're too late.'' Jim slapped a hand on Jake's shoulder.

Yancy pulled Felicity daringly close and touched his cheek to hers. Her sweet scent was intoxicating and her body felt good, real good. It was damn hard to control his urges when a woman's soft curves were pressed so sensuously close. The drinks he'd had failed to numb his desire. If anything, the liquor was making him forget his intentions to proceed cautiously with her. He nuzzled Felicity's ear and whispered, "What do you say we leave now before the road gets clogged up with all the wagons?"

There was something in Yancy's tone that worried Felicity, but before she could form an answer, Yancy was rudely tapped on the shoulder.

"Sorry, Parnell, but Miss Howard promised me a dance tonight and it looks like this is it." Yancy glared icily at Jake, but he stepped away from Felicity without a word. He didn't want to do anything to ruin the evening when it had gone so well. Besides, he'd be taking her home, and it was a good hour or more back to her cabin. It would be very dark and very chilly, and he was looking forward to keeping the little lady very warm.

Jake swept her up in his big arms, not giving her a chance to protest. But protesting was the last thing on her mind. All evening she had been praying for this moment and had despaired of it actually happening. No, she was of no mind to protest.

He took her right hand into his left and eased his other hand around her tiny waist. Her movements were stiff and awkward and he knew that she was nervous. He bent his head and whispered into her hair, "Relax, lady, I'm not gonna bite you. Dance with me like I'm one of your suitors . . . your favorite suitor."

She gazed up at him in astonishment but he just smiled. His large hand flattened against her waist and moved languidly up her back as they began to move to the haunting strains of a solitary violin.

Her reserve melted away like hot wax as she let the music weave its spell around her. Goose bumps danced up her spine. Jake placed her right hand on his shoulder and let his newly freed hand slide slowly up her arm, down the side of her breast, and come to rest at her waist. He gently pressed her closer. Her eyes widened in alarm at his intimate touch, but somewhere in the back of her mind a small voice kept whispering, *Enjoy yourself. You're not a nun anymore.*

A strange yearning throbbed at the center of her being, making her shiver.

Jake almost groaned aloud when he saw her eyes light with desire. Somehow, he'd known she'd be like this. Maybe that's why he'd fought so hard to stay clear of her. But now he knew with startling clarity that he'd lost the fight. With her soft curves pressed against his hard length, her sweet scent drugging his senses, and those emerald eyes beckoning him, his besotted mind reeled with but one thought—he wanted to possess this woman as he had never wanted another. Nothing that had passed between them before mattered. Only this moment existed.

Felicity closed her eyes and reveled in his nearness. She felt dangerously vulnerable, gloriously beautiful, unforgivably and wonderfully wicked.

His mouth was close, so very close. His warm breath caressed her lips. She leaned further into his embrace and suddenly she knew. She was falling in love with Jake McCullough.

The music stopped. Loud applause, catcalls, and foot-stamping finally broke the spell that bound the two. Felicity opened her eyes and gradually became aware that hundreds of faces were staring at her. She and Jake were the only two people still on the dance floor.

Chapter 7

Felicity pulled back on the reins and brought the wagon to a halt on the outskirts of Silverton. "I made it," she sighed aloud in relief. It had taken her over an hour just to get the horses hitched up. Then she'd checked and rechecked every step Jake had shown her to make sure she hadn't forgotten anything. Finally satisfied, she'd climbed onto the high seat and headed for town.

The treacherous places on the pass, combined with her fear of heights, had caused her to move so slowly and cautiously that she was exhausted from the strain.

She removed a canteen from beneath the wagon seat and uncapped it. She took several gulps, then dampened her handkerchief, wiping perspiration and dust from her face. Two whole days, she fretted. Where on earth is he?

She'd been disappointed Sunday morning when she found that Jake hadn't come home from the dance, but she'd gone about her day, confident that he'd show up for supper. But by midnight, he still wasn't home. She had paced back and forth across the length of the cabin floor, not knowing if she should be furious or worried sick. Anger at his inconsiderate behavior finally won out and she'd given up and gone to bed. He had, after all, promised to take her to town on Monday morning for supplies. Surely he'd come home sometime during the night.

Monday morning came and went and still there was no sign of Jake. By that evening, her anger had turned into real alarm. She spent the night on the settee, hoping that she'd hear him riding up to the lean-to during the night.

Now it was Tuesday and she was too overwrought to sit and wait anymore. Something *must* have happened to him. And so here she was outside of Silverton. God, she prayed, please don't let him be lying somewhere hurt and alone. Her heart wrenched painfully at the thought. One simple dance had opened her eyes to her true feelings, and now she might never know what could have been. It was just too cruel. He had to be all right! She lifted her chin defiantly, determined not to fall victim to her rising panic. Giving the reins a hard shake, she guided the horses into town.

Felicity pulled the wagon up in front of Gunderson's General Store. Jake had told her that they had an account there and that Ole Gunderson was "a square dealer." She jumped down from the wagon seat and then turned at the sound of a familiar voice. "Felicity Howard, it's about time you got yourself back here into town."

Roxie Wilson saw Felicity's face light up. Setting her packages down, she opened her arms wide to Felicity, who stepped into her hearty embrace and planted a warm kiss on her powdered cheek. Then, to Roxie's surprise, Felicity's words flooded forth in a headlong torrent. "Roxie, you don't know how glad I am to see you. Jake's gone. He's missing. I'm so afraid that he's lying hurt somewhere. He was supposed to take me into town for supplies yesterday but he hasn't been home since Saturday. Oh, Roxie, I'm so scared! Where can he be?"

Roxie smiled in bewilderment at Felicity's babbling and pushed herself back from the girl's panicked clutch. "Hold on there, sweetie. You're goin' way too fast. Now, slow down and say all that over again."

"Oh, Roxie!" Felicity wailed. "I haven't seen Jake since Saturday night. He promised to bring me here on Monday for supplies but he never came home after the Howardsville dance. Then, one of his men stopped by this morning looking for him because he hasn't been at the mine either. I decided to come to town on my own to get the supplies and see what I could find out. I just *know* something awful has happened to him!"

Roxie put her arm around Felicity's shoulders. "Now, don't you worry none, sugar. I know where he is. The inconsiderate fool is holed up in one of the rooms upstairs at the Last Chance."

"What did you say?" Felicity gaped at her in disbelief. "Are you telling me that Jake's been in town all this time? I've been worried sick for nothing? By the blessed saints, Roxie, I swear I'll kill him for this!"

Roxie just smiled benignly and continued as if Felicity hadn't interrupted. "I don't know what's botherin' Jake, but he was already skunked when he come draggin' in just before closin' time Saturday night. He had a couple more drinks, then he took Rena upstairs with him."

Felicity stiffened with rage.

"Next thing I knew," Roxie continued, "Rena came stompin' out of her room, madder than a wet hen. Jake didn't come out though. He spent all day Sunday and Monday up in that room with a bottle. Then, last night, he finally came down and picked a fight with Yancy. Before Dan, the bartender, could stop it, all hell broke loose. Chairs were flyin', bottles breakin', and noses bleedin'. You should have seen it, Felicity! It was the biggest ruckus we've had in a long time."

"Oh, how awful!" gasped Felicity. "Was anyone hurt?"

"Nah, just a few cuts and bruises is all." Roxie chuckled and looked at Felicity speculatively. "Been worried about him, have you?"

Felicity sighed and nodded."Yes, I admit it. I was afraid maybe he had gotten drunk and walked off the side of the mountain or something. Now I think it would have served him right."

"What happened between you two that put him in such a cantankerous mood?" Roxie questioned.

"Oh, it's a long story."

"Do I detect a romance in the makin'?" Roxie prodded, her eyes wide with eager curiosity.

"Absolutely not!" Felicity protested vehemently. "In fact, Jake's trying to marry me off to somebody else as fast as he can."

Surprised by this revelation, Roxie patted Felicity's hand sympathetically. "Well now, honey, it sounds like you and I need to have a long talk."

"I'd like that, Roxie. I'm so mixed up. I really need the advice of an expert."

Roxie chuckled. "If you mean an expert on men, then I reckon I'm one of the best. Males ain't all that hard to figure out, Felicity. You just gotta pet 'em and give 'em a treat once in a while like you would a good dog. Then you can wrap 'em right around your little finger."

Felicity smiled at Roxie's earthy wisdom. She especially liked the idea of treating Jake like a dog. She watched as Roxie retrieved her packages. "I see you've been doing some shopping, too," Felicity observed. "Could we meet later, after I finish ordering my supplies?"

"Sure. Just come on up the back stairs. You know the way." Roxie winked. "We'll have lunch and some serious girl talk."

"I'd love it!" Felicity said enthusiastically. "I won't be long." Roxie turned to leave, but stopped when Felicity called, "Roxie, before you go, I have to ask you something."

"What's that, honey?"

Felicity moved closer and whispered in her friend's ear. "Do some of the women here really wear men's pants in the winter?"

Putting her hand next to her mouth and imitating Felicity's conspiratorial countenance, Roxie answered, "Well, I ain't seen 'em dressed that way for town visits, but I hear they do up in the mountains when they're at home. Seems it's the only sure way to keep your backside really warm." Felicity stepped back and giggled. "Though one time I did see old Granny Willard wearin' britches under her skirt here in town," Roxie added. "Why do you ask?"

"I met Marion Gorton at the Howardsville dance and she said I should get myself some men's clothes for the cold weather. What do you think?"

"Sounds like a good idea to me," Roxie agreed. "The first time you go out to the woodpile in November and that wind blows up your skirts, you'll wish you had more than just pantalettes coverin' your bottom.

"Well, I guess I better get myself some pants then." Felicity laughed.

"And I better get goin' if I'm gonna arrange lunch for us. See you later, honey."

Felicity smiled as she watched Roxie hurry up the street. There was a refreshing frankness about Roxie that always managed to lift her spirits. Felicity was anxious to finish her business so she could enjoy her friend's company and obtain some much-needed advice. Still smiling to herself, she entered the general store.

Half an hour later, Felicity was finally finished placing her order with the Gundersons. Minnie Gunderson had been more than happy to help her pick out some warm clothes and had advised Felicity to purchase a flannel coat, rubber boots, and several pairs of thick, woolen socks. After trying on several sizes, Felicity found that boys' clothes fit her small figure best. She purchased several plaid flannel shirts and two pairs of heavy denim pants. Mrs. Gunderson assured her that even *she* occasionally wore men's apparel when the weather turned especially frigid.

"Don't you worry none, Miss Howard," Mrs. Gunderson said, "my husband will load up the wagon for you. I'll see to it that these clothes are wrapped up for you, too. Ole!" she bellowed. "I got another package to go into Miss Howard's wagon."

"Thank you, Mrs. Gunderson, you've been very helpful." Felicity smiled. "I'm going to have lunch with a friend, but I'll be back later this afternoon."

Minnie Gunderson nodded, acknowledging Felicity's compliment. She liked the polite young woman and wondered what her relationship was to that giant, Jake McCullough. Despite some of the gossip in town, she could tell a real lady when she saw one, and Felicity Howard was every inch a lady. Whatever was going on at that cabin, Minnie was convinced it was nothing improper.

Felicity stepped out into the sunshine, and, after her eyes adjusted to the brightness, she saw a familiar figure coming toward her. "Mr. McCullough?"

Jake's head shot up. Damn, he groaned to himself, what's she doin' here? Didn't he have enough to handle right now with the problems that were suddenly occurring at the mine? He stopped in front of Felicity and scowled at her upturned face. "What in tarnation are you doin' in town?" he demanded.

Felicity shook an angry finger at him. "Jake McCullough, where do you get the nerve to ask me that? You just up and disappear for two whole days without so much as a by your leave." Though she was mad, she was also vastly relieved to see that he was all right. He was still wearing his Saturday night dress clothes which were, by now, hopelessly wrinkled. His hazel eyes were bloodshot and rough, dark whiskers shadowed his face. Other than that, though, it appeared that Monday night's brawl had done him little harm.

Jake couldn't help but grin at the incongruity of this tiny woman shaking a finger at a man his size. Was he supposed to be scared? The gall of the girl was unbelievable! Still, he detected a note of concern under her bravado and it secretly pleased him. He couldn't help but notice that she'd evidently been busy the past few days remaking her clothes. Her simple blouse and brown twill skirt fit her body like a glove. The memory of that soft body pressing against him while they danced caused an uncomfortable tightening in his trousers. He stiffened abruptly and his smile was quickly replaced by a frown. Those very same curves were responsible for the monstrous headache he was now nursing. "Do you always answer a question with a question, Miss Howard?"

Felicity glared at him angrily. "You promised to bring me into town for supplies on Monday. Remember?" He had the good grace to look shamefaced. "Then, too, Jim Cranston stopped by this morning looking for you. There's trouble up at the mine and he wouldn't even tell me, your partner, what it is."

Steering her away from the subject of the mine, Jake apologized. "I'm sorry for forgettin' my promise. I, ah, got called into town on business." Felicity rolled her eyes but didn't argue. This was not the appropriate time or place to air their domestic problems. "You don't need to worry about Jim," Jake continued. "He found me a while ago and I'm on my way up to the mine now."

"Mr. McCullough, I have the supply wagon here." She gestured to where the wagon sat. "I need you to drive me home because I don't think I can get a loaded wagon up that pass myself. I barely managed to get it down here when it was empty."

Jake kicked at a dirt clod on the boardwalk and hooked his thumbs into the pockets of his rumpled trousers. "Christ, woman," he muttered, "you are a trial."

"What was that?" she asked testily. "Are you blaspheming again?"

"Never mind. I can't wait around here all day. I'll have Jim wait here in town for you and drive you back to the cabin when you're ready. Where are you headed now?"

Not wanting to tell Jake that she was on her way to see Roxie at the Last Chance, Felicity lowered her eyes. After the worry he'd caused her, not to mention his own lie about having business in town, what was one little fib going to hurt? Besides, it would prevent an unpleasant scene. "I promised to meet a few of the ladies over at the church for a couple of hours," she said innocently.

"Fine. Then I'll have Jim pick you up there in two hours."

"No!" she blurted in alarm. He raised his eyebrows questioningly. Recovering, she added, "That is, I don't want to trouble him. Just tell him to meet me right here."

"All right. It makes no never-mind to me. I've got to get goin' now." He shoved his hat further down over his forehead and stepped off the boardwalk into the street.

"Jake! Wait!" He stopped and turned around impatiently. "Will you be home for supper tonight?" she asked shyly.

He grimaced at her pleading expression. Home for supper, he mused. It sounded real nice. She'd called him Jake, too. Did she realize she'd done it? He took a step toward her, then remembered himself and stopped. "Yeah, I'll be home for supper . . . Felicity." He watched as she smiled happily and then turned away and headed down the street.

Felicity smiled all the way to the Last Chance. He'd called her by her first name again. She knew she should be angry with his uninvited familiarity, but for some reason she wasn't. The man had definitely wormed his way into her heart.

Her mind told her that Jake would never love her. At this point he didn't really even *like* her, but her heart just refused to listen. If what Roxie had said about men was true, perhaps she could at least gain his friendship by changing her tactics a little.

As Jake rode toward the mine, he tried for the thousandth time to force the vision of Felicity Howard from his mind. He'd been trying to forget about her ever since the dance, but it was useless. Even Rena hadn't been able to help. In fact, the incident with Rena had been the most embarrassing moment of his life and he fervently hoped it never happened to him again. If word ever got out that Jake McCullough had drunk so much that he hadn't been able to . . .

He shook his head. He had to concentrate on the problems at the mine. There had been two minor cave-ins last week, and now, last night, someone had set fire to the new shoring timber. So far, no one had been hurt and for that he was grateful, but his men were starting to get jumpy. He couldn't blame them.

He hadn't mentioned the cave-ins to Felicity and he was thankful Jim had also kept quiet about the fire. Whoever was perpetrating these ''accidents'' was serious and he didn't want her sticking her nose into something she had no business messing with. He knew it was a breach of their agreement not to tell her about the incidents, but there was nothing she could do to change the situation anyway, so why worry her?

Even though Yancy Parnell had adamantly denied having anything to do with the cave-ins, Jake still suspected him. Jake had also told him to stay away from Felicity and then had demanded to know if Yancy had touched her after the dance. That's when the free-for-all had broken loose at the Last Chance.

''Hell,'' Jake cursed aloud, ''I'm back to thinkin'

about her again." He just couldn't seem to get what happened at the dance out of his mind. All the men had laughed and pounded him on the back as Felicity had disappeared with Yancy. At the time, he had been too stunned by his own passionate reaction to the girl to say or do anything. But when one of the miners laughingly said that he'd thought Jake was going to make love to his partner right on the dance floor, Jake had hauled off and knocked him cold. Then he'd hurriedly left the dance and gone to a saloon in Howardsville. When they finally threw him out, he'd bypassed the cabin and gone on into Silverton where he'd gotten falling-down drunk. He shook his head in disgust at his own behavior. That damn little nun was going to be his downfall—he just knew it!

" 'Bout time you got here." Roxie grinned. "The hotel just brought over the food and the coffee's good and hot."

Felicity took a seat at Roxie's little table. "I'm sorry I'm late," she apologized. "I just saw Jake in front of Gunderson's. He was on his way up to the mine."

"Yeah, I saw Jim Cranston goin' to Jake's room when I got back here." Roxie set a plate of roast beef and gravy in front of Felicity, poured them each a cup of coffee, and sat down at her own plate. "Is Jake comin' back to take you home?"

"No, he was anxious to get up to the mine, but he told me he'd be home for supper."

Roxie nodded, her mouth full of food. "I'm not surprised he's in a hurry to get up to his mine. I heard about the cave-ins. Jake even accused Yancy of havin' somethin' to do with them. That's what caused the fight last night."

"What cave-ins?" Felicity's voice was icy.

Roxie looked up guiltily. "You mean you didn't know? Jake didn't tell you?"

"No, Jake didn't, but you better."

"I don't know much about it, Felicity, except that

I heard someone's causin' trouble up at the Silver Lady." Roxie looked uncomfortable. "Are you sure Jake didn't say nothin' to you?"

"No, he didn't, and he's going to be sorry! He agreed to keep me informed of any problems that came up at the mine. Why, I'm so mad at him, Roxie, I could just . . . just spit!"

Roxie couldn't help the smile that split her face. "Do nuns spit?" she teased. Felicity frowned and stabbed a chunk of beef with her fork. "Suppose you tell me what's been goin' on up there between you two," coaxed Roxie. "This is beginnin' to sound real interestin'."

Felicity looked up from her plate and sighed. "You know, Roxie, life outside the convent sure is different from what I expected." For the next several minutes she poured her heart out to her friend, telling her all that had happened. When she got to the part about Jake telling her to get rid of the breast binders, Roxie's brows drew together.

"Hold on a minute, honey." She held up her hand. "How did he know you wore them things, anyway?"

Felicity's face went blank. "Why, I don't know. I never gave it a thought." She cocked her head to one side, and suddenly it dawned on her . . .

"What is it?" Roxie asked excitedly.

"I just remembered something. About a week ago, when I went out to get my laundry off the clothesline, I found two of my binders missing. I thought that maybe the wind had blown them away, but I couldn't find them anywhere. Do you suppose that somehow Jake saw them hanging there? If that's true then he must have . . ."

Roxie burst into gales of laughter. "Oh, this is too much!" she guffawed. "That big, handsome hulk snatched 'em, Felicity. I just know he did!" She broke into another round of hilarity, tears streaming from her eyes.

"It's not funny," Felicity protested indignantly. "In fact, I think it's positively outrageous."

"Honey, you may think Jake McCullough hasn't noticed you, but you're dead wrong. He must have wanted to see what you looked like without them binders real bad. Oh, Lordy, wait till I tell the girls about this! Rena will die!"

Felicity looked stricken. "Roxie! Don't you *dare* tell anyone about this. Why, it's . . . it's mortifying!" In her agitation, Felicity knocked over her coffee cup, dumping its steaming contents into her lap. She gasped and jumped up. "Oh! Now look what I've done! I've probably ruined my skirt." With that, she burst into great wailing sobs.

Roxie leaped up to pull the clinging skirt away from Felicity's legs. "Are you burned, sweetie? Are you hurt bad?"

"It's all right." Felicity sniffed. "The coffee wasn't really that hot."

"Well, just the same, let's get those clothes off you and wash them out. I reckon the coffee went clear through, and your underthings are gonna stain, too, unless we wash 'em right away. I'll take everything down to Dora."

When Roxie returned, Felicity had donned one of her friend's wrappers and was sitting on the settee, her eyes still wet with tears. "What am I going to do, Roxie?" she moaned.

"Oh, don't cry, sugar. The skirt will be all right. Dora will get it clean."

"No," wailed Felicity. "It's not that. I mean, what am I going to do about Jake and me? He said that I look like a boy and that I should fix myself up so that I can hurry up and find a husband. He said I need protecting and that he doesn't want to do it. He even gave me a list of marriage prospects to memorize before I went to the dance. I was so embarrassed, I wanted to die, Roxie. I fixed up my clothes and did my hair different, and all he said was that I looked good enough to attract some man named Walter Beasley who didn't even show up at the dance!'' Felicity cried harder and buried her face in her hands while Roxie stared at her, unable to believe her ears.

"Why, that no good son of a . . .'' Roxie cursed. "If I'd known he said all that, I'd have given him a piece of my mind that he wouldn't soon forget. I hope you clobbered him good, Felicity. You did clobber him, didn't you?''

"No, I just tried to act like it didn't matter. But then, when Jake danced with me Saturday night, it was like he'd never said all those awful things. He was like a different man. He held me so close I could hardly breathe and I think he wanted to kiss me.''

"Well, I'll be damned!'' exclaimed Roxie. "You got it real bad, don't you, honey?''

"Got what?'' Felicity wiped her eyes dry with the edge of the wrapper.

"You're in love with Jake McCullough, ain't you?'' Felicity shook her head in protest, but Roxie was having none of it. "No use denyin' it, sweetie. It's written all over your face. And from what you've told me, Jake's fallin' for you too . . . real hard. Only he's like most men, scared to give up his freedom. So what does he do?'' Felicity stared at Roxie blankly and shrugged. "I'll tell you what he does,'' Roxie went on. "He tries to marry you off to somebody else so he won't fall into the trap himself!''

"Trap?''

"Yeah, marriage. Most men think marriage is like a trap.''

"No, it's different with Jake, Roxie. He can't stand me.''

"I don't believe that for a minute, sugar, not if what you say happened at the dance is true.''

"Then what can I do? I'm afraid I'm falling in love with him, but it's hopeless. I'm just not the kind of woman he's attracted to. He thinks I'm plain and homely. He tells me so all the time!''

Roxie leaped on an idea. Springing out of her

chair, she stared hard at Felicity for a moment and then snapped her fingers. "I got it! Jake sure don't think the girls here at the Last Chance are plain and homely, so why don't we fix you up a little? You can surprise him tonight. How does that sound?"

"Do you really think it would work?" Felicity asked hopefully.

"Sure it will! Come on, honey, we got work to do!" Roxie grabbed Felicity's hands, pulling the reluctant girl to her feet. She looked Felicity up and down and then turned her around appraisingly. "You know what you need?" Not giving Felicity a chance to answer, Roxie ran to her chest of drawers and rummaged through them until she found what she wanted. When she turned around, she wore a wide grin and held a large pair of scissors in her hand.

At Felicity's worried expression, Roxie laughed. "Don't worry, sweetie. Surely you know that all the fashionable ladies are wearin' a fringe."

"What's a fringe?" asked Felicity warily.

Roxie pointed to the short curls across her forehead. "This," she said.

"Well, I *have* seen a lot of women with their hair bobbed in the front like that," Felicity admitted, "but do you think it would look good on me?"

"Of course it will," Roxie assured her. "Now sit down over here and I'll cut it for you. You'll love it!"

Felicity wasn't at all sure she was going to love it, but she was so desperate that she was willing to try anything. She sat down in a straight-backed chair as Roxie took out a comb and parted off a small section of hair at her forehead. Felicity cringed as she watched more than a foot of her hair fall to the floor. But, despite her growing panic, she held her tongue.

Roxie stood back and studied her handiwork. "Why, it don't even need the hot iron taken to it, Felicity. It just curls up on its own." She retrieved a hand mirror from her dressing table. "Here, have a look."

Felicity took the mirror with a trembling hand, but what she saw was a pleasant surprise. A slow smile of delight spread across her face as she glanced up at Roxie. "I like it! It makes my eyes stand out. And it does curl nicely! Well, don't stop there, Roxie. Do whatever else you think needs to be done."

"Oh, this is gonna be fun," Roxie trilled gleefully. "Come on over to the dressin' table. Jake Mc-Cullough ain't gonna know what hit him when he lays his eyes on you tonight!" Roxie's enthusiasm was infectious and Felicity smiled with anticipation.

An hour later Felicity surveyed herself in the mirror in disbelief. "Do you really think Jake will like the way I look, Roxie?" she asked hesitantly. She stared at the stranger in the mirror and batted her heavily coated black lashes. Her long hair was pulled back to the crown of her head and pinned into a profusion of long, spiraled curls. A bright red bow topped them off. Her cheeks were powdered and rouged, her lips painted a shiny red. On her eyelids was a bright green paste which Roxie assured her enhanced her eyes. Roxie had used a special pencil to draw a thick black line around her eyes, and, for good measure, she had added a beauty mark at the corner of Felicity's crimson mouth.

Felicity stood up and studied the revealing dress that Roxie had insisted she borrow. Her waist was cinched even tinier than usual and the tight corset pushed her breasts up so high that the red satin bodice barely covered her nipples. Felicity feared that the slightest wrong move would be her undoing. She was decidedly uneasy.

"There's only one way to see." Roxie smiled in answer to Felicity's question. "We'll get a man's opinion." Roxie went to the door and yelled down the stairs, "Dora, send Yancy up here."

Two minutes later Yancy Parnell stood in the doorway, his mouth hanging open as he strained to see Felicity who had backed into a shadowy corner of the room. "Roxie, I don't know who she is or where you found her, but give her the room at the end of the hall. The men will line up at the end of her bed to enjoy that body. I'll make a fortune!" Felicity flushed bright red at Yancy's crude words.

"Why, Yancy, don't you recognize who this is?" Before Roxie could inform him, Felicity desperately shook her head at her friend.

Roxie smiled her understanding and quickly ushered Yancy to the door, assuring him that he could take a closer look at the "mystery woman" later. Yancy hungrily eyed Felicity's exposed bosom one last time before the door closed in his face.

"Roxie, do you have a shawl I can wear?" Felicity asked apprehensively. "I don't think I should walk down the street by myself. I feel almost naked. Jim Cranston is taking me home and I feel uncomfortable meeting him dressed like this."

"Don't worry, honey. You look great! Why, Yancy couldn't take his eyes off you! Didn't you hear what he said about how the men would want to take you to bed?"

"I'm afraid I did," Felicity mumbled in embarrassment.

"Well, whether you know it or not, sugar, once a man decides he wants to bed a lady, he's halfway to the altar. After all, any man knows that he's gotta marry a lady like you before he can put his hands on you. It's all part of the game. You gotta work up a man's appetite before he'll be willin' to pay for the banquet." Roxie chortled at her own witticism. Felicity smiled weakly and continued to stare in the mirror.

Roxie pulled a lace shawl out of one of her drawers and draped it around Felicity's shoulders. "There's still something missin'," she murmured as she gazed speculatively at Felicity. "Oh, I know! Hold on a second." Roxie opened several perfume bottles and sniffed each one. Inhaling deeply from the last bottle, she smiled in satisfaction. "Ah, yes, my favorite: Midnight Desire. This will be perfect."

Roxie tilted the bottle over her finger and hastily dabbed the strong perfume behind Felicity's ears. Then she upended the bottle and let a generous amount splash down between her breasts. Felicity shivered as the cool liquid trickled down her cleavage, wrinkling her nose at the cloying scent.

"Don't worry none, sweetie. It's kinda strong at first, but it fades after it's on a while. Why, you look so sexy and smell so good, you'll be lucky if Jake doesn't try to sample you tonight, but don't you let him!"

"Oh, Roxie!" Felicity gasped in horror. "How could you even *think* such a thing? Why, I'd never, *ever* consider doing . . . that!"

Roxie winked broadly. "Honey, 'that' is what makes the world go 'round. Jake McCullough's mighty temptin', so you just be careful."

Felicity, holding her breath so as not to pop out of the top of the dress, nodded solemnly.

When Felicity met Jim Cranston at the loaded wagon, she had to tell the flabbergasted man who she was. All the way out of town she caught him casting knowing, sidelong glances at her. Finally, embarrassed and outraged, she pulled the shawl tighter and tersely ordered him to keep his eyes on the road.

Several hours later, Felicity proudly surveyed the meal she had just finished preparing. Ham, baked potatoes, beans, and chocolate cake. It was enough to please any man, especially one with an appetite the size of Jake's.

Hearing Jake ride in, she quickly lit two candles and set them on the table. Then she ran into the bedroom to make a last-minute check of her appearance. Yanking her apron off, she prayed that he would approve of her new look. The back door creaked open and she heard his low-timbered voice speaking to Boozer.

Jake wrinkled his nose. The food smelled wonderful, but what was that other odor? He glanced around the kitchen but saw nothing out of the ordinary. Then he noticed the candles on the table and wondered why Felicity had lit candles when the lamp was sitting right on the counter. Shrugging, he pulled his stool out and was about to sit down when she made her entrance.

Jake was halfway into his seat when he saw her. He instantly halted his descent and straightened to his full height. His mouth unhinged and his brows knitted in disbelief. Felicity smiled in what she hoped was a seductive, sophisticated manner and walked toward him.

"Felicity? Is that you?"

He's really surprised! she silently rhapsodized. "Of course it's me, Jake." She stopped a few feet away from him in order to give him the full effect of her appearance. Jake reached out and gently ran a finger down her cheek. Pulling his hand away, he rubbed his fingers together to remove the heavy powder. Then he sniffed the air around her.

"It's you that stinks!" he exploded. "My God, what have you done to yourself?"

Felicity's elation crumbled. Tremulously, she answered, "I did it for . . . that is, you said to fix myself up and Saturday night you seemed disappointed with my efforts, so I got some help." The last few words were uttered with a gulp. "Roxie said you love the way the girls at the Last Chance look. I just thought . . . "

"Well, you thought wrong! You look like some two-bit hussy! Phew! You even smell like one! The whole goddamn place stinks like a whorehouse," Jake shouted. He looked down at the red satin dress and sucked in his breath. "Jesus, woman, did Jim Cranston see you in that getup?" Felicity, who was now staring at the floor, slowly nodded her head.

"Well, no wonder he was givin' me those sly looks all afternoon!"

Felicity looked up at him with tears welling in her eyes. "I'm sorry, Jake," she whispered. "I just wanted to please you. Just once, I wanted you to think I was pretty, but I guess there's no hope for me, is there? She picked up the satin skirts and fled, slamming the bedroom door behind her.

Pouring water into the basin, she grabbed a bar of soap and feverishly scrubbed her face. Then she tore the pins out of her hair, savagely throwing the red bow to the floor. The satin dress was ripped off, along with the tight corset and the rest of her underclothes. She washed every inch of her body to rid herself of the cheap perfume's nauseating aroma. Her body was chafed red from her relentless scrubbing before she finally pulled on her wrapper and collapsed onto her bed. Only then did she release the salty, stinging tears. She cried until there were no more tears to cry.

Jake sat down at the table and watched the candles slowly melt. Whatever had possessed her? After several minutes of deep thought, it finally dawned on him. Hating himself for his thoughtlessness, he shoved his plate away, leaned his elbows on the table, and cupped his hands against his forehead. "What a cowardly bastard I am," he muttered. "I'm so damn afraid of her that I treat her like dirt. She looked beautiful Saturday night but I couldn't admit it. I had to spoil it for her." He groaned. Despite his callousness, Felicity had still tried to please him and had gone to hell of a lot of trouble to do it. And still, his only reaction had been to tell her that she looked like a whore. He'd beat another man senseless for even insinuating such a thing.

You're an ass, McCullough, he chided himself. Every woman likes to be told she's pretty, but all you can think about is the possibility that she might be tryin' to put a weddin' ring on your finger. And did that worry come from somethin' she said or did? No! It's because you acted like a goddamn Peeping Tom and then got scared that you couldn't keep your hands off her.

Jake shook his head in utter self-disgust. He studied Felicity's closed door for a moment, then walked resolutely toward the bedroom.

Felicity ignored the light tap on her door. It came again more insistently and she heard Jake's concerned voice. "Felicity, can I come in? I want to talk to you."

"Well, I don't want to talk to you, Mr. McCullough. Go away!"

"Please, Felicity, give me a chance to apologize." He waited and listened, but there was no answer. After a long moment, he turned to leave, but then, remembering his resolve, he quietly eased the door open.

Felicity lay on her stomach, her head turned toward the far wall. Jake crept over to the bed and looked down at her. She looked so small lying there in the middle of that big bed. He carefully sat down on the edge of the mattress. As it sagged under his weight, Felicity rolled over and scrambled to sit up. "What do you think you're doing?" she demanded shrilly. "Get out of my room this instant!" She tugged the edges of her wrapper closer about her neck, her hands clutching at the lapels.

Her wide emerald gaze was Jake's undoing. "Felicity," he breathed. The pounding of his heart blocked out all rational thought. He reached out, clasped her shoulders in his big hands, and pulled her across his lap. His mouth swooped down on hers, smothering any protest with a hard kiss. His lips were insistent, demanding that she open to him and accept his questing tongue.

At first Felicity tried to struggle against his iron embrace, but her hands were trapped between their bodies. Then a strange sensation slowly began to envelop her. A warm tingling unraveled at the tips of her breasts and moved down her belly to torment the core of her womanhood. Caught up in the sensual mystery, Felicity relaxed and gave herself over to the pleasure of this new, misty world of passion.

Jake felt her rigid body surrender to the desire he was creating within her. His mouth gentled to a searching caress, tenderly coaxing her to respond. He loosened his viselike grip and Felicity's arms slid around his neck. She trembled as erotic sensations wrapped their intoxicating tentacles about her, her body instinctively arching to meet his.

Jake gasped as Felicity's aroused nipples pressed hotly against his chest. His own desire swelled and he realized that he had to stop while he still could. Her untutored kiss was proof of her innocence, and he knew she wouldn't part with that innocence lightly. She'd demand, and she deserved much more than he was willing to give.

Shaken, Jake wrenched away from Felicity's embrace. She opened her eyes and searched his face in complete bewilderment. Suddenly aware that she was still languishing in his arms, she quickly sat up and wiggled off his lap. Her hurried movement brought Jake to his senses. She was too close, dangerously close! In a flash he was on his feet and headed for the door. Felicity watched his hasty departure in a speechless daze.

Jake grasped the door handle, halted, and muttered a curse. Looking back over his shoulder at the vulnerable young woman, he rasped, ''I'm sorry, Felicity. I didn't mean to hurt your feelin's. But you don't need all that stuff on your face to be pretty. You're already pretty just the way you are.''

Then he was gone.

Chapter 8

Jed Croft pushed through the bat-wing doors of the Last Chance and scanned the smoke-filled room for his boss. Spying Yancy Parnell descending the staircase, he hailed him, and the two men headed for Yancy's small office at the back of the saloon.

Yancy closed the door behind Croft, shutting out the bawdy piano music. He motioned his mine foreman into a seat in front of his large, paper-strewn desk. Yancy eased back into his own chair and casually settled his feet atop the cluttered surface, his jet-colored eyes appraising the other man. Pulling two long cigars from his inside breast pocket, he offered one to Croft. "Cigar?"

"No." Croft shook his head. "I can't stay long."

Yancy lit his cigar. "It's about time you showed up here. I was beginning to get worried."

"Ain't you heard the news?" Croft asked. "I been real busy. Two cave-ins and a fire that burned all of McCullough's new shorin' poles. Ought to set him back a pretty penny, not to mention the time it'll take him to make the mine workable again." Jed Croft leaned back in his chair, a self-satisfied grin wreathing his homely face.

Yancy nodded in approval. "Was anyone hurt?" he asked casually, drawing on his cigar and exhaling a cloud of smoke toward the ceiling.

"Naw," replied Croft. "Nobody was around."

"Good." Yancy smiled. "McCullough's already suspicious and I don't want him getting any evidence that I'm involved in this. Remember, all I'm trying to do right now is make things uncomfortable enough that he's willing to sell out. So take it easy and don't get caught."

"Quit worryin', Parnell. You just do your part and I'll do mine. Hell, I'm the one takin' all the chances. All you gotta do is charm that Howard bitch into givin' you what you want." Croft chuckled at his double meaning and winked slyly. "You get anywhere with her yet?"

Yancy's eyes narrowed at Croft's insult to Felicity, but he clamped down on his temper and shook his head. "Not yet, and after what happened at the Howardsville dance the other night, I don't know if I ever will. It's obvious she's in love with McCullough." Yancy frowned, remembering his irritation with Felicity the night of the dance. She had cleverly evaded him when he'd tried to kiss her at the cabin door, and, stammering an excuse, had quickly disappeared inside.

"Well, you better try harder," Croft persisted. "It shouldn't be hard, Parnell. From what I've heard about her, she should be damn flattered you'd even glance her way."

"Well, you heard wrong," Yancy snarled. "Felicity Howard is a lady. And with women like her, you have to take it slow, otherwise you'll scare them off."

"Just don't louse it up," Jed warned. "If McCullough won't sell out, we gotta get our hands on her share of the mine as quick as we can."

"You think I don't know that?" Yancy barked. He stood abruptly, signaling an end to the meeting. "Don't ever tell me what I should be doing, Croft. Just remember who works for who around here. Now get out."

Jed Croft gave a curt nod and left. Yancy stared at

the closed door for a long time, furious at Croft's high-handed attitude. The scum was too eager, too demanding, and yet, despite his loathing for the man, Yancy knew he needed him. Croft was one of the few men in the area who knew enough about mining to effectively sabotage McCullough, and yet was too shiftless and dissolute to stake his own claim and set up an honest operation. Shrugging away his revulsion, Yancy crossed the room and returned to the rowdy scene in the saloon.

Roxie watched from her faro table as an angry Jed Croft bolted out of Yancy's office. When Yancy emerged a moment later, she asked one of the other girls to relieve her and walked over to where he stood at the bar. "Somethin' wrong, Yancy?" she asked in concern. "You look kinda down at the mouth."

Yancy's eyes swept over Roxie's voluptuous figure. Her turquoise satin gown clung to her lush curves and the raw sensuality she exuded made his heart race. "There's nothing wrong that a good shot of whiskey with my favorite gal can't cure." He grinned. "How about it?"

Yancy seldom shared a drink with any of the girls who worked in the saloon and Roxie's face lit up with pleasure. "Thanks, Yancy, don't mind if I do."

Yancy glanced over his shoulder and quietly summoned the bartender. "Dan, send a bottle of my personal stuff over to the back table." Then, taking Roxie's elbow, he escorted her to his private table, where he graciously seated her.

Felicity stood in the cabin door and gazed at the lean-to. The spicy scent of pine and the rhythmic sound of Jake's axe as he chopped wood lent a peaceful air to the evening. All week, Jake had come home early from the mine so he could begin the arduous task of increasing their store of wood. The nights were already getting cooler and he had told her that a great deal of wood was needed to see them through the long winter months.

It was Saturday, four days since he had grabbed her and kissed her so passionately. Felicity still didn't know quite what to make of the incident. At times, she felt gloriously happy, and yet, at the back of her mind, it niggled that perhaps Jake had just felt sorry for her. The thought pained her, but she feared it was true. Since he had made no further attempts to touch her, it was the only explanation that made sense. Felicity sighed despairingly. She wanted Jake's love, not his pity. Right now, more than anything else, she just wanted to know how he really felt toward her. But his aloof manner and her own lack of courage had forestalled her desire to approach him. Perhaps it was better to forget what had happened. She could still try to win his friendship and she silently reminded herself that friendship was all she could really hope for. The question was, could she settle for simple friendship after knowing the ecstasy she had felt in his arms?

She reluctantly entered the cabin and closed the door behind her. Ed Banyon, a man she'd met at the dance, was coming to call on her that evening and she had to get ready. Although Mr. Banyon was pleasant and attractive, Felicity could rouse little enthusiasm for his visit. It seemed like such a waste of time to encourage one man to court her when she was in love with another. I mustn't think that way, she chided herself. Jake wants to be rid of me and no moment of weakness is going to change that. Lifting her chin a notch, Felicity strode into her bedroom, determined to look her prettiest when her suitor arrived.

Sunday was the only day of the week that Jake allowed himself a few hours of relaxation. On this late summer afternoon, he sat on an old log outside the lean-to, contentedly whittling. Boozer barked noisily as he chased a butterfly across the yard, and one of the hens squawked indignantly as she scurried out of the dog's path. Jake glanced up, chuckling at Boozer's antics.

Hearing the cabin door slam, he looked over to see Felicity strolling toward him. Boozer bounded to her side and dropped a large stick at her feet. She stopped, and after giving the huge dog an affectionate pat on the head, picked up the stick and gave it a hearty toss. Boozer tore after his prey, barking excitedly at their game.

Although she was wearing one of the plain calico dresses she'd purchased soon after her arrival, Jake noticed that she'd let her hair down. It hung loose and flowing, a narrow white ribbon restraining it from her face. The sun glinted through the trees and reflected golden highlights off the top of her head. He had a sudden and almost unbearable urge to take her in his arms and bury his face in that soft, thick mane. It took every ounce of willpower he possessed to drag his attention away from his tempting partner.

He had avoided her all week and he was immensely grateful that, the few times they'd been together, she hadn't mentioned his impulsive and unexplainable actions on Tuesday night. He doubted she would understand the subtle difference between a man's simple lust for a woman and his desire to marry her. She was too innocent to know how it was for a man. To women like Felicity Howard, love and desire were one and the same. With this in mind, he had deliberately remained aloof, basing their conversations on business matters, and absenting himself from her presence as much as possible. He had no doubt that she felt something for him, but it would be cruel to let her believe there could ever be anything serious between them.

Still, despite his desire to see her safely married, it inexplicably nettled him when men came to call. She and Ed Banyon had sat outside the cabin for a long time last night, sipping tea and visiting, while he had been relegated to the lean-to. He'd felt like a damn chaperone!

Ed was two years younger than himself, handsome and successful. In short, he was everything that Felicity should look for in a man. Given time, Jake was sure that Ed could win her affections. However, it was infuriating to have to stand by and watch Banyon fawn all over her. The chaste goodnight kiss he had witnessed had so angered him that he'd had to take a long walk to cool down. A volcano of jealousy had erupted within him when Banyon had drawn Felicity close, and his feelings confused and frightened him. It didn't matter that she had quickly turned her head so Banyon's kiss had landed on her cheek. The man had no right to put his hands on her and attempt to kiss her the first time he came to call. Jake didn't know who he was more angry with: Ed Banyon for touching Felicity, or himself for caring that he had.

His troubled thoughts were suddenly interrupted as he felt something thump against his boot. He looked up to see Boozer lope over, pick up the stick at his feet, and race back toward Felicity.

She gave the dog's toy one last toss, and sauntered over to where Jake sat whittling. His handsome face was in a shadow that hid his expression, but as she approached, he looked up at her. She was surprised at the welcoming warmth revealed in his hazel eyes. Despite a desperate attempt to appear nonchalant, her heart leaped into her throat. She had been lonely sitting by herself in the cabin, but had been reluctant to venture outside for fear that Jake would resent her intrusion. She finally decided, however, that it was much too lovely a day not to be enjoyed and shared.

She stood before him, unsure of her welcome, and smiled timidly. "Hello. Mind if I join you?"

He smiled back and patted the place beside him. She sat down, leaving a discreet distance between them. Merciful heavens, she thought, I'll *never* get used to how handsome he is. She was suddenly reminded of the old fairy tale, *Beauty and the Beast*. Well, Jake was most definitely the beauty and that meant she was . . . Felicity laughed out loud.

Jake glanced up from his carving and grinned. "What's so funny?"

She blushed and smiled in embarrassment. "I can't tell you," she demurred. "I was just laughing at a private joke on myself."

He set his knife aside. "Well, I reckon we all need to be able to laugh at ourselves once in a while. It ain't healthy to take ourselves too serious all the time. I've sure had a lot of good laughs on myself."

She nodded in agreement and then looked down at the carving in Jake's hand. "What are you making?"

"Nothin', just whittlin'."

"May I see it?" He opened his hand and she shyly plucked the carving from it. "Why, it's a horse! Jake, this is beautiful. I didn't know you had such talent." She held the carving up to inspect it more closely, tracing the smooth lines with an appreciative finger.

He had never thought of his whittling as anything more than a pastime to while away a lazy afternoon. "It's nothin', really," he denied self-consciously. "My pa always whittled on Sunday afternoons and I guess I just picked up the habit from him."

Handing the carving back to him, Felicity protested, "It is too something! It's a talent to be proud of. You're a real artist, Jake."

He quirked a brow in amused disbelief. "You think so, huh?"

"Yes!" Felicity stated firmly. "Back East, rich people pay a lot of money for carvings like this. They're called 'primitive art.'"

"Well, I'll be damned. You learn somethin' new every day, don't you? Primitive art, eh? Well, I guess 'primitive' is probably the right word to describe me."

"Don't laugh, Jake, it's the truth," she insisted.

"Oh, I believe you." But he was laughing anyway. "So," he teased, "now that I've had a lesson, tell me what you've learned today."

She thought for a moment. "Nothing . . . yet. But I've learned an awful lot since I left the convent. One of the first things I learned was how ignorant of the real world I am." She smiled. "I've changed the way I think about almost everything. It's been good for me, though. I love meeting all the different types of people who live out here and learning about their ways. I felt out of place at first, but for the most part, everyone has been very warm and friendly."

He nodded. "I can understand how strange this all must seem. I felt like a damn fool over there in England. I stood out like a cow in a herd of sheep. But you know what?"

"What?"

"Those Brits said I was a 'bloody good chap.' " He laughed and she joined him, amazed at how relaxed and comfortable she was feeling.

Jake enjoyed the way her eyes lit up when she laughed. He, too, was surprised at their easy camaraderie and found himself relishing her company. The most he'd ever wanted to share with a woman was a bed, and then only for a short time. It was astonishing to realize he actually wanted to know more about the intriguing little package who sat next to him so companionably.

"Can I ask you somethin', Felicity? I mean, somethin' sort of personal?"

She threw him a wary glance. "I . . . I suppose so," she answered hesitantly.

"Why did you leave your convent?" At her sharp intake of breath, he quickly amended, "You don't have to tell me if you don't want to, but I always wondered. Did you just get sick of it and decide to leave?"

She sighed and looked off at the distant mountains. "No," she said slowly, "I didn't decide to leave. I was dismissed."

Jake was incredulous. "You're kiddin'! What did you do?"

"I was found with a man in my room," she murmured.

To her dismay, he burst into laughter. "You? I don't believe it! Why, you won't even let me sleep in the *house*, much less let a man into your bedroom."

She couldn't help but smile. "It was all a terrible mistake. I didn't even know who the man was. He was hiding under my bed, but I guess he had sneaked into the convent to see someone else. He'd just gotten into the wrong room. Unfortunately, Reverend Mother decided to make an example of me and I was dismissed."

"That's awful, Felicity," he said, sobering. "I know you well enough to know you were innocent. Why couldn't your Reverend Mother see that?"

"I don't know, Jake. But what's done is done and I have to put it behind me."

He looked at her speculatively for a moment and then said, "You know, Felicity, maybe what happened was for the best. I don't think you would've been happy bein' a nun."

"Whatever do you mean?" she protested. "I was very happy in the sisterhood."

He shook his head. "Nope. You're too friendly to be a nun. You like to laugh and dance and have fun. I saw what a good time you were havin' at the dance at Howardsville. You wouldn't have been happy over the long haul. I think you're better off now."

She was thunderstruck. It was the first time since they'd met that Jake had ever said anything so flattering and she was speechless with delight.

Her prolonged silence made him shift uncomfortably in his seat. He took one last swipe at his carving and turned the tiny horse over in his hand, saying,

"Now look at it. I've got the mane and tail finished."

Felicity again took up the intricate little carving and smiled. "It really is wonderful, Jake. It's hard to believe you could do that with just a little block of wood."

"Do you want it?" he blurted.

Her eyes widened with pleasure. "Could I really? Why, I'd love to have it! Are you sure you want to give it away?"

He looked embarrassed. "Sure I'm sure. It's just a stupid little carvin', but since you seem so partial to it . . ."

"Thank you, Jake," she murmured.

He stared off into the woods and nodded. Again, silence ensued as they both tried to think of something to dispel the sudden awkwardness between them. Finally, Felicity spoke. "You mentioned your trip to England. Roxie said you went over there to learn about how they mine in Cornwall. Is that right?"

He nodded and told her about the techniques he'd seen in England and how he planned to put some of them to use at the Silver Lady. At the mention of the mine, she decided that now was as good a time as any to bring up the subject of the accidents she'd heard about.

"Jake, now that I've answered your question, there's something I want you to tell me. Now, please don't get angry, but I want to know about the accidents at the mine." For the sake of their newfound camaraderie, she didn't remind him of their previous agreement.

He frowned at this sudden turn in the conversation, but he had known she was bound to find out sooner or later. Obviously someone had talked to her, but perhaps he could downplay the severity of the problems. He studied her expectant face, trying to gauge how best to begin. "I guess I should have said something sooner, but the trouble really didn't seem all that serious."

"How can you say that? Isn't a cave-in very dangerous?"

"It can be," he admitted, "but the two we've had were minor and no one was hurt."

"But how did they happen, Jake? Was it carelessness?"

He hesitated before replying. "Look, Felicity, workin' in a mine of any kind is hazardous. There are bound to be occasional accidents."

"I understand that, but there have been two cave-ins within a very short time, and I know that Jim was bringing news of more trouble when he came looking for you on Tuesday. I'd like to know what that problem was too." Though he was hiding his concern well, she sensed that things were much worse than he was letting on.

He bowed his head and raked his hand through his hair in frustration. Damn! She wasn't going to let this alone. He sighed in resignation and turned toward her. "Someone set fire to the new shoring timber Monday night. We lost all of it. The whole load."

Her hand went to her throat. "Good heavens, Jake! Why? Was anyone hurt?"

"No one was hurt. As to why, I honestly don't know."

"Do you think all these accidents are connected?" she asked. "And, if they are, do you have any idea who's behind them?"

"I don't have any answers, Felicity, and I don't want you jumpin' to conclusions. It's like I said, accidents happen, and it could be that we were just overdue."

"I don't believe that, Jake, and I don't think you do either. That fire didn't just happen. Someone must have set it."

He groaned. Why did she have to be so damn clever? he thought in annoyance. Why couldn't she just be like other women, too occupied with choosing the next frilly dress to bother with anything else?

But Felicity wasn't like other women and he knew she wouldn't be satisfied until he told her the truth. "All right," he acquiesced, "I guess I might as well level with you. I think someone is tryin' to run us out of business, get us so far in debt that we have to sell out."

"But why would someone do that? Is our claim that valuable?"

"No, at least not right now. Maybe someone's got the wrong idea about how much the mine is worth—you know how miners talk—or maybe someone's got a grudge against me. If I knew *why* someone was doin' it, then I'd probably be able to figure out *who* was doin' it and I could put a stop to it. I wasn't really tryin' to keep this from you. It's just that . . . well, there's nothin' you can do about it anyway."

"Still, we did agree that I should be kept informed, Jake."

"I know that," he acceded, "and I guess I should have told you right away. But whoever is behind this means business. I didn't want you gettin' mixed up in it and risk havin' somethin' happen to you."

She looked at him in complete bewilderment and Jake decided that he might as well confess all of his suspicions. Maybe then she'd realize the danger involved. "Like I told you before, I've never been totally convinced that my father's death was an accident. Pa was a careful man and too good with explosives to make the kind of mistake that was made. I think someone murdered him and tried to make it look like an accident."

"Jake, no!"

"I could be wrong, but I don't think so. Especially now, with all that's happenin'." He took her shoulders in his hands and gave her a gentle shake. His eyes bored into hers. "I want you to promise me right now that you'll stay out of this. You won't discuss it with anybody and you won't go around askin' any questions."

"But I . . ."

"Felicity, promise me!" he demanded.

"I promise, Jake. Only please, don't keep anything else from me. I'm not a child."

He loosened his grasp, but he continued to stare at her. "All right. I'll tell you everythin' that happens as long as you stick to your word and don't get involved."

"I'll keep my word, Jake." She nodded earnestly.

"Good. I'm glad we're agreed because if my suspicions are right, there's gonna be more trouble and I don't want to have to worry about you jumpin' into the middle of it."

There was a sudden restless movement among the horses stabled nearby, and she twisted around to see what was exciting them. One of the hens had wandered too close to a mare's hind hooves. Just as the horse positioned herself to kick at the annoyance, the bird squawked and fluttered out of harm's way.

"Damn hens," Jake muttered. "One of these days some horse is gonna break a leg trippin' over those stupid birds. Maybe I'll slaughter all of 'em and we'll have a big chicken dinner." He grinned at Felicity's appalled expression.

"Don't you dare touch my hens," she warned. "Why, I don't know what I'd do without their eggs. What would I feed you for breakfast?"

He shrugged. "I'd just eat biscuits and cream gravy. That's my favorite breakfast anyway."

"I know," she replied, "and that brings up another matter I want to talk to you about."

He cringed, knowing that Felicity's "matters" usually resulted in discussions he didn't want to have.

Undaunted by his anxious expression, she said, "We need a cow."

"A cow!" he exploded. "What the hell do we need a cow for? I'm a miner, not a farmer, and we don't need no cow!"

"Now, Jake, be reasonable. Once winter comes, you're not going to be able to go to Silverton to get supplies. How am I supposed to make those biscuits and that cream gravy you like so much without milk? And you won't have any butter all winter, either," she reminded him.

"Now, Felicity, you be reasonable," he argued. "How am I supposed to get a cow up this mountain? Besides, we don't have room in the lean-to, what with the horses, the hens, and me livin' in it. No. Enough is enough. This ain't no farm and I'm not sleepin' with no cow! I'll make do without biscuits until spring. We'll just eat potatoes."

"Yes, but without butter," she replied wryly.

His expression remained mulish and she decided not to spoil the afternoon by pressing her point any further. Instead, she smiled sweetly and asked, "When are you going to teach me to ride?"

Jake was caught off guard by her sudden change of topic and took a moment to answer. "Well, how about a lesson this afternoon?"

She couldn't hide her excitement. "You really mean it? We could do it right now?"

He grinned and reached for his hat. "I can't think of a better way to spend the rest of the day. The weather's perfect for a ride. There is one problem though." He frowned. "I don't have a lady's saddle and you can't ride in that." He gestured at her dress.

Her face fell. "What should I wear then?"

He thought for a moment, then shrugged his shoulders. "What you need is one of them split skirts. Maybe we'll have to put off teachin' you to ride until you can go to town and get one."

Felicity's shoulders slumped in abject disappointment, but almost immediately she brightened. "Wait a minute! I almost forgot! I have some pants. I bought them in town on Tuesday." His shocked expression made her laugh out loud. "Oh, don't be such a prude, Mr. McCullough," she teased. "I have it on good authority that lots of women wear pants in the winter to stay warm. Several of the ladies at the dance suggested that I get some before the cold sets in, so I took their advice and bought several pairs and some flannel shirts too.''

"Oh . . . well . . . I suppose that's probably a good idea.'' He was having difficulty picturing the prim Miss Howard wearing a pair of pants. The image of Felicity in baggy trousers and an ill-fitting flannel shirt was hilarious and the corner of his mouth tilted in a half-smile.

She noticed the twitch of his lips, as well as the amused glimmer in his eyes, but she was too excited to remark on it. "I'll go change while you get the horse ready, all right?''

"No.''

"No?''

"You get changed and eventually we'll go ridin', but first, you gotta learn the parts of the horse and its equipment and how to saddle and bridle one. Go on now, hurry up.''

Thrilled that she was finally going to have a riding lesson, she raced into the cabin. In her eagerness to get changed, her fingers fumbled clumsily at the buttons on her clothing but she still managed to complete the task in record time.

Jake threw a saddle over the top rail of the paddock fence and turned at the sound of her light footfall. "I'm ready!'' she called excitedly.

His eyes bulged at the sight that greeted him. This wasn't at all what he'd expected. His gaze roamed slowly down Felicity from her smile of anticipation to her sturdy shoes . . . and everything in between. He swallowed hard.

"Yeah, I guess you are,'' he returned distractedly. God in heaven, those pants fit like a second skin! Jake watched as Felicity moved closer. The sexy turn of her slim hips and tiny waist were greatly emphasized by the tight-fitting jeans. Beneath the flannel shirt, her lush breasts jiggled freely with her slightest movement. Like a lightning bolt it struck him that she couldn't possibly be wearing anything under that shirt. My God, he thought, what I wouldn't give to be in that damn shirt's place! He groaned inwardly, thinking about what she was going to look like bouncing along on a trotting horse. He never should have agreed to teach her to ride. This was going to be pure torture!

She glimpsed his pained expression and asked, "Is something wrong? Did I forget something?"

"Ah, no. Everythin's fine," he croaked, and quickly turned back toward the mare. He took a few deep, calming breaths, and willed his inflamed body to cool down. If he didn't get control of himself immediately, he was going to give little Miss Howard an anatomy lesson on far more than just horseflesh. "Come on over here and I'll show you how a horse is put together and how to tack one up."

She obediently stepped to his side with rapt attention. After explaining the proper terms for the various parts of the horse's body, he lifted the saddle off the fence rail and placed it on the mare's back. Then he took it off, threw it back over the fence, and directed her to do it. She smiled confidently. This wasn't going to be so hard after all. She couldn't understand why he suddenly seemed so nervous and edgy. Walking over to the railing, she took hold of the saddle and after several struggling attempts, finally heaved it off the railing. The next thing she knew, she was flat on her backside with the object of her efforts sitting in her lap. She threw an embarrassed look up at Jake. "What did I do wrong?"

He grinned at her befuddled expression. "Nothin'." He laughed. "You just have to get used to the weight of the saddle." He leaned over, removed the saddle from her lap, and placed it back over the fence. Offering her his hand, he pulled her to her feet. "Try again," he ordered.

She shrank inwardly, but she was determined not to give up. On the third try, she finally got the saddle tossed across the horse's back.

"I did it!" she cried jubilantly, jumping up and down in excitement.

He nodded absently, his eyes glued to the movement several inches below her smile. He cleared his throat and said, "That you did, little girl, that you did. Now I'll show you how to tighten the saddle and keep it from slippin' off." He then proceeded to demonstrate how to cinch the saddle. She watched with concern as he gave the bay mare a firm nudge in the belly with his knee.

"Doesn't that hurt her?" she asked.

"Nope. Did you see the way she puffed out her belly when I tightened the cinch?" Felicity nodded. "If you don't jab her belly a bit and make her let that air out, the saddle won't fit tight. Then, when you start ridin' and she lets it out, you know what happens?" She shook her head. "Before long, the saddle will slide sideways, takin' you with it. So pay close attention."

Hiding her impatience, Felicity tried to concentrate. She wished he would hurry and get to the good part, the actual riding of the horse.

He pointed out the pommel, stirrups, latigo, fender, and what seemed like a hundred other parts of the saddle. Next he showed her how to put the bridle over the horse's head and secure the bit. When the entire tacking procedure was completed, he unfastened everything and made her repeat the whole process.

When do we get to the riding part? Felicity wondered in annoyance. But she held her tongue and concentrated on his instructions. To her immense relief, cinching and bridling was much easier than lifting the saddle.

Jake grinned with satisfaction when she finished. "Good. Now you gotta learn how to mount." With an ease born of long experience, he placed his foot in the stirrup and threw his leg over the horse's back, settling himself in the saddle. It looked simple, but after her first attempt, it became obvious that she was too short to reach the stirrups and he had to find a bucket for her to stand on. Once she got her foot hoisted into the stirrup, he placed his hand on her round little bottom and boosted her into the saddle.

Felicity's face flamed at this intimate contact and she turned toward him with a reproving look. But he was staring off toward the woods and smiling, and she decided that he probably hadn't even noticed where his hand had touched her. After all, he was just being helpful. He adjusted the stirrups to fit the length of her legs, then made her dismount and remount several more times until she could do it without his helpful boost.

Finally, he saddled his stallion and they slowly proceeded out to the road. Jake watched Felicity's every move, instructing and correcting her as they rode. "Can we go up to the mine?" she asked. "You told me you'd take me sometime and I really would like to see it."

"I guess there wouldn't be any harm in it. You seem to be doin' pretty good for a tenderfoot." He grinned and Felicity glowed with pride at his praise. He seldom offered compliments, which made them all the more treasured. Pointing out the direction, Jake let her lead the way. Twice they stopped along the narrow road and he pointed out interesting landmarks.

They were stopped, looking at an unusual rock formation, when the accident happened. Her mare suddenly leaped sideways, reared on her hind legs, and screamed in terror. Her hooves hit the ground with bone-jarring force, hurtling Felicity out of the saddle.

She felt the air whoosh out of her lungs just as the back of her head struck the ground. Stars danced before her eyes and she closed them, trying to block out the nauseating dizziness. She lay absolutely still as the world spun crazily. Her body jerked at the thunderous crack of a gunshot, but she was too dazed to fully comprehend what was happening.

Jake had watched in horror as Felicity's spooked

horse threw her and galloped off, up the trail. She'd barely hit the ground before he was off his own mount and kneeling beside her. Suddenly, he heard the tell-tale rattle. Turning and drawing his gun in one swift motion, he shot the snake's head off. He holstered his gun without further regard for the viper, and turned his attention back to Felicity's inert form.

He noted her closed eyelids and ghostly pallor as he carefully checked for broken bones. Finding none, he gathered her into his arms and held her close. "Felicity, sweetheart, are you all right? Wake up, darlin'." Lifting his head, he pushed her hair back from her smudged cheek and gently searched her scalp for wounds. His fingers found a rapidly swelling knot on the back of her head and his heart leaped into his throat. "Oh, Christ, little girl, don't die," he pleaded.

As if from far away, Felicity heard his tender en-treaties, but couldn't summon the strength to open her eyes. His endearments sounded too wonderful to be true, and the sensation of his lips against her ear was heaven. Still, it wasn't right to worry him. His warm breath brushed her cheek and her eyes fluttered open.

Jake sighed in profound relief. A strange rasping sound escaped from somewhere deep in his throat as his mouth dipped gently to cover hers. She eagerly welcomed his kiss, arousing all the pent-up desire he'd tried so hard to control. Jake pulled back slightly and looked down at her, unable to believe her response.

His eyes were glazed with fear and something she was only just beginning to understand. She blinked to clear her head as she heard him ask, "Are you all right, sweetheart? Where does it hurt?"

"I . . . I'm fine, Jake, I . . ."

Before she could complete her sentence, he was crushing her to him once again. He was at once both tender and savage, and he kissed her like a man who'd nearly lost his most precious possession.

His tongue flicked at the corners of her mouth, seeking and finding entrance into her moist warmth.

He rained kisses across her eyes, her cheeks, and moved down her neck, her sweet scent enticing him almost beyond the limits of his control. *God, I want her so much!* he thought desperately.

She arched her back to allow him greater access. Gooseflesh rippled her skin as his caresses engulfed her in passion's flame. She emitted a low groan of pleasure that she didn't even recognize as hers.

He gently pushed her back onto the bed of soft grass, his body half covering hers. Deft fingers easily dispensed with the buttons on her shirt and pushed it open. As he'd already guessed, she wore nothing underneath. Her green eyes widened with fear but Jake brushed her hindering hands aside and feathered his tongue over the tip of an erect nipple.

Felicity lost her grasp on reality as his mouth sucked hungrily and his hands roved everywhere at once. She clasped his head to her breasts and rubbed herself against him. Never would she have believed that such pleasure was possible. He slowly slid down her body, his hands and mouth tracing a sensitive trail over her womanly swells and dips.

She barely noticed when he unfastened the buttons on her jeans. His lips kissed and nibbled her hip as his hand journeyed downward toward the most intimate part of her body. But as his fingers entwined in the downy curls at the juncture of her thighs, she suddenly came to her senses. She cried out, shoved hard against his chest, and twisted her body beneath him in a desperate attempt to move him off of her.

Jake felt like a starving man at a banquet and it took a moment for her frantic protests to register in his besotted brain. At first he thought she was begging him to hurry. His body's reaction to what he assumed was passionate fervor urged him to seek his release and he moved boldly to remove her jeans.

"Jake, no! Stop!"

The panic in her voice finally penetrated his drugged senses. He halted his caress and stared at her with glazed eyes. Her body was stiff beneath him and her eyes were wild with fear. Jake shook his head, dissipating the cloud of passion that enveloped him. Pushing himself off her, he leaped to his feet and pinned her with an icy stare.

She shivered and shrank away from his frosty gaze. "I'm sorry, I . . . I can't!"

"Get up and fix your clothes," he ordered hoarsely. "Somebody might come along this trail any minute."

Felicity got slowly to her feet. She looked down at her exposed breasts, swollen from Jake's caresses, and hurriedly turned away from his cold scrutiny. Suddenly, her knees buckled and she swayed with a rush of dizziness. Her hand flew to the back of her head as, cursing, Jake rushed forward to steady her. She lowered her eyes from his condemning glare and the heat of humiliation washed over her cheeks.

Jake roughly rebuttoned her shirt, tucked it back into the top of her jeans, and fastened them. Scooping her up in his arms, he unceremoniously set her onto his horse. Climbing up behind her, he circled her waist with his arm and angrily kicked the stallion's flanks.

She tried to keep from touching him, but her body ached with the effort it cost her. She heard his exasperated sigh as he gently took her shoulder and pulled her back against his broad chest. "Lean back, little girl, and relax." His harsh tone belied the gentle words. Felicity did as she was ordered and Jake tightened his grip around her waist. Her head was still swimming and she gratefully closed her eyes.

When she next opened them, he was settling her into her bed and pulling the sheet up over her. His brows were knit in concern and his mouth was set in a tense line.

"Jake?"

"It's all right, Felicity, you're home now." He walked over to the pitcher of water sitting on the chest and dampened a cloth. Returning to her side, he carefully wiped her face.

The cool cloth was reviving.

"Jake, we have to talk."

"No, we don't. Not now. You need to rest. You've got a mean bump on the back of your head. For a minute there, girl, you had me scared to death."

"I feel much better and we need to talk *now*," she protested. "I'm so ashamed at the way I behaved, Jake. I don't know what came over me."

"Don't apologize, Felicity. It was my fault. There's nothin' for you to be ashamed of." He sat down on the edge of the bed and set the cloth aside.

"But I *am* ashamed. No man has ever touched me the way I let you. We almost made love, didn't we?"

He felt like a villain, but at the same time, his unsatisfied desire made him surly. He didn't respond to her question. It wasn't necessary. She had to know the answer.

After a long, silent moment, she spoke again. "This must never happen again. Never! I was raised to believe that a woman should keep herself pure for her husband. Though you've never come right out and said so, I know you don't want a wife." Her voice cracked slightly. Her love for Jake made the words difficult to voice, but she knew she must say them. "If you want me to find a husband so you can be free of me, then you have to leave me alone."

Jake's confusion and impatience over his inability to control the desire he felt for her was unleashed in his angry retort. "That's just fine with me! You're right, I don't want a wife. And I also don't want any little bastards of mine runnin' around."

She sucked in her breath at his crude remark. He stood up abruptly and looked down at her with frustrated fury. "You have my word that I won't touch you again. Good night, Miss Howard."

Felicity heard him slam out of the cabin. She squeezed back threatening tears and prayed for God's forgiveness. For even now, her traitorous body burned for Jake McCullough's enslaving touch.

Chapter 9

Felicity walked across the yard, happily swinging an empty milk pail. Her grin spread from ear to ear as she approached the lean-to and its new boarder, whose name, like so many of her profession, was Bess.

Bess looked up at her with soulful brown eyes and mooed a morning greeting. Felicity gave the brown-and-white cow an affectionate pat on the flank and sat down on a stool. Leaning her head against Bess's side, she gently squeezed the animal's heavy udders. It was a technique she had been practicing for a week now and the sound of the fresh, warm milk hitting the bottom of the bucket made her smile with contentment.

Jake had disappeared for five days after that momentous riding lesson. Although Felicity was a little concerned by his unexplained absence, she instinctively knew that he had not come to any harm, but merely needed some time alone to get over his anger with her. She was actually grateful for the solitude, as she, too, needed time to recover from the emotional upheaval.

Continuing with her milking, she chuckled at the thought of Jake's return home. Never would she forget the sight of the frowning, exasperated man dragging the tired, resisting cow up the mountain pass. She heard his cursing long before he ever rounded the bend and appeared in the yard.

Boozer immediately set up a ruckus, causing Jake to yell at him and the unhappy cow to bawl plaintively. Felicity just stood there, dumbfounded, as Jake tethered the cow and marched into the house carrying two large sacks. Without a word, the scowling man set the bags down on the kitchen table. She peeked curiously inside the bags and squealed with delight. "Oh, Jake! Oranges!" She threw herself into his arms and gave him an enthusiastic hug. "Oranges and a cow! What could be more wonderful? Now we'll have milk and butter all winter. Thank you so much!"

Jake was somewhat embarrassed by her outpouring of gratitude, and, shrugging his shoulders, he said gruffly, "Well, you wanted a cow so damn bad, and I was in Durango anyway . . ."

What he didn't mention was that he'd ridden like a madman all the way to Durango just to buy a cow in the hopes of mending the rift between them. Nor did he mention that he'd practically threatened a hapless storekeeper's life in order to force the man to part with a portion of a crate of oranges which had been specially ordered from California for a wedding celebration.

"Well, it was very thoughtful of you," Felicity said as she eagerly peeled an orange, "and I promise you won't regret it when I fix you biscuits and gravy for breakfast this winter." She popped an orange wedge into her mouth, closing her eyes in ecstasy and sighing, "Mmmm, so good!" She opened her eyes, grinned, and handed him a wedge, delighted that he had remembered her fondness for the fruit.

Felicity pulled herself back to the present, picked up her now-full pail of milk, and headed for the cabin. Placing the bucket on the counter, she gazed proudly at the heavily laden shelves above it. Jars of wild raspberry jelly, canned beans, tomatoes, peas, and corn were neatly stacked in rows on the shelves.

Her hands had been stained for days after picking the berries, but she and Jake would have jelly all winter.

He had helped her store sacks of potatoes, onions, apples, and parsnips in the cellar his father had dug the previous fall. He'd told her he would bury the parsnips in a snowbank after the first storm, saying that the longer they were buried, the sweeter they'd be. He had chopped wood until the stack behind the cabin extended several feet out from the back wall and ran the entire length of the building. Felicity was astonished when he said they'd be lucky if it was enough to last the winter. After re-chinking the cabin walls and patching the roof in several places, he declared them ready for the season.

As September progressed, the nights became cooler and Felicity began to worry about Jake sleeping in the lean-to. Although he hadn't mentioned his sleeping arrangements, she knew he couldn't continue to stay in the drafty shelter much longer.

It was a week later when one evening, as Felicity was preparing supper, Jake walked in the back door, sneezing loudly. A shock of damp chestnut hair fell over his forehead as he sniffed the air. "Smells good, whatever it is," he said by way of greeting. Then he threw his head back and sneezed again.

"Bless you," Felicity said. He nodded his thanks and broke into a series of hacking coughs. "You sound like you're getting a cold." Concerned, she was around the table and at his side in a flash, reaching up and placing her hand on his forehead. "You don't have a fever, but you will if you don't take care of yourself." She took a step backward and eyed him speculatively. "Your eyes are red. Is your throat sore?"

He snorted. "I'm fine, Felicity. I'm just tired and hungry and the cold air makes me cough. Is supper ready yet?"

She threw him a doubtful look but went back to the big iron stove. Removing a venison roast from the oven, she set it on top of the stove and stirred up some gravy from the pan drippings. Jake helped himself to a cup of coffee and sat down at the table. He watched her put a large dollop of butter on a huge mound of mashed potatoes and smiled as he thought of how happy she'd been over that cow.

Despite his claims of hunger, his appetite was not up to its usual capacity. Felicity was surprised for she seldom had any food left over. He really is sick, she fretted.

They ate in silence and immediately after finishing, he rose, saying, "I'm gonna turn in early tonight. I'm real tired." He turned toward the back door but was halted by her words.

"Jake, you can't sleep out there tonight. It's too cold."

He turned around, put his hands on his hips, and lifted an eyebrow. "Do you have any suggestions about where I *can* sleep, Miss Howard?" He watched her expressive face and knew she was wrestling with her earlier resolve not to let him sleep in the cabin with her. That thought made him wonder if she was still blaming herself for their passionate encounter a few weeks before. Although he'd tried not to think about it, the memory of her hot little body pressed intimately against his crept up on him at the oddest times. Once his men had caught him staring into space and smiling for no reason at all. Corny had jokingly asked him if he was moonstruck. Jake had laughed it off with a red face and a rather vague reply. It had been damned embarrassing.

He knew that she hadn't forgotten the incident any more than he had. She might seem prudish, but Felicity Howard had wanted him as much as he had wanted her. She could deny it all she liked, but her body didn't lie. Like opposite ends of a magnet, they were attracted to each other with a force that was impossible to ignore.

Felicity cast a glance at Jake from beneath her lashes. For the past few weeks, he'd acted like those passionate moments between them had never occurred. Even when they'd worked side by side preparing the cabin for the winter, he had been politely distant and respectful. Gradually, she'd grown less wary in his presence and decided that he was just as determined as she to put the disgraceful episode behind them. He had admitted he didn't want marriage and he was obviously doing his best not to compromise her.

With this last encouraging thought, she quickly made up her mind. "I guess there's no help for it. You'll have to bring your cot in here and set it up by the fireplace."

Jake could hardly believe his ears. "Are you sure? I could probably move in with my crew for the winter. Of course, that would leave you here all alone and if you get snowed in, which is bound to happen, it could get mighty lonesome. Not only that, but if you get sick or hurt, no one would even know, let alone be able to get to you." He paused and said earnestly, "It's up to you, Felicity. It's your cabin. But, if you decide later that you've made a mistake lettin' me stay here, I don't want you blamin' me."

She did not miss that, for the first time, he had admitted that the cabin belonged to her. She shook her head and answered, "No, Jake, I won't blame you. I know I'm not ready to stay here alone all winter. You need a roof over your head and, greenhorn that I am, I need your protection. I think the only solution is for you to stay here with me for the winter."

"There is one other solution," Jake offered. "You could go live in town for the winter. I'd miss your good cookin', of course, but I'd get along all right. Pa and I always fended for ourselves."

She shook her head. "We can't afford that. I know that the accidents at the mine have almost stopped production and we can't deplete our funds paying rent for me. We need to save our money to buy another load of shoring timber to replace the poles that burned.''

''What about gossip, Felicity? There's bound to be talk in town once word gets out that I've moved in with you.''

She shrugged. ''I know, Jake, but there's nothing we can do to prevent that. I'm sure there's already been gossip about us being up here together. I don't think anything is going to be said that hasn't been said already. Maybe the fact that I'm being courted by several suitors will squelch the rumors. After all, if you and I were involved with each other, I certainly wouldn't be encouraging the attentions of other men, would I?''

He wasn't totally convinced that this whole arrangement wasn't going to backfire, but, at the moment, he didn't have a better solution. Besides, right now, he felt too miserable to care. Another night spent in that freezing lean-to might well be the death of him. ''Well, who knows?'' He smiled. ''Maybe you'll get married soon and the problem will solve itself.'' He bent over to tug on his boots and didn't see Felicity's stricken look. When he straightened up, her face was an impassive mask. ''I'll go get the cot and my belongin's.'' He hurried from the cabin before she had time to reconsider.

Felicity wasn't sure her decision was the right one either. The reasons for making Jake sleep in the lean-to in the first place hadn't changed. There was still her reputation to consider. What would her suitors say when they found out that Jake had moved in with her? She blushed just thinking about it. Oh, well, she'd just have to make it clear that everything was most proper.

She cleared the table and washed the dishes while he made several trips to the lean-to. After stoking the fire, he lay down on the cot. Felicity handed him a cup of hot tea mixed with honey. ''Here, drink this,'' she ordered gently. ''It will warm you up, and the honey will soothe your cough.''

He took the cup and wearily nodded his appreciation. She heard Boozer scratching at the door and crossed to let him in. The big dog shook off the evening's dampness, trotted over to the fire, and curled up on the rug. She sat down next to Boozer and stared pensively into the flames while her hand glided over his thick winter coat.

Jake watched the firelight shimmer over Felicity's hair, the intimate scene reminding him of another time and place. His mother used to sit before a fireplace much like this one, her knitting needles softly clicking as she rocked back and forth and quietly chatted with his father. It seemed a lifetime ago, and yet the pain would never go away.

He angrily shook off the tender memory, concentrating instead on the sight of his father crying and begging his mother not to leave them as Maryanne walked out of their lives forever. No matter how alluring the girl curled before the fire looked, he would never open his heart to another woman. He knew from tragic experience that a woman's love for a man wouldn't withstand hard times, and he would not allow himself to be emotionally destroyed as his father had been.

Stifling a yawn, Felicity gave Boozer one last pat and stood up. "I think I better go to bed before I fall asleep in front of the fire. Would you like another cup of tea before I go?" she asked solicitously.

"No, thanks. I'm ready to hit the hay too."

Her brow knitted with concern. "If you need something for your cough later on, just wake me. I'll be happy to fix you some more tea." She turned to leave.

"Felicity?"

She turned. "Yes?" she said, surprised. There was a strange light in Jake's eyes. He seemed about to confide something and yet he just lay on the cot looking at her.

After a long moment, he shrugged. "Nothin'. Good night."

She swallowed her disappointment. "Good night, Jake. Don't forget what I said about the tea. I'll be right here if you need me."

Long after her bedroom door closed, he lay on the cot and stared at the ceiling.

Felicity was surprised to find Jake still sleeping soundly when she awakened the next morning. It must be his cold, she reasoned. She slipped into a pair of boots and pulled on the flannel coat over her wrapper. A light dusting of snow had fallen during the night, making the ground sparkle. She hurried out to the lean-to, the crisp air chilling her cheeks and nose. Confronting the hens without hesitation, she edged her hand under their warm bodies and produced several eggs. Shivering, she scurried back into the cabin to prepare Jake's breakfast. By the time the meal was on the table, he was up and dressed.

Although she tried to talk him out of going to the mine, he stubbornly insisted that he was well-rested and fit for work. She finally decided she was wasting her breath and sent him on his way with three huge venison sandwiches for his lunch.

Having planned to make a trip into town today, Felicity dressed quickly. Jake had given her several more riding lessons in the past weeks and she felt confident that she could safely make the journey down the mountain.

In the short time it took her to get ready, the snow had melted. She saddled the mare and was about to mount when she heard another horse approaching. She glanced up to see Ed Banyon trot into the yard. Ed had been a frequent caller since the Howardsville dance, and though several other men had come courting as well, Ed was the most persistent.

" 'Morning, Felicity." He tipped his white Stetson. "I see I got here just in time. Are you going into town or just getting some exercise?"

She smiled a greeting. "I'm so happy to see you, Ed! I'm on my way to town and since this is my first trip alone on horseback, I'd be grateful if you'd accompany me. I must confess, I'm still a little nervous about riding all that way by myself.''

He grinned, his perfect white teeth gleaming against his bronze face. 'Why, I'd be delighted! I can think of nothing I'd rather do than be of service to you. I was hoping to take you riding anyway. I couldn't concentrate on my accounts this morning and I realized the day was just too beautiful not to spend it with you.''

She laughed. She was used to Ed Banyon's flowery compliments and wondered if he truly meant anything he said.

Ed watched Felicity's denim-clad figure appreciatively as she dragged the bucket over to her horse and mounted. The first time he'd seen her in those pants, he'd had to cut his visit short for fear she'd notice his lustful state. Lord, but she has a gorgeous body, he thought. And to think I almost didn't come today!

As they trotted companionably down the pass, Felicity commented, ''I hope you won't be sorry you came with me. Besides posting a letter, I plan to stop at the Ladies' Bazaar. I've been told that the owner, Mary Real, has lovely dress material and I'd like to look at some. I don't suppose you know where her shop is, do you?''

''Certainly. My sister trades there all the time. It's on Thirteenth Street. Quite an eccentric woman, that Miss Real.''

''Eccentric?'' she echoed. ''I've never heard that. I have heard that she's a shrewd businesswoman and that she owns an interest in several claims around here.''

''That's true,'' Ed said. ''She's very successful and has become quite wealthy. Of course, I've never approved of a woman being in business.''

Felicity shot him an arch look. ''Why, Ed Banyon!'' she exclaimed. ''Have you forgotten that I own half of the Silver Lady?''

Banyon had the good grace to look sheepish. "Well, I just meant . . . well, in your case it's different."

"And how is that?" Felicity asked.

"For one thing, you inherited the business. You didn't go out looking for an investment. Not only that, but McCullough runs the operation."

"Don't tell me that Miss Real works in her mines," she teased.

He caught the mischievous glint in her eye. "Felicity Howard, you're playing games with me," he chided.

"Yes, I am." She laughed. "But you really must stop being so old-fashioned, Ed. Back East, there are lots of women who own their own businesses."

"I'm sorry, Felicity, but you'll never convince me to change on that score. A woman should be taken care of by a man."

She shook her head. "Ed, you're impossible."

Banyon grinned and nodded. "So I've been told."

On the outskirts of town, Felicity suddenly pulled her horse over to the side of the road, dismounted, and handed her reins to Ed.

"Will you hold her while I change?"

"While you what?" he questioned.

"While I change," she repeated. Reaching into her saddlebag, she pulled out a dress and continued, "I can't very well ride down the mountain in a dress, but it certainly wouldn't be proper to be seen in town in pants either. So I brought a dress along to change into. Then I'll just lead my horse the rest of the way." She giggled at Ed's incredulous look and disappeared into the woods. Several minutes later she reappeared, dressed in a high-necked, long-sleeved dress. She stuffed her jeans and shirt into the saddlebag, took the reins from Ed, and said, "All right, I'm ready now."

He burst out laughing. "Felicity, you're a wonder!"

She grinned at him and nodded. "So I've been told."

Outside the dress shop, Ed took Felicity's letter, promising to mail it and return for her in an hour. She entered Mary Real's small establishment and was soon entranced by the little woman's kindly manner and large selection of materials.

After choosing a length of wool and a pattern for a new skirt, Felicity asked to see the fashion books containing designs for dresses to wear visiting or to church.

The front door opened and Felicity looked up from where she sat surrounded by bolts of brightly colored cloth. "Oh, Ed, has it been an hour already?" she asked. "The time went by so quickly."

He smiled indulgently. "You must be enjoying yourself."

"Oh, I am!" she said enthusiastically. "Tell me, Ed, which do you like better, this rose color or this emerald green?" Felicity held up two pieces of material for his inspection.

He stepped closer, took the piece of rose material and held it up to her face. "This is lovely, Felicity. It brings out the blush in your cheeks." Then he held the emerald cloth up. "Ah, but this is the one for you," he proclaimed. "It just matches those beautiful eyes of yours." She blushed and cast an embarrassed glance at Miss Real.

"Take his advice, my dear," advised Mary Real with a wink. "This man knows how to dress a lady."

Ed's brows twisted in a perturbed frown and Felicity chuckled at Miss Real's implication. She had already surmised that Ed Banyon was a lady's man; Miss Real had only confirmed her suspicions.

"Very well, I'll take the green." Felicity followed Mary into the fitting room to have her measurements taken while Ed patiently thumbed through a newspaper. In a short time, both women reemerged.

Miss Real said, ''The garments will be ready for a fitting in three days, Miss Howard.''

Felicity was all smiles. ''Thank you. I'll be here bright and early.''

''It certainly doesn't take much to please you, Felicity,'' Ed commented as they left the dress shop. ''Most women wouldn't have been happy with only two new outfits. I know my sister would have ordered half a dozen, at least.''

''I'm not nearly that extravagant.'' Felicity laughed. ''Two will do just fine!''

The couple walked their horses out of town until they came to the spot where Felicity had changed her clothes. They stopped while she redonned her jeans and shirt, then rode on up the trail.

As they neared the cabin, Felicity asked, ''Ed, would you like to stay for supper? It won't be fancy, but I'd love to have you.''

He couldn't believe his luck. He'd been waiting all day for the opportunity to spend some time alone with Felicity and he jumped at the chance. ''I'd like that very much. I'm sure anything you cook will be delicious.''

The evening was a disaster. The meal was excellent, but after dinner, when Jake didn't immediately excuse himself and leave as Ed expected him to, Banyon became increasingly irritated. Worse, Jake seemed to sense the man's desire to be alone with Felicity and took perverse pleasure in seeing that Ed didn't get his wish. Jake didn't bother to ask himself why he was being so ornery. He only knew that some devil in his gut was compelling him to spoil this man's plans for the evening.

When Ed finally decided to give up and take his leave, he made it a point to suggest that Jake depart as well. Jake was about to inform him that he wasn't going anywhere when he detected Felicity's warning glare. He wisely held his tongue, not wanting to jeopardize his warm bed by the fire.

She held her breath, praying Jake wouldn't tell Ed

that he was sharing the cabin with her. The two men walked to the door and stopped, both waiting for the other to exit first. Felicity frowned at Jake, but he tossed her a devilish wink over Banyon's head and threw his arm around Ed's shoulder. "You know, Ed, I've been meaning to talk to you about some business matters," he said as he guided the other man through the door.

Ed dug his heels in stubbornly. "Can't this wait, Jake? I'd like to say good night to Felicity."

"Oh, sure. Me too. 'Night, Felicity, and thanks for another fine supper." He smiled innocently and propelled a very frustrated Ed Banyon out the door.

Felicity was furious at Jake's outrageous behavior. For all his claims of wanting her to find a husband, he wasn't helping much.

After seeing Ed well down the trail, Jake returned. He grimaced at Felicity's angry expression and started coughing loudly while holding his chest. "Guess I better get some rest. This cold seems to be gettin' worse."

She rolled her eyes and stalked off toward her bedroom. "Good night, Jake."

Three days later, Felicity returned to Silverton for her fittings. Her trip down the trail was uneventful and, even though she was alone, she enjoyed the cool, clean air and brilliant autumn colors festooning the mountainside.

She found Mary Real busily putting the last touches on a bright orange dress trimmed with black lace which looked like it might be destined for one of the saloon girls.

"Good morning, Miss Howard."

"Good morning, Miss Real," Felicity returned. "Are my dress and skirt ready to be fitted?"

Mary pushed aside the dress form and took Felicity's hand. "Yes, and I think you'll be most pleased with them. In fact, after we have fitted them, if you can wait, I could have them ready in a couple of hours and save you another trip to town."

"Thank you. I'd appreciate that." Felicity smiled and followed the bustling little woman into the fitting room. A short time later, she left the dress shop feeling excited and a little guilty, for Miss Real had talked her into buying a pair of green shoes that just happened to match her new dress perfectly.

Felicity decided to pay Roxie a visit while she waited for her new clothes to be finished. As she was about to duck into the alley behind the Last Chance, Yancy Parnell hailed her. "Felicity!" he called as he ran across the street to join her. "How are you? What brings you to town today?"

"Yancy, how nice to see you," she replied warmly. "I was just having some new things fitted at the Ladies' Bazaar. I thought I'd drop by to see Roxie while my clothes are being finished."

Yancy was pleased to see that Felicity was alone. He'd seen her three days earlier leaving town with Ed Banyon. It appeared that he now had more than just Jake McCullough to worry about in competing for her favors. "Come have a cup of tea with me at the café, Felicity. It's been so long since I've seen you."

"Thank you, Yancy, that sounds wonderful."

Grinning triumphantly, he took her elbow and escorted her across the street to the small café.

By the time she returned to Miss Real's shop, it was nearly dark. She'd spent an hour visiting with Yancy and the rest of the afternoon with Roxie. Roxie had insisted that Felicity have Yancy escort her back to the cabin. "It'll be dark soon, honey," she had said. "Some crazy, drunken skunk could attack you up on that trail. It's not safe for a woman alone." Yancy had been more than willing to accompany her home and Felicity had to admit she felt safer with him riding beside her.

All in all, it had been a very pleasant day and she was looking forward to wearing her new skirt tonight at supper. Since Ed's visit, Jake had been on his best behavior and Felicity truly enjoyed their evenings together. Sitting in front of the cozy fire at night, petting Boozer and chatting with Jake, it seemed almost as if they were a happy, married couple. She sighed and, as usual, berated herself for her foolish dreams.

October came and went and still autumn seemed reluctant to yield to winter's grip. Jake repeatedly told Felicity how unusual it was for the weather to remain pleasant so late in the season. For her part, she was grateful for each balmy day, feeling that every one that passed meant one less day she would have to face the icy winds and paralyzing snowstorms everyone had warned her of. The first Saturday of November dawned bright and cool. Felicity prepared Jake's breakfast as usual and was surprised when he didn't leave for the mine directly afterward. Instead, he hung around the cabin doing little, inconsequential jobs. She was further astonished when, at mid-morning, he suggested that she fix lunch and they have a picnic at the creek.

At noon, she packed a basket and strolled down to the stream. The aspen trees had shed their leaves, the wildflowers had gone to seed, and the large, V-shaped formations of birds were no longer visible in the sky, having long since departed for the south. Though the day was mild, Felicity shivered in apprehension. Winter wouldn't stand in abeyance forever, and she knew that any day now, she would be forced to deal with its terrifying fury.

Shaking off her apprehension, she dropped to her knees not far from the creek's edge and spread a checkered tablecloth on the grass. As she unpacked their lunch, Jake walked quietly up behind her. Startled, Felicity's head snapped around to find him towering above her. "I see you're all ready to eat." He smiled. His shirt was slung over his shoulder and she caught her breath at the sight of his brawny chest. Seemingly unaware of her dumbstruck expression, he quipped, "I could eat a horse. What've you got in there that's good?" He pulled on his shirt, then folded his long legs and sat down at the opposite edge of the cloth.

She dragged her eyes away from his chest and chuckled. "Now I *know* your cold is gone for good. Your appetite's back." She handed him a chicken leg and a cup of coffee, jerking her hand away when his calloused fingers grazed hers.

Jake nodded his thanks, the crescent-shaped dimple appearing at the corner of his mouth. As he proceeded to make the piece of chicken vanish, he studied the play of the wind in Felicity's hair. She had pulled it back with a ribbon and it hung down her back to her waist, the breeze teasing a few strands loose to caress her cheeks. She still wore the jeans and shirt she'd put on that morning to wash the cabin windows. He knew he should be used to seeing her in that outfit, but the sight still heated his blood. Forcing his eyes from her shirt and the twin points of interest, he cleared his throat. "Felicity, would you have supper with me in town tonight?"

Astonished, she choked on a bite of chicken. "Supper? In town? Why?"

He smiled encouragingly. "Well, I thought we might try out the restaurant at the new Grand Hotel. You know, have a real elegant dinner."

Felicity frowned. She desperately wanted to accept his invitation, but she was afraid. "Jake, I thought we agreed it would be better if we stayed away from each other."

"Look, Felicity, I'm invitin' you out for dinner, not askin' you to share my bed." At her shocked expression, he added, "I've been sleepin' in the same house with you for weeks now and nothin's happened, has it?"

She couldn't help but smile at his logic. "That's true, Jake, but it's still not a good idea."

He stared at the slow-moving creek for a long moment. Then, determinedly, he turned to her again. "You know, winter's gotta come soon, and once we get snowed in here, there may not be any trips to town for months. I thought we could each get a room at the new hotel, have supper, and enjoy a little luxury for a change. Come on, Felicity, say you will. It'll be fun and we deserve it."

She wanted to say yes so badly. It would be like a dream come true to spend a romantic evening with him. And that was exactly why she knew she had to say no. "I'm sorry, Jake. I just can't."

He tried once more. "Look, Felicity, if you'll go with me tonight, I'll go to church with you in the mornin'. We'll both be in town anyway and we'll already have our Sunday clothes with us. That way, you won't have to drive the wagon in tomorrow."

"No, Jake. I can take the wagon and go to church alone. You don't have to escort me."

Jake rose to his knees, exasperation written all over his face. "Damn it, Felicity, it's my birthday, and I *don't* want to spend it sittin' alone in a saloon gettin' drunk. Please have supper with me!"

"Oh, Jake," she gasped, "today's your birthday? I'm so sorry, I didn't know. Of course I'll have supper with you. But I feel terrible! I don't have a present for you, I didn't bake a cake, nothing! Why didn't you tell me?"

He beamed. "Oh, hell, Felicity, I don't need no cake. It's enough that you'll celebrate with me."

"Your birthday," she mused. "Is that why you didn't go to the mine today?"

"Yup." He nodded. "It's the one day of the minin' season that I play hooky. Nobody should have to do a lick of work on their birthday."

"I'll remember that when mine comes around," Felicity teased. She paused a moment and then shyly asked, "How old are you, Jake?"

"Twenty-eight," he responded. "That probably makes me an old man to you."

She smiled. "No, not an old man. I think twenty-eight is the perfect age for you to be."

He looked at her in bewilderment for a moment, but shrugged away her puzzling comment. "Can you be ready to go by six o'clock?"

"Yes, that should give me plenty of time to get ready."

Jake grinned in satisfaction and bit into another piece of chicken.

Chapter 10

Roxie Wilson gazed happily out her bedroom window. For the hundreth time that day she smiled, thinking that Silverton was the most beautiful town on earth.

The past few weeks had been the happiest Roxie had known since her husband had died seven years before. Ever since the evening when Yancy had invited her to share a drink with him, the two of them had been almost inseparable. They had gone on picnics, taken rides up into the hills to view the autumn splendor, and had shared cozy, private suppers in Roxie's room. About the only thing they hadn't done was spend any time in bed together, and Roxie found that to be the most wonderful thing of all. For the first time in many years, a man was looking at her as something more than a receptacle for his momentary desire. Yancy treated her like a real person, not just a female body. He wanted to *talk* to her. He was interested in her thoughts and dreams, her hopes for the future.

Roxie smiled dreamily, realizing that Yancy made her feel like she was little Emma Roxanne Gray Wilson again. It had been a long time since Roxie had thought of herself as Emma, Hank Wilson's pretty little wife and Roy and Rachel Gray's talented daughter. But somewhere, buried deep inside her, Emma was still alive, and suddenly, Roxie wanted

Yancy to know her . . . the girl who dwelt beneath the powder and rouge and feathers.

Yancy was coming for supper that evening and she quickly made up her mind that tonight was the night she would let him meet the real Roxie, the woman no one in Silverton had ever known.

She whirled away from the window and yanked open the doors to her wardrobe, reaching far into the back and pulling out a demure gray velvet dress. The hem reached the floor, the sleeves reached her wrists, and the neckline reached her throat. Roxie chuckled, thinking that tonight Yancy was going to see less of her than he ever had before, but by the time he left her room that evening, he would know her more intimately than anyone in town.

She sat down at her dressing table and eagerly pulled the pins from her upswept, ribbon-bedecked coiffure. Her long red tresses tumbled to her waist and she grabbed her hairbrush, vigorously applying it until her hair streamed down her back like a molten river.

Shaking her head to throw the flaming mane behind her shoulders, she reached for a jar of cream and liberally applied it to her face, wiping away layer upon layer of powder and kohl. Next, she walked over to the china basin by the bed and dipped her hands into the water, scrubbing her face clean of the last traces of makeup. She pinched her cheeks to add a little color and gazed hard at her clean, naked face, trying to see herself as Yancy would. Would he think she was plain? She hoped not. Rather, she hoped he would see, perhaps for the first time, the rose and cream of her complexion, and the bright blue depths of her unadorned eyes. She felt light, free, and young. It had been a long time since she had really looked at herself and she was pleased to see that the years had treated her kindly. Her uncorseted waist was small, her large breasts still high and firm. Her skin was smooth and her eyelids almost transparent in their delicacy. Best of all, she didn't look like Roxie, the saloon girl. She looked like Emma.

She stepped into the gray dress and fastened the tiny pearl buttons that ran up the front. She hadn't worn this dress in years. It belonged to that other girl . . . the girl she suddenly, desperately wanted to be. It belonged to Emma.

Checking the small brass clock that sat on the tiny table by the window, Roxie realized that Yancy would arrive at any moment. She felt like an innocent with her first gentleman caller. It was wonderful. She was in love.

Yancy Parnell meandered down Greene Street toward the Last Chance and his supper date with Roxie. He almost wished that he hadn't accepted her invitation. He didn't feel much like socializing.

His leisurely chat with Felicity the day before had dealt a stunning blow to his plans. But, try as he might, Yancy could no longer deny the truth. He *liked* Felicity Howard. He genuinely liked her. She was sweet, trusting, gentle, and honest. How could he continue with his sordid plans to dupe her into marrying him? He couldn't. He cared too much for her. Besides, it was painfully obvious that Felicity was head over heels in love with Jake McCullough. Every time the man's name came up in conversation, her eyes lit with a fire that was impossible to miss. Yancy had long and intimate experience with women and he knew when one was in love. Even if he wanted to pursue Felicity, he doubted he could turn her head. She loved Jake and Yancy knew that it was not in his power to change that.

So, he thought dismally, where did that leave him? He *had* to get his hands on the Silver Lady mine. It was his ticket back to respectability. He could put this sleazy, deceitful existence behind him and return to his proper place in society, where honest people lived quiet, sedate lives of wealth and grace. After years of being an outcast, he desperately wanted to return to the culture that was his birthright.

What was he going to do? He felt trapped, knowing the only way he could get his hands on the mine was to continue his odious relationship with Jed Croft. Somehow, he *had* to bankrupt McCullough. It was the only option left to him. If he could just buy Jake out, he could proceed with tapping the vein he knew led into the Silver Lady. His problems would be solved. He could sell the saloon, establish himself in another community as a man of wealth and power, and marry a respectable woman. It was his dream. It had to happen. Whatever it took, he would *make* it happen.

As he neared the saloon's entrance, Yancy pushed aside his troubled thoughts and smiled in anticipation. The past few weeks spent in Roxie's company had been the happiest of his life. He astutely realized that there was much more to Roxie than she allowed most people to see. She was intelligent, beautiful, and a witty companion. Although Yancy ached to sample her charms, he knew it could destroy the fragile relationship they had recently built. No, he would not approach her in that way. When the time was right, if ever, she would come to him. Until then, he would continue to fight his lust and treat her with the respect a decent woman deserved.

He sighed wistfully. If only Roxie had come from a different background. If only she had ever been given the chance to be something other than a painted harlot. Yancy knew he could happily spend the rest of his life with Roxie. But she was not the right kind of wife for a respectable businessman. The style of her hair, her clothes, and her makeup attested to that. Still, he couldn't help but wish that things could have been different, that he had met Roxie before life had dealt her such a bad hand.

He climbed the back stairs of the saloon with the comforting thought that at least they would have the winter together. Now that November was upon them, his plans for bankrupting McCullough would have to wait until spring. That gave him six months to spend with Roxie before he had to make any more decisions about his future.

He smiled. Six months was a long time and he planned to spend every available moment with the beautiful woman who was, even now, waiting for him. He hastened his steps. He couldn't wait to see her.

When Emma heard the soft knock on her door, she leaped out of her chair like a shot from a gun.

She caught the image of her panicked face in the mirror and thought with dismay, I can't answer the door. This is a mistake. Yancy's going to think I'm ugly . . . plain. He'll feel like he's spendin' the evenin' with a schoolmarm. Oh, why did I think I could still be Emma?

A second, more insistent knock sounded and she knew it was too late to change her mind. Resolutely, she smoothed the folds of her velvet dress and headed for the door.

For a long moment, Yancy Parnell just stared at the vision who opened Roxie's door. Finally finding his voice, he blurted, "Roxie, is that you?"

"Well, sort of." She giggled nervously. "Do I really look that bad?"

"Bad? You think you look bad? My God, you're the most beautiful creature on earth!"

She smiled shyly and responded, "Do you really think so, Yancy?

"Yes," he said sincerely, "I really think so."

For an endless moment the couple stood on either side of the doorway and stared at each other. Yancy finally chuckled, breaking the spell. "Aren't you going to invite me in?"

She stepped back and threw the door wide. "Of course," she stammered. "I don't know what I'm thinkin' of, makin' you stand out in the hall."

He entered the room and tossed his hat, gloves, and walking stick on the bed.

"Would you like a drink?" she asked. "Supper won't be here for a few minutes yet."

Yancy nodded agreeably. His eyes were riveted on the gentle sway of her long skirt as she glided gracefully around the room preparing their drinks. When she handed him his glass and sat down across the table from him, he said, "Roxie, you're exquisite. I could just sit and look at you all night."

"Yancy, you're embarrassin' me."

"Don't be embarrassed. You're beautiful. I never would have guessed what you keep hidden under all those cosmetics. Why do you wear them, Roxie? You're much prettier like this."

She shrugged. "It's part of the act. It's expected. Besides, Roxie would wear them."

"What do you mean, *Roxie* would wear them?" he questioned.

She smiled. "Just what I said. Roxie would wear them. Emma wouldn't." Her voice had dropped to almost a whisper.

He shook his head in confusion. "Who's Emma?"

"I'm Emma," she replied softly, "or at least I used to be."

"Are you telling me that your real name is Emma?" Yancy asked, aghast.

She nodded. "Emma Roxanne Gray Wilson."

"I love the name Emma," Yancy mused aloud, "and the way you look tonight, it suits you perfectly." He paused. "You know, suddenly I don't feel like I really know you at all. Tell me about yourself, Roxie. Tell me about Emma Roxanne Gray Wilson."

She hesitated. "It's not a pleasant story, Yancy."

"I want to know anyway," he said gently.

"Well, I was raised in Wichita, Kansas, and I got married when I was sixteen. Hank was a good man and I really loved him. We had a farm and the first year everythin' went real good for us. Then, the second winter we were married, Hank took sick and died.

"I wanted to die too, Yancy, I missed him so bad. I couldn't run the farm alone, so I sold it. My folks were dead by that time and I wanted to get out of Wichita, so I went to Kansas City to stay with my sister. But when I got there, I couldn't find a job. I'd already used most of the money I'd gotten for the farm, so I moved on. I went to Denver and got a job in a ladies' dress shop. It didn't last long, though." She chuckled at the memory. "I just can't add.

"Then I tried to be a waitress, but I could never keep the orders straight and the customers were always gettin' mad and complainin' about me. So that only lasted about three months. I tried to think of somethin' else I could do, but I really didn't have any talent for anythin' . . . except singin'. I knew I could sing and everywhere I worked, men told me I was pretty, so I started workin' in a saloon."

There was a knock at the door, signaling the arrival of their supper. Yancy went to accept the tray from the delivery boy while Emma poured them each a glass of wine. When they were once again seated and had started their meal, Yancy asked, "How did you end up here?"

"I don't know." She shrugged. "Itchy foot, I guess. I thought maybe I could start fresh here, but every place is pretty much the same." Her voice trailed off.

"Do you want to change your life, Roxie?" he asked quietly. "Do you want to be Emma again?"

She stared at her plate in silence. When she raised her head, tears glistened in her blue eyes.

"Yes." She nodded as a tear escaped to slowly trace down her cheek. "More than anythin'."

His meal forgotten, Yancy rose from his chair, circled the table, and gathered her in his arms. He kissed her gently on her soft lips, holding her close and crooning, "Don't cry, baby. If you want to be Emma again, we'll make it happen."

"Oh, Yancy," she sobbed, lifting her eyes to his, "it feels to good when you hold me."

Feelings of tenderness unlike any he'd ever felt before tore loose from somewhere deep inside his soul. Suddenly, he couldn't get close enough. Pressing her tighter to him, he kissed her eyes, her cheeks, trailed his lips down her neck, and then back up to gently explore her mouth.

She responded with a passion and yearning that Yancy knew was genuine. This was not the calculated response of an experienced prostitute feigning desire for a client. This was Emma, kissing him with an honesty that spoke of emotions long suppressed.

Finally, he gently pushed her away. "Our supper is getting cold," he teased.

"Do you care?" she whispered.

"Aren't you hungry anymore?"

"Oh, yes . . . I'm hungry," she breathed.

Yancy's pulse pounded. "Do you mean it? Are you really sure?"

She slanted a provocative look at him and drew him over to the bed. "I've never been more sure of anythin' in my life."

Much later the couple lay bathed in the serenity of love's afterglow. Both of them felt awed by what had passed between them and knew, in that moment, that their lives would never be the same. It was a new beginning, the promise of a new life, and their happiness and contentment was boundless.

"I want you to stop working," Yancy whispered. "I never want another man to be in your bed again."

She felt as if her heart might burst. "But Yancy—" She giggled. "—think of how much money you'll lose without me at the saloon."

"It doesn't matter." He shrugged. "I have some business to take care of in the spring, then I'm going to sell the saloon and you and I are going home to New Orleans."

"Home?" she questioned. "Are you from New Orleans?"

He nodded in the darkness. "Yes."

"Tell me," she whispered. She heard him sigh and it was a long time before he spoke.

"Mine's not a pleasant story, either. Except, unlike you, I brought all my problems on myself. My folks were rich planters in the Louisiana Delta. I was the younger of two sons and, somehow, as far as my father was concerned, nothing I ever did was quite as good as my brother."

"How terrible, Yancy. Why did he feel that way?" she asked.

"Who knows," he replied. "He just did. It was when I was at the university that the final break came. I wasn't studying and I was failing just about every course. I was much more interested in playing cards and chasing women."

"I can believe that!" she giggled and snuggled closer.

"Well, anyway, I knew I was going to fail my final exams . . . so I cheated on them."

"Oh, Yancy," she moaned, "why?"

"It was stupid, I know, but I thought I could get away with it, and I didn't want my father to be disappointed in me. Of course, I got caught and they expelled me. When I returned home, my father was in a rage. We had a terrible argument and he threw me out. That was fifteen years ago and I haven't been home since. I swore I'd never go back until I was rich and successful."

"So what did you do?" she asked.

"Hopped a riverboat and played cards for a living. I went from one boat to another and the years just went by. When I got tired of that, I gave up the boats and wandered from town to town, taking suckers for all I could get. Actually, I haven't done all that badly. I've made a lot of money over the years. I finally ended up here, won the saloon and the mine, and decided to stay. All I need now is one more big score and I'll have enough to go home and face my family.''

''Life's been pretty rough on us, hasn't it?'' She sighed.

Yancy turned on his side toward her. ''Yes, but that's all over now. I have a feeling that everything is going to work out for us, Emma. Come spring, you and I are going to blow this town and go back to New Orleans in style. Would you like that, honey?''

''Yes,'' she breathed, her lips brushing his, ''I'd like that just fine . . .''

Chapter 11

❧❧❧

Wearing his best suit and whistling a bawdy tune, Jake strutted jauntily toward the cabin. A brisk breeze ruffled his hair and tumbled dry leaves across his boots. The late afternoon air was cold and he inhaled its invigorating essence with relish. He felt good, real good. The stock was fed, the bags were loaded, and the horses were hitched to the wagon. Everything was ready for their departure.

Entering the cozily lit cabin, Jake found that Felicity had not yet emerged from her room. He took a cigar from the breast pocket of his dark brown tweed jacket and struck a match to it, easing down onto the settee. He lifted one foot to inspect the glossy shine on his new boots and grinned. Nothin' like a new pair of boots to make a man feel like a gentleman, he thought with satisfaction. Puffing contentedly on his cigar, he pulled his watch from his waistcoat and checked the time. He grunted and shook his head. Felicity was sure taking her sweet time getting dressed. What could a woman do that took so long?

No sooner had the thought crossed his mind than the bedroom door clicked open and his question was answered. He stood up slowly, his eyes glued to the angelic vision before him. Felicity glided into the room and stood quietly waiting for his reaction.

Jake could hardly believe that the woman standing before him was his plain little business partner. The dress, a soft emerald wool, seemed to shimmer as it caressed her feminine curves. Gentle folds of material draped down the front and the bodice held a cream-colored satin inset that rose to her chin with a delicate, lacy, piecrust collar. The long, tight sleeves were cuffed with a narrow band of the same creamy lace.

"Felicity, you look . . . lovely," he stammered.

A blush reddened Felicity's cheeks as her wide green eyes met his warm, admiring ones. She lowered her lashes under his bold appraisal, after noting his handsome attire and virile physique. His high-heeled boots made him a veritable giant. Beside him, she felt tiny and feminine, and for once, she reveled in that femininity.

She tilted her head to one side, sending a long curl cascading over one shoulder. Jake drew a deep breath, steeling himself against the temptation to reach out and run his fingers through the silken fall. She'd fixed it the way he liked it best: pulling it back from her face to the crown of her head, she'd secured it with a length of green ribbon, allowing it to hang loose down her back in an undulating, honey sea. Saucy curls breezed across her forehead.

"And you, sir, look very handsome." She smiled, returning Jake's compliment.

He nodded graciously and held out his arm. "Shall we, madam?"

Her smile broadened as she hooked her hand into the crook of his arm.

Suddenly she paused. "Our bags?"

"I've already put 'em in the wagon," he assured her. "Everythin's ready."

When they reached the wagon, he stopped and, before she could protest, scooped her into his arms. Trembling, she drew a halting breath as his hand brushed against her breast. Carefully depositing her on the wagon seat, Jake grinned. "Can't take the

chance of tearin' that beautiful dress, now can we?''
he teased. ''Besides, I don't get many opportunities
to play the gentleman.''

Felicity smiled nervously as he took his seat beside her. He clucked to the horses and the wagon
lurched forward, causing her hands to flail outward
in an attempt to keep her seat. One hand inadver-
tently grasped Jake's thigh. His head snapped
around toward her as she yanked her fingers away
in dismay. With an outward tranquility she was far
from feeling, she smoothed invisible wrinkles out of
her skirt. She forced herself to adopt a composed
facade, folding her hands in her lap and looking
straight ahead.

Jake's skin burned where her hand had touched
him, but he ignored the erotic, tingling sensation
and Felicity's obvious embarrassment, saying simply, ''Sorry for the rough start.'' She remained rigid
in her seat.

Pulling back on the reins, he turned and faced her.
''You're still worried about us goin' out together,
aren't you? I promise you, Felicity, nothin' is gonna
happen. Stop lookin' like a scared rabbit.'' At her
continued silence, he smiled and chucked her playfully under the chin. ''Come on, Miss Howard, relax! It's my birthday and how can I enjoy it if you're
gonna sit there all evenin', tied up in knots won-
derin' when I'm gonna pounce on you?''

She threw him a chagrined smile. ''I'm sorry, Jake.
I'll try. To be honest, I'm just as afraid of myself as
I am of you.'' She blushed at her admission but she
didn't want him to think that she thought of him as
a beast and herself as the prey. After all, it wasn't
his fault that just being near him caused such strange
yearnings within her. ''I promise I'll do everything
I can to help you enjoy your birthday to the fullest,''
she added earnestly.

''Good.'' He grinned. ''I can hardly wait to sink
my teeth into a big steak.''

* * *

The Grand Hotel was as elegant as its name suggested. Backed by the Crown Perfume Company of London, the British owner, W. S. Thomson, had spared no expense. After parking the wagon, Jake took Felicity's arm and escorted her through the lobby to the front desk. She stared in awe at the beautiful, ornate furnishings, many of which were constructed of precious cherry wood. She was surprised to discover that the ground floor of the hotel was devoted almost entirely to shopping emporiums, including a haberdashery, a dry-goods shop, and two hardware stores. The second floor was rented to the San Juan County government for offices and courtrooms. The third floor held the only rooms available to let.

She was peering around, trying to locate the dining room, when Jake turned to her and said, "Henry says our rooms are ready, Felicity, so why don't we put our bags away and freshen up before dinner."

As the bellboy set her valise inside her room, Felicity glanced apprehensively at a door which appeared to connect directly to Jake's room. After the young man handed her the key and took his leave, she tiptoed over to the door and cautiously tried it, feeling relieved when she found it was locked.

She was enchanted by the grandeur of her room. It was decorated in peacock blue, including the thick carpet and brocade swagged drapes. She walked over to the large, canopied bed and ran her hand along a smooth, mahogany poster. Her eyes lit on the intricate Indian cotton coverlet and she smiled, thinking that the bed was entirely too beautiful to sleep in. At the same time, she could hardly wait to try it out.

She had just finished washing her hands and face and repairing her wind-blown curls when Jake knocked on the outside door. "Are you ready?" he called eagerly.

She opened the door and turned to fetch her reticule. "I haven't seen any place this fancy since I left England," Jake said, looking around her room with interest. "Are you comfortable here?"

Returning with her evening bag, she nodded. "Oh, yes, Jake. It's lovely! I've seen pictures of rooms like this but I've never stayed in such elegant surroundings. Are you sure we can afford this?"

His face lit with pleasure at her approval. "Don't worry. One night in this hotel isn't goin' to break us." Without further comment, he took her elbow and escorted her down the hall, remarking that the desk clerk had told him the dining room and bar were located in the basement of the hotel. They descended to the dining room where they were shown to an intimate table in a secluded corner. Felicity glanced at Jake curiously as she saw him press a large coin into the maitre d's hand. He answered her look with a disarming smile and pulled out her chair.

"Oh, Jake, isn't it wonderful?" Felicity breathed as she looked around. Small gas-lit chandeliers were scattered about the room and on each table was a crisp white tablecloth and matching napkins. The marble-topped, dark walnut sideboards and dim light lent a quiet, romantic elegance to the richly appointed restaurant.

An impeccably attired waiter interrupted their examination of the dining room as he handed each of them a large, impressive menu. After several minutes of silence, Jake peered around his menu at Felicity, who was still studying hers. "Have you decided what you want yet?"

She lowered her menu and looked up. "There are more selections here than I've ever seen. It all looks so delicious that it's difficult to decide."

"Well, personally, I'd recommend the steak. It may not be the fanciest thing they've got, but a good steak is hard to come by, way up here." Felicity took one last look at her menu and laid it aside.

"I think I'll take your advice." She nodded. "I've never even heard of most of these dishes, let alone eaten them. The food at the convent was hearty, but very simple. The only problem I have is everything sounds like more than I could possibly eat. At these prices, I wouldn't want to waste anything.''

''Don't worry about that,'' he assured her. ''I won't let it go to waste.'' Knowing his voracious appetite well, she chuckled and decided to go ahead and order the steak.

He signaled to the waiter, who immediately came to their table. After ordering their meals, Jake added, ''And we'll have a bottle of your best champagne.'' At Felicity's shocked look, he grinned, his dimple flashing. ''It's my birthday!'' he reminded her.

''Please remember that I don't drink, Mr. Mc-Cullough,'' Felicity remarked primly.

''Have you ever tasted champagne, Felicity?'' She shook her head in adamant denial. ''Then I insist you try a little so we can have a birthday toast. Don't worry—'' He held up a hand to cut off her protest. ''—no one ever got drunk on a champagne toast, and if you don't like the taste, you don't have to finish it. All I ask is that you try it. Fair enough?''

She wrinkled her nose but conceded, ''Well, I suppose it wouldn't hurt to try a little, just to toast.''

Jake nodded to the waiter who had patiently stood by during their discussion. At Jake's nod of assent, the stiff-lipped man scribbled on his pad and marched away.

Jake gazed at Felicity from across the small table. God, but she's beautiful tonight. Was he crazy or did she really get prettier every time he saw her? As always, he was drawn to her eyes. True, they were an unusual color, but it was more than that. They reflected her whole character: clear, bright, gentle, and honest. As he covertly watched her, he realized that she was different from any woman he'd ever known. He'd seen something in those eyes the first day he'd met her, but his cynicism had not allowed him to admit it. Felicity Howard wasn't a gold digger, nor was she shallow and deceitful, as his mother had been. Felicity was the type of woman most men only dreamed of finding, and the man who married her would have a mate for life: a woman who would stand by him regardless of the blows life might deal them; a woman who would love him until the day he died.

Jake shook off his philosophical thoughts and laughed wryly to himself. The tiny female sitting across the table was putting the lie to all of his long-held views about women. This revelation was not only startling but frightening. Jake knew he was changing and that Felicity Howard was responsible. He was able to admit that, perhaps, his early cynicism toward her had been misdirected. Still, he wasn't prepared to place his heart in this woman's hands, or any other's, for that matter. The wounds left by his mother's abandonment were just too deep to ever really heal.

Felicity was blissfully unaware of Jake's tumultous thoughts as she sat gazing about the restaurant. She recognized several ladies she'd met at church and graciously returned their nods of greeting. At one table she saw the banker, Mr. Werkheiser, and her lawyer, Mr. Ford, in a serious discussion with two other businessmen she didn't recognize. Why, I'm actually getting to know people, she thought with delight. I'm beginning to feel like a member of this community. The thought filled her with a pleasurable sense of well-being.

She surreptitiously glanced over at Jake and found him studying her thoughtfully. His intense regard was disconcerting and Felicity's gaze faltered as she contemplated Jake's strange mood. Although he had been attentive and charming all evening, there was now a faraway, pensive look in his eyes. His visage, as he stared at her, held an expression akin to respect. She risked another measuring glance. There was something else in his eyes . . . a look almost like yearning. She told herself that her imagination was playing tricks on her, that it was just her own longing that she saw reflected in his hazel gaze.

Their long, pensive silence was broken by the waiter and his assistant appearing with their meals. As the plates were set before them, the waiter lifted a large bottle of champagne from a silver bucket and, with a great flourish, popped the cork. He poured a few drops into Jake's glass and waited as Jake tasted it and nodded his approval. When their glasses were filled, the waiter asked, "Will that be all for now, sir?" His words were clipped and Felicity was immediately reminded of the little Cornishman she'd met at the Howardsville dance.

Jake nodded and the man disappeared. "Snobby, isn't he?" Jake commented with a smile. "He reminds me of the waiters in London."

Felicity chuckled. "I think that's the whole idea. You know—" She lifted her nose in the air and jutted her chin out. "—so veddy, veddy propah."

Jake burst out laughing. It was the first time he'd ever heard Felicity make a real joke. Feeling decidedly content with the surroundings and the company, he raised his glass for a toast. Felicity followed suit, intrigued by all the little bubbles that kept floating to the top of her glass. "This first toast is to you, Felicity, for agreein' to help me celebrate my birthday."

She smiled with delight as he touched his glass to hers, and then took a small sip of the effervescent wine. "Oh!" She looked at Jake in astonishment and rubbed her finger over her upper lip. "It tickles!"

"Sure it does." He grinned. "That's why people like it." He set his glass aside. "Now I'm gonna try this steak."

She looked down at the huge piece of beef covering her plate. It was so large that her potato had been put on a smaller side plate. "It looks delicious," she said.

Jake swallowed his first bite, rolled his eyes, and

declared, "Best steak I ever tasted." He waited while Felicity tried hers. "Well, how is it?"

"It's *very* good, Jake. We never had anything like this at St. Margaret's." He threw her a satisfied grin and raised his glass once again. "Another toast?" she asked.

"A man can't toast enough on his birthday," he assured her. She picked up her glass and waited for him to speak. He looked thoughtful for a moment and then proclaimed, "To the steak!" Again, they touched glasses and drank.

"You know, I think the second sip tastes better," Felicity stated. She took another small swallow to test her theory. "Yes," she went on firmly, "it gets better and better. But I don't think steak deserves a toast, Jake."

"You don't?" he asked.

"Of course not. The credit should go to the cook."

Jake picked up his glass and held it in readiness. "Then, by all means, a toast to the cook!"

"To the cook!" Felicity echoed and took another swallow.

Their meal continued companionably for several minutes until Felicity suddenly set down her fork and said in dismay, "Jake, shouldn't we be toasting you? After all, it's *your* birthday."

"I thought you'd never ask." He chuckled. "After all, a man can hardly propose a toast to himself, now can he?"

"I guess not." She laughed. It was a soft, musical sound that washed over Jake like fresh spring rain. "I've never toasted before." She cocked her head to one side and asked, "Can a lady propose a toast?"

"I don't know why not."

"Then . . ." She lifted her glass. ". . . I propose a toast to you, Jake. May you have a full and happy life and live till you're one hundred." They drained their glasses for a second time, and after Felicity set hers down, Jake refilled them.

As the meal progressed, Felicity felt more and

more relaxed. It was as if the whole restaurant was suffused in a warm, rosy glow. Laying her knife and fork aside, she delicately wiped her mouth on the linen napkin and said, "I don't think I can eat any more of this—" She hiccoughed. "—steak." She blushed and touched her fingertips to her lips. "Excuse me." She giggled.

Jake fought hard to suppress his amusement. He'd never dreamed that a couple of glasses of champagne would turn the tight-lipped Miss Howard into such a gay and charming companion. I should have put a shot of whiskey in her tea a long time ago, he thought irreverently.

He reached over and exchanged plates with her, finishing off her steak with relish. Felicity, as always, marveled at his huge appetite. With no provocation whatsoever, another giggle bubbled out of her. Startled, her hand flew to her mouth. Jake grinned at her baffled expression and asked, "What's so funny?"

She contemplated his question for a long moment, her brow wrinkled with thought. Then she shrugged and smiled sheepishly. "Everything. Goodness, is this what a few sips of champagne does to you? Makes everything seem funny?" She cast him a doubtful look. "Are you *sure* one can't become intoxicated from this?"

He smiled at her rosy, flushed face. He couldn't bring himself to point out to her that he had refilled her glass numerous times as the meal progressed. That admission might end the evening on a sour note and too many of their evenings had ended that way. He was enjoying her company too much to risk spoiling this one. His mouth quirked in a lopsided smile. "Champagne has been known to make ladies giggle," he noted. "Somethin' to do with the bubbles, I think."

She pondered his explanation for a moment and nodded her acceptance. "Well, I guess that's all right if that's all it does." Her speech was slightly slurred.

"It's not like I was drinking real spirits that might really intoxicate me."

Jake was feeling a bit ashamed of himself for encouraging Felicity to drink so much. As much as he hated to end the evening, he knew it would be best to do the gentlemanly thing and escort the lady back to her room while she could still walk. Right now she was just feeling tipsy and relaxed, but another glass and he might end up carrying her out. That, he knew for sure, she'd *never* forgive. "I think that unless you want some dessert, we'd best retire to our rooms now, Felicity."

She looked around the restaurant and noted with surprise that it was nearly empty. "Oh, I didn't realize it was so late. By all means, we better go upstairs. I have to get up early for church in the morning."

He seriously doubted that she was going to make it to mass the next morning, but he remained silent. He hailed the waiter and paid the bill.

Felicity felt like the room was tilting as Jake assisted her out of her chair. Grabbing for the edge of the table, she swayed slightly and gasped, "Oh, my! I must have gotten up too quickly. I feel a bit dizzy."

He smiled benignly and took her by the elbow, guiding her out of the restaurant and up the first flight of stairs. Embarrassed by her reeling gait, but seeing no help for it, she accepted his assistance and leaned unsteadily against him. Jake swallowed hard as he tried to ignore the sensation of her soft breast rubbing against his arm.

When they reached the landing on the second floor, Felicity came to an abrupt halt. "Are we there yet?"

Try as he might, he couldn't suppress his amusement. "Nope, not quite there." He chuckled.

She looked up into his handsome face and grinned. "You know, Jake, I like it when you smile like that. You have this wonderful dimple that—" She poked her finger into his dimple. "—just magically appears when you smile. And you know what else?'' She giggled.

He laughed and removed her probing finger, but continued to hold her hand. She was leaning closer now and the heady scent of her perfume made a jolt of desire course through him. He closed his eyes for a moment, gritted his teeth, and answered, ''No, I don't know what else. Tell me.''

Her breast brushed intimately against his shirt-front and he bit his bottom lip hard. ''You're very charming when you're not mad at me,'' she declared with a crooked smile. ''I really like you when you're in a good mood.''

He blinked in surprise but chalked up her compliment to the liquor. She tugged gently on the sleeve of his coat and Jake felt as if he would drown in the depths of her soft eyes. God, why is she lookin' at me like that? Doesn't she have any idea the power she wields with those eyes?

''Do you like me at all, Jake? I mean, just a little?''

His breath caught in his throat. ''Yes, Felicity,'' he answered softly, caressing her hand. ''I like you a lot. Now, come on, sweetheart, let's get you to your room.''

She nodded agreeably and said, ''That's a good idea. It's so *hot* out here in the hall.''

As they approached the third flight of stairs, Felicity again came to a dead stop. ''Where are we going?'' she asked in annoyance. ''We *must* be there by now!''

Jake looked at her limp little body leaning so heavily against him. Glancing around to ensure that there was no one in sight, he scooped her up in his arms and took the last flight of stairs two at a time, setting her down in front of her door. ''Sweetheart, where's your key?'' he asked.

She held up her reticule and smiled. ''Right in here.'' She opened the tiny purse and began fumbling inside it to find the key. After a few fruitless minutes, Jake reached out and plucked the bag from her hand, then removed the key and unlocked the door.

As the portal swung open, she stumbled into the room, nearly upsetting a small chair. Jake leaped forward, grabbing her around the waist and righting her before she fell. "Whoa there, honey. You're gonna hurt yourself."

Felicity looked at him groggily and shrugged. Shaking his head, he again picked her up, traversing the width of the room and depositing her carefully on the bed.

He tried to straighten, but Felicity refused to unlock her arms from around his neck, causing her to come up off the bed with him. Quickly, he sat on the edge of the bed, relieving the pressure of her dead weight. "All right, darlin', let go. You need some sleep and I need to get out of here."

"Is our evening over?" Her voice was plaintive.

His breathing became labored as he looked down at her alluring figure lying on the bed. Her arms were still locked around him and as he bent in one last effort to untangle them, her lush breasts grazed his chest. Jake groaned aloud, feeling a familiar tightening in his loins. He redoubled his efforts to remove her arms and release her fingers from where they had wound themselves into his hair.

"Felicity," he pleaded, "let go of me *now*. For God's sake, girl, I know I promised you I'd be a gentleman, but I'm only human and you're not helpin' much."

She looked at him in complete bewilderment and withdrew her arms. "I'm sorry, Jake. I didn't mean to hurt you."

His mouth twisted in a wry smile as he thought of how shocked she'd be if she knew where he was really hurting.

"Go to sleep, honey," he whispered. "I'll see you in the mornin'."

Turning, Jake silently exited the room. As he closed the door behind him, he shook his head in wonder. Christ, he thought, I should get a goddamn medal for this!

The small mantle clock on the fireplace struck two times. Felicity's eyes fluttered open and for a long moment she stared at the ceiling, wondering where she was. Then she remembered. She was in her room at the Grand Hotel. Her mind was hazy as she tried to reconstruct the events of the evening. She remembered eating the huge steak and sipping a few drops of champagne as she and Jake toasted his birthday. But somehow the end of the evening was a blur. How had she gotten back to her room, and why was she lying here on her bed completely dressed? She had a vague recollection of being carried up some stairs and there was a distorted vision in her mind of Jake's face bending close to her. Had he kissed her? Surely not, she thought with a smile, she'd *definitely* remember that. Feeling groggy and somewhat uneasy, she rose. She lit a small lamp and undressed, pulling on her nightgown and wrapper and kneeling to stir up the fire in the chilly room. Her feelings of unease regarding the previous evening's events remained with her. Had something bad happened? Had she gotten sick? She did feel a little light-headed, even now, but she wasn't ill.

She sank into an overstuffed chair before the fire and pondered the perplexing situation. She clearly remembered starting up the stairs with Jake. She had felt a little dizzy . . . and that was the last she remembered.

Suddenly, she had a clear vision of Jake telling her to get some sleep and leaving her room. Why, she hadn't even wished him a final happy birthday or thanked him for the lovely dinner! Her breach of manners was unforgivable. It must have been the champagne. Even though Jake had repeatedly assured her that she couldn't become intoxicated from it, those bubbles must have had some strange effect on her. What must he think of her? After bringing her to town, and spending so much money on dinner and lodging, she hadn't even thanked him! She had just . . . just passed out!

Felicity stared into the fire, wallowing in a mire of self-derision. Well, there was only one thing for it. She would go apologize and thank him for the wonderful evening, right now.

She gazed over at the connecting door between their rooms and saw the faintest glimmer of light coming from Jake's room. He must still be up, she thought with relief. Crossing to the door, she tapped on it softly. There was no answer. She tapped again but was still met with silence. He must be up, she thought in annoyance, he wouldn't go to sleep with candle still lit! Was there something wrong with *him*? Was *he* ill?

Without a second's pause, she turned the key and tried the door. It was not locked on Jake's side and opened easily. Stepping into his room, she realized that the light she had seen was not a candle, but the still-glowing coals of his late-evening fire.

As her eyes adjusted to the darkness, she could see him lying on his back in the bed, asleep. Gasping in embarrassment that she had almost awakened him, she quietly backed through the doorway.

He sat up with a start as he struggled to focus on the shadowy figure standing in the doorway to the adjoining room.

"Felicity?" he murmured in a sleepy voice. "Is that you, sweetheart? What's the matter, are you sick?"

She stood as if riveted, staring in dumbstruck awe at the Adonis sitting in the bed. The dim glow of the waning fire cast giant shadows across the chiseled planes of his bronzed chest. His thick, chestnut hair was tousled, his eyes limpid with sleep.

Felicity knew that the sight of Jake at this moment would forever remain etched in her mind. She thought he was the most beautiful man God had ever created and, regardless of what the future might bring, she would love him till she died.

It was several moments before she could find her voice to answer his simple question. "No, Jake," she whispered, "I'm fine. I came in here to—well, I thought you were still up and I just wanted to thank you for the lovely evening."

A soft chuckle rumbled from deep in his chest. "Well, you're welcome, Felicity. Come over here where I can see you. I feel like I'm talkin' to a ghost."

She shyly walked over and stood next to his bed, her eyes widening and her heart pounding as she saw he was naked from the waist up. "I . . . I shouldn't be here, Jake," she stammered. "I'll go back. I just woke up and realized that I didn't even say good night. I'm sorry about how I behaved. I guess there are some people who *can* become intoxicated from champagne."

Jake winced, thinking again of how he had intentionally misled her about the effects of the bubbly drink.

"Anyway, I just wanted to thank you, say good night, and . . ." Her voice trailed off.

"And what, Felicity?" he asked quietly, his heart in his throat.

"Well, in my family, we had a tradition that a person must receive at least one kiss on their birthday to ensure a year of good health and prosperity."

"Sounds like a wonderful tradition," he said. "And God knows, I need all the help I can get on the prosperity end of things." He paused and looked at her, his hazel eyes fathomless. "Are you goin' to kiss me, Felicity?"

"Yes," she breathed.

He gently pulled her down onto the edge of the bed, gathering her in his arms and twisting her body so that she was lying across his lap. She lifted her lips to his, feeling as if she might swoon as his warm, firm mouth covered hers. The kiss went on endlessly as he deepened the caress, his hand meandering up her spine. He heard her breathy sigh as she surrendered to his embrace and parted her lips to his questing tongue.

Jake knew his battle was lost. He wanted her so badly, and she had come to him. *She had come to him!* What was happening between them couldn't be wrong. He had never felt anything more right in his life than the sensation of this woman nestled against him, running her fingers through his hair and sighing with desire.

His tongue met hers, and Felicity's mind was filled with the erotic memory of these same inflaming caresses on a lonely mountain trail. For the slightest moment she hesitated, waiting for the warning voice in her head to sound an alarm. But, strangely, there was only silence. Silence, and a sense of pleasure she had never known existed.

His big hand cupped her breast and his thumb glided sensuously over her hard, excited nipple. As he caressed her, he placed his mouth against her ear, his voice a husky whisper. "Baby, I want you so bad . . . but if you don't want me, then you better get off this bed and out of this room as fast as you can."

"I want you, Jake," she moaned in surrender. "I don't want to leave."

He felt a rush of desire so powerful that it took his breath away. Expelling a long, shaky sigh, he groaned, "Oh, God, Felicity, you're so beautiful." Burying his head in the soft hair at her temple, he trailed kisses over her eyelids and down her nose before capturing her mouth again.

Drowning in his passionate embrace, Felicity was hardly aware when he pulled off her robe and nightgown. But suddenly, she was naked against him, feeling the heady sensation of his skin rubbing against the length of her body while he lowered his mouth to worship the rosy tip of one breast.

Streaks of pleasure raced through her body as his

hot mouth fondled and sucked at her nipple. She arched against him in a silent plea to get closer, clutching his head to her.

Jake never wanted this moment to end, but her reaction to him was so eager, and he was so starved for her, he could barely control himself. He knew he had to slow down or he wouldn't be able to give her the pleasure she deserved. Rising on his knees above her, he hungrily feasted his eyes on her naked body, his gaze burning a trail over every curve as if to sear them into his memory.

If possible, her body appeared even more beautiful than the first time he'd viewed it through her window. He ran his hand slowly down between her breasts, pausing at her tiny waist and continuing on to her flat stomach. He rested his hand on her belly and lifted passion-glazed eyes to hers. "Did you know your name means happiness, Felicity? Let me make love to you, sweetheart. Let me show you the happiness of a lifetime."

She shivered, her mind rejoicing at the apparent meaning in his sensuous words. Raising on her knees to face him, she whispered, "Oh, yes, Jake, but let me look at you first. Turn toward the fire and let me see you."

He eagerly complied. Her eyes made a slow tour over the splendor of his muscular body. He gasped in reaction as her eyes settled on the bold evidence of his desire. Her breath quickened and her teeth unknowingly caught at her lower lip as she stared in awe and fear at the threatening magnificence of his impassioned manhood.

He gently pulled her back down onto the bed, half covering her body with his. She jumped in alarm as his rigid shaft pressed against her thigh. "Shhh, sweetheart," he whispered hoarsely, brushing at the short curls on her forehead. "I won't hurt you, little one. Relax and let me love you." At her dreamy nod, he began a tender assault on her sensitive body, licking, touching, and tasting all of her until she was mindless with need.

"Jake, please!" she whimpered, not even knowing what she was asking for.

He smiled and shook his head. "Not yet. Touch me, Felicity."

"I . . . I can't."

"Yes, you can." He gently took her hand and guided it down. As she tried to pull away, he kissed her, softly coaxing, "Don't be scared, sweet. Please, I want you so much."

His soothing, encouraging words relaxed her and she stretched her hand forward to shyly explore the heat of his passion. The skin there was hot and satiny. She looked up at him in wide-eyed wonder as he drew a shaky breath, closing his eyes in sheer bliss. Then, trembling, he moved atop her, parting her thighs with his knee. His kiss betrayed his urgency as he removed her hand from him and placed it on his shoulder.

His fingers again cupped her breast and she arched to meet his touch. Then he was inside her, hard and hot. She gasped at the sudden sharp pain of his entry and he paused to give her body time to adjust to the invading fullness of him. Feathering his fingertips along her temple, he murmured soft words of love until she relaxed once again. Then, with slow deliberation, he set a gentle rhythm within her moist warmth.

A fierce yearning budded within her. The sensation grew and grew until she could stand it no longer. She moaned in ecstatic torment, and her desire sent Jake past the brink of his control. His thrusts gained momentum, casting them both onto a swirling sea of passion.

Jake felt Felicity's body tense. She dug her nails into his shoulders and clenched her eyes shut, crying out with the ecstasy of her release. He joined her, and together they exploded into thousands of fiery, shooting stars.

Afterward, he lay watching as she sank into a deep, love-drugged slumber. Her head rested on his shoulder, and her leg was thrown intimately over his thigh as he held her close against him. He remembered commenting to someone, not long ago, that Felicity Howard was full of surprises. Until this moment, he hadn't realized just how accurate that statement had been.

Chapter 12

⟨~⟨⟨⟨⟨◯○○⟩⟩⟩~⟩

Jake slowly opened his eyes and gazed over at the soft, warm woman snuggled next to him. He still couldn't believe that Felicity was in his bed. Even more incredible was the fact that *she* had come to *him*. He propped himself up on an elbow and studied her lingeringly. Her long lashes turned up at the ends, casting a slight shadow on her cheeks. Rich, honey-colored hair haloed her head and lay in wanton disarray across the pillow. Her lips were still soft and kiss-swollen. Little girl, Jake mused, you sure took me by surprise. He grinned, thinking that Felicity Howard had made his twenty-eighth birthday one he'd remember for the rest of his life.

How could I ever have thought she was anything but beautiful? he wondered. Lifting a soft, silky curl in his hand, he touched it to his cheek and inhaled its sweet scent.

Felicity moved slightly so she lay on her back. The sheet had worked its way down to her waist, revealing her creamy breasts to Jake's hungry gaze. His fingers tingled with the memory of how their satiny fullness had overflowed his hands. How could she ever have contemplated being a nun? he marveled. The girl was made for a man's loving. He drew a shaky breath and watched the slow rise and fall of her chest.

Her innocence hadn't detracted in the least from

the intense enjoyment he had found in her arms. In fact, no woman had ever pleased him more. Beneath her prim exterior, Felicity was seething with passion and Jake was secretly delighted he'd been the one to introduce her to the ultimate intimacy between a man and a woman. His manhood suddenly throbbed to life, the lusty recollections rekindling his desire. Would Felicity let him make love to her again? He worried that she'd wake up in a fury and claim he'd taken advantage of her. He didn't want to believe that she'd regret what had happened between them last night, but with her quicksilver temperament, he couldn't be sure. She'd always sworn that she was saving herself for marriage, and yet, here she was in his bed. What had made her change her mind?

He pushed the troubling question aside as desire surged hotly through him. He wanted her again, and there was only one way to find out if she felt the same.

Felicity lay on the precipice of wakefulness, gradually becoming aware of something tickling her cheek. She lifted a hand to brush it away. The tickle moved to the corner of her mouth. Surely there isn't a fly in here at this time of year, her sleepy mind reasoned. She drowsily opened her eyes just as Jake settled a soft kiss on her lips.

"Good mornin', darlin'."

For a moment she just stared at him. Then she smiled shyly as memories of the previous night came flooding back. "Good morning, Jake," she whispered. She lowered her lashes, wondering what he must be thinking of her wanton behavior the previous night. Noticing that the upper half of her body was exposed to his view, she gasped in embarrassment and yanked the sheet up to her chin. He might have seen all there was to see last night, but, somehow, it wasn't the same in the light of day.

His reaction was instantaneous. "Don't," he whispered, and slowly pulled the sheet back down to her waist. He reached over and cupped one of her breasts in his big, work-hardened hand. At her sharp intake of breath, he released her and gently took her chin between his thumb and forefinger, turning her to meet his eyes, ''Are you sorry, Felicity?''

He waited for what seemed an endless, silent moment. Finally, she shook her head and murmured, ''No. I know I should be . . . but I'm not.''

He exhaled a strangled breath. He hadn't realized how much her answer meant to him until that moment. ''I'm glad,'' he breathed. ''Want another lesson?''

''In the morning?'' she exclaimed, shocked. ''But it's so *bright* in here! Do people do this in the daytime?''

He chuckled, and despite herself, her body reacted to the low, sensuous timbre of his voice.

''Felicity, sweet, day or night is okay. There ain't any rules about lovemakin'. You can do it anytime you want to.''

Her eyes widened. ''Do you mean we can do this as often as we want?''

''Yup,'' he teased, ''as often as we want. Unless, of course, you make so many demands on me that you wear me out.''

The lustful flame in his eyes belied his words and made her feel weak and shaky. Before she could think of a tart response, Jake grabbed her in his arms and threw one of his legs possessively over hers. All thoughts of conversation fled. She encircled his shoulders with her arms and his teasing grin faded as he lowered his head and claimed her waiting lips.

Felicity felt like she was melting. His kiss was searching yet tender, and a throbbing ache spread through the core of her being. She groaned, now fully aware of the pleasure that awaited her. Jake's breathing quickened and she could feel his heart pounding against her breasts. In a husky whisper, he asked, "You do want me again, don't you, sweetheart?"

She touched her fingers to his temple and slid them down the strong line of his jaw. She didn't know what it was about this man that made her lose all reason, but right now, all she could think of was satisfying the hunger he'd so easily aroused. "Yes, Jake," she breathed, "I do want you again."

He shivered in reaction to her soft words and branded her lips with a searing kiss. Her mouth parted in surrender and he pulled her closer to taste her more fully. He moved lower, his tongue tracing a hot, wet path in the valley between her breasts. She caught her breath as he captured one hard-tipped nipple in his mouth and gently kneaded its mate between his fingers. Pausing briefly, he looked into her love-softened eyes. "You're so beautiful, Felicity," he whispered. He slowly trailed his hand up and down her rib cage. "I love your skin. It feels like warm satin." He raised his head and kissed her lips. "Lord, sweetheart, but you're somethin'."

Her smile was soft and seductive. She threaded her fingers through the thick mat of hair on his chest. "I like the way this feels against me," she whispered. "Especially here." She moved her hands down to her breasts and boldly lifted them to rub against his naked chest.

Jake went wild. He buried his face in her breasts and rubbed his parted lips back and forth across her nipples as she held them pressed close together.

Gradually, he moved down her body, kissing and licking every inch of her. Felicity surrendered completely to his passionate worship and wondered if she would survive the torturous pleasure of it.

Just when she thought she could endure no more of his sensuous assault, he slid between her legs, fusing his body with hers. He moved in a slow, deliberate rhythm; enflaming her womanhood until she writhed beneath him. "Please, Jake, now!" she panted.

His thrusts quickened and he felt her body stiffen and arch higher, taking all of him. Her cry of release sent him hurtling over the edge with her. Waves of pleasure streaked through his body as, together, they reached for and found sweet surcease.

Much later, after his heartbeat and breathing had finally returned to normal, Jake opened his eyes. He glanced toward the window and noticed that although the sun had risen, the sky had hardly lightened from the predawn darkness. He slowly edged off the bed and walked over to the window. Sighing with regret, he turned back to awaken Felicity. "Come on, baby, it's time to get up."

She stretched languorously and murmured, "What time is it?"

"Time to head for home. It's really snowin' out there, and the way that sky looks, we could be in for a bad one. Guess we should skip church." She moved to get out of the big bed, but he held up his hand. "Wait a minute. Stay there till I get a fire built up. This room is freezin'."

Felicity snuggled back under the quilt and sighed contentedly. After building a fire, Jake leaped back into the bed and pulled her to him. She squealed and tried to wiggle out of his grasp as he pressed his cold body against her. Her efforts caused her bottom to rub against him and he gave her a playful smack. "You better quit that or I'll forget all about leavin' and we'll get snowed in here for the winter and your cow will starve."

Felicity felt his mounting erection against her bottom and quickly rolled away, gaping at him in astonishment. Jake gave her a sheepish grin and shrugged. Burying his hands in her tousled hair, he gave her one last, hard kiss. "Come on, you vixen, let's get dressed."

Felicity watched as Jake concentrated on the snowy road in front of the horses. It had taken them less than an hour to get dressed and eat a light lunch. Now she sat snugly bundled in two blankets, one across her lap and the other wrapped around her shoulders over her coat. Her long hair was tucked into her collar and Jake's muffler covered her face so only her eyes were exposed. He had acted like a fussy old grandmother, wrapping her up so tightly that she felt like one of those Egyptian mummies she'd read about. Still, she had been thrilled by his obvious concern for her comfort.

Her eyes sparkled over the top of his muffler. He loves me! she thought rapturously. Even though he hadn't come right out and *said* so, she had no doubts. The words he'd whispered last night had said it all. *Let me show you the happiness of a lifetime.* A lifetime! That phrase could only mean one thing. Jake wanted to spend his life with her and that meant he wanted her for his wife.

Felicity knew she should feel guilty for letting him make love to her without benefit of marriage. It *was* a serious sin, after all, and she dreaded facing Father Thomas when next she went to confession. But how could something that felt as right as being in Jake's arms be wrong? The night had been so perfect and her happiness was so complete that it was impossible to feel the guilt and regret her religious teachings demanded. Besides, she rationalized, we'll be married soon.

She smiled dreamily as she mentally planned her wedding. I wonder if I'll have time to make a wedding dress? she mused. Well, if he's really anxious, I can always wear my new green wool. After all, what difference does the dress make when you're about to marry a man like Jake McCullough? She spent the rest of the long ride up the mountain happily pondering the arrangements . . . who she'd invite, what refreshments she'd serve, where they would hold the service . . . Everything would be perfection.

Momentarily dragging his eyes off the dangerous, icy road, Jake stole a quick glance at Felicity. Her expression was contented and happy; like a woman who'd just been made love to . . . and enjoyed it. He was delighted that she didn't regret her impulsive decision to come to his bed, and that his earlier worries had been for nothing. He was curious, though, to know her feelings about the new direction their relationship had suddenly taken. Curious and apprehensive. She hadn't mentioned marriage, but he knew she strongly believed that sex and marriage went hand in hand. So why hadn't she said anything? And why had she let him make love to her again this morning?

He smiled to himself as memories of the last day washed over him. Never had he experienced such bliss in a woman's arms. It was so good between them. So goddamn, amazingly good! There was a depth of passion in the girl that he would never have believed if he hadn't experienced it himself. Just the thought of her naked and writhing beneath him, whispering his name, and shyly offering herself to him was enough to make him shift uncomfortably on the hard wooden seat of the wagon. Watch it, man, he silently warned himself, this is no time to think about pullin' over and takin' another taste. He chuckled at his own licentiousness. He hadn't thought so much about sex since he'd been a green kid. How had Felicity managed it? One day he couldn't stand the sight of her, and the next thing he knew, he couldn't keep his hands off her. There was something about the girl that ignited a fire in his blood and he wondered if he'd ever be able to get enough of her. He'd thought at one time that if he could just take her once, he'd get her out of his system and be done with her. Now he knew how mistaken he'd been. His appetite had only been whetted and he didn't know how he was going to make it the rest of the way up to the cabin without throwing her into the wagon bed and satisfying his suddenly raging desire.

His face turned red with embarrassment as he no-

ticed Felicity staring at him curiously. She must have
noticed how much he was squirming on the seat.
He groaned inwardly, willing himself to sit still.
Think about something else, he silently commanded. The storm, the road, the snow you're
gonna have to shovel, the damn cow and hens
you're gonna have to feed! His pounding heart
slowed and he let out a shaky breath. He could wait.
Felicity was worth waiting for, and the notion of taking her in the back of a wagon during a snowstorm
was just plain insane. Exciting, but insane.

He stole another glance at her and marveled at the
serene loveliness of her profile. There was a lot more
between them than just good sex. For the first time,
he admitted to himself that he truly enjoyed her
companionship. She was a good woman; a kind,
gentle, caring woman. She was forever baking a pie
for that priest of hers, cooking a meal for some luckless miner's widow, or working like a slave to polish
all the pews at St. Patrick's. Again the thought
struck him that she was exactly the kind of woman
that a man wanted to marry: pretty, sexy, loving,
and, he now knew, passionate. For all these reasons, Felicity Howard was also dangerous.

Dangerous? Jake asked himself. Would marriage
to Felicity be so bad? Somehow, he didn't think so.
But still, he wasn't about to rush into something just
because the girl had given him the best twenty-four
hours of his life. Better to let things go along as they
were, he reasoned. Winter was obviously upon them
and no decisions could be made until spring anyway, so why worry about it now? There were a lot
of long, cold, secluded months ahead of them.

He felt a thrill of anticipation as he contemplated
spending those months lying in front of a warm fire,
making love to Felicity. By spring, they'd both be
sure of how they felt. Until then, they could just
relax, enjoy, and really get to know each other.

Yup, he nodded to himself, spring was time
enough to decide what their future might be.

* * *

The wagon pulled into the yard in front of the cabin and Jake jumped down and hurried over to help Felicity. Boozer bounded up to greet them and Felicity gave him an affectionate pat. She pulled the scarf away from her mouth and asked, "Did you miss us, boy?" The big dog galloped around her legs, barking excitedly. "Well, come on, then," she said, laughing, "let's go inside, warm up, and get you something to eat!"

Boozer happily followed them into the cabin. Jake set their bags down by the door and knelt in front of the fireplace. "I'll get this fire goin', unhitch the horses, and feed the stock. Then I need to set a few traps. I'll try to be back before dark."

"You're going to set traps in this weather?" asked Felicity as she pulled off her wet blankets and flannel coat.

"Have to. I should've set 'em sooner but there was too much work up at the mine." She frowned and glanced apprehensively out the window. "C'mon, Felicity, don't scowl at me," he coaxed. "You'll be plenty glad to have fresh meat when we get snowed in here."

"I suppose you're right," she conceded. "I just hate to see you go out when it's so miserable."

He pinched her cheek and grinned. "Don't worry, I'm used to it. Just keep the fire goin' and have a big, hot supper ready for me when I get back." He bent down and stole a quick kiss. "I'll bring in some more wood before I leave."

He disappeared out the front door and headed for the lean-to. Felicity watched him through the window for a moment and then dragged the kitchen stools over to the fire, draping the soggy blankets over them to dry.

After tending the stock and bringing in several armfuls of wood, Jake pulled Felicity to him, gave her a hot, hard kiss, and left to set his traps. Felicity stood before the fire and rubbed her cold hands to-

gether, smiling down at Boozer a who lay contentedly curled up on the rug, enjoying cozy nap. She
sighed and looked around the silent cabin. Her eyes
fell on Jake's bag sitting next to hers, but unsure of
what to do with it, she left it there, picking up her
own and taking it to her room to unpack.

She was removing a roasted chicken from the oven
when Jake finally came through the door, stomping
snow from his boots. She set the chicken on the
counter and turned to see a large puddle of melting
snow forming beneath his feet. She raised a scolding
finger, but quickly lowered it at the sight of his half-
frozen face. His lips were blue and his clothes were
completely sodden. She rushed over to help him remove his coat. "Jake, you're freezing! Get those
boots off and come over by the fire." She hung his
dripping coat and hat on a hook behind the door.

He pulled off his boots and walked over to the
fire, holding his hands out to its welcome heat. Felicity was right behind him. "Your shirt is dripping,
too. How did you get so wet?"

"I slipped and fell. Some snow went down my
back and it soaked through my clothes. Lord, but
it's gettin' cold out there. I swear it would freeze a
witch's tit. I mean, um . . ."

She rolled her eyes in reproof. "I think I get the
idea," she said wryly. "Now, you better get those
clothes off before you catch your death." Like a
mother with a recalcitrant child, she started to un-
button his shirt. Jake stood and watched in amusement as she pushed it off his shoulders and tugged
it out of his jeans. Turning, she removed one of the
now-dry blankets from the stool and replaced it with
the shirt. Handing him the warm blanket, she said,
"Here, wrap this around you. Your skin feels like
ice." Then, without waiting for him to do it himself,
she pulled the blanket tightly about his shoulders.
Her hands were soft and warm as they brushed
against his chest. Jake sucked in his breath and
caught her hands to stay them. She lifted her eyes

to his, and was startled to see the hazel orbs darkening with desire. "Jake, you have to get the rest of these wet clothes off."

He leered at her suggestively. "You want to help me, Felicity?"

"I, ah . . ." She stepped back, blushing and flustered. "I have to get supper on the table.

His plaintive voice stopped her as she turned away. "Come on, Felicity, I need help. I'm so cold. I'll have to let go of this blanket in order to get these wet jeans off. They're already stiff and colder than hell."

She clucked her tongue in mock reproach as she again turned to tend their supper. "You're a devil, Jake McCullough. I know what you're up to."

Holding the blanket with one hand, he reached out and yanked her back against him. Before she could protest, he whirled her around and imprisoned her mouth with his. His kiss was long and thorough and Felicity felt a shudder of desire ripple through her. Her knees grew weak and she leaned into his body, wrapping her arms around his waist. Abruptly, he ended the kiss and tangled his hand possessively in her hair. "There's all kinds of ways for a freezin' man to get warm," he whispered. "Sure you don't want to help me?"

Her mind reeling from his passionate kiss, she nodded dumbly and reached with shaking fingers to unfasten his belt. The leather was stiff and resisted her efforts, forcing her to drop to her knees to get a better view of what she was doing. She finally released the buckle and slid the belt free. It dropped, unheeded, to the floor. She tried to unfasten the top button on the jeans but the heavy, wet material made it almost impossible. As she slipped one hand inside the fly to push the reluctant button through its hole, she suddenly became aware of Jake's rapidly swelling manhood. Her face flushed as the material pulled tighter, making it even more difficult to work.

The back of her hand caressed Jake intimately as she continued to push the buttons through the holes. As the last button finally gave way, he gulped in mounting anticipation. It had started out as a teasing game of seduction on his part, but the tables had quickly been turned. Had Felicity taken much longer, he was certain that the last button would have just popped off from the sheer strain of his throbbing arousal.

Tossing the blanket to one side, he tore his jeans off himself. At the sudden release from imprisonment, his manhood stood rigidly out and away from his body, glancing against her cheek as he stepped free of the encumbering clothing.

Felicity was awestruck by the boldly intimate proof of Jake's desire. She reached up and gently touched the velvety skin of his rigid length, letting her fingers trail sensuously down to the firm roundness below. A tiny drop of crystal-clear liquid appeared at the end of his shaft and, unable to help herself she leaned forward and caught it on her tongue.

The touch of her tongue sent a surge of primitive lust coursing through him. Dropping to his knees, he pushed her down onto her back, kissing her with a savage hunger. His mouth was hot as his tongue entered her in imitation of the ultimate consummation he desired. The tender pulse point at her throat beckoned him and he ran his lips across it, excited by her rapid heartbeat. "Jake," she moaned against his neck, "supper is getting cold."

"Supper? To hell with food, girl, there's only one thing I'm hungry for right now."

His provocative words awakened a fury in Felicity and she writhed against him, lost in her own wanton desire.

In seconds, he had her clothes off and she lay naked beneath him. Her hands traced the hard, flexing muscles in his back as she kissed and sucked on the sensitive skin behind his ear. Her hand moved around his body, caressing him lower and lower until she boldly wrapped her fingers around his hot, velvety shaft.

Jake gasped as waves of exquisite pleasure rolled over him. He shifted his body slightly so that her hand slid down his engorged length, then rubbed the wet, pulsating tip against her sensitive palm.

Felicity let out a little shriek of surprise at the highly erotic sensation. She lifted her arms, placing her hands on Jake's shoulders as he began to kiss her soft belly. He glanced up at her briefly and rasped, ''Put your hand back where it was.'' She instantly complied, her heart pounding in reaction to his heated request.

His mouth and tongue continued their downward path, sensuously exploring her abdomen and coming to rest in the soft, fleecy triangle at the juncture of her thighs. He buried his hand in the soft curls, finding them moist with her desire. His fingers teased at her small, sensitive bud, making her cry out and buck against him, her whole being straining toward the ultimate pleasure she knew he would give her.

But Jake was not ready to release her from the erotic torture he was inflicting. Moving his mouth downward, he dipped his tongue into her honeyed essence, tasting her intimate nectar as his tongue glided up and down her hot, wet sheath.

She screamed in shock and ecstasy, begging him to stop even as her fingers entwined in his hair and she pressed his face closer to her.

He felt her muscles begin to convulse and knew she was at the brink of fulfillment. He raised himself to his knees and sat between her legs, grasping her buttocks. Lifting her hips, he entered her with one swift, powerful thrust. His body pounded against her, immediately bring her to a mind-shattering climax. Groaning and shuddering, Jake succumbed to his own release. He poured himself into her, finally collapsing against her soft breasts as they blended into one.

* * *

It was hours later when Jake awoke. The fire had burned low and the room was cold. He disengaged himself from Felicity's arms and threw several logs onto the glowing coals, blowing gently until they caught and ignited. As he turned around, he saw that Felicity had curled herself into a small ball against the chill of the room. Tenderly, he bent down and scooped her into his arms. With a small sigh, she snuggled close to him. Using his foot to nudge the bedroom door open, he carried her to the bed and gently laid her on it. He pulled down the covers on the opposite side, then picked her up and tucked her beneath them. He hesitated only a moment before climbing in next to her. She automatically nestled close to his warm body and, within moments, they were both sound asleep, arms and legs entangled.

Chapter 13

Felicity slowly opened her eyes. She looked sleepily out the window at the predawn darkness, wondering what had awakened her. Suddenly she knew. She smiled and turned to look up at Jake. He was propped on an elbow, staring at her with hooded eyes as one finger lazily circled a taut nipple.

She gasped at his heated regard and whispered throatily, "Again?" Jake's smoldering gaze was his only reply. "What woke you? It seems like we just went to sleep."

"Boozer." He chuckled. "Seems we got kind of sidetracked last night and I forgot to put him out."

She lifted her head to see the gigantic dog standing at the end of the bed, a hopeful expression on his face. "Oh, the poor thing," she murmured. "Don't you think you should let him out now?"

Boozer walked over to Jake's side of the bed and scratched at the mattress, whining plaintively. Jake ignored him and lowered his head to tease her breast with his tongue. "Nope," he drawled, "he can wait a little longer."

Felicity groaned as his hand fanned downward over her bare stomach, his fingers tangling in the soft curls below. She could already feel his manhood pulsing against her thigh and she shivered in anticipation. She rolled her head against the pillow, and her tongue unknowingly passed over her lips. Jake's fingers moved down to gently stroke her wet, satiny core, causing her to almost jump off the bed.

Throwing one leg over her body, Jake sat up, bracing himself against her thighs as he rhythmically rubbed the tip of his throbbing shaft up and down her hot, moist womanhood. She whimpered and pushed herself toward him.

"Is there somethin' I can do for you, lady?" Jake rasped, as she wiggled her hips in an effort to further his penetration. He pulled back just enough to prevent her from attaining her desire and whispered hoarsely. "Ask me, Felicity, ask me for it."

"Oh Jake, Jake, please . . ." Felicity panted. Firmly grasping his hips, she hooked her ankles behind his thighs and thrust herself onto his turgid staff.

Jake's reaction was instantaneous. "You want me, girl? Tell me you want me."

Felicity bit down hard on her lip as Jack seductively undulated his hips and waited for her answer. Her eyes snapped open and she jerked spasmodically. "Yes, I want you. Oh, please, Jake. Now."

"Now, Felicity? Now?" His hips undulated faster. "Is this what you want?" He thrust hard twice and stopped.

"Yes," shrieked Felicity. "Oh, God, Jake, don't stop. Please, no more teasing."

Jake threw his head back in exultant laughter. "All right, baby," he growled. "I never could deny a lady."

He set a frenzied pace, thrusting into her until she was sure he must be touching her womb. Her head rolled back and forth on the pillow in ecstasy until suddenly, a strange sound from the far corner of the room penetrated her drugged senses and drew her gaze from Jake's heaving shoulders. After a moment of confusion, she located the source of the noise.

It was Boozer, who was now frantically scratching at the bedroom door. Looking back toward the bed, the dog noticed Felicity's gaze on him and trotted eagerly over to her, nudging the mattress with his nose. Felicity closed her eyes against the distraction, but involuntarily opened them again when Jake snarled, "Get away, dog."

In horror, Felicity felt her concentration waning and a giggle forming deep in her throat as she again looked over Jake's shoulder. The quilt was sliding off him, exposing his back and thrusting hips. Felicity lifted her head and saw one corner of the blanket firmly clamped in Boozer's jaws as the dog backed slowly toward the door. Her hips stopped rotating as she watched Jake's gradual undraping in fascination.

"Boozer!" Jake shouted, making a grab for the blanket. "Cut it out!" The dog obediently dropped the quilt and sat down, his tail thumping the floor. He waited patiently for a moment but when his master still made no move to answer his pleas, he threw back his head and emitted a deafening howl.

Felicity was lost. The giggle she was trying so hard to suppress forced its way up her throat and she opened her mouth in a hearty guffaw.

"Felicity, stop it!" Jake thundered. "What the hell's the matter with you?" His head snapped around and he glared at the dog. "Boozer, damn it, shut up!"

Boozer was, by now, practically dancing in his anxiety and Felicity thought that the rhythmic click of his nails on the wooden floor sounded just like a military drum roll. This thought caused her to break into renewed peals of laughter.

"God damn it, Felicity, stop laughin'!" Jake yelled.

"I can't." She giggled. "Get off, Jake, and let Boozer out. This is never going to work."

Jake looked as if he wanted to strangle her. "Let him out! Now? Ah, *shit!*" Pulling out of her, he leaped off the bed, and in one giant stride, threw open the window, grabbed Boozer by the nape of his neck, and shoved the luckless dog over the sill and onto the porch. Felicity screamed with laughter, rocking back and forth and holding her sides.

Jake whirled to face her, his erection enormous, his face mottled with frustration. "Quit laughin', damn it. We're gonna finish this."

Tears streamed down Felicity's face. "No, we're not," she gasped. "I can't." She dissolved in a new wave of giggles.

He gaped at her in disbelief. "What the hell do you mean, you can't? I'm dyin' here, Felicity. Look at me! You can't leave me like this!"

"I'm sorry, Jake," she panted. "It's too late. If you could have seen what that looked like . . ." Another shriek of laughter escaped her and she turned onto her side, burying her head in her pillow as her entire body shook with mirth.

"I don't believe this!" he shouted. "I'm gonna kill that mutt!"

Weak with laughter, she rolled onto her back and gazed through tear-filled eyes at the furious man. He impatiently jerked on his trousers and tore out of the room, nearly yanking the door off the hinges in his anger. She heard the front door open and Jake yelling ferociously, "If you value your hide, dog, you better get the hell out of here. First you drink my whiskey and now you're ruinin' my love life. You better move 'cause if I step off this porch, you're dead."

A new wave of hilarity floated out the window. "And you, Felicity," Jake thundered from the porch, "you better quit laughin' because one of these days I'm gonna stop in the middle and tell *you* to forget it . . . and then we'll see how you feel!"

She seriously doubted that he would ever make good his threat, but she clapped a hand over her mouth and struggled to regain some semblance of sobriety. When she heard him stomp off to the lean-to, muttering and cursing about giggly women and idiot dogs, she withdrew her hand and expelled a long, shaky sigh. She was exhausted from her laughing fit and wanted to go back to sleep, but knew she'd better get up and make Jake some breakfast before he came back in the house. No sense in giving him something else to rage about. He was mad enough already . . .

She dressed quickly, went to the kitchen, and filled the coffeepot. As she tried to concentrate on frying bacon and stirring up biscuits, her mind kept replaying the sight of Boozer pulling the quilt off Jake. Try as she might, little eruptions of laughter continued to escape from her throat.

She heard the object of Jake's fury scratching at the back door and hurried out to give him breakfast, knowing that if she left it to Jake, the dog might get throttled instead of fed.

A half hour later, Jake slammed back into the house, glaring at her and declaring, "That dog never sleeps in the bedroom again. Understand?" Her lips trembled. "I mean it, Felicity," he warned. "If I ever see him anywhere near the bed again, so help me, I'll throw him off the side of this mountain. Quit laughin', damn it. It ain't funny. My God, I was hurtin' so bad, I thought it would never go away!"

Felicity nodded meekly, her mouth twitching. She placed Jake's breakfast on the table and, willing herself to be serious, said, "I'm really sorry, Jake. I promise I'll make it up to you."

His angry expression immediately turned into a leer. "Now?" he asked hopefully.

"No!" she exclaimed. "Sit down and eat your breakfast. I swear you're *never* satisfied."

"Yeah, well, another incident like this mornin' and you'll never be satisfied again either because I'll be worthless."

She bent over him where he sat at the table and rubbed her breasts against his back. "Don't worry," she whispered, "I'll make sure Boozer stays in the kitchen tonight."

Jake glanced at her from over his shoulder and

tried hard to control the smile that threatened the corners of his mouth. "You better quit rubbin' on me, sweetheart, or you're gonna find yourself back in that bed a hell of a lot sooner than tonight. If you've got anythin' you want to do today besides play with me, you better sit down on the other side of this table right now and change the subject."

Felicity's breath caught in her throat, but realizing they both had work to do, she obediently walked around the table and sat down.

"The weather seems better today," she said in a desperate attempt to cool the fire in Jake's eyes.

"Yeah." He nodded, staring at her bosom. "At least it's quit snowin' for now. Looks like it could start up again anytime, though."

"Will this snow melt?" Felicity asked.

He shrugged. "Maybe. Hard to tell. It's still pretty warm durin' the day so it might. Why?"

"Well, I was just wondering if we would be able to get into town this week."

"Why do you want to go to town?"

She looked at him in surprise. "To see the priest, of course."

He gazed at her for a long moment. "Why do you want to see the priest?" he asked quietly.

Felicity felt a cold chill creep up her spine. "To talk about the wedding . . ." she whispered.

Jake put his fork down and stared at his plate. "What weddin'?"

She rose to her feet, her face flushing crimson. "You know perfectly well what wedding."

He said nothing. The silence grew and grew until it roared in Felicity's ears. "Jake! Say something!" His continued silence echoed through the room. "Oh, my God," she shrieked. "Say it, say it, you coward!"

Jake raised his head, his face a mask of misery. Looking into her panicked eyes, he whispered, "I can't marry you, Felicity."

The roaring in her ears increased until she knew

she was going to faint. She grabbed the edge of the table, her knuckles turning white as she gulped, trying not to get sick. Her voice was suddenly very quiet. "Are you telling me you're already married?"

"No!"

"Then why?" She could barely whisper.

"I just can't. It wouldn't be fair to you and it wouldn't be fair to me."

"Fair? What do you mean, fair? After everything that's happened between us the last two days, you can sit there and tell me it wouldn't be *fair*?" Her voice rose again, reaching a pitch very near hysteria.

"You don't understand," he said softly.

"You're right, I don't." She drew a deep, shuddering breath and collapsed onto her stool. "But, Jake McCullough, you're going to explain it to me."

He nodded slowly and reached out to take her hand. She jerked it from his grasp and hissed, "Don't touch me, just talk."

"Bein' the wife of a miner's no life, Felicity. My ma taught me that. I always thought she and Pa loved each other, but as soon as the mine we had in California played out and the money was gone, that love ended real quick. When we moved here and Pa couldn't find a claim that would pay, she got fed up and left. She ended up hatin' Pa. There was never any money, no luxuries, just work and disappointment. The bad times killed any love she'd ever had for him or me, and all she wanted was out. So she left, and she never even wrote Pa a letter to tell him where she was or ask about me. It nearly killed him. I hated her for what she did to my father. I decided a long time ago that no woman would ever do that to me."

"I'm sorry, Jake, I didn't know," Felicity said slowly. "I can understand your feelings, but I'm not your mother."

"I know you ain't." A hint of a smile played around his mouth. "You're a fine woman, Felicity, and you'll make someone a fine wife. You're everythin' a man could ever want. But I know I couldn't live through the pain that Pa did and I'm not willin' to risk marryin' a woman and havin' her walk out the door and never come back. I'm sorry, Felicity. I never meant to hurt you, but you gotta understand. I just can't marry you.''

Her anger rose within her like a rolling sea. "What I understand, Jake McCullough, is that you've ruined my life. You've taken my virginity and spoiled any chances I might have had of finding a husband. Who'd want me now? I'm used goods, as they would say at the convent. By the saints, Jake, I trusted you! I gave you everything a woman can give a man. Why would you do this to me?''

"My God, Felicity, do you think I planned this?'' His face was a study in remorse. "Sweetheart, I fought against how bad I wanted you for months. But the other night when you came to my room at the hotel, I knew you wanted me too. I even told you that if you didn't, you'd better get out. You remember that? But you stayed, Felicity. And what we did wasn't wrong. And what we've done since hasn't been wrong either. The last two days have been the happiest in my life and I think you feel the same. How can that be wrong?''

"It's wrong,'' she whispered, "because nice women don't make love to men they're not married to. Or, if they can't help themselves and do, they get married! You told me that night in town that you wanted to show me the happiness of a lifetime. I thought you were committing yourself to me, Jake. And yes, you've made me happy. I didn't know it was possible to feel the way I do when we make love. But if I'd known that I was nothing more than a plaything for the night, like some hussy you'd paid off with a nice dinner, I'd never have let you touch me. For years, I was warned about the weakness of the flesh, but I guess you made me forget. And I'll spend the rest of my life paying for that mistake.''

Jake closed his eyes in agony, unable to face her

ravaged countenance. "I'm sorry, Felicity. I don't know what to say."

With an angry swipe at the tears streaming down her face, she set her jaw and said coldly, "There's nothing to say, Jake McCullough. It's over between us. Forever. I never want to see you again, I never want to talk to you again, I never want to hear your name again. You are going to pack your gear and move out of my house. Now. Take your horse, your clothes, your tools, and get out. Don't ever come back here and don't ever try to contact me. If we're unlucky enough to see each other in town, then just pretend you don't know me. If the mine starts paying, I will trust you to put half the proceeds into my bank account. If something comes up at the mine that requires my attention, you can get in touch with Mr. Ford and he can relay the message to me. But this is the last conversation you and I will ever have. Now, get out."

Jake shook his head. "I can't do that, Felicity. I can't leave."

"What do you mean, you can't leave? Haven't you listened to a word I've said? *I want you out!*"

"I can't leave," he said simply. "I don't have any place to go."

"I remember saying those very words to you once, Jake, and your response to me was 'That's not my problem, lady.' Well, your not having any place to go is not my problem, mister. I want you out of my house, and if you have to sleep in a room above the Last Chance saloon tonight, then so be it."

"Felicity, be reasonable," he pleaded. "That was July. This is November. I told you a couple of months ago that I'd go live at the mine for the winter, but you told me I could stay here with you. Well, it's too late to change your mind. I won't be able to get back up to the mine for months now that it's snowed. And, as you said durin' that same conversation, we can't afford for me to rent a room in town."

"Oh, I don't think you'll have to *rent* a room," she sneered. "I'm sure your friend Rena would put you up."

Jake's face flushed with embarrassment. He'd had no idea that Felicity knew anything about Rena and he silently vowed to wring Roxie Wilson's neck. Clamping down hard on his temper, he tried one more tack.

"Felicity, honey, I don't want to stay with Rena. I want to stay here. Couldn't we just leave things the way they are for the winter?"

"What?" she gasped in disbelief. "You expect me to keep your bed warm all winter after what you've said to me today? How *dare* you insult me like this!"

"Jesus Christ, Felicity, I'm not tryin' to insult you!"

"Quit swearing!" she snapped.

He took a deep, calming breath. "Listen, sweetheart . . ."

"Don't call me 'sweetheart'!"

"Felicity!" Jake shouted. "Shut up and listen to me! It's time to face facts. We're here for the winter, do you understand? Nobody's goin' anywhere till spring. We're stuck in this cabin together and we might as well enjoy it, because that's the way it is. Now, I know how much you like to negotiate deals, so I've got one for you. Let's just leave things the way they are and give ourselves a chance to really get to know each other. Hell, by spring, I'll probably be *dyin'* to marry you! I think I just need some time to get used to the idea. I care for you a lot, Felicity, more than any woman I've ever known. Don't you see, sweetheart? Bein' here together all winter is the perfect opportunity to see if marriage can work for us. By the time spring comes, we'll both know, and then we can decide what we want to do." He looked hopefully at her expressionless face. "Well, what do you think? Is it a deal?"

"No," she said, her voice like ice. "It is *not* a deal. I want you out. I'm not going to live here with you and play your fancy woman while you decide if you want to marry me. No." She shook her head emphatically. "You either marry me now or you get out. That's your choice and there will be no negotiations."

"You're the stubbornest, orneriest woman I've ever met!" Jake thundered. "You want a commitment that I can't make yet. But you won't give me a chance to see if, maybe, in four or five months, I *can* make it. Well, lady, I've got news for you. I'm not leavin'! And there's not a damn thing you can do about it unless you're gonna ride through four feet of snow into town and get the sheriff to come up here and throw me out. I'm stayin' until spring and, since you can't leave either, I guess we're stuck with each other. Now, we can spend the winter makin' love and really gettin' to know each other, or you can be a bitch and make us both miserable.

"Tellin' you that I'll probably be dyin' to marry you by springtime is the best I can do right now. Three days ago, I never dreamed I'd say that. But after spendin' a couple of nights huggin' you up to me, I've realized that it might not be so bad havin' that to look forward to for the rest of my life. But I need some time and if you ain't willin' to give it to me, then you're a fool. I can't believe that you'd throw away what might be the best thing that ever happened to either one of us just because you're in a fit of temper. Think about it hard, Felicity, because how you want to handle this situation is up to you. But I'm stayin'."

Her mind was swimming. She was so astounded by Jake's outburst that she was speechless. He was refusing to leave! This might legally be her cabin, but she knew there was nothing she could do to make him leave. It was beyond belief! Well, there was more than one way to get around this problem. She couldn't stay here with him all winter, and if he wouldn't leave, then she would.

An alarm sounded in her mind, warning her not

to tell him of her decision. She had no doubt that he would try to stop her, and she wasn't about to be stopped. She had to get away from him. She knew she didn't have the strength to resist him if he was with her every day, and she couldn't continue to sleep in his bed when he was unwilling to make a commitment to her. Leaving was the only solution, and at the first opportunity, she'd go. She'd ride into Silverton and beg Roxie to take her in. She could stay with her for the rest of the winter and then, come spring, she'd return to Philadelphia and try to start a new life. She'd be safe at Roxie's. Safe from Jake's overpowering presence: his laughter, his kisses, his passion.

"I don't want to discuss this any more right now, Jake," she said tiredly. "I need time to think . . . alone."

"Fine." He smiled. "I need to go check my traps before it starts snowin' again, anyway. That'll give you some time alone and when I get back, we can talk about this some more."

She nodded, hoping her face didn't betray the devastating sense of loss she was feeling.

Jake pulled on his heavy coat, hat, gloves, and boots. He walked toward the front door, but hesitated before opening it. He turned back and said, "Sweetheart, will you do me one favor before I leave?"

"What?" asked Felicity in annoyance. Oh, why doesn't he just go, her mind screamed.

He looked at the floor for a long moment and then, in a voice so soft that she almost didn't hear him, said, "Will you give me a kiss?"

Her heart dropped into her stomach and she fought back the urge to throw herself into his arms. Very slowly, she walked over to him and put her arms around his neck, knowing this would be the last kiss they'd ever share. She reached up and gently placed her lips on his, breaking the union almost immediately and trying to step backward out of his embrace. Instantly, she felt herself being crushed against his chest as his mouth covered hers with a fever too hot to cool.

Her knees started to buckle and she felt that if he released his grip, she might fall. He nuzzled his lips against her ear and in a soft, pleading voice, said, "Please, honey, give it a chance. I'm scared. I'm scared to death of how I feel about you. I need some time. Please, please give it to me."

With that, he released her, yanked the door open, and disappeared into a cloud of swirling snowflakes.

Felicity leaned against the door and burst into tears. If there had been any doubt in her mind about the necessity of leaving, it was gone now. This last kiss had sealed her fate. The man wasn't going to leave her alone if he stayed, and she knew she couldn't make him leave. There was no help for it. She would have to go.

Chapter 14

Felicity dashed madly back and forth between the bureau and the open valise lying on her bed. Frantically, she crammed dresses, nightgowns, and underwear into the small bag. Hurry, hurry! her mind screamed. She had to be gone before Jake returned from checking his traps. She knew, without a doubt, that she'd lose her chance to escape once he returned. He'd never let her leave with another snowstorm threatening, and she had to get away today. She couldn't spend another night in this cabin with him.

Squeezing the tightly packed valise shut, she snapped the latch. Grabbing her coat, she hastily pulled it on over the flannel shirt and jeans she'd donned for the treacherous journey down the pass. She tied Jake's woolen scarf around her head and shoved one of Joe McCullough's old slouch hats down over it. After pulling on her boots and gloves, she grabbed the heavy bag off the bed. She was ready.

She paused briefly at the bedroom door, heaving a sigh of regret for what might have been. For a moment, her eyes rested on the bed and her mind was flooded with bittersweet memories. She blinked back a tear and took a deep breath. This was no time for wistful yearnings. She had to get a good head start in case Jake came after her. Bolstering her faltering resolve, she turned determinedly on her heel and firmly closed the bedroom door behind her.

Boozer lifted his head and peered at her from his place by the fire. His tail thumped against the floor and Felicity bit her lip hard, willing herself not to cry. 'Good-bye, boy,'' she whispered raggedly. "I'm really going to miss you.'' Boozer cocked his head to one side, but she was already out the door.

Snow was falling in light, gusty flurries as she raced toward the lean-to. She snatched a bridle off a hook and headed for the bay mare. She briefly considered saddling the horse, but discarded the idea. Although the thought of riding bareback all the way to Silverton was terrifying, she just couldn't take the time. Besides, Jake had told her that it was warmer to ride bareback in the winter, and safer too. She shivered apprehensively as she remembered his warning about how easily horses slipped on snow and ice. Well, there was no help for it. At least, without a saddle, there was no danger of getting her foot caught in a stirrup if the horse suddenly went down.

''Okay, Miss Ornery,'' Felicity said firmly, ''you're going to get me to town and you're not going to throw me and you're not going to fall. If this weather gets any worse, we're both in a lot of trouble, so let's go, and no nonsense.'' She led the mare to an overturned milk bucket and mounted awkwardly, pulling her valise up after her and settling it between her thighs. With the reins in one hand and a hank of mane in the other, she left the shelter and headed down the road. She smiled in grim satisfaction, confident that she had enough of a head start that she would be safely in town before Jake discovered her absence.

The snow was already four feet deep in places and the going was much slower than she had anticipated. A prickle of fear crept up her spine when, after an hour, she calculated that she'd traveled less than a quarter of the way into town. Already, both she and the mare were chilled to the bone and exhausted. To make matters worse, the wind had again picked up and the gentle flurries had increased into a whirling sea of white. The bitter wind tore viciously at her scarf, exposing her neck to a deluge of stinging, icy pellets, and the blinding white curtain was fast erasing all traces of the road. She fought back the panic threatening to grip her as she acknowledged the very real danger of riding off the side of the mountain.

A wolf howled in the distance and Felicity gazed warily up at the trees and boulders high above the trail. She gave the laboring horse an impatient kick, begging the 'mare to increase her pace. The high-strung, confused animal was startled by this new demand and took three quick leaps sideways. Felicity felt herself slipping, and the next thing she knew, she was on her back.

Unhurt, but half buried in a snowdrift, Felicity struggled to her feet and brushed the icy snow from her face. She floundered out of the drift and reached out to recapture the mare's dangling reins. ''Nice girl,'' she crooned, ''good horse. Just stand still.''

The terrified horse lunged backward, wrenching the reins out of Felicity's grasp and whinnying shrilly. The animal's hindquarters suddenly slipped underneath her and, with a scream of pain, the mare fell backward. She thrashed wildly in a valiant attempt to regain her footing. Felicity stood, staring in horror through the swirling wall of snow as the horse flopped over on her side and ceased struggling.

Jake still had several traps to check when he noticed the wind picking up. He stood still and listened alertly as its keening howl increased, then wisely slung his catch over his shoulder and headed for home. Experienced in mountain winters, he knew he had to hurry or he'd be caught in the middle of the season's first, full-blown blizzard.

A short time later, he arrived safely at the cabin. He led his horse into the lean-to, but it wasn't until he hung up his saddle that he noticed the bay mare was gone. He cursed the flighty animal, wondering why on earth she would leave her shelter in such god-awful weather. Something must have spooked her, he concluded. Swearing in frustration, he vowed to sell the stupid creature come spring. Hungry, cold, and angry, he bent his head against the punishing wind and waded through the snow to the cabin.

The minute he stepped into the dark, chilly room, he knew something was dreadfully wrong. There was no delicious aroma of supper being prepared and Felicity was nowhere in sight. He warily set his rifle down by the door and scanned the empty cabin.

Boozer stood up and stretched, drawing Jake's attention to the dying embers in the fireplace. A hard knot of fear formed in his belly as he called Felicity's name, knowing she wasn't going to answer.

Jake ran toward the bedroom and yanked the door open, coming to a dead halt as his worst fears were confirmed. The empty bureau drawers gaped at him. He stooped and picked up a lace handkerchief lying forgotten on the floor, staring at it in dumb disbelief. She was gone.

The wind shrieked around a corner of the cabin, rattling the windows. His head jerked up and he grimly noted the worsening weather. "My God, she's out in this!" he said aloud. "The little fool!" Abruptly, he turned and raced out of the room.

Running to the front door, he grabbed his gun and called, "Boozer, come on, boy. I may need that nose of yours." Sensing his master's distress, the big dog jumped up and dutifully followed him out into the storm.

Jake knew a horse would be of little use, but he stopped at the lean-to and pulled on a pair of snowshoes. He tied a second pair around his waist, thinking that if he found Felicity, she would need them for the trek home. A combination of fear, worry, and anger caused adrenaline to surge through his body, vanquishing his fatigue. "Come on, Boozer, find Felicity." As if he understood, Boozer barked once and tore off down the trail toward Silverton.

Felicity had never been so frightened in her life. She was almost positive her horse had broken its leg and she knew that if the animal died, her own foolishness would be to blame. No longer able to discern any landmarks, she didn't dare proceed toward town, but neither was she sure of how to get back to the cabin. She only knew that if she was to have any hope of surviving this ill-fated escapade, she'd have to find some way of keeping warm.

Somewhere, in the back of her mind, Felicity recalled once reading a story about a trapper who had been caught in a blizzard. She searched her memory, trying desperately to remember what he had done to survive. Slowly the story came back to her. The man had forced his mule to lie down, enabling him to use the animal's body as a wind block. The trapper had then curled up next to the mule for warmth.

She hurried over to the downed horse and dug the snow out from around her back. She climbed into the small space and pressed herself against the mare.

Stupid! I'm so stupid! she chided herself tearfully. And this time my impetuousness just might be the end of me.

She took a deep, shuddering breath and willed herself to remain calm. Think of something else, she commanded herself. Think about Jake. Had he discovered she was gone yet? Surely he must have returned to the cabin by now. He wouldn't stay out in the woods in this storm. Then where was he? Was it possible he was so angry with her that he didn't care? Maybe he was actually relieved to know that, at last, he was done with her and she was out of his life.

My God, what if he doesn't come? She rejected that thought, realizing that she was hovering dangerously close to hysteria. Be calm. He'll come, she assured herself. The words drummed through her mind like a litany. Wedging herself closer to the mare, she tried to recall if the story about the trapper was fact or fiction. Perhaps it was better that she couldn't remember.

Her mind began to wander. She was so cold . . . so very, very cold. So cold she almost felt hot. She giggled at that thought. How could you be so cold that you were hot? And she was sleepy. So sleepy. She gave her head a hard shake, trying to stay awake. Pray, she told herself. Say your rosary. She concentrated on saying ten Hail Mary's in a row, but her mind kept drifting off. She just couldn't think. It really didn't matter, though. Now that visibility was so poor, even if Jake was searching for her, he would never find her. Better just to go to sleep. Then she wouldn't feel the cold and if Jake did find her, he could just wake her up. She would just close her eyes for a little while. If she rested a few minutes, maybe she would find the energy to get up and start walking again. Just a little while . . . Her eyes closed.

Jake was frantic. He'd been searching for the better part of an hour and still there was no sign of Felicity or the horse. He cursed himself for not realizing she would try something like this. Hadn't she said there was no compromise, that she wouldn't spend another minute alone with him? But she'd also said she wanted to think things over. You should have expected this, he chided himself for the hundredth time. Did you think she'd tell you she was plannin' to leave when she knew you'd stop her? You're a fool, McCullough. You never should have left her alone!

He suddenly heard Boozer barking. He stopped

and listened intently, but the howling wind made it difficult to determine which direction the sound was coming from. There! He heard it again. Had the dog found something? Jake ran in the direction of the barking as fast as the awkward snowshoes would allow.

He finally spotted Boozer standing near a large hump in the snow. Jake drew a deep breath and tried hard not to panic as he hurried over to investigate. Drawing closer, he recognized the prostrate body of the bay horse. Dear God, where was Felicity? A vision of her broken body lying at the bottom of some ravine washed over him and he cried out, "Felicity! *Felicity!*" He ran toward the horse, his heartbeat escalating with his fear. "Felicity, for God's sake, answer me!"

Something warm and wet nudged Felicity's frozen cheek. She didn't want to wake up. She was so warm and comfortable. Why was she being bothered? She brushed at the continuing irritation. Suddenly her shoulders were seized in a punishing grip and she was roughly shaken back to wakefulness.

"Felicity! Goddamn it, Felicity, wake up! *Wake up!*"

She slowly opened her eyes and stared groggily into Jake's ravaged face. Why was he shaking her? And *why* was he so angry? "I'm tired, Jake," she murmured. "Let me sleep."

"No!" he shouted, shaking her again. "Wake up, *now!*" He watched with relief as she again opened her eyes and stared at him in bewilderment. The life he saw returning to her emerald gaze made him very aware of how close he'd come to losing her. Dragging her out of her small burrow, he crushed her to his chest, rocking her back and forth in his arms. "Oh, baby, baby." His voice was choked and ragged against her ear. "Sweet Jesus, I thought I'd lost you!" Tears welled up in his eyes, blurring his vision. He couldn't remember a time since he'd become a man that he'd cried, but as the tears overflowed and ran down his cheeks, he was powerless to stop them.

Felicity looked around in bemusement. "Where are we?" she asked weakly.

"Out in the snow, sweetheart, and we've got to get home."

She nodded, her mind slowly clearing. "Oh, yes, the storm. How . . . how did you find me?"

Still cradling her, Jake fought to get hold of his emotions. When he finally answered her, he was amazed at how calm his voice sounded. "I know this pass like the back of my hand, but, actually, Boozer found you. I might have passed right by you if it hadn't been for him. How'd you stray so far off the main road?"

"I didn't realize I had," she replied simply.

He stood up. "Come on. I've got to get you and the horse out of here."

At the mention of the mare, Felicity's foggy mind snapped back to reality. "Oh, Jake, I think she's broken her leg. I'm so sorry. I never intended to . . ."

"Don't worry about that now," he interrupted. "We're all gonna freeze out here if we don't get movin'. Do you think you can walk?" He reached down and pulled her to her feet. She leaned heavily against him, trying to stand, but her knees buckled and she cried out in pain as blood rushed through her numb legs.

"I don't think so," she moaned.

He put an arm around her waist to support her. "Come on, baby, you gotta try. Now, walk!"

She took a tentative step forward, gritting her teeth against the excruciating pain. Tears welled up in her eyes and she turned toward Jake. "I was so afraid you wouldn't come," she blurted. She buried her face in the fur collar of his coat and sobbed as if her heart was breaking.

He took her cold face in his hands and placed a quick, gentle kiss on her nose. "C'mon now, there's no time for this." He untied the extra pair of snowshoes from his waist and bent down to fasten them onto her boots. "You ever walked on these?"

"No, what are they?"

"They're snowshoes and once you get the hang of 'em, you can walk a lot easier in the snow. They keep you from sinkin'."

"I don't think I can do this, Jake," she wailed, staring at her feet.

"Yes, you can," he insisted. "Now watch. You just lift your knee and bring your foot down flat. That's all there is to it. Try it."

She took several halting steps. "Am I doing it right?"

"Good enough." He nodded. "It'll be easier once you get used to them." He walked over to the mare and stooped down, running his hands along her legs. Straightening, he shook his head, picked up his rifle where it lay in the snow, and fired one bullet into the mare's brain.

Felicity screamed and buried her face in her hands. Jake returned to her side and put a comforting arm around her heaving shoulders. "There was no other way, Felicity. It had to be done."

She sagged against him, feeling sick from the overwhelming guilt descending on her. If it hadn't been for her stupidity, she and Jake would be safely inside their cozy cabin and he wouldn't have been forced to destroy an innocent animal. She hung her head in despair, plowing along behind Jake as he dragged her away from the scene. Boozer leaped through the snow behind them, totally oblivious to his heroism.

The trip on foot was a nightmare, and several times they were forced to stop when Felicity insisted she couldn't go on. Jake shouted, threatened, cajoled, and pleaded with her, using every tactic he knew to force her to continue walking.

Just as the cabin finally came into sight, she grabbed for his sleeve, moaned softly, and sank to her knees. Jake knew she had reached the end of her endurance, and, stooping, he gathered her in his arms and carried her the short distance to the cabin.

He kicked the door open, and after depositing her on the settee, returned to shut and bolt it. Removing her snowshoes and boots, he vigorously rubbed her blue feet, blowing on his hands in an attempt to manipulate his stiff fingers. Turning away briefly, he quickly built up the fire, then lifted the unconscious Felicity off the settee, carrying her into the bedroom and placing her on the bed.

He hastily removed her soaked clothing, noting with alarm the ashen pallor of her skin. He'd have to get her warmed up fast or risk her getting pneumonia. With that thought in mind, he pulled a flannel nightgown over her head, tucked her under the blankets, and stripped off his own clothes. Climbing into bed with her, he pulled her hard against him, encircling her body with his arms and placing his leg over hers. He roughly massaged her until her skin finally began to assume a more normal color.

Despite his vigorous ministrations, she didn't move or open her eyes. When Jake was finally assured that her breathing was deep and normal, and her skin was again pink with restored circulation, he closed his eyes and fell into exhausted slumber.

Felicity woke slowly, aware that every muscle in her body was screaming with pain. Shifting her position slightly, she moaned, feeling as if she had been bludgeoned. Sunlight streamed through the window and she squinted against its piercing glare. Why did she feel so miserable? Suddenly, the memory of the previous day's trauma flooded over her. Her argument with Jake, the storm, the horse, the snow, Jake yelling at her to walk. It hadn't been a nightmare. All of it had really happened.

A soft, deep voice whispered against her ear. "Mornin', sweetheart. Are you feelin' all right?"

She turned in shock toward the naked man

pressed so intimately against her back. The feeling of his body next to her was becoming so familiar that she hadn't even thought about it until he'd spoken. "What are you doing in my bed?" she shrieked. "I thought I made my feelings clear to you yesterday morning. Get out!"

Jake stared at her, stunned. His eyes narrowed dangerously and his voice impaled her like a lance as he rasped, "What I'm doin' in your bed, you ungrateful little bitch, is tryin' to keep you alive!" His sentence ended with a hoarse shout of rage as he threw back the blankets and leaped from the bed.

Grabbing a pair of pants from the chair, he yanked them on, snarling, "You really think a lot of yourself, don't you? It would never occur to you that I'd get into your bed for any reason except to ravish you. Well, let me tell you somethin', lady. You ain't that pretty and you ain't that sexy." He winced at the devastated look on her face, hating himself for the lie. But he was deeply hurt by her callous opinion of him and he rushed on heedlessly. "The *only* reason I got in bed with you last night was 'cause I thought you were freezin' and for some stupid reason, I was tryin' to prevent it. I'm sorry if you found my presence offensive." He threw her a furious look and stormed out of the room.

She knew she was wrong. Very wrong. But, hang the man, did he always have to act so superior? Bolting out of bed, she flew through the doorway after him. "Well, why shouldn't I think that?" she railed. "It's the only reason you ever got in bed with me before!"

He whirled toward her, his eyes flaring with rage. "I beg your pardon, ma'am, but if you will recall, the first time we were ever in bed together, you came to me!"

She had the good grace to look chagrined. "Be that as it may," she answered in a self-righteous voice, "I told you yesterday morning that I never wanted you to touch me again and, yet, that very same night, you crawl into bed with me.''

''I don't believe this!'' he thundered. ''The only reason I got in bed with you was to save—your—goddamn—life! If it wasn't for your stupid, pious sense of right and wrong, none of this would have happened! Do you have any idea of how close we both came to dyin' in that blizzard yesterday?''

Felicity had never seen Jake so angry. The spectacle of his full-blown wrath was daunting and she took an involuntary step backward. ''I know now,'' she began quietly, ''that what I did yesterday was inexcusably stupid and I'm very grateful that you saw fit to save me from what was probably certain death. I deeply regret what happened to your mare and I will reimburse you for the cost of a new horse out of my proceeds from the mine.''

His anger evaporated. He shook his head and took a step forward as if to reach for her, but she held up her hand to stop his advance. ''But, even though I'm sorry about the incident yesterday, the reasons for my leaving haven't changed. You refused to go, so I felt I had to. I just couldn't stay here with you any longer. Please remember, also, that your refusal to cooperate with my wishes was what forced me to leave in the first place.''

Jake crossed his arms over his chest in disgust. ''Now, that makes a whole hell of a lot of sense,'' he growled. ''What makes you think I would have made it to town any better than you did? In case you didn't notice, the pass is completely blocked with snow and *nobody* is gonna get through it till spring.''

She nodded her head in agreement. ''I know that now, but I had to try.''

He sank down on the settee and buried his face in his hands. When he spoke again, his voice was so low that she could hardly hear him. ''Is the thought of bein' here with me so terrible that you were willin' to risk your life to get away?''

"Oh, Jake, it's not that!" she protested. "It's not *being* here with you that's the problem. It's what I know will happen if we stay here together."

He couldn't resist a small smile. "Is havin' that happen really so bad, Felicity?"

Her eyes narrowed. "I won't stay here and be your whore."

His ire flared again. "Now, wait a goddamn minute!" he shouted. "I never said you were a whore and I haven't treated you like one either. I'd shoot the first son of a bitch who dared suggest such a thing."

Felicity shook her head in dismay. Jake didn't understand at all what she was trying to say, that she'd be betraying everything she'd ever believed in. Somehow, she had to make him see that she wouldn't accept his amorous attentions. Then, come spring, she'd be able to escape him with at least a modicum of pride left.

"There's no sense arguing about it," she said quietly. "I realize that we're stuck here together for the winter, and I promise that I won't put either one of us in jeopardy by trying to leave again. But I've decided to go back to Philadelphia in the spring and you must promise me that you will leave me alone in the meantime."

He groaned in exasperation. "And just how do you propose for me to do that? This cabin isn't big enough for us to be able to avoid each for the next four months."

"We don't have to avoid each other," she explained patiently. "I know that's impossible. What I propose is that we treat each other like a landlady and a boarder."

"Oh, come on, Felicity!" Jake snorted. "Be realistic. You and I both know that way too much has passed between us to be able to pretend we hardly know each other. It would never work and it's senseless to try. Do you truly think we can live this close all winter and not touch each other? At least

I'm honest enough to admit that you light a fire in me every time I look at you. It's a miracle that I kept my hands off you as long as I did. *And*," he added, pointing a finger at her for emphasis, "you know you feel the same way about me. You're just not grown up enough to admit it."

She blushed at the truth in his words, but stubbornly shook her head. "I'm sorry, but if you can't control your base impulses, Mr. McCullough, then you will have to leave, snow or no snow. I will remind you once more that this is *my* cabin and you will either behave yourself or you will get out." At his frown, she continued vehemently, "I mean it, Jake. You touch me again and I'll get a gun, I swear I will."

He shook his head in disbelief at her words, then stomped over to the hearth, grabbed the poker, and crouched down, jabbing viciously at the logs. Damn her! he thought in frustration. She had him backed into a corner and she knew it. There was always the slight chance that he could still make it up to the mine and spend the winter there, but it was just too risky to try. Besides, he silently admitted, he couldn't desert her. Not now. Not after everything they had shared. She had no idea of how to survive a Colorado winter and he'd never forgive himself if something happened to her.

Cursing under his breath, he stood up and turned to look Felicity straight in the eye. "Okay, lady, you win."

She breathed a sigh of relief. What would she have done if he'd called her bluff and actually left? Chances are, he would have found her next spring either frozen or starved to death. But never, ever would she let him know how glad she was that he was staying. She steeled her voice. "Good enough. But remember what I said. You make one move to touch me and you're out! I'll shoot you if I have to, but you will never touch me again."

Jake turned his back on her and gave the logs another jab. Tossing a surly look over his shoulder, he gritted, ''Fine. I hope you mean what you're sayin' because I'm through tryin' with you. The only way I'll ever touch you again is if you crawl all over me and beg me to. Go ahead and enjoy your cold, empty bed all winter. But think about it, Felicity, before you close the door on us. I guarantee you'll be thinkin' about it in January when it's about thirty below outside. You'll realize then how nice it would be to have me cuddled up next to you under the quilts. And maybe then, you'll also realize what a damn fool you're bein' and come to your senses. If you do, you know where to find me. I'll be right out here, sleepin' on my cot next to the fire. Just come crawl in with me. I won't throw you out.'' He sighed. ''But until then, you're nothin' more than my landlady and you couldn't be safer if you were livin' with a monk. If you ever want to get made love to again, little girl, then the next move is yours.''

He threw down the poker, grabbed his coat, and stormed outside, slamming the front door so hard that the windows rattled in their frames.

Chapter 15

Felicity lounged lazily on the settee, knees pulled up, an old Denver newspaper resting against them. Her eyes moved over the paper sightlessly and her mind wandered, as it always seemed to these days, to thoughts of Jake. Seeing a shadow, she glanced out the window, catching a glimpse of him as he walked across the yard to the lean-to.

After the first strained week following his birthday, they had settled into a polite but distant relationship. Surprisingly, the past six weeks had passed quickly, and, true to his word, Jake had not tried to touch her. Although she was loathe to admit it, there'd been times when she'd almost wished he had.

Even though their intimate relationship had been brief, she found she sorely missed his warm presence in her bed. Worse, her body had been awakened to the delights of erotic pleasure, and she spent many sleepless nights aching to feel again the sensual fulfillment Jake had given her. She was embarrassed by these yearnings, but, loving him as she did, she couldn't seem to control her feelings of desire.

Fueling this torment were their evenings spent by the fire. Often their mere proximity caused the air between them to become so highly charged that she was tempted to give in to her heart and throw herself into his arms. But she would ferociously crush her desire by reminding herself that Jake didn't want her for his wife, nor did he love her. This painful knowledge would cool her blood faster than a dip in the icy creek. She was trapped. She couldn't leave, and yet the enforced incarceration with the man she loved was a cruel punishment.

Despite these occasional electric moments, a daily routine had gradually evolved. Felicity would rise early, dress, milk the cow, and collect the eggs. While she was about these chores, Jake would use the privacy to clean up and dress. Immediately after breakfast, he would leave the cabin to tend the stock and check his traps. He'd return at noon for his meal and then hurry away to busy himself with tasks that kept him out of her presence until suppertime.

Scanning the wintry scene outside the window, she sighed with boredom. Concentrating on the old newspaper in front of her was impossible and she was too restless to sit and knit. The cabin was as neat as a pin and a stew was simmering on the stove. She smiled fondly as she watched Boozer tear out from behind the cabin, rooting in the snow. Suddenly she was struck with the need for some fresh air and exercise. She was tired of sitting in the tiny cabin, feeling sorry for herself. Tossing the paper away, she leaped to her feet and headed for her bedroom to change into warmer clothes.

Ten minutes later, she emerged outdoors, bundled up in her jeans and heavy coat. She could hear the steady whack of Jake's axe as he chopped wood behind the lean-to. She took a deep breath of the cold, invigorating air, relishing the sound of her feet crunching across the snow.

Crouching down, she cupped some snow between her gloved hands, packing it together until she had a good-sized ball. Then she rolled it forward, adding to its size. When the ball was so large that she could hardly budge it, she started on a second one. Boozer ran up and watched her progress curiously for several moments. He sniffed at the large snowball, but, finding little of interest, took off for the woods to chase a rabbit.

She hefted the second, smaller snowball on top of the first, packing more snow between the two to hold them together. The third, smallest snowball was finished in no time and she put it on top of the other two to make her snowman's head. She stood back to survey her work and frowned, deciding something was missing. She hurried back to the woodpile and began searching for a couple of twigs among the scraps Jake had set aside for kindling. She picked up a long twig and measured it against several others. When she finally found a twig that closely matched the length of the first, she smiled in satisfaction and disappeared around the corner of the house.

Jake, who'd stopped his chopping and watched as she rummaged through the kindling, arched a brow. What's she up to? he wondered. Intrigued, he leaned his axe against the woodpile and followed her to the front yard. He grinned at the sight that greeted him. It had been a long time since he'd built his last snowman, but, as he recalled, he'd made some of the best. He watched quietly as Felicity placed the twigs just so, giving her creation a pair of skinny arms.

"Pretty decent snowman you got there." She spun around as he approached. He stood before the snowman, his chin propped in his hand, a contemplative expression on his face. "He needs a face, don't you think?" he suggested.

"Well, I suppose he does, but I don't know what to use. Got any ideas?" she asked.

"Maybe. Hold on a minute." He disappeared around the back of the cabin and was gone for a long time. When he returned, he triumphantly held up a potato and a carrot. Felicity watched in amusement as he reached into his coat pocket, produced a knife, and sliced the potato neatly in two. Pushing the flat sides into the snowman's face, he gave him eyes. Next, he pressed the carrot into the center of the snowman's head, creating a large, protruding nose. "There, how's that?" he asked with a proud grin. "Damn good, wouldn't you say?"

Felicity chuckled at his pleased, arrogant expression. "Not bad," she conceded, "but he still doesn't have a mouth."

"Ah, yes," he said, "He must have a mouth, of course." Stooping down, he dug in the snow until he'd gathered several pebbles. Placing them in a half-moon shape, he gave the snowman a happy, slightly lopsided smile.

"There! Now he's perfect!" Jake crowed triumphantly.

Felicity was suddenly seized with a fit of giggles. Somehow, the idea of a full-grown woman teaming up with a big, burly miner to create a perfect snowman struck her as ridiculously funny. Their eyes met, each reading the other's amused thoughts, and a simultaneous burst of laughter pealed across the frozen landscape. It was the first time they had laughed together in a long time and she delighted in the rare, carefree moment.

Suddenly, they were both silent. Their laughter dwindled to smiles, the smiles to looks of hungry yearning. How easy it would be to step into his arms and kiss him, Felicity thought longingly. What difference would one little kiss make?

Jake saw the longing in her eyes and stepped closer. His movement broke the spell, and as he reached out a hand to touch her, she knelt abruptly, then rose, clutching a large snowball in her hands. He realized her intention a moment too late. The icy missile scored a direct hit, right in the middle of his face.

Spitting and sputtering and wiping snow from his eyes, he quickly recovered and moved to retaliate. "Why, you little . . ." Felicity turned to flee, but almost instantly felt her back being pummeled by a barrage of snowballs.

The battle was on! The air rang with wild shrieks, blustering protests, and triumphant guffaws. Not until Boozer came rushing up, barking a protest at seeing his two favorite people engaged in warfare, did they both collapse on the ground in surrender.

Felicity shoved Boozer away and launched into a good-natured argument with Jake about who had been winning. Finally, tired and hungry, she conceded the victory and went inside to get their supper on the table.

Happily exhausted, he watched her snow-plastered figure disappear into the cabin. God, how he missed being with her! True, he slept in the same cabin and ate at the same table, but he wasn't really *with* her. She was always polite and considerate, but then, he'd seen her show that same polite consideration to complete strangers. The most frustrating thing of all was that he had brought this on himself. It was *his* actions that had condemned them both to this intolerable situation . . . *his* cursed, stubborn pride and *his* quick temper. How could he have been so stupid as to vow never to approach her again, to swear she'd have to crawl to him?

Damnation! Just being near her made him swell with desire. Every fiber of his being ached to take her in his arms and remind her just how good it had been between them. But that was impossible. He was caught in his own trap.

He knew that she wasn't immune to him. He'd have to be blind not to notice the flame that leaped into her eyes whenever they happened to accidentally touch one another. But she was a strong woman and Jake realized she'd stick to her moral convictions and would never come to him on his terms. Oddly enough, he felt a grudging respect for her resolute character. Despite her delectable body, Jake knew that he wouldn't find her half as desirable were she lacking this quality. And so, they were at an impasse. He, too, had his pride, and since he'd laid down the rules, he'd have to live by them.

A cold gust of wind sent a shiver down his back, startling him out of his reverie. He shook his head in self-disgust. Why do I torture myself like this? Felicity wants a husband and all I want is a warm body in my bed. Come spring, I'll just visit Rena down at the Last Chance. It's better that way: no promises, no shackles, just plain, simple sex. He shook his head, knowing he didn't believe a word he was thinking.

"You're a damn fool, McCullough!" he cursed aloud as he headed around the back of the cabin. "You got yourself so confused, you don't know what you're sayin' or doin' half the time." He stopped and picked up the axe where he'd left it leaning against the woodpile. Hefting it up to rest on his shoulder, he stomped back to the lean-to, threw the axe angrily in the corner, and slammed the door shut with a resounding bang.

Later that night, Felicity lay in bed remembering the day. She'd enjoyed the afternoon romp immensely. The air had been crisp and invigorating, but it was the playful interlude with Jake that had lightened her heart. Never mind that he'd been withdrawn and uncommunicative after supper. For a little while, at least, they'd laughed together.

The following morning she woke bright and early, feeling more rested than she had for a long time. It wasn't until she rose to get dressed that the mysterious stomach ailment that had plagued her for the last two weeks sent her dashing for the washbasin, retching miserably.

Moments later, pale and weak, she wiped her face with a wet cloth and set the odorous washbasin outside her window to be cleaned up when she felt better. She sank down on a corner of her bed, feeling drained and more than a little worried. She'd concealed her illness from Jake easily enough, since it only seemed to plague her in the early morning. But it had been going on too long, and she was beginning to fear that it was serious.

What's the matter with me? she wondered. Why am I only sick in the morning? Could it have something to do with the fact that her monthly time was overdue? For as long as Felicity could remember, she'd never been late. Perhaps that was the answer. She reached for the small calendar she kept on her bedside table. She always marked the day when she should begin her woman's time with a small, barely discernible X. Extremely fastidious about her personal hygiene, she'd made it a point to keep track of her cycle so that she'd never be caught in an embarrassing situation.

She turned the page back a month and realized with a start that she hadn't circled the X for the month of November. Frowning, she tried to think back. Dear God! She'd missed her time in November too. She hadn't even realized it till now. Her hands shook as she turned the page forward to December. As of today, she was again five days late. Skipping a month wasn't cause to panic, but to miss twice in a row! What could be wrong? Her heart started pounding in her ears and she felt hot all over as her mind dredged up the memory of something that had happened at the convent long ago.

She had been only thirteen when a pretty girl named Ruth Colbert had been brought to the convent by her mother. Felicity hadn't thought about Ruth in years, but suddenly, the girl's sad story flooded her mind like it had happened yesterday.

Ruth's parents had brought her to the convent to prevent the sixteen-year-old from eloping with a young man they didn't approve of. However, two months later, it was discovered that Ruth was carrying a child. The man, by this time, was nowhere to be found, and so, to prevent embarrassing her family, Ruth had stayed at the school until her child was born. Felicity had briefly shared a room with

Ruth and now she remembered that the other girl had shown the same symptoms she was experiencing. Ruth had stopped having her woman's time and she was frequently nauseated, especially in the early morning.

Felicity's calendar dropped from numb fingers. "Lord, please don't let this be," she pleaded in a whisper. As much as she wanted to deny the possibility of such a disaster befalling her, the evidence was nearly irrefutable. She was going to have a baby.

She buried her face in her hands. "Why me?" she cried softly. "I make one little mistake and look what happens. I should have known I'd be punished for my weakness. What am I going to do now? I'm going to be a mother and I'm not even a wife yet! *Yet*? Who am I kidding? I'm *never* going to be a wife! Dear God, what *am* I going to do?"

She cried until there were no more tears. Finally, she blew her nose, put a cold wet cloth against her eyes, and again sat down on her bed. She had to think. There was no help for her problem, so she just had to pull herself together and think about what she was going to do next.

Now, more than ever, she had to leave, and as quickly as possible. She couldn't tell Jake about her condition. She knew he'd feel that he had to marry her and she didn't want him on those terms. Guilt, remorse, and obligation were poor reasons to get married. She also knew she couldn't stay in Silverton and bear the fruit of her sin. Though her acquaintances from church probably wouldn't openly condemn her, neither would they welcome her into their circle as they once had. After all, no one wanted to associate with one of *those* women. There was only one person whom she could confide in. Roxie. When the time came to leave, she knew she could depend on Roxie for understanding and help.

Until she could find a way to leave Silverton, though, she'd have to be extremely careful. Her mind wandered back to Jake and what his reaction would be if he found out. He'd insist on marrying her. He might not want a wife, but she instinctively knew that he'd never let her suffer the shame of bearing his bastard. Nor would he shirk his paternal responsibility toward his child. He might be stubborn and insufferably arrogant at times, but he was an honorable man. Felicity shook her head despairingly. She didn't want him to feel obligated to her. She wanted him to love her and she knew that would never happen. Jake had made it perfectly clear what he wanted their relationship to be, and love had nothing to do with it.

So she was alone with her problem. She could only pray that her pregnancy wouldn't become obvious too soon. If she let her dresses out carefully and wore aprons, maybe she could camouflage her condition until she could leave for Philadelphia. I *can* hide this, she assured herself. I *have* to!

On Christmas Eve morning, Felicity sat in the middle of her bed, putting the last touches on a sweater she had knitted for Jake. She finished sewing on the sleeves and held up the garment to admire her work. The sweater was a rich, burnished brown and she knew it would suit Jake's coloring perfectly.

Scooting off the bed, she pulled out the bottom drawer of her old chest and removed a precious piece of white tissue paper and a scrap of bright red ribbon. She quickly wrapped the sweater and hid it away in the chest.

Just as she was finishing her task, she heard a loud thumping on the outside door. "Felicity! Come open the door, will you? My arms are full."

She hurried to the door, surprised that Jake was back so early in the afternoon. She pulled open the portal to find the doorway filled with a large evergreen. "What on earth?" she exclaimed.

From behind the tree, she heard his deep chuckle. "Haven't you ever seen a Christmas tree, Felicity?"

She laughed with sheer delight. "Of course I have, but this is such a surprise. It's beautiful, Jake!"

He parted the branches and peered through them, grinning. "It's not really Christmas without a tree. So, if you'll just move out of the way, ma'am, I'll bring it in."

She stepped aside, directing him as he wrestled the tree through the door. After scattering pine needles all over her freshly polished floor, they finally agreed to place the tree in the corner between the fireplace and the settee. Jake leaned it up against the wall and went back outside to retrieve two pieces of wood he'd nailed together, one across the other. Felicity noticed that a long, thick nail protruded from the center of the brace where the pieces of wood crossed. For several minutes, Jake struggled to twist the tree's trunk down onto the nail. When he was finally finished, he stood back and gave a satisfied nod. "That ought to do it."

She had never seen a more perfect tree. Tears welled in her eyes at Jake's thoughtfulness. She remembered all the times he'd balked at some request she'd made, only to end up going out of his way to see that she had what she wanted. He'd moved her kitchen shelves down, bought her oranges, taught her to ride a horse, drive a wagon, and even bought her a cow. And now this.

Jake turned around and caught sight of the tears trickling down her cheeks. "Felicity," he said with concern, "is somethin' wrong?" He stepped closer, his hand outstretched. Then, remembering himself, he let his hand fall to his side. "What's the matter, sweetheart?"

She winced at his endearment. He hadn't called her that for a long time. She knew that he hadn't even realized he'd said it. "Nothing's wrong, Jake." She smiled tremulously. "It's the tree. It's so lovely and it was so thoughtful of you."

Relieved, he grinned down at her. "I'm glad you like it. But just wait till we get it decorated. Then it'll *really* feel like Christmas.'' He gazed at the tree and reflected wistfully, ''My pa always loved Christmas. He took a lot of pride in pickin' out and cuttin' down a tree. He said it was *his* job and he never let anyone else do it. Even—'' Jake hesitated. ''—even after Ma left. Pa went to extra trouble to make sure Christmas was special for me. I just hope that someday I'll be able to do the same for my . . .'' He stopped in mid-sentence, astonished at what he'd been about to say. He'd almost admitted that he hoped to do the same for his own children. What a crazy thought, he mused, considerin' I never figured on havin' a wife, much less kids. So why now? It must be Christmas Eve makin' me feel sentimental. Yet, somehow, the idea of making a little Christmas magic for a tiny son or daughter touched a tender spot somewhere deep inside him.

Felicity had held her breath when Jake had almost mentioned children. How wonderful it would be to give him the special gift of her secret. But he hadn't finished what he'd been about to say, and now, he was just standing there, staring out the window with an enigmatic expression on his face. She stepped closer to him and placed her hand on his arm, unable to hide her tender feelings. He gazed down at her and for one thrilling moment, she thought he might kiss her. Her lips tingled at the thought but he just smiled and turned away toward the door. ''Wait here, I have another surprise for you.'' She masked her disappointment with a weak smile.

When Jake returned, he was carrying a large wooden box which he set down in front of the settee. ''You're gonna love this!'' Caught up in his boyish enthusiasm, Felicity sat down on the arm of the settee and eagerly watched as he pried the lid off the box.

She gasped as the box's contents were revealed. Sitting on top of a layer of straw was a vast array of colored cloth bows. Some were faded with time, but, nevertheless, they would look very festive on the tree. Beneath this was another layer containing several long white lace garlands and a wealth of small candles with holders.

He carefully lifted the second layer of straw out of the box and her hands flew to her cheeks as she saw what lay beneath. Jake smiled at her reaction. "These belonged to my mother's grandmother." He carefully lifted one of five delicate hand-blown glass ornaments. "My mother's people came from Germany and one of them had apprenticed with a glassblower. These ornaments are all that's left of his collection. Ma told me once that there used to be twelve but I guess, over the years, most of them got broken by excited children on Christmas mornin'. I know I was responsible for the loss of one. Pa said I almost knocked down the whole tree tryin' to get to it."

"Oh, Jake, I don't think we should use them. They're a precious keepsake."

"It wouldn't be Christmas without them. We always hung them on the tree. Ma said it would be an insult to our ancestors not to use them. When they're gone, they're gone. They were meant to be enjoyed."

"Then we shall enjoy them, Jake. I think it's wonderful to be able to carry on such a lovely family tradition."

With the question of the ornaments settled, they set about decorating their tree. When it was finished, Felicity thought it was the most glorious Christmas tree she'd ever seen.

By suppertime that night, the little cabin smelled like heaven. Fresh cinnamon bread, sugar cookies, and even a small pan of candy had emerged from her oven. Jake had playfully snitched bits and pieces all afternoon while she scolded him and slapped at his hands. She warned him to save some for tomorrow, but, even so, by the end of the day, he had devoured half of everything. He teased her unmercifully with threats of a midnight raid, and walked around all evening with a sugary smile.

She woke early on Christmas morning and, after battling down her usual queasiness, she dressed quickly. Before leaving her room, she pulled open the bottom drawer of her chest and took out Jake's sweater.

Not wishing to awaken him, she crept out to the Christmas tree. But, to her surprise, his cot was empty and he was nowhere in sight. Felicity jumped when he noisily kicked the back door open.

With a load of wood in his arms, and a smile spread across his face, he greeted her cheerfully. "Merry Christmas, Felicity." She smiled shyly and hid his present behind her back.

She waited until he bent down to dump the wood into the box by the stove and then stealthily slid her gift under the tree. "Merry Christmas to you, Jake," she returned as she straightened up to face him. "I'll get my coat on and get some eggs for breakfast. I thought I'd fix flapjacks this morning."

"Sounds great, but there's no need to get the eggs. I brought 'em in earlier and there's a pail of milk sittin' outside the door." He dusted his hands off and grinned. "I've been up for hours and since it's Christmas, I figured I'd give you a hand with the chores so we could both enjoy the whole day."

She couldn't suppress the teasing smile that tilted the corners of her mouth. "You mean you actually faced those hens all by yourself?" She watched as Jake, pointedly ignoring her question, set the coffee-pot on the stove. It was then that she saw the wicked scratches on the back of his hand. She hurried over to him, taking his hand in hers. "What happened to you?" She reached for a cloth, dipping it into a pail of water that sat on the counter. "Here, let me clean it for you."

Self-conscious and more than a little shaken by her gentle touch, he took the damp rag from her, mumbling that it was nothing.

"It was the hens, wasn't it?" With a look of concern, Felicity reclaimed his hand and examined it more closely.

He nodded in resignation. "I told you those damn chickens hate me. They start raisin' a racket every time I go near them." God, he thought with a shiver, her skin is so soft. He snatched his hand out from between hers and continued raggedly, "You should see the floor of the lean-to. There's enough feathers on it to make a couple of pillows. I was lucky to get out alive!"

"Well, I truly appreciate you braving those monsters just to help me out." Inwardly, she was struggling mightily to keep her amusement from showing. Men! she thought. They're such babies! And, oh, how I'd love to baby this one right now! Shocked by her lusty thoughts, she quickly turned toward the stove and pulled out the skillet. "Why don't you build up the fire in the fireplace while I mix up the flapjacks?" She held her breath until he left her side to do as she suggested.

As they were finishing breakfast, Boozer scratched at the door. Jake let him in and Felicity gave the dog a special Christmas treat consisting of a huge flapjack covered with thick, sweet maple syrup. Boozer licked at his sticky chops the rest of the morning, searching for any drop of the delicious syrup that he might have missed.

Throughout the day, Felicity labored happily over the sumptuous Christmas dinner she was preparing. She'd removed a ham from the root cellar the day before and its sweet, smoky aroma permeated the house all day.

Outside, the evening sky darkened to indigo, and the temperature dropped steadily. But, inside the homey little cabin, all was cozy and warm. Felicity hummed a Christmas carol as she removed ham, sweet potatoes, and creamed vegetables from the oven. Jake smiled as he watched her from where he sat on the settee. "Why don't I slice that ham for you?" he suggested.

"Thank you. I was hoping you'd offer." She smiled. "I'm not very good at wielding this big knife. I'm afraid I'll hack the meat apart and it's just too beautiful to ruin."

Jake joined her at the counter and removed the large knife from her hand. "I was thinkin' more about sparin' your fingers." He chuckled. He leaned over the ham and smelled it appreciatively. "Mmmm, if this tastes half as good as it smells, I'm gonna eat myself sick!" He straightened and proceeded to cut the ham, neatly piling the slices on a plate while Felicity set the rest of the food on the table.

True to his word, he stuffed himself on her delicious meal. He could only groan when she asked him if he wanted some dessert, but somehow, he managed to eat two pieces of pie. "I won't need to eat for at least three days," he declared, patting his stomach.

"You say that now, Jake McCullough, but I'll wager that by tomorrow night, there won't be one bit of this ham left." He groaned again, but nodded sheepishly, knowing she was probably right.

Felicity was very touched when he insisted that she allow him to clean up the dishes while she relaxed by the fire. She declined his offer, however, afraid that he would destroy her kitchen. After a halfhearted argument, they finally agreed to clean up together, making short work of the job.

Later, they sat contentedly before the fire, recalling past holidays and sharing childhood memories. Jake lit the candles on the tree and the small tapers flickered merrily, casting dancing shadows on the cabin walls. When the conversation lulled, Felicity finally got up the nerve to reach beneath the tree and present him with her gift. "I should have given this to you this morning, but I must confess, I was too shy." She smiled in embarrassment. "Somehow, it seems more appropriate now, anyway." The pleasure in Jake's eyes made her heart pound.

He looked down at the package in his lap and then back up at Felicity. "For me?" he asked unnecessarily.

She hoped the shadows hid her blush as she nodded and watched him tear the paper away. He held the sweater up and grinned delightedly. "This is beautiful! Did you make this?"

"Yes. I hope it fits. I used one of your old shirts to measure by."

Jake jumped up and unbuttoned his flannel shirt, pulling it out of his jeans. Tossing the shirt aside, he drew the sweater over his head and pulled it down over his big chest. He adjusted the sleeves and looked down at her with a melting smile. "It fits perfect, Felicity. I know it must have been a lot of work for you to make." His voice was low and husky. "Thanks, darlin', I love it."

Her eyes were glued to his and she didn't even notice that he had pulled a small box out of his pocket until he pressed it into her hand. "For you, Felicity. It's not much, but I hope you'll like it. I found it in Durango when I went to get Bess. It just seemed to have your name on it."

She forced her eyes from his and stared down at the velvet-covered box in her hand. She slowly lifted its lid and gazed in awe at a small, oval cameo. "Oh, Jake," she breathed, "it's lovely! I've never owned anything so beautiful." Carefully, she lifted the pin from its plush bed and held it up to the light. The head of a beautiful woman was embossed on the amber oval, which, in turn, rested in a delicate gold setting. She unfastened the pin on the back of the brooch and attached it to the neck of her dress.

Seeing that she was having difficulty fastening the clasp, Jake gently brushed her hands away and finished pinning on the cameo. His hands glided down her shoulders and rested there. Felicity lifted her eyes and gazed at him with a questioning expression. "It's not half as pretty as you are," Jake murmured.

With eyes full of yearning, they stared at each other. She felt his hands tremble where they rested on her shoulders. Her lips parted and she was hardly aware that she was leaning into his body, nor did she hear his soft, agonized moan. The space between them seemed to evaporate. Later, she couldn't recall how it happened; her only awareness was being pressed against the rocklike wall of Jake's chest and kissed senseless. It was an endless caress as his tongue sought and found every soft crevice in Felicity's mouth. When his lips finally left hers, they were both weak and shaken by their emotions.

"Felicity, I . . . I'm sorry," Jake stammered.

She could only stare at him dumbly. Finally, reason returned, and knowing she mustn't let herself get carried away with the moment, she lowered her eyes and forced herself to concentrate on the glowing embers in the fireplace. "I think it's time to say good night, Jake."

"Felicity, I . . ."

She held up a hand to stop his words. "I really enjoyed the day, Jake, and I'll cherish your gift always. Thank you so much." She stepped away abruptly, not trusting herself to linger any longer in his virile presence. Pausing at her door, she turned, an expression of naked longing in her eyes. "Good night, Jake. Merry Christmas."

Stunned, he watched her as she seemed to dissolve from his sight. For a long time, he just stood and looked at the closed bedroom door. Then, sighing heavily, he sank down onto his cot, resting his elbows on his knees and dropping his head into his hands.

How did it happen? When had it happened? Jake raised his head and stared into the shadows, knowing that the how and when didn't matter. "Sweet Jesus, help me," he whispered, "I love her."

Chapter 16

"Just a minute, I'm comin'!" Emma yanked open the door of her room above the Last Chance and immediately broke into a huge grin. "Felicity! I certainly didn't expect to see you! What are you doin' in town?" She eagerly grabbed Felicity's arm and pulled her through the doorway, exclaiming, "Come on in before you freeze to death!"

At this enthusiastic welcome, Felicity stepped into the cozy little room, her eyes alight with pleasure. She had known it would be worth the long, cold trip down the pass, and she wasn't disappointed. Thirty seconds in her friend's company and already Felicity felt better than she had in weeks.

"Gosh, sweetie, it's good to see you." Emma beamed. "How've you been doin' locked up there in that cabin? Can you believe it's almost February?" Before Felicity could answer, she rushed on. "Here, let me take your coat. I don't know where my manners are! Have a seat."

Felicity handed over her coat and sank gratefully into a chair. Emma studied her friend's drawn face. "You look plum tuckered out, honey. Was the trip down that bad?"

Felicity nodded. "It took us an awful long time and it was so cold! I didn't think we were ever going to get here."

247

"Well, you just sit here by the fire and warm up. How 'bout a cup of coffee? One of the girls just brought me up a pot."

"It sounds wonderful, Roxie, but I'm afraid coffee hasn't been agreeing with me lately. Would it be too much bother to send down for a cup of tea?"

"No bother at all," Emma assured her. She stepped out into the hall and called for Dora to bring up some tea, then hurried back inside her room. Pouring herself some more coffee, she sat down across the table from Felicity and settled in for a chat. It was then that Felicity noticed the difference in her friend's appearance.

"Roxie, I've never seen you look so wonderful. What have you done to yourself? Your hair isn't so . . . it's not so red. And you aren't wearing any makeup, are you?" She also noticed the prim little calico dress Emma was wearing, but didn't mention it for fear of embarrassing the other woman with her observations. She watched in astonishment as Emma's face flushed. Felicity had doubted that anything could ever make the seasoned saloon girl blush, but that was exactly what she was doing.

"A lot has happened since our last visit," Emma explained. "For one thing, I don't work downstairs anymore."

"What's wrong?" asked Felicity in bewilderment. "Were you fired? Why, I can't believe Yancy would do such a thing!"

"Wait a minute!" She laughed, holding up her hand. "It ain't nothin' like that, honey. Yancy, well, he . . . well, we've started seein' each other. Courtin', I guess you'd call it." Her face was animated. "Oh, Felicity, I'm so happy! Yancy wants me to go to New Orleans with him in the spring, and I'm goin'. He hasn't come right out and proposed, but I think he might. This has all happened so fast between us and we're tryin' to just sorta take things one step at a time. Yancy hasn't had an easy life and neither have I, but I think, together, we make a pretty good team.''

''You're in love, then.'' Felicity smiled.

''Honey, let me put it this way. I haven't felt like this since my husband, Hank, died. All of the sudden, it just seems like everythin's finally goin' my way.''

Felicity's smile broadened and she reached across the table to give her friend's hand a small squeeze. ''I'm thrilled for you, Roxie. You deserve the best life has to offer and I'm so glad you've found someone to share it with. Yancy has always been so kind to me. He's a good man.'' Felicity mentally dismissed the time he had tried to kiss her at the door of her cabin. She supposed it was only natural for a man to try his luck with a girl, especially if he was a gambling man like Yancy.

''I have to tell you that, for a while, I thought you and Yancy might have somethin' goin,'' Emma confessed. ''I was kinda jealous, but, at the time, I didn't even know why. I guess I didn't figure anyone would ever consider courtin' me. I don't mind admittin' that I was gettin' pretty tired of the life I'd been leadin'. Saloon life makes a woman old real fast.''

There was a knock at the door and Emma called for the maid to enter. The girl cast Felicity a shy smile of greeting and set a pot of tea on the table. ''Thank you, Dora,'' Felicity said warmly. ''I hope I didn't cause you too much trouble.''

''You're welcome, Miss Felicity, and it weren't no trouble at all. Anything else I can get you?''

''No, thanks, this is just fine.'' Dora glanced at Emma, who shook her head. The little maid quietly took her leave.

As soon as the door closed, Emma continued her story. ''By the way—'' She winked. ''—you might not want to call me Roxie anymore.'' Felicity looked at her questioningly. ''You see, my real name is Emma.'' She chuckled and splayed her hand over her chest, indicating her dress. "This dress was mine before little Emma Roxanne Wilson became Roxie, the saloon girl. Yancy calls me Emma now and he won't let anyone around here call me Roxie anymore. He says I'm never playin' that role again, so I should use my real name. To tell you the truth, it makes me feel real special when he yells at people for callin' me Roxie."

"Emma it is, then." Felicity laughed. "I think it's wonderful that Yancy is so protective of you." This time it was Felicity's turn to wink. "And to tell you the truth, in my mind, you've always been Emma, just dressed up in Roxie's clothes."

Emma smiled with delight. "Why, Felicity, I think that's just about the nicest thing anybody's ever said to me. But enough about me. What brings you to town? Got cabin fever?"

"Well, that too," Felicity began slowly, "but mostly I'm here because I need some advice. When the thaw started a few days ago, I decided to take advantage of it and talked Jake into bringing me to town with him so I could talk to you. He's over at Gunderson's buying supplies that he plans to take up to the men at the mine tomorrow. He also wants to check the mine out to make sure no one has tampered with anything."

"It's great seein' you, sweetie, but I'm surprised Jake agreed to bring you," Emma said. "A January thaw always brings every miner from miles around into town to get the stink blowed off and have a good time. Whiskey and women are all they can think about, and some of 'em go plum crazy." Felicity could easily believe that, for despite the early hour, the Last Chance was resounding noisily below them. Emma shook her head. "It ain't safe for a decent woman to be on the streets. Most of 'em stick to the saloon girls, but there's a few damn fools that don't give a hoot if a woman is a lady or not. Jake didn't let you walk over here by yourself, did he?"

"No," Felicity assured her. "In fact, he wasn't at

all happy about bringing me into town, but I insisted. He walked me all the way to the bottom of your stairs.''

''Well, it'll take him a while to get his supplies, so we got plenty of time for you to tell me what's on your mind.'' Emma leaned back in her chair expectantly, puzzled by Felicity's wan countenance. She had seen that kind of forlorn desolation before and she guessed if there was trouble, it was spelled J-A-K-E.

''I hardly know where to begin.'' Felicity sighed. She poured a cup of tea as if to fortify herself for what she was about to confess.

''Why don't you start at the beginnin'?'' prompted Emma. ''It's somethin' about Jake, isn't it?'' Felicity nodded. ''Then maybe it will save time if I tell you what I already know.'' Felicity's eyes widened. ''Now, don't get yourself in a dither, honey.'' Emma chuckled. ''You ought to know by now how fast gossip travels in this town. I heard that you and Jake came into town a while ago and spent a night at the Grand Hotel.''

Felicity almost choked on her tea. ''You know that?'' she asked in horrified astonishment.

Emma laughed out loud. ''Yeah, and so does everybody else, but don't worry. Word is, you only went to dinner and you and Jake had separate rooms.''

Felicity blushed to the roots of her hair. ''I'll *never* get used to this small-town gossip. How did all this information leak out?''

''Well, Mrs. Granger, who's got to be the town's biggest gossip, saw you at dinner with Jake. Her brother is a desk clerk at the hotel, and knowing her, she probably badgered him to death until he finally told her all he knew.''

''Well then, I guess that's where I can start.'' Felicity's face was suffused with color and her voice was shaky. Though Emma was fairly sure she knew what Felicity was about to tell her, she kept quiet, aware that Felicity needed to talk.

"Jake and I came to town to celebrate his birthday and it all started out very innocently." Felicity cleared her throat. "Dinner was lovely and we had a wonderful time drinking champagne and toasting each other, and the food, and the restaurant, and . . . well, just about everything we could think of."

Emma's eyebrows shot up at the mention of champagne and it was all she could do not to interrupt. Good God, had Jake gotten Felicity drunk so he could take advantage of her?

"Anyway," continued Felicity, "those little bubbles in the champagne made me dizzy and I'm afraid Jake had to help me back to my room." Suddenly, her hands flew to her cheeks. "Good Lord, I hope *that* fact isn't all over town!" Emma shook her head adamantly, assuring Felicity that that part of the evening had been missed by the gossip mongers.

"Jake was a perfect gentleman. He saw me to my room and left me there."

This wasn't what Emma expected to hear. If Jake acted like a gentleman, what was the problem? Intrigued, she leaned forward, hanging on Felicity's every word.

"I woke up in the middle of the night," Felicity continued, "and realized that I hadn't even thanked Jake for the lovely evening. I saw a light under his door so I went into his room to thank him. As it turned out, he was asleep, but my knocking woke him and by the time I realized it, I was standing next to his bed, and . . . and . . ."

"And he pulled you into bed with him and made love to you," Emma finished knowingly.

Felicity hung her head and nodded. "Yes, and again in the morning too." She took a long, shuddering breath. "This is . . . hard for me to talk about."

Emma reached across the table and placed her hand over Felicity's. "Honey, there ain't much that can shock me and I ain't your judge. We're friends, and sharin' problems is what friendship is all about. So you made love with the man. You're not the first girl who's ever done that without a weddin' ring on her finger. Then what happened?''

Felicity raised tear-filled eyes and murmured, ''It was wonderful, Roxie, I mean Emma, and at the time, it didn't seem wrong. Jake said he wanted to show me the happiness of a lifetime, and, well, I guess I didn't understand his meaning. I thought he was telling me he wanted me forever, and that meant he wanted to marry me.'' Felicity exhaled a deep breath and shook her head. ''But that wasn't what he meant at all.'' She paused. ''I guess the misunderstanding was my fault. I love him so much that I just heard what I wanted to hear.'' Emma nodded sympathetically.

''On the other hand,'' Felicity went on, ''I've always made it perfectly clear to Jake that I would never sleep with a man who wasn't my husband. He *had* to know what I expected. But, when I asked him when we could go talk to the priest about getting married, he nearly fainted from shock. We had a terrible argument because he actually had the gall to suggest that I spend the winter in his bed first! He said that maybe by spring, he'd be sure he wanted to get married. Can you imagine the nerve of him? You'd think I was a piece of mining machinery that he wanted to try out before he paid for it.'' Tears of humiliation coursed down Felicity's face.

Emma leaned back in her chair and pinned Felicity with a frank gaze. ''Yes, I can imagine him sayin' that to you.'' Felicity gasped at her friend in horrified disbelief. ''Felicity, girl,'' she said firmly, ''it's time for you to grow up. Now, think about what you just said to me. You tell this man that you'd never sleep with anyone you weren't married to. Then you go to *his* room, climb into *his* bed, and let him make love to you, not once, but twice! Don't you think that might have confused him a little?''

"Four times," Felicity murmured.

"What?"

"We made love four times, not twice."

"Four times in one night?" gasped Emma.

"Oh, no!" Felicity exclaimed. "Not all in one night. But there was the next morning, and then again that night after we got back to the cabin, and then again the next morning, but we didn't really finish that time because Boozer interrupted us." Felicity trailed off and looked at Emma in embarrassment. "Is that a lot? I mean, more than normal?"

Emma was silent for a moment, then she suddenly burst into uproarious laughter. "And you wonder why Jake wanted you in his bed all winter? Honey, he must have thought he'd found Venus! Well, I can tell you one thing. The man's head over heels in love with you."

At Felicity's blustering protest, she held up a finger sagely. "Sweetie, take it from one who knows. Men don't make love four times in twenty-four hours to women they don't care about. They take you once, fast, and then they leave you. Now, don't be embarrassed, but I want to know somethin' else. When you were finished, did he roll over and go to sleep or did he hold you?"

"He held me all night," Felicity whispered.

"That's what I thought." Emma nodded. "The man loves you."

"No, you're wrong," Felicity argued. "If he loved me like you think, he'd marry me."

"But honey—" She laughed. "—he didn't say he *wouldn't* marry you. He just said he needed time, right?"

"Yes," Felicity admitted, "but I don't have any time. I'm used goods. I can't marry anyone else now." Her face crumpled and she ashamedly hid her face in her hands.

Emma stiffened and sat back in her chair. Leveling an intense stare at her anguished friend, she asked,

"Felicity, what do you mean you don't have any time?" Emma winced at the sharpness in her voice, knowing it was a direct reflection of her worst fears for her friend.

"Well, I . . . I . . ."

"You're gonna have a baby, ain't you?" She sighed. She got up and went around the table to lead Felicity to the settee. "Sit down here and tell me about this. Maybe you're wrong."

Felicity allowed herself to be eased down into the settee's cushions. Emma kept her arm around Felicity's shoulders and gave her an affectionate hug. "Now, what makes you so sure you're pregnant?"

"Because I've got all the same signs Ruth Colbert had," Felicity wailed. At Emma's bewildered look, Felicity rushed on. "She was a girl at the convent who found herself in the family way. Every symptom that she had, I have. I've missed my monthly cycle three times and I'm sick in the morning. I'm tired *all* the time and if I'm not vomiting, then I'm starving. I have these terrible cravings, mostly for oranges."

Emma couldn't contain the smile that flickered across her face at this last bit of evidence. "Oranges, huh? Well, honey, I hate to be the one to confirm bad news, but you sound very pregnant to me. What does Jake have to say about this?"

"I haven't told Jake!" Felicity exclaimed.

"What?" she gasped. "You haven't told him? Well, don't you think you should? After all, it's his baby too. You're what, about three months along?" Felicity nodded. "Well, you're not showin' yet, but you soon will be and Jake's gonna figure it out all by himself."

"Oh, no, that mustn't happen!" Felicity declared. "Jake must never find out!"

"You're talkin' crazy, girl. Of course he needs to know. You two have to get married and give this little tyke—". She patted Felicity's stomach. "—a name."

"No!" Felicity declared. "Regardless of what you think, Jake doesn't love me and I won't have him marry me out of pity. I've decided to go back to Philadelphia in the spring. I can tell everyone that I was married while I was here and then widowed."

Emma stared at her friend thoughtfully. "Felicity, did you know that Jake McCullough never even *looked* at a woman before you came here? Why, with that body and that smile of his, half the women in this town, both single *and* married, would have walked down Main Street naked if they'd thought it would catch his eye. But he never noticed any of 'em. Rena was the only woman he ever spent time with, and we all know what he wanted *her* for. Even *she* was smitten with him. I heard that she didn't even charge him!"

At Felicity's horrified look, she smiled sheepishly. "Sorry, honey, didn't mean to shock you. What I'm tryin' to say, is that for Jake McCullough to tell you that he wants you to give him a little time to think, is more commitment than any woman's ever come close to with him. All men need some time to get used to the idea of bein' married. Jake will come 'round. Tellin' him about his baby will just speed his thinkin' up a little. I bet once he knows, he'll be so proud, he won't be able to find a preacher fast enough!"

Felicity looked at her dismally. "Oh, Emma, you make it all sound so easy. But Jake isn't like other men when it comes to marriage. I haven't told you everything yet."

Emma rolled her eyes skyward. What else could there be?

"You see, Jake told me he'll never marry *anyone*. His mother walked out on his father and him because she couldn't take the life of a miner's wife. It hurt his father terribly and it left a scar on Jake as well. He doesn't trust women and he won't risk suffering the way his father did for so many years. I thought that if I could make Jake love me, he'd change his mind. But he hasn't. I've made my decision, Emma, and nothing you can say is going to change it. I may not be able to give my baby his father's name, but I can spare him the stigma of being called a bastard. And I'm going to do it, even if it means living a lie for the rest of my life. Can you understand at all how I feel?''

''I only understand that your pride is gettin' in the way of your happiness,'' Emma replied flatly.

''Okay—'' Felicity relented. ''—let's say I tell Jake about the baby and he marries me. Can you promise me that he won't come to resent being trapped into marriage with a woman he doesn't love? I don't think you can. Sooner or later, he'd come to hate me. I can bear a lot of things, but not that. Better that I simply sell my share of the mine, take my money, and leave.''

''I still think you're wrong not to tell Jake,'' Emma asserted stubbornly. ''He has a right to know, Felicity.''

Ignoring Emma's persistence, Felicity asked, ''Will you help me leave Silverton, Emma?''

She sighed. ''I guess if you insist on makin' this terrible mistake, I'll have to help you. There's no gettin' out of here till spring, though. The train won't be runnin' until April, and, by then, you're not gonna be able to hide your condition.''

''I know that,'' Felicity said, ''but I'm counting on getting away from the cabin before that. I was hoping to move into town when my condition starts showing and maybe stay with you for a while till the train is running again. Would that be all right?''

''Yes, of course. But . . .''

''And you won't tell Jake my secret, will you?''

''No, though heaven knows, I'd like to. But it's not my place to tell him. That news can only come from you.''

Felicity smiled in profound relief. ''Thanks, Emma, you're the best friend anyone ever had—

sometimes I feel like you're a sister to me. I wish I didn't have to burden you with this, but I had nowhere else to turn."

"Felicity Howard! I'd be mad as hell if you felt you couldn't come to me after all this time. Now, I'm gonna go get Doc Brown to come have a look at you just to make sure everythin' is progressin' the way it should."

"No, you can't do that!" Felicity jumped up in a panic. "I can't take the chance of a doctor knowing. He might tell someone about the baby and then it would be all over town."

"Felicity." Emma laughed. "Doc Brown probably knows some secret about every person in this town, but he'd *never* tell. He prides himself on bein' a professional and he'd be real insulted if he thought you were worried that he had a loose tongue. Now, I've agreed not to tell Jake about the baby and to help you leave Silverton, but I won't let you talk me out of this. You just go lie down there on my bed and rest. I'm goin' to fetch the doc and that's all there is to it."

Seeing that Emma would not be swayed and lacking the will to disagree further, Felicity acquiesced. "All right," she sighed, "you win. To be honest, I'd feel better knowing for sure that the baby is doing well." Felicity sat down on the edge of the bed, catching Emma's satisfied grin. "I want you to know something, Emma," she said quietly.

"What's that, sweetie?" She moved to stand at the foot of the bed.

"Despite everything, I love this baby. I'm only trying to do what's best for him."

"I wouldn't have expected any less from you, Felicity. And now that I know I'm gonna be an 'aunt,' I love him too."

Lying back on the pillows, Felicity smiled sleepily. "I wouldn't have expected any less from you, Emma."

* * *

Jed Croft watched Jake McCullough walk through the door of Gunderson's General Store. He waited until Jake disappeared into the back of the store and then scrambled across the slushy street to investigate why McCullough was in town.

Sauntering into the store, Croft idly leaned against the counter. One of Gunderson's tall, gangly sons hurried over. "Anything I can get for ya, Mr. Croft?"

"Shore can, boy. You got any of them fancy cigars I bought in here last time?"

"No, sir, we don't. All we got till the train starts runnin' again is chewin' tobaccy. Will that do ya?"

"Reckon it'll have to, now won't it?"

The lanky boy took a tin of tobacco down from the shelf behind him. "Will that be all, sir?"

"Yup, that'll do it. Say, boy, tell me, ain't that Jake McCullough that just went in the back with your pa?"

"Yes, sir, sure is."

"Well, what d'you suppose brought him to town?"

"Heard he's takin' some supplies up to his men tomorrow. Said he wanted to check his mine to make sure no one's been messin' around. Guess they had a heap of trouble up there last fall."

"You don't say. Real sorry to hear that." Croft stashed the tobacco in his coat pocket and tossed down a coin. "Thanks, son, I'll be seein' you."

Jed Croft walked quickly in the direction of the livery stable. He was tired of waiting around for Yancy Parnell to make a move. Several times, he'd sneaked into the Silver Lady to check on the miners' progress before they closed down for the winter. Come spring, McCullough was going to hit that silver vein for sure unless he, Jed Croft, took matters in hand and put Jake out of business permanently. That'd put a fire under Parnell!

Croft chuckled as he entered the stable. Yes, sir, he thought, by this time tomorrow, McCullough would be only a bad memory. Maybe he'd even get a chance to have a taste of that little gal that was shackin' up with him.

Felicity watched from the warmth of the cabin as Jake tied the last pack onto his horse's back. The pass to the mine, being further up the mountain, had not thawed out enough to get a wagon through, but Jake was sure he could make his way with a horse. Dawn was just breaking, and, barring a sudden storm, he thought he'd be back by suppertime. He put on his snowshoes and led the heavily laden animal up the steep path toward the mine.

She turned away from the window and sank down onto the settee. She knew she should clean up the breakfast dishes, but she yearned to go back to bed. Well, why not? she thought. Jake would be gone the whole day and wouldn't be around to question her inactivity.

It hadn't been easy trying to act like her usual energetic self. Early afternoon was the worst. With a warm meal in her stomach, all she wanted to do was curl up and go to sleep. The one time she'd indulged herself, Jake had come home early for supper and had caught her in bed, sound asleep. He'd obstinately insisted that she must be sick. The more she argued that she felt fine, the more he'd demanded that she stay in bed and let him prepare supper. Tired of arguing, she had finally conceded. That night, they had dined on burned venison and shriveled, scorched potatoes. The biscuits were as hard as rocks and even dunking them in coffee didn't help. Boozer was offered one, but he'd turned up his nose in disgust. Felicity had laughed so hard at that, she'd nearly fallen off her stool. Jake had scowled throughout the entire meal, insisting that the food wasn't that bad. Since then, all she had to do to revive herself after lunch was remember that fiasco.

The doctor had said that her fatigue was perfectly

normal. He'd confirmed her pregnancy and quietly told her what she could expect over the next few months. He'd warned her to be careful that she didn't fall when she went outdoors, and had advised her to get plenty of rest. Not once did he ask any embarrassing questions, for which she was extremely grateful.

She trudged over to the washtub and set about her task, promising herself a morning nap as soon as she was finished.

Jake plowed through the snow, his horse in tow. He'd left the supplies with his men, and, after sharing the noon meal with them, had continued up the mountain to the mine. Everything appeared to be as they'd left it before the first snow. He headed into the mine, lighting the lantern which hung just inside the entrance. Holding the lamp aloft, he carefully made his way into the cavernous darkness. The cold, dank air enveloped him, sending a shiver down his spine. His mind gradually strayed from the business at hand as he recalled his ride back to the cabin with Felicity the day before.

Despite his protests, she'd insisted on wearing a dress into town. On their way home, the temperature had dropped considerably, and although she'd said nothing, Jake knew she had to be freezing. He'd tried to wait her out, thinking she'd eventually give in and move closer to him for warmth, but she'd stubbornly clung to the far side of the wagon seat. He'd finally stopped the wagon, reached behind the seat for a blanket, and wrapped it around her shivering form. Then he'd hooked his arm around her shoulders, pulling her tight against him. She'd flung him a withering look, but had stayed where she was.

Jake smiled into the darkness, remembering their Christmas kiss and his startling realization that he loved her. He'd almost broken down and told her on several occasions, but she had been so aloof and unapproachable lately that he wondered if maybe it was too late for them. She'd kept to her room a lot since that kiss and every time he moved close to her, she shrank away from him, busying herself with some inconsequential task on the other side of the cabin. How could a man tell a woman he loved her when she treated him like he had the plague? Jake shook his head. Why did life have to be so damn complicated?

His mind snapped back to reality as he tripped over something lying on the mine floor. He lowered the lantern to better focus on the obstruction, but by the time he realized what it was, it was too late.

The blast flung him backward like a rag doll. Rocks and debris flew everywhere. He felt a white-hot pain searing his chest. A large shoring timber trembled, snapped, and then crashed to the floor directly behind where he lay, filling the air with dust and making it almost impossible to breathe. Before blackness claimed him, his last, fleeting thought was that his mine, which had held so much promise for a secure future, would now be his grave.

Chapter 17

"God in heaven, what was that?"
Five heads snapped around in the direction of the earthshaking explosion.

"The mine! Jesus Christ almighty, Jake's up there, ain't he?" Chaos broke out in the cabin as the miners scrambled over each other, climbing into coats and yanking on boots. Two men grabbed horses, the rest took off on foot in a mad dash up to the mine. Panic was plastered on every face as they saw smoke and debris rolling out of the mine's entrance.

"It's no use," yelled the first arrival, turning back to the others who were clambering up the path behind him. "Jake must be dead if he's in there. No one could live through an explosion like that."

"Don't say that!" Jim Cranston bellowed. "Don't you *dare* say that! Just shut your mouth and start diggin'!"

The men attacked the tons of fallen rock and timber relentlessly but, despite their efforts, it was still hours before they reached Jake. At their first sight of him, they fell quiet, everyone thinking the same thought. He was too still, too silent, too ashen. Pete removed his hat, pressing it against his chest and shaking his head in disbelief. "I think he's gone, boys," he whispered.

"Don't just stand there gaping," yelled Corny. "Let me through. This is nothing to guess about!"

Corny knelt beside Jake, checking for a pulse in his throat. Nodding his head in grim satisfaction, he raised blazing eyes to Pete and barked, "The boy's alive, but he's not going to be if you just stand around gawking. Find something to make a stretcher out of! We've got to get him back to the cabin before he freezes to death."

Two of the miners fled to do the little Cornishman's bidding as he leaned closer to Jake's inert body. "Well, laddie," Corny whispered raggedly, "you've gone and done it good this time."

Directing the silent miners to pull off their shirts and tear them into strips, Corny fashioned a makeshift bandage and tied it around Jake's bleeding chest. The men who had gone to get a stretcher finally returned and began the arduous task of loading Jake's unconscious body on to it. It was slow, exhausting work, but they finally managed to get him back to the cabin. Corny carefully cleaned and dressed the wounds on Jake's chest, easing everyone's mind when he pronounced that the boss would live as long as infection didn't set in.

"How come he looks so bad, Corny?" asked Jim Cranston.

"The lad's been hit by about a thousand rocks. I dug out all the pebbles and dirt I could. Now we just have to wait and pray that he doesn't get a fever. That'll kill a man faster than any wound."

"What's all this talk about dyin', Corny?" interrupted a weak voice from the cot.

Corny looked down at Jake and beamed. "For sure, it isn't you that will be dying, lad, but just lie still and take it easy. Your face and chest are cut up pretty bad."

"My face?" Jake questioned.

"Yeah, your face," chuckled a much-relieved Jim Cranston. "Don't figure it'll hurt you much, though, Jake. You always was too pretty for your own good."

Jake closed his eyes in confusion. "Where am I?"

he said feebly. "God, somebody give me a drink, I'm dyin' of thirst." He struggled to raise himself on one elbow but sank back with an agonized gasp as burning pain sizzled across his chest.

"Lay back, boy!" yelled Corny. "Are you trying to kill yourself? I told you, just stay where you are and don't move."

"But where am I, Corny?" Jake asked groggily. "What happened?"

"You're hurt, son. There was an explosion at the mine and you got hit by some rocks. The boys and I brought you back to the cabin. You're safe now, so just close your eyes and rest. You've got a lot of healing to do."

"Take me home, Corny," Jake rasped.

"Can't, Jake," replied the Cornishman. "It would be too dangerous to move you."

"Damn it," Jake growled as he again tried to sit up, "I've gotta get home. She's there all alone."

"What's he goin' on about?" asked Jim.

"I think he's talkin' about Miss Felicity," Pete supplied.

"Jim, take me home. She'll take care of me." Jake drew a painful breath and whispered, "She'll worry herself sick. She's that way. I've gotta get back to her. Please, somebody help me get home." His voice trailed off and he lay panting from the effort it cost him to speak.

"All right, Jake, just relax," Jim said soothingly, "we'll get you back to your lady."

"He shouldn't be moved, Jim," warned Corny.

"I know." Jim nodded. "But I also know Jake McCullough. If we don't take him, he'll get up and walk back. I figure it's safer if we put him on that travois the boys made and haul him there ourselves. Besides, he's right about one thing. Miss Felicity is alone and probably worried sick by now. We'll have to go down to her cabin to give her a hand while Jake mends, so we might as well take him with us."

"All right," Corny agreed reluctantly. "But wrap

him up warm, and dose him good with whiskey. The weather is starting to look mean again.''

A worried frown etched Felicity's features as she paced back and forth in front of the window. She hadn't been concerned when Jake didn't show up for supper, thinking that his trip to the mine had taken longer than he'd expected. But now it was nearly nine o'clock and there was still no sign of him. Her thoughts raced in a wild circle as she tried to seize upon a logical, inconsequential reason for his delay. Inconsequential, because she couldn't bear the thought that something might have happened to him.

A new possibility for his continued absence suddenly tore through Felicity's mind. She gasped, her hand flying to her throat even as she tried to quell her panic. What if he wasn't coming back? What if he'd decided to stay up at the mine with his friends for the rest of the winter?

She drew several deep breaths, willing herself to remain calm as she frantically rationalized that he wouldn't have made that kind of decision without telling her. Besides, she reminded herself, he'd specifically requested venison stew for supper before he'd left that morning. But could that have been a ruse so she wouldn't suspect his real plans? No, she told herself firmly, he wouldn't just leave her all alone to fend for herself. She couldn't believe that he would be that unfeeling. And yet she knew better than anyone how unbearable she'd been lately. Even yesterday, during the cold ride home from town, Jake had tried to warm her up and her only response had been to glare at him. Releasing her breath in a tiny, distressed moan, Felicity again gazed fretfully out the window.

''Oh, no,'' she whispered aloud. ''It's starting to snow again. Where *is* he? Something *must* have happened to him!'' Her fingers plowed through her tangled hair and then slid down to circle her aching temples. "I've *got* to stop this," she told herself. "I'm just wearing myself out and if something has happened, I'll be no good to Jake or anyone else. None of this is doing any good."

She sank down onto the settee and curled her feet up beneath her. Resting her head on the cushions, she stared bleakly into the winter night, keeping her worried vigil.

It was an hour later when Boozer lifted his head and cocked it to one side, listening intently. He got up, trotted over to the door, and barked. Felicity crawled wearily off the settee to let him out. The second the door opened, Boozer tore out of the cabin, barking and growling. Bess bawled a long, mournful note and a chill of apprehension skipped down Felicity's spine. She stood in the doorway, carefully scanning the snowy landscape, but when Boozer quieted and disappeared into the darkness, she shrugged off her feelings of foreboding. Knowing the dog would scratch when he wanted back in, she started to push the door shut, but Boozer made a sudden reappearance and again started barking excitedly. Felicity's brow creased in bewilderment as she pulled the door back open. She glared at the dog in annoyance as he pranced around at the edge of the light spilling from the cabin, until finally, her eyes were able to discern what was exciting him. She let out a small shriek of surprise as two men leading a horse materialized out of the night.

All Jake's warnings about letting strangers into the cabin when he wasn't home came flooding back. She ran over to the fireplace and pulled down an old rifle from over the mantel, not having the slightest notion of whether the gun was loaded, or how to shoot it even if it was. Nevertheless, she flew back to the doorway and boldly hefted the gun to her shoulder, trying to appear that she knew what she was doing. "Hold it right there, or I'll shoot," she shouted.

The men came to a dead stop. One of them cupped his hands around his mouth and called, "Miss Howard, it's Jim Cranston and Pete Brady from the mine. We got Jake on a travois behind the horse here. He's been hurt and we brought him home."

Felicity's sense of caution evaporated as a new fear gripped her. "Jake? Hurt? Merciful heavens, bring him in!" She lowered the gun, setting it inside the doorway as she stepped aside to allow the men entry.

At the sight of Jake's cut and bruised face, Felicity clapped her hand over her mouth, and stood motionless, staring at him in horror. It was several moments before she realized that the men were waiting for instructions. Forcing back her feelings of panic, she directed them to follow her into the bedroom. As she hurriedly pulled back the blankets on the bed, the men lifted Jake from the makeshift stretcher. It was all Felicity could do to keep from screaming with anxiety and fear.

As soon as the men deposited Jake on the bed, she stepped closer and scrutinized the wounds on his face. Turning to Jim, she asked in a small voice, "Is he hurt anywhere except his face, Mr. Cranston?"

"Please, ma'am, just call me Jim. And, yes, ma'am, he's got a bad chest wound. He was hit with a lot of rocks during the explosion."

"Explosion!" she gasped. "What explosion?"

"Up at the mine, ma'am. Jake was alone up there and all of a sudden, we heard an explosion. We ran up there quick as we could, but part of the mine had caved in and it took us a long time to dig him out. He's in pretty bad shape, ma'am, but Corny thinks he'll make it, and he's as good as any doctor."

"He's not going to die," Felicity returned fiercely. "Move, please. I want to see for myself." She started to reach toward Jake but Jim gently restrained her, knowing she was too upset to do Jake any good.

"It's okay, ma'am. Corny's already seen to

cleanin' up and wrappin' the wounds. I think all Jake needs now is rest."

She nodded reluctantly, struggling mightily to get a grip on herself. She stared at Jake's chalky face, then pulled the quilts up tightly under his chin and ushered the two miners back out to the kitchen. "Please sit down and I'll fix you something to eat."

Nodding in appreciation, Jim and Pete shed their heavy coats and sat down at the table. Felicity lit the stove and put the cold pot of stew on top of the burner.

Turning back toward the men, she clasped her trembling hands in front of her and said, "Please tell me everything that happened."

Jim shook his head. "We really don't know much. Jake dropped off some supplies for us and said he was goin' up to the mine to check on things before he headed home. A few minutes later, we heard the blast. It sounded like the whole mine was goin' up. We ran up to see what happened and that's when we realized that the explosion had caused a cave-in and Jake must be buried inside. Took us hours to find him and dig him out. It was a good thing he was near the entrance or we never would've gotten to him in time."

"What I can't figure," Pete interjected, "is what caused the blast. Someone musta rigged a charge. We found dynamite casings all over when we was diggin' Jake out and none of us left it there last fall."

Felicity gasped. "Are you saying that someone was out there and blew up the mine on purpose, knowing Jake was inside?"

Pete shrugged his shoulders. "It kinda looks that way, but who woulda known he was gonna be up there? We didn't even know he was comin', so how could anybody else?"

Felicity reeled with shock. This situation had gone way past someone just trying to run them out of business. Someone wanted Jake dead.

"Please try not to worry, Miss Howard," Jim said

soothingly. "Me and the boys will do some investigatin' and see what we can come up with."

"I'll be grateful for anything you can find," she responded. "If someone is trying to kill Jake, they're going to try again when they find out he's still alive." She turned back toward the stove, gripping its edge with shaking hands. "You say Corny cleaned all the stones out of his chest?" she inquired.

"Yes, ma'am," Jim replied. "He has one real bad wound in the middle of his chest. Looks like he was hit by a big rock during the blast." Felicity's dismay was apparent on her face and Pete hurried to reassure her.

"Corny said Jake should be fine if infection don't set in. I just hope we didn't hurt him none by bringin' him home. We should've left him where he was. He passed out when we got him back on the travois and hasn't woke up since."

Pete sipped the coffee that Felicity set in front of him and added, "We knew we shouldn't move him, but Jake was so set on gettin' here that we figured if we didn't bring him, he'd try to get here on his own. He never woulda made it, but he woulda died tryin'."

Felicity nodded, understanding their dilemma. "I know how stubborn Jake can be and I don't blame you for giving in to him. However, the fact that he's been unconscious all this time doesn't sound good at all." She turned back to the stove and ladled up huge bowls of stew for the men.

"Thanks, Miss Howard." Pete smiled. "This smells real good."

"You're welcome, Pete. It's the least I can do." Jim added his thanks and then Felicity, unable to contain her concern any longer, excused herself to go check on Jake.

Her worried gaze swept over his pale features as she drew back the quilts and unbuttoned the borrowed shirt he was wearing. She gently unwrapped his bandages to make sure his wounds had been properly cleaned and attended to. Though she knew little of nursing, the sisters at the convent had been of the belief that many serious infections and illnesses could be prevented if proper sanitation was adhered to.

Felicity's stomach lurched at the frightful sight of Jake's bloody chest. There were many small cuts and one large gash that looked especially serious. She shivered at the thought of how much pain he must be in. Half conscious, he groaned and clawed at his bandages. Her heart twisted as she leaned forward and took his big, calloused hand in both of hers. With soft reassuring murmurs, she told him that he was home, that he was safe. Her gentle tone seemed to have a calming effect on him and he relaxed, sinking again into oblivion.

Satisfied that Corny had known what he was about, Felicity pulled the heavy quilt back over Jake and quietly returned to where the two men sat eating.

Pausing at the bedroom door, she lifted her chin and pasted a smile over her tense features before walking back into the kitchen. It wouldn't do to upset the men by letting her terror show. "Would either of you like some more stew?" she offered graciously.

Pete shook his head. "Thanks, ma'am. Hope you don't mind, but we already helped ourselves. Please don't feel like you have to wait on us. Jim and me are used to takin' care of ourselves."

"I don't mind at all, Pete. Please make yourselves at home, and please call me Felicity. I'm afraid I can't offer you a warm bed, but you're more than welcome to stretch out in front of the fire tonight."

"We should be gettin' back to our cabin, Miss Felicity," Pete demurred. "We thought we'd make sure you had all you needed for the next few days and then head on back. It's snowin' pretty heavy now and if we don't leave soon, you might be stuck with us for a while."

"You can't mean to strike out in this terrible weather!" she protested. "It's freezing out there and it's well past midnight."

Pete pushed back from the table. "She has a point, Jim. We worked most of the day diggin' Jake out of the mine and then walked all the way down here. Maybe we'd be better off if we got a little shut-eye, took care of some of the chores in the mornin', and then lit out for home."

Jim looked out the window warily but finally nodded his head in agreement. "Maybe you're right. I have to admit, I'm really beat."

Felicity smiled, relieved that they were staying. "Good," she said, nodding. "I'll fetch you some blankets. I'm going to stay up with Jake tonight, but before you retire, there's one more favor I'd like to ask of you."

"Anything, Miss Felicity, just name it." Pete smiled.

Even in the dim lantern light, both men noticed the rosy blush that crept up Felicity's cheeks as she determined how best to word her request. "I was wondering if you could help me get Jake out of his clothes and into some clean long johns. I think he'd be more comfortable."

"Sure thing, ma'am." Jim said, happy to aid the pretty, blushing woman. "There's no need for you to help. Jake's too big for a little gal like you to handle anyway. You just set out some clean drawers and me and Pete will do the rest." Felicity thanked them and hurried off to fetch the clean clothes.

As she disappeared into the bedroom, Jim gave Pete a sly wink and said, "I think that little lady has some special feelings for the boss."

Pete gave Jim a conspiratorial wink. "I think you're right, my friend. I just hope Jake knows how lucky he is."

"Oh, I don't think we need to worry 'bout that. Jake got downright mean about gettin' back down here to her."

"If you had a nurse like her, wouldn't you be bellyachin' to get back to her too?" Pete asked enviously.

Jim opened his mouth to reply but shut it and gave Pete a kick under the table as Felicity reappeared. She shyly told them that she'd laid out fresh garments for Jake and he was ready to be tended to. Both men gave her courteous smiles as they rose, leaving her to pick up their empty dishes.

Pete moved Jake's cot into the bedroom and placed it at the end of the bed for Felicity, insisting that she couldn't do Jake any good unless she also got some rest.

She felt as if she'd barely closed her eyes when Jake groaned loudly and jettisoned his covers. Her eyes instantly flew open. She sprang off the cot and rushed to his side, placing her hand on his head as he twisted it from side to side on the pillow. Scorching heat emanated from his brow and Felicity's breath caught in her throat as she drew back her hand in alarm. He was burning up. His arm suddenly flew out like a battering ram, nearly knocking her off her feet as he thrashed wildly in his delirium.

She raced into the front room and shook Jim awake. After directing him to fetch her some water, she ran to the kitchen and grabbed several soft cloths. Jim stumbled to his feet, pulled his boots on, and hurried off for the water. He quickly returned, carrying the bucket to the bedroom and waiting for more instructions.

Felicity poured a little water into the basin she'd placed on the bedside table and set about trying to bring Jake's fever down.

While Jim held Jake still, Felicity murmured softly to him and cooled his flaming face with the wet cloths. Pushing his sleeves up as far as they'd go, she ran the cloth over the corded muscles of his arms, repeating the process over and over until he finally quieted and fell into a restless sleep. She touched the back of her hand to his brow and was reassured that the fever was down a bit. Nodding to Jim, she moved away from the bed and set the cloth aside. "I think he'll be all right for a while now," she whispered. "Why don't you go get some more rest."

Jim's gaze traveled to the window and then returned to Felicity. "It's almost dawn, ma'am. I think me and Pete best get up and see to your stock so we can get an early start back. I want to start checkin' the mine for clues that might help us figure out exactly what happened."

She looked at Jim speculatively. "Do you think this accident has any connection to the other incidents at the mine?" she asked.

Jim hesitated, unsure of how much Jake wanted Felicity to know. Then he put a comforting hand on her shoulder. "Please, ma'am, don't worry. Me and Pete will get to the bottom of this trouble."

She nodded, well aware of Jim's deliberate vagueness. His reluctance to discuss the explosion further served to confirm her suspicions. Jim shuffled his feet uncomfortably and she relented, knowing it was unfair to place the man in such an awkward position. She'd just have to wait until Jake was well enough to explain things for himself.

As she looked up into Jim's uneasy face, she smiled and patted the hand that rested on her shoulder. "Very well, Jim, I'll let you off the hook. I'm very grateful for all the help you've given Jake and me. I can't thank you enough." Jim's hand slid off her shoulder and he stepped away, smiling his relief.

"You're mighty welcome, Miss Felicity. Me and Pete were happy to do it."

After the men finished with the last of the morning chores, they came to bid her good-bye and ask one more time if she was sure she could handle things alone. Felicity assured them that she would be fine and handed Pete a large bag stuffed with food, including a loaf of bread and a jar of her homemade jelly. Thanking them one last time, she watched from the window as they disappeared up the path to the mine. Then she turned and walked into the bedroom to take up her vigil at Jake's side.

Shortly after Jim and Pete left, a blizzard moved in and blanketed the area beneath several feet of new snow. Fortunately, Pete had carried enough wood into the little cabin to last for several days. The men had also made sure that Bess, Jake's stallion, and the wagon horses had three days' worth of hay in their mangers, thus freeing Felicity from that chore. She was grateful for this reprieve for she spent the next three days fighting a life-and-death battle with Jake's raging fever. Time dragged by endlessly, filled with a never-ending succession of cooling sponge baths and exhausting attempts to force water and broth through Jake's parched lips.

On the morning of the fourth day, Felicity knew she had no choice but to leave Jake for a short time and tend to the animals. The chores took her over an hour, and by the time she'd finished, it had started to snow again. She hurried back to the warm haven of the tiny cabin to find Jake sprawled on the floor, delirious with pain and fever. It took her another hour to get him back into bed. She was nearing the end of her endurance, but there didn't seem to be any sign of his fever breaking and she knew she wouldn't be able to rest until it did.

For three more grueling days, she nursed him. Between morning sickness, chores, unrelenting snow, and her own desperate need for sleep, there were moments when she wondered how much longer she could go on. But one look at his ravaged face—pale, bewhiskered, and wracked with pain—renewed her resolve. Felicity knew she could withstand anything if her efforts would save him.

Several times, while in the throes of delirium, he called her name, pleading with her not to leave him. Her heart leaped with joy on these occasions, but always she'd tell herself it was just the fever talking and that he didn't know what he was saying.

Finally, eight days after the accident, he awoke, tired and weak but clearheaded. Felicity was asleep, sitting in a chair she'd pulled up next to the bed. She was slumped over onto the edge of the mattress, her head resting on her crossed arms. Jake was astonished at the effort it took him to lift his hand as he gently caressed the top of her head. "Felicity, sweetheart, come lay down," he rasped. She looked so tired. He knew she'd worn herself out caring for him. In the few lucid moments he'd had in the past week, he'd realized that it was her soft voice and gentle touch that soothed him.

She raised her head and stared at him uncomprehendingly. She thought she was still dreaming when she saw his hazel eyes gazing back at her with an awareness she hadn't seen for many days. She smiled and laid her head back down on her arms to continue the pleasant delusion.

"Felicity, darlin', come to bed."

She groaned, annoyed at being disturbed. She felt a gentle tug on her arm and raised her head again. Somehow, through her grogginess, she perceived what it was that Jake wanted. Too exhausted to argue, she crawled into bed next to him.

Jake smiled and drew her closer as she curled up against his big, warm body and sank into a deep sleep.

When Felicity finally awoke, she was aghast to find herself in bed with Jake and even more shocked to realize that the sun was well past its zenith and evening was fast approaching. Greatly relieved that he was asleep, she crept out of the bedroom and set about doing the day's chores and making some broth for Jake's supper.

After apologizing to the animals for her neglect, she fed and watered them, milked poor, miserable Bess, and returned to the cabin. She could hear Jake stirring in the bedroom and although she wanted to go in and check on him, she hesitated.

Was he aware that she'd spent hours cuddled up with him? She whispered a fervent prayer that he wasn't. If he asked her why she'd done it, she wouldn't even know how to respond. She had no recollection whatsoever of getting into bed with him.

Please, God, she pleaded, I can't be blamed for something I didn't even realize I was doing. Please don't let Jake remember it. Everything we've gained will be lost if he thinks that I want to go back to being lovers.

Even as she tried to concentrate on her chaste prayer, she felt guilty for the thrill that shot through her. There was nothing in the world that she wanted more than to be Jake's lover. But it was impossible. A lover was all he wanted and as wonderful as it had been to again awaken in his arms, she would not allow herself to be seduced back into that role. That was a decision she had made months ago and she would never again surrender to her passions.

With this resolution in mind, she picked up his soup and walked into the bedroom. The sight that met her made her beam with pleasure. Jake was awake, and from the expression in his eyes, she knew his fever had broken and that he was lucid. Placing the bowl of soup on the bureau, she smiled happily and walked over to the bed.

"How are you feeling?" she asked.

"Better," he answered. "How are you holdin' up?"

"I'm all right. A bit tired, but all right. Do you think you'd like some soup?"

He nodded.

She carried the bowl of broth over to the bed and sat down on the edge. He said nothing, but smiled at her warmly as she placed a napkin around his neck and began spooning the broth into his mouth.

"I don't like layin' on my back when I'm tryin' to

eat," he grumbled. "Let's see if I can sit up a little. It would be easier for both of us."

His complaints were like music to her ears. He's going to be all right, she thought joyfully. He's going to be all right! Setting the bowl down, she placed her hands under his arms and helped him to raise himself. He gritted his teeth against the pain the movement caused, but nodded in assent when she asked if he was comfortable. Much to her delight, he ate the entire bowl of broth and even remarked that it tasted good.

After finishing his meal, Felicity asked him if he felt well enough to allow her to check his wounds. He nodded tiredly and again lay down.

As she removed the bandages from around his chest, he said, "Do I look terrible? My face hurts so much I know I must be cut up. Do I look awful?"

"No, Jake," she said, hoping he couldn't hear the laughter in her voice, "you don't look terrible. Your face is cut, but it will heal."

"Good." He sighed wearily. "The boys at the mine told me my face was a mess and I wondered if the damage was gonna be permanent."

She could no longer contain the giggles that threatened. "What's the matter?" she teased. "Did they tell you you weren't handsome anymore?"

"Somethin' like that," he muttered. "Not that it makes any difference to me," he added hurriedly.

Felicity smiled at his lie. "Don't worry," she assured him, "you look just fine."

He nodded matter-of-factly, but she had seen an expression of relief flit across his face.

"I just wish I was clean," he complained. "I feel so dirty, I don't know how you can stand me."

"We'll give you a bath as soon as you feel up to it," she promised.

"Well, it better be soon or I'm not gonna be able to tolerate bein' in the same room with myself."

"Hush, now." She chuckled. "You're going to

wear yourself out with all these complaints. Just lie back and take a nap."

"Good idea," he murmured. He closed his eyes and as Felicity secured his bandages, she thought he'd again fallen asleep. As she got up to leave, however, his voice stopped her.

"Felicity?"

"Yes, Jake," she responded, turning back toward the bed.

His eyes were open again as he spoke to her. "Thank you, sweetheart. Thank you for everythin'."

You're welcome, Jake," Felicity whispered. She quickly left the room so he wouldn't see the tears of joy spilling down her cheeks.

Late that evening, after donning her warmest nightgown before the fire, Felicity quietly pushed open the bedroom door to check on Jake one last time before retiring.

He was sleeping soundly, his chest slowly rising and falling, his big body motionless. Felicity padded over to the bed and lightly pressed her fingertips to his forehead. He still felt cool, and there was no sign of the fever returning. She sighed with relief and cast her eyes heavenward in a heartfelt prayer of thanks.

She gazed down at the sleeping man, her heart tight with the intensity of the love she felt for him. Unconsciously, she caressed her slightly rounded stomach and wished for the thousandth time that she could tell him of their child—that things could be different between them. Shaking her head to dispel her forlorn thoughts, she leaned over and pulled the blanket down to check his wounds. During the course of his delirium, Jake had torn off his long johns in an effort to cool his scorching body, and even now, he lay naked under the covers. Little rivulets of dried blood traced down his chest and stomach to his thighs. Perhaps, thought Felicity, now would be a good time to give him a bath. Since he was sleeping so deeply, there would be little chance of him feeling any pain, and—she smiled ironically— little chance of her being embarrassed since he wouldn't be aware of her ministrations.

She left the bedroom and filled a basin with warm water from the pot simmering on the stove. She fetched a clean cloth and reentered the bedroom, setting her supplies on the small table by the bed. She thought about lighting a candle, but decided that the glare might wake him, and that the moonlight streaming through the window would have to suffice.

Sitting down carefully on the edge of the bed, she dipped the flannel into the basin, drawing it gently across the taut muscles of Jake's stomach. She smiled to herself, loving the feel of his skin beneath her fingers. She continued to tenderly wash him for several moments before rinsing the dried blood from the cloth and pulling the blanket down to expose his loins and upper legs.

Her eyes greedily drank in the sight of his masculine perfection. To her dismay, Felicity realized that her heart was hammering against her ribs and her breath was coming fast and harsh. Shocked by her reaction to his nudity, she turned and clasped her shaking hands in her lap. Stop this, she chided herself, it's just a body—a wounded, pain-wracked body that needs tending.

After several moments of self-reproach, she felt that she had sufficiently subdued her wanton thoughts, and turned back toward Jake to continue his bath.

She brushed the warm cloth against his thighs, but drew back with a small gasp as his manhood stiffened and rose boldly before her eyes.

For a long moment, Felicity stared in fascination, then she slowly raised her eyes to his face. His eyes were open and he was staring at her so intently that she turned away in embarrassment. Jake reached over and lifted her hand to his lips, murmuring, "Love me, Felicity. Don't deny me again."

"But Jake," she protested weakly, "we can't. You're still sick and I might hurt you."

"You're not gonna hurt me." He smiled wryly. "It's my *chest* that's wounded. Please, sweetheart, I want you so much . . . Don't walk away and leave me."

She knew that she was lost. She could no longer deny what they both so desperately wanted. With a shaky sigh, she wrapped her cool fingers around his rigid length, marveling at its heat and size. It felt heavy in her hand, almost as if it was overburdened with the passion it contained, and she could feel Jake trembling beneath her touch. As she rubbed a finger along the sensitive underside of his throbbing shaft, she whispered, "May I kiss you . . . there?"

He was nearly unable to answer, so overwhelmed was he by her boldness. "Yes," he rasped. "Oh, yes, baby, you can do anythin' you want to."

She dipped her head and rubbed her slightly parted lips up and down his hot, hard erection. Jake nearly arched off the bed.

Sinking into an abyss of desire, Felicity was hardly aware when her tongue passed her lips, licking and sucking at the wet, pulsating tip of the engorged organ.

Jake could take no more. The months of abstinence had sparked an inferno of need within him and Felicity's intimate caress was his undoing. Forgetting the agony of his lacerated chest, he raised himself on his elbows and groaned, "My God, Felicity, stop! Please, sweetheart, no more!"

She raised her head worriedly, thinking she had somehow hurt him, but seeing his eyes aflame with lust, she smiled provocatively, pulled her nightgown over her head, and flung it aside. "All right, sir." She laughed. "I will torture you no more." With that, she crawled forward on her knees, straddled his hips, and sat down hard.

She was wet and ready for him and a harsh cry escaped Jake's lips as he slipped easily into her silken body. He bucked against her, almost unseating her in his excitement.

Felicity's response was a cry as primitive as a she-wolf calling her mate. Jake's eyes flew open and he stared in wonder at the heady sight of his cold, untouchable landlady impaled on him in glorious, naked abandon.

She leaned back and placed her hands on his knees as she arched her back. Her head was thrown back and her curls brushed his loins, tickling him intimately and nearly sending him over the edge. He reached up to grasp her breasts and she rocked forward, pressing their passion-swollen tips against his lips in open invitation. Jake eagerly pulled a rose-hued nipple into his mouth while rubbing his face back and forth against the exquisite softness. Then he reached for her hips, encouraging her to seek love's rhythm and grant him release from his sublime torment.

Breathless, shaking, but ecstatically aware of the pleasure she was giving this magnificent male, she clenched her thighs against him and moved up and down with increasing rapidity.

Jake erupted with a hoarse shout of release while Felicity threw her head back and screamed her delight. The cabin walls fairly shook with the fury of their unabashed joy in each other.

As she slowly returned to reality, Felicity collapsed on the bed next to Jake, careful not to brush against his chest. Still panting and gasping, he gingerly pulled her against his heaving side and whispered raggedly, "I love you, Miss Howard. I don't want you to leave. I want you to stay here and marry me."

She froze in shock at his soft plea, but before she could gather her wits to reply, he buried his face in her hair and fell into exhausted slumber.

Chapter 18

I love you, Miss Howard. I don't want you to leave. I want you to stay here and marry me.

Jake's words drummed like a litany in Felicity's mind as she nervously prepared his breakfast the next morning.

Had he meant it? Would all her dreams be realized? She desperately hoped it wasn't just his sated passion talking, but how could she be sure? Would he repeat his whispered proposal this morning? And if he didn't, did she dare mention it to him? She shuddered at the thought of how uncomfortable and embarrassing that conversation could be if he didn't remember his words or if he had, during the night, regretted his proposal and changed his mind. Or, worst of all, what if he had never meant it at all and had merely said it so that she would not regret their fiery lovemaking?

Felicity paused in her cooking and gazed out the front window. It was odd that she felt no guilt over what had happened between them the previous night. She had wanted Jake as much as he had wanted her, and, as she had languished in his arms in the aftermath of their passion, she had felt only a sense of rightness.

Although she had sworn Jake would never again touch her outside the bonds of wedlock, she could not berate him or herself. It had been inevitable . . .

like the moon and the tides. And afterward, she had felt only an overwhelming love for the man who cradled her close to him.

Maybe it had been Jake's proposal that justified their actions in her mind, but somehow, the sense of contentment she felt in his embrace seemed to have little to do with the legalities of marriage.

Of course, she thought with dread, she would again have to confess her immoral sin to Father Thomas at St. Patrick's. Despite the darkness of the confessional, she couldn't be absolutely sure that the priest didn't recognize her and, after her first confession in November, she had found it difficult to look him in the eye when he greeted her with his other parishioners after Sunday mass.

Felicity pushed the thought of the embarrassing confession to the back of her mind, and again addressed the problem closer at hand. She knew that her doubts would not be allayed until she walked into the bedroom and faced Jake. If he regretted his proposal, she would just return to her original plan and leave for Philadelphia as soon as possible. A familiar twinge of guilt shot through her at the thought of leaving without telling Jake that he was going to be a father. I'll write him and tell him after the baby is born and I'm settled, she rationalized. That way, he'll know I wasn't trying to trick him into marriage by getting myself with child.

Feeling that this was the best plan of action, she finished Jake's breakfast tray and resolutely headed for the bedroom to face whatever fate awaited her.

The enticing aroma of bacon penetrated Jake's dreams, coaxing him to wake. He smiled as his mind drifted back to the previous night's encounter. He still couldn't quite believe Felicity's uninhibited seduction, and a jolt of renewed desire shot through him at the memory of the pleasure they had shared. At that moment, the object of his musings shoul-

dered the door open and walked into the bedroom,
carrying his breakfast tray and smiling shyly.

He gingerly pushed himself up to a sitting position, grimacing as his healing skin pulled tightly
across his chest. Setting the tray down on the bedside table, Felicity stacked the pillows behind his
back. "There, how's that?" she asked.

"Good. Thanks, sweetheart." He reached out for
her hand, placing a soft kiss on her knuckles. "God,
you look good for so early in the mornin'."

"Thank you." She blushed. He continued to gaze
at her searchingly until she turned away, feeling embarrassed. She quickly picked up the plate and fork
off the tray, saying, "Here, I want to you to eat all
of this."

"I don't think that'll be any problem this mornin'.
I'm so hungry, I could eat a grizzly—and from the
smell of that bacon, I see you've finally fixed me
some real food."

She nodded and handed him the plate. "I thought
it was time we worked on building up your
strength."

He eyed the plate hungrily and began to fork up
eggs and fried potatoes with an enthusiasm that
made Felicity beam. "Sure tastes good after all that
damn broth. I don't care if I ever see another bowl
of that stuff as long as I live."

She bent down and tenderly brushed a lock of hair
back from his forehead. "Just be careful and stay
well," she murmured. "Then you'll never have to
eat that awful stuff again."

He stared at her and she held her breath, hoping
he'd repeat last night's words of love. Finally, she
dropped her gaze and said, "Enjoy your breakfast.
I'll go get you some coffee." He nodded and turned
back to his food as she hurried out.

Finishing his meal, Jake set the plate down and
leaned back into his pillows. Had Felicity heard his
declaration of love the night before? More impor-
tantly, had she heard his marriage proposal? He'd

fallen asleep so quickly, he wasn't sure if she'd answered. It was obvious from her shyness this morning that their relationship had again taken a new turn, but he couldn't quite discern her feelings. Well, he thought, I'll just ask her again this mornin'. He grinned as he realized how happy that thought made him. He *wanted* to propose to Felicity again. He wanted to hear her say she'd be his wife. For the first time, he was completely aware of his own feelings and, more than anything in the world, he wanted to spend the rest of his life loving Felicity Howard.

She bustled through the door again, the coffeepot in one hand, a cup in the other. "Are you ready for some coffee?" she asked.

"In a minute." He smiled. "Come sit down." He patted the bed next to him. "I want to talk to you."

A rush of fear flooded through her. This was it. He was going to tell her he hadn't really meant what he'd said about wanting to marry her. She set the coffee down with shaking hands. Sitting down on the edge of the bed, she tried valiantly to assume a composed air, but fear wrung at her heart, clouding her vision.

"Move a little closer, baby," Jake gently urged. "I'm not gonna bite you." He reached over and took both her hands in his. "I asked you a question last night and I don't remember you givin' me an answer, so I'm gonna ask you again."

She held her breath as he drew a deep breath of his own and let it out slowly. "Will you marry me, Felicity? I want you to be my wife and if you'll have me, I promise I'll try to be a good husband to you."

Tears trickled down her cheeks. "Oh, Jake!"

His heart leaped into his throat. Why was she crying? Was she going to say no?

She jerked her hands free and launched herself into his arms. He winced as she unthinkingly threw her weight against his wounded chest, but a pleased smile hovered on his lips.

She wrapped her arms around his neck and hugged him ardently. "Yes! Yes, you big handsome man. Yes, I'll marry you!" She gave him another enthusiastic squeeze and then sat back to better see his expression. "Oh, Jake, I was so afraid that you hadn't really meant it when you asked me to marry you last night."

He gaped at her astonishment. "Hadn't really meant it? Little girl, I love you! You belong to me, weddin' or no weddin', so you might as well let me make an honest woman of you," he teased. "Felicity, why are you bawlin'?"

"Because—" She sniffed. "—I'm so happy! I can't believe this is happening to me!"

"Believe it, baby," he murmured. "You're mine, and as soon as I can get out of this bed and down the side of this mountain, we're gonna make it legal for the whole world to know. Especially that damn Ed Banyon."

She looked at him in surprise. "Why, Jake, were you jealous of Ed? There was never anything between us, I swear!"

"I know," he muttered. "But I hated the way he ogled you. I hated the way all the men ogled you. So if that's being jealous, then, yeah, I guess I was jealous."

"Well, you had no reason to be," she assured him. "I never wanted anyone but you."

She moved closer, and he covered her lips with a long, drugging kiss. When he finally pulled away, she was close to swooning, and from the sound of Jake's ragged breathing, he was as shaken as she by the instant flaring of passion between them.

He gazed into her limpid eyes and then reluctantly let her go, gently pushing her away. "Don't look at me like that. I want to talk to you and if you keep lookin' at me like that, I'll never get this said."

She gazed at him in confusion, trying to gather her scattered wits. "Talk to me?" she asked stupidly.

"Yeah, you hot little baggage," he chuckled, "talk to you. Now sit up so I can keep my mind on what I want to say."

She obeyed, sitting up and primly folding her hands in her lap. "Is this satisfactory?"

"Better." He nodded. "Just quit lookin' at me as if you want to eat me."

"I'm not!" protested Felicity. "I've never looked at you like I want to eat you. A lady would *never* do such a thing!"

"Honey—" He smiled. "—if you ever *stop* lookin' at me like that, I swear I'll divorce you." At her startled expression, he laughed and chucked her under the chin. "Now, don't get mad. I like the way you drool every time you see me."

She gasped in embarrassed outrage. "I don't drool!"

"Yes, you do," he assured her, "and I do the same thing every time I see you."

"You do?" asked Felicity in astonishment. "But that's different. Men drool over every woman they see."

His smile faded, his expression suddenly serious. "This one doesn't, and that's what I want to talk to you about."

Her teasing grin also disappeared and she was suddenly as serious as he.

"Felicity, I've never felt anythin' for a woman like I feel for you. I adore you, sweetheart. I want to marry you, I want to live with you the rest of my life, and I want us to be happy, but I'm scared as hell that you'll get tired of this life like my ma did."

She opened her mouth to protest, but he held up his hand. "No, don't say nothin'. Just hear me out. I know you're in love with me now and you think it'll last forever between us, but how will you feel after we've been married a couple of years and you're used to me? Will you still love me if the mine doesn't pay and there's no money, if we have to move on, if there's kids to take care of, and work that never ends? Will you still want me when you've made love to me a thousand times and the thrill isn't new anymore? Think about it, Felicity, because if you have any doubts, then don't marry me. I know I couldn't live through what Ma did to Pa. I'd rather lose you now."

She sat on the edge of the bed, her eyes boring into his with a look he'd never seen before. A long silence hung between them until finally, in a calm, quiet voice, she asked, "If all those bad things happen, will you still love me, Jake?"

"Of course!" He nodded vigorously.

"Then why do you think my love for you is any less enduring than yours for me?"

He was completely nonplussed and it was a long time before he answered. "Well, because of my mother . . ." he began.

"I'm *not* your mother!" she blazed.

He stared at her, amazed at her vehemence. "No, you're not," he agreed. "You really love me, don't you?"

"Yes!" answered Felicity fiercely. "And I have something for you to think about too. If you aren't prepared to be married to me for the next fifty or sixty years, then don't do it. Because once we say those vows, Jake McCullough, you'll *never* get rid of me!"

He leaned forward and pulled her down onto the bed with him. "Damn it, woman, but you are somethin'!"

Laughing and breathless, they rolled on the bed, embracing, kissing, and whispering promises of never-ending love. Now, thought Felicity, now I'll tell him about the baby. She turned toward him, full of purpose as she planned how to phrase her confession. But before she could utter a sound, Jake brushed his hand seductively up the inside of her thigh and whispered, "Why don't you get back under these covers with me?"

She was so startled that all thoughts of her confession

fled, and she sat up abruptly, smoothing her skirts and patting her hair. "I think not, sir," she admonished. "You shouldn't be exerting yourself so much. You haven't even been out of bed yet. Before you get yourself too excited, you better get some strength back."

Snorting a denial, he made a grab for her, but she twisted nimbly off the bed. "Felicity," he groaned, "there's one part of me that is definitely *not* weak, and is, without question, already excited. Now, come back here! You can't leave me like this!"

Ignoring his plea, she poured a cup of coffee and extended it toward him. "Here, drink this and behave yourself."

He scowled, making no effort to take the coffee. "Felicity, have a heart! Are you gonna make me get up and chase you around the bedroom?"

"No," Felicity responded with assurance, "and don't argue with me. I meant what I said. You need to rest and get your strength back." She picked up his breakfast tray and turned toward the door. "Now, just lie back and relax. Take a nap and maybe you can get up for a while this afternoon."

Before he could protest further, she was out the door. He cast a forlorn glance down at the throbbing bulge beneath the quilt and squeezed his eyes shut. Relax? Take a nap? The woman was crazy! Picking up the coffee cup, he took a swallow and leaned back with a wry smile. He'd get his strength back, all right, and when he did, he was going to take that little vixen to bed for about a week!

It was late morning when Jake awoke to the soft sounds of Felicity moving about the room, a dust cloth in her hand. Her back was turned to him and she was obviously so lost in thought that she didn't hear him stirring.

She had spent the entire morning contemplating just when and how to tell Jake about his impending fatherhood. She had come to no concrete decisions as to when, but she had convinced herself that she should wait until he was completely recovered. She was unsure of what his reaction would be to such startling news and the moment had to be perfect. Although she had no idea when that perfect moment might present itself, she didn't think it would be while he was lying in bed, wounded. No. Better to wait and hope that she'd recognize the moment when it arrived. After all, there was still plenty of time.

Jake had slumped down in the bed when he'd fallen asleep, but the pillows still remained propped against the headboard and he struggled to push himself up to a sitting position. He knew that if he was going to regain his strength anytime soon, he'd have to start doing a few things for himself. Gritting his teeth against the pain, he finally managed to get himself situated comfortably.

Felicity turned at the rustling of the covers. "Oh, you're awake," she said in surprise. "Why didn't you say something? I would have helped you." She walked to the side of the bed and laid her palm against his cheek and then his forehead. "No fever. That's good. I think you're finally on the road to recovery."

"You should have figured that out after last night," he teased.

She rolled her eyes, ignoring his lecherous look and returning to her dusting. Jake watched the provocative sway of her skirts and the unsatisfied lust that had plagued him earlier shot through him again. "Felicity," he complained, "I'm cold. Why don't you quit that damn cleanin' and come warm me up?"

Her back again turned to him, she smiled in amusement. She set her cloth down on the chest and pivoted to face him. "You know," she said thoughtfully, "I think I almost liked it better when you were too sick to annoy me with your constant demands. Have you always gotten what you wanted, when you wanted it?"

A smug smile settled over his features. "Pretty much," he affirmed, "at least until I met you. But—" He sighed dramatically. "—that's all changed. I *never* seem to get what I want anymore. It's a terrible thing for a man to have his most basic needs denied by the woman he loves."

"Oh!" Felicity blustered. "You're impossible! I can't *believe* how spoiled you are! I would remind you, sir, that your basic needs were *more* than fulfilled less than twelve hours ago!"

"Yeah." He grinned. "You hit the nail right on the head, sweetheart. Twelve long hours ago!"

"Oh, you . . . you're . . . insatiable!" She bit her lip hard in an effort to control the laughter that threatened to escape.

"I'm not sure what that means, baby, but if it means that I can't make love to you often enough to ever be satisfied, you're right!"

Felicity was shocked speechless by Jake's bawdy confession, causing him to laugh harder. Wrapping his arms around his shaking chest, he pleaded, "Quit makin' me laugh, woman. You're givin' me a terrible ache."

Her eyes narrowed and she glanced boldly at the enormous bulge which was again evident under the quilt. Shooting him an arch look, she retorted, "Yes, I can see that, and I know just *where* you're aching."

It was his turn to look shocked.

"So," she continued in a husky voice, "I suggest that you be *very* nice to me today and maybe, just maybe, tonight I'll see what I can do to massage that ache." With another meaningful glance at his towering erection, she spun on her heel and exited the room, ignoring his stunned expression.

Covering her mouth, she ran toward the kitchen, aghast that she had actually made such a risqué suggestion. Good Lord, what would Sister Angelica say? Picturing what the nun's expression might be upon hearing such words coming from one of her pious novices, Felicity ran to the counter, grabbed a towel, and smothered her uncontrollable laughter. When she finally sobered, she glanced over at the clock, her eyes widening as she realized where her own licentious thoughts were leading her. It was almost noon . . . only nine more hours till she could climb into bed . . . and massage Jake's ache.

Chapter 19

~~~~~~~~

The month of February flew by. Jake's injuries healed, and under Felicity's watchful eye, he slowly but steadily regained his good health. He and Felicity continued to share her bed and Jake never ceased to be amazed at the passion she displayed in his arms. Despite her convent upbringing, she was eager for him to teach her new ways to enjoy their intimacy and, on more than one occasion, she initiated her own beguiling and highly pleasurable experiments in the art of love.

Jake inhaled the unseasonably mild March breeze, exhaling with a smile of utter contentment. Felicity sat next to him on the wagon seat, reacquainting herself with the bustling streets of Silverton. She still wore her flannel coat, but the weather was warm enough that her hair was uncovered and hung loose down her back. She had drawn the sides neatly up to the crown of her head and secured them with a delicate pink ribbon. Anticipation of today's errand made her cheeks flush with excitement. Jake had brought her to town to set up an appointment with Father Thomas so that they might meet with him to discuss their wedding plans.

Felicity knew that she had never been so happy, despite the nagging guilt which constantly plagued her. She still hadn't told Jake about the baby, and

with each passing day, the telling became harder.
They were so happy now, but what if he wasn't glad
about the baby? What if he didn't want a family immediately? She was so worried that her confession
might change things between them that she just
couldn't bring herself to share her secret with him.
She needed help, counseling, and she felt the best
person to guide her was Father Thomas. She would
somehow find the courage to tell him of her situation, and once he had chastised her for her immoral
behavior, she was confident that he would advise
her on how to properly approach her touchy and
sometimes intimidating husband-to-be.

Jake tugged on the reins, bringing the horses to a
halt in front of the church. He hopped down and
hurried over to assist Felicity. Wrapping her in a
gentle embrace, he gave her a quick kiss. "I'll be
back in a little while, sweetheart," he promised. "If
you're done before I get here, just stay put. Everybody and his dog is in town and it wouldn't be safe
for you to be on the streets alone."

"All right," she agreed, "but this meeting won't
take long, so please hurry."

"I will," he assured her. "I've got one stop to
make and it'll only take a few minutes." He guided
her around the wagon and up to the church door.
"See you later, baby."

She gave him a last hug and hurried inside, anxious to see Father Thomas and tell him her happy
news.

Jake walked back to the wagon with long, determined strides. He had intentionally neglected to tell
Felicity exactly what his business was, knowing she
would try to talk him out of it. But he had a score
to settle with Yancy Parnell and this confrontation
was long overdue. He climbed into the wagon and
grabbed the reins. "Get up there," he called impatiently to the dozing horses.

Several people waved and called out greetings as

he made his way down the street, but he was in too much of a hurry to do more than nod in response.

He tied the horses to the hitching rail outside the Last Chance and shouldered his way through the bat-wing doors. A piano player thumped out a bawdy tune, but it was nearly drowned out by the din of raucous laughter and calls for more beer. He strode up to the bar and leaned against it.

"What'll it be, Jake?" asked Dan, the barkeeper, congenially.

"Where's Parnell? I need to talk to him."

Dan tugged at one end of his long mustache speculatively. He had seen Jake McCullough's temper before and knew from the grim set of the miner's mouth that his current state of mind didn't bode well for Yancy Parnell.

Shrugging, Dan told himself that Parnell was a big boy and could take care of himself. He was not about to bring McCullough's wrath down on his head by refusing to reveal Yancy's whereabouts. "Hmmm, let's see now. He was here a while ago, but I think he went upstairs with Emma. Just a second, Jake, I'll check."

Dan turned and walked down to the end of the bar where Rena Roland was plying her trade with a young miner who'd just struck a rich vein. "Hey, Rena! Go up to Emma's room and tell her there's someone down here who wants to see Yancy."

Rena flung the barkeeper a disgusted sneer, angry at being called away from the wealthy miner before she had a chance to entice him up to her room. As she flounced off toward the stairs, she spied Jake and detoured to his side. "Hi, Jake, lookin' for me?" she purred.

"Nope. Lookin' for your boss and I think you're supposed to go fetch him for me."

Except for his last visit to her room, which had ended disastrously, Rena had never had a man who was as good in bed as Jake McCullough. She had long harbored the hope that, someday, Jake would see her as something more than a saloon woman for hire, and she was distressed and annoyed at his indifference. "Sure thing, honey. I guess you wouldn't be interested in seein' me. I forgot that you can't . . . well, you know what I mean." The words dripped from her lips in a sarcastic drawl.

He ignored her insult and replied in a bored tone, "Just go get Parnell, Rena."

She turned away in a huff and sashayed up the stairs, swinging her hips provocatively in one last attempt to catch Jake's attention. But he turned away in disgust, wondering what he had ever found attractive about the woman.

A few minutes later, she reappeared and coldly directed Jake up to Emma's room. He took the stairs two at a time, anxious to have it out with Parnell. When he knocked on the door, however, it was neither this Emma person nor Yancy Parnell who met him, but Roxie Wilson.

"Jake, come in!" the redhead greeted him. "Yancy isn't here right now, but maybe I can help you."

Somewhat confused, Jake stepped inside the door and looked around in surprise at the rich, tasteful furnishings. Removing his hat, his gaze scanned the homey room. "I was supposed to see someone named Emma, Roxie, but you seem to know why I'm here, so I guess it doesn't matter. I can't wait, though, so I'd be obliged if you'd give Parnell a message for me."

Emma smiled at his confusion. "I *am* Emma, Jake. I don't use the name Roxie anymore; it's just plain Emma Wilson now. I'm not workin' at the saloon anymore, either. I guess Felicity didn't tell you. Now then, you said you were in a hurry. What message do you want me to give Yancy?"

As surprised as he was to hear that Roxie was now called Emma and no longer worked the floor below, he brushed the news aside. He was too impatient to relay his warning to Parnell and get back to St. Patrick's to worry about Roxie's new name and status. An intimidating frown darkened his handsome features, causing her to suck in her breath in alarm.

"Just tell Parnell that the next time he tries to kill me, he should come face me like a man. Maybe, that way, he'll get the job done right."

She gasped at his accusation and took a shaky step back from his menacing presence. "Someone tried to kill you and you think it was Yancy? There must be some mistake, Jake. I know Yancy hasn't led the most honest life, but murder? No, you're wrong. Why do you think Yancy tried to kill you, anyway?"

"Silver, Roxie, pure and simple. He's tried to talk me into sellin' my mine to him ever since I got back from England last summer. And, before that, he tried to buy out my pa."

"Maybe, Jake, but that's hardly a reason to suspect a man of attempted murder!"

"There's more to it than that," he snapped. "I went up to my claim in January to check some things out and found a little surprise waitin' for me. As soon as I got back into the mine a ways, there was an explosion that came damn close to killin' me. If I hadn't stopped to look at somethin' I'd tripped over, I'd be a dead man. My men checked out the mine after the accident and found a charge had been mounted between some rocks near the roof. The murderer gave me just enough time to get close to the dynamite before he set it off. I figure it was the detonatin' line, buried in the dirt, that I tripped over. Funny, ain't it, that the line saved my life."

"Oh, Jake!" Her face was ashen. "I can't believe this! Why would anybody want to kill you? I remember the day Felicity came to town to visit me and she told me you planned to go to the mine the next day. But Jake, Yancy was with me all that week. He never left town, and that's a fact. Besides that, he and I are leavin' here in the spring, so why would he still be wantin' to buy the Silver Lady?"

"I don't know, Roxie," he growled. "But, for a

man who's plannin' to leave Colorado, he's been damn persistent. Maybe you better ask him that question.''

"Jake, you've got to believe me," she pleaded. "I know Yancy didn't try to kill you. I just know it!''

"Maybe he didn't do it personally, Roxie, but there's no doubt in my mind that he was behind it," he returned tightly. ''There's not many people who knew I'd be up at the mine that day. I figure Felicity told you and you innocently told Parnell.''

"I might have mentioned it to him," she admitted. "I don't rightly recall. But I still don't believe Yancy was involved.''

Jake slammed his hat back on his head, discounting her continued defense of the gambler. "I gotta go. Felicity's waitin' at the church and I don't want her gettin' impatient and startin' down the street by herself. I'm sorry if I upset you, Roxie, but it couldn't be helped.''

She nodded absently and moved to open the door. Turning back toward Jake, she looked at him curiously. ''Did you say Felicity's waitin' for you at the church? What's she doin' at church in the middle of the week?''

Jake smiled and relaxed. "Since you and Felicity are such good friends, I guess there's no harm in tellin' you. Felicity and I are gettin' married soon. That's the one good thing that came from the attempt on my life. We had plenty of time together and both of us finally came to our senses.''

Emma's worried expression melted into a smile that wreathed her pretty features. "Married? Really?" Jake grinned proudly and nodded. "Oh, Jake, that's wonderful! I'm so happy for you both. And your baby too. Now he'll have his father's name and everythin' will be as it should.''

She kept chattering, but Jake didn't hear anything past the words "your baby" and "father's name.'' A myriad of emotions hurtled through his mind, ranging from stunned surprise to thunderous fury.

His body stiffened and he grabbed the bewildered Emma by the shoulders, giving her a rough shake. "What did you say, Roxie? *What baby?*"

The blood left her face as she realized what she'd done. Good Lord! Hadn't Felicity told the man he was going to be a father? Whatever was she waiting for? "I, ah, well . . ." She frantically searched her mind for some kind of explanation but panic entangled her thoughts and her tongue. "Well, you see, Jake, um, Felicity needed someone to confide in. Please don't tell her I told you, okay?"

He crossed his arms over his chest and glared down at the pale woman, his expression menacing. "I don't want to hear your excuses, Roxie. You've spilled the beans: now, you're gonna tell me exactly what you know."

Emma tried but failed to swallow the lump in her throat, so she simply nodded her head.

"When did Felicity tell you about this?" he demanded furiously.

"Jan . . . January," she squeaked.

"January!" Jake thundered. "She's known she's gonna have a baby since January and she hasn't told me? Even after . . ." His voice trailed off as it suddenly dawned on him that if he hadn't asked Felicity to marry him, she would have gone back East, leaving him totally ignorant of his child. "That heartless little bitch!" he exploded. "I swear, I'm gonna wring her neck!" Spinning on his heel, he yanked the door open and stomped down the hall toward the stairs.

"Jake!" cried Emma desperately as she rushed after him. "Come back! Let me explain! You don't understand!"

He never broke stride as he threw back over his shoulder, "I know all I need to know. She was gonna leave Silverton carryin' *my* baby and I never would've known. God *damn* her!"

Emma ran after him as he charged, bull-like, down the stairs. Like the parting of the Red Sea, everyone in the saloon shrank back, clearing a path for the

man whose black countenance bore a distinctly mur-
derous expression. Unfortunately, that path filled
back in immediately, and by the time Emma had
pushed her way through the melee and reached the
wooden boardwalk outside, Jake was in his wagon
and rolling, hell-bent, down the street.

Emma headed back into the saloon, intending to
cut through the alleys in an attempt to beat Jake to
the church, but when she finally reached the back
door, she had changed her mind. Leaning against
the door frame, she took a deep breath, trying to
calm her racing heart.

Although she was concerned for Felicity, she
couldn't deny that Jake had every right to be angry.
She knew that he wouldn't hurt Felicity, no matter
how angry he was with her, and she was confident
that after he gave Felicity a much deserved tongue-
lashing, all would be well between the couple. In
fact, Emma smiled to herself, it would probably be
a most intimate and romantic evening up at that little cabin. Once he calmed down, Jake would, no
doubt, be overjoyed at the prospect of gaining a wife
and a baby all at one time.

She sighed deeply, envying the couple being able
to share the joy of what they had created together.
She only wished that she could give Yancy the same
gift. But, so far, the fates had not been kind.

She walked back into the saloon, confident that
Jake and Felicity would work out this misunderstanding without her interference. After all, she had
never seen two people more deeply in love . . .

Halfway to the church, Jake slowed the horses to
a walk. He knew he had to get control of himself.
He wasn't about to have this out with Felicity in
front of her priest and everyone on the streets of
Silverton. No, he thought, drawing a calming
breath, he'd wait until they were alone at home, but
then, by God, he'd have some answers!

Jake brought the wagon to a halt in front of St.

Patrick's, wrapped the reins around the brake, and leaped down from his seat. Felicity was just saying farewell to Father Thomas at the church's front door as he approached.

Jake offered a polite but hasty greeting to the priest and reminded Felicity of the urgency to head home before they found themselves traversing the treacherous mountain pass in the dark.

Baffled by Jake's odd behavior, Felicity cocked her head to one side and stared up at him curiously. It was still early afternoon and there was plenty of time to get safely back up the pass before darkness fell. What was the hurry? Sensing his agitation and guessing that something was wrong, she bid the priest good-bye and allowed Jake to hustle her to the wagon. She was further bemused and slightly disgruntled when Jake lifted her off the ground and practically threw her onto the wagon seat. Her eyes widened with alarm as she watched him pull himself onto the seat beside her, grab the reins, and crack the whip over the horses' backs with a vengeance. The wagon took off like a shot and nearly sent her somersaulting over the back of the seat into the wagon bed.

She was too busy holding on to attempt to find out what was wrong with Jake. The careening wagon wove through the streets at a perilous pace, sending several pedestrians scurrying out of their way and hurling angry curses after them. Jake's face was scarlet with rage and she was immensely grateful that she had done nothing to provoke his temper and wasn't the object of his wrath. Just being caught in the tail wind of his fury was bad enough! She'd never seen Jake so angry and thought it prudent to stay quiet and let him work it out in his own way. She just hoped they lived that long, as once again, they narrowly escaped collision with another wagon. She sucked her lip in and squeezed her eyes shut, praying their terrifying flight would end soon.

As they started up the pass, the rough terrain

forced Jake to slow down, allowing the wheezing horses to get their wind back. He glanced over at Felicity, noticed the terror etched on her face, and tersely announced, "You can open your eyes now, Felicity. I'm not gonna kill you."

She slowly opened her eyes and sought his with a questioning look. At his silence, she finally dared to venture a question. "Jake, did something go wrong in town?"

"Yeah, you might say that," he snarled.

"Well, for heaven's sake, what?"

He continued to brood, staring at her coldly until, finally, she tried again. "Jake, please tell me! You scare me when you're like this! What's wrong?"

"For your own sake, Felicity, just let it go until we get back to the cabin. I need some time to cool down."

"But Jake!" He flung her a warning glare, silencing her protest. Deciding that discretion was perhaps the wisest choice for the time being, Felicity kept her counsel for the remainder of the trip home.

When they finally arrived in the yard, Felicity, anxious to leave Jake to his anger, was about to jump down from the wagon when he suddenly leaped from his seat and ordered her to stay put. He stalked around to her side and gently grasped her around the waist, lowering her to the ground. He studied her face for a moment and then dropped his gaze to her waistline where his hands still rested. "Puttin' on a little weight, ain't you, Felicity?"

She was astonished at his sarcastic tone, and stared at him in complete bewilderment. She opened her mouth to reply, but he quickly dropped his hands from her waist and turned his back. "Go in the cabin and put on some coffee," he ordered. "Make it good and strong 'cause we're gonna need it."

As Felicity opened the cabin door, the cause of his foul temper hit her. She stepped inside, leaning weakly against the door after it closed. "He knows," she murmured to herself. "He knows and he's furious with me. That remark about putting on weight . . . God help me, how did he find out? Oh, Emma, you were wrong about him being happy about a baby. It's obvious that now he doesn't want either one of us."

Throwing her coat down on the settee and removing her boots, she trudged dispiritedly into the little kitchen and set the coffeepot on the stove. Mechanically, she filled it with water and threw in a large handful of beans. She lit the stove and turned around just as Jake made a noisy entrance. She froze, waiting for the storm to break.

"You got that coffee on?"

She nodded and watched apprehensively as his coat joined hers. "Come here, Felicity," he commanded quietly. Although his voice no longer sounded threatening, she hesitated. When she didn't respond, his hazel eyes riveted hers and he ordered more loudly, "I said, come and sit down. I think you have somethin' to tell me, don't you?"

With trepidation, she walked over to the settee and gingerly took a seat as far away from him as possible. "It's obvious you already know, but Jake, you must believe me. I was going to tell you!"

His bark of cynical laughter sent a cold chill shooting down her spine. "Oh, yeah? And just *when* were you plannin' to tell me, lady? When it was time to fetch the doctor? More important, what were your plans if I hadn't asked you to marry me? Were you gonna go back East and dump my child at some orphanage?"

"Oh, Jake," she gasped, "how *could* you think such a thing? I love my baby!"

"Right!" he interrupted. "There's the truth of it. *Your* baby. That's how you think of it, ain't it, Felicity? *Your* baby, not *our* baby. And just how were you plannin' to explain *your* baby to your friends in Philadelphia?"

She averted her gaze. "I was going to tell them

that I was married while I was out here but that my husband died in a mining accident; that I was a widow.''

''How convenient!'' he sneered. ''Just pretend that I'm dead and that way, you'd never have to feel guilty about robbin' me of my child.''

Her head snapped around. ''No, Jake, you're wrong,'' she insisted. ''I had decided even before you proposed that I would tell you about your child. I thought that after the baby was born and I was settled, I'd write you and let you know about him. That way, you wouldn't feel any pressure that you had to claim him. I knew you didn't want a wife and I loved you too much to make you think that I'd trapped you into marrying me.''

As he watched a tear course down her cheek, his expression softened. ''I thought you loved me, Felicity,'' he murmured. ''People who love each other don't have secrets, especially not one as important as this. Whether you want to admit it or not, that baby in there is mine too. Didn't you think I had a right to know?''

''I just didn't want you to feel trapped,'' she whispered.

''Trapped? *Trapped?*'' His anger surfaced again. ''Woman, I asked you to marry me *weeks* ago. What possible explanation can you have for not tellin' me *after* I proposed? Is it that you were never really sure you wanted to marry me? Maybe you just wanted to wait as long as possible to tell me, so if you changed your mind at the last minute, I wouldn't do anythin' to try to keep you here.''

''Please, Jake,'' she pleaded, dropping her head into her hands, ''please forgive me. You're right about everything except me not wanting to marry you. I should have told you sooner. I know that now. Father Thomas told me this morning that he wouldn't consider marrying us until you knew the truth. There just never seemed to be a good time, and the longer I waited, the harder it got. But after talking to Father this morning, I knew the time had come and, whether you believe it or not, I was going to tell you today."

He stood up and walked over to the fireplace mantel, leaning one arm against it and bowing his head in defeat. "Christ, you even told your priest before you told me. You told Roxie Wilson, you told Father Thomas. Who else did you tell, Felicity? For all I know, everybody in Silverton knows about this baby except me! Did you tell your friend Ed Banyon or were you savin' him for last? Maybe you figured that if things didn't work out between us, you could pin the fatherhood on him!"

Felicity was speechless. After a tense silence, she shook her head and said, "I think the reason I didn't tell you was that, deep inside, I expected this kind of reaction from you. You don't even believe the baby's yours."

He closed his eyes, struggling against the despair that threatened to engulf him. "I'm sorry, Felicity. I didn't mean that. I know as much as any man ever can that this baby's mine. In fact, I feel like a damn fool for not figurin' it out on my own. My God, girl, I know every detail of that sexy little body of yours. When we started makin' love again in January, I noticed you were fillin' out in places, but you never said nothin' and I just figured it was from sittin' around the cabin this winter."

She gazed into the pained hazel depths of his eyes and saw reflected there the terrible hurt she had inflicted. "What can I say, Jake?" she asked quietly. "What's done is done. I know now that I was wrong, but I wish you could believe that I never meant to hurt you. I wanted so badly to tell you. I knew I should. Even Emma told me that you deserved to know. But somehow I could just never bring myself to do it. I thought you'd hate me for being careless and feel that I'd done it on purpose to wangle a marriage proposal from you. I just didn't want you to think that."

His mouth dropped open. "You thought I'd accuse you of gettin' pregnant on purpose? What kind of man do you think I am? You didn't get this baby by yourself, and I knew every time I took you to bed that there was a chance of this happenin'. Did you honestly think I'd abandon you? Do I seem like the kind of man who would do that? Christ, Felicity, what have I ever done to you to make you think so little of me?"

Her face was a study in remorse, but she didn't answer. He waited expectantly, hoping she'd say something, *anything*, that would explain why she hadn't wanted to share this most intimate of experiences with him. What was lacking in him that made women shut him out? First his mother and now Felicity. The correlation caused his anger to erupt again.

"Damn it, Felicity!" he yelled, pounding his fist on the mantel. "I trusted you! For the first time since I was a kid, I put my heart in a woman's hands and trusted her, and this is what you do to me. I should have known. God, you *are* like my mother . . . and every other woman. You just take a man's heart and stomp on it till there's nothin' left. Well, it's the last time you'll do it to *me*, lady. I know about you now."

She looked at him tiredly and then shrugged. "If that's the way it is, Jake, then there's no hope for us. If you feel you can't trust me, then you obviously can't love me either. And I love you far too much to accept anything less from you. I think it would be best if we both admitted that marriage would be a tragic mistake and just end this torture now." Felicity stood up, and, with great dignity, walked toward the bedroom.

"We've had this argument before, Felicity, and my mind hasn't changed, I'm not leavin'," he bellowed.

"You don't have to," she responded softly. "*I'm* leaving."

"Felicity," Jake warned, "don't close that door. We gotta settle this!"

She looked at him over her shoulder and said with resignation, "No, Jake. There's nothing more to say. We were doomed from the start. I'm just glad we found out before it was too late."

Jake's head throbbed with pain, anger, and frustration. "Yeah, well, if that's the way you feel, then so am I, *Miss Howard*. All I want to know is where the hell you think you're gonna go?"

"I'll stay in town with Emma until the train starts running again. Then, I'm returning to Philadelphia. We'll decide what to do about the baby before I leave, but after I'm gone, please don't try to see me or contact me, Jake. I'll send you an address where you can send my share of the mine's profits, or perhaps it would be better if I tried to sell my half before I leave Silverton. That way, we can avoid having any further contact with each other."

"Fine!" Jake shouted. "I don't care what you do or where you go as long as you're out of my life! You've screwed me up for the last time, lady, and I don't care if I ever see you again, either."

She winced at his words, but lifted her chin a notch and closed the bedroom door. Once in the privacy of the room, her silent tears fell as she again filled her well-worn bag with her meager belongings. A defeated smile flitted across her face. How many times had she packed and unpacked this same bag since arriving at this cabin? Well, this was the last time. It was really over between them. This rift was just too big to ever be mended. She should have known that it would never work between her and Jake. The nuns had always said that you couldn't hold onto a tiger's tail, and Jake was a tiger if ever there was one. She had been foolishly naive to think that she had the power to tame him.

A half hour later, she dropped her valise next to the settee and drew on her coat. Jake was not in the cabin and she was grateful for this small reprieve. She didn't think she could bear to look into his handsome, beloved face ever again. She pulled on her boots, picked up her bag, and without a single backward glance, left her home and all the dreams that had once filled it.

As she pulled a saddle down from the rack in the lean-to, a huge hand clamped down on hers. "Just what do you think you're doin'?" The chill in Jake's voice was every bit as frosty as the nip of the mountain air.

She refused to look up at him and kept her eyes on the rough, weathered hand covering hers. In a small voice, she replied, "I'm leaving. Surely you're not going to force me to walk into town. If you're worried that I might steal one of your horses, don't be. I swear to you that I'll leave him at the livery or make arrangements for someone to bring him back here."

"You can't take my horse," he said flatly. "I need him here and I can't wait for someone to bring him back up the pass."

She nodded. "All right, then. Would it be all right if I borrowed a pair of the snowshoes?"

He released her hand and watched dispassionately as she pulled on the heavy snowshoes, picked up her valise, and tramped clumsily out of the lean-to. His heart stopped when she slipped and almost fell. Cursing, he struck out across the yard after her.

Without warning, Felicity felt herself being swept off her feet in his muscular arms. "What are you doing?" she shrieked. "Put me down this instant!" She squirmed, kicking and fighting him, but she was powerless against his strength. Her struggles ended abruptly when she found herself rudely flung onto the wagon seat.

"Just stay there," Jake snarled. "Don't move, don't talk, don't do nothin'." He disappeared into the lean-to and returned leading both wagon horses. Making short work of hitching the team, he threw himself onto the seat next to her. At her furious glare, he growled, "You may not give a damn, but I'm not lettin' you take any chances with *my* baby.

You want to break a leg after he's born, that's your business, but while you're carryin' him, *you'll be careful!''*

''Don't you tell me what to do!'' Felicity raged.

He glared at her as if he could strangle her. ''I told you before, Felicity. Don't move and don't talk. Just shut up and enjoy the ride!''

She felt an overwhelming desire to punch him in the stomach, but knowing the futility of such a childish gesture, she kept her clenched fists tucked beneath the blanket he had wrapped around her and stared straight ahead.

Chapter 20

Yancy Parnell threw down his pen and frowned at the avalanche of paperwork cluttering his desk. "That damn bookkeeper of mine is worthless," he muttered. "Look at this mess. I'll never get through it if I work for the next ten years!"

Shaking his head in annoyance, he checked his pocket watch and rose from his chair, blowing out the lamp on the corner of the desk. He walked out of the office and locked the door behind him. He had ordered a sumptuous dinner from the Grand Hotel and it would be delivered any moment. With the early lessening of winter's grip, the Last Chance was booming and he hadn't had the opportunity to spend an evening alone with Emma in days. Yancy was sure she would be delighted with his plans and strode eagerly toward the staircase.

Halfway across the saloon, he spied a waiter from the hotel carrying a large covered tray. With a pleased smile, Yancy beckoned the man to follow him up the stairs.

Reaching Emma's room with the waiter close behind him, Yancy knocked briefly and pushed open the door. "Em? Look what I've got for you. Baby, are we gonna have a night . . ." His words faded as Emma whirled toward him with a stricken look. Behind her, sitting at the small table, was Felicity

Howard, and from the looks of her tearstained face, something was very wrong.

"What's going on here?" asked Yancy.

"Nothin'!" Emma assured him, pushing him backward into the hall. Just before the door slammed shut, Yancy peered over Emma's shoulder and caught the briefest glimpse of Felicity hiding her face and crying.

"Emma," Yancy demanded as they stood facing each other in the hall, "*what* is going on?"

"I can't tell you here!" Emma hissed. "Let's go to your room and I'll explain."

"But I have dinner here!" Yancy protested, gesturing to the waiter who stood patiently holding his heavily laden tray. "I thought we'd eat in your room and spend a romantic evening together!"

"Well, we can't do anythin' in my room!" Emma exclaimed in exasperation. "Have the man bring the food to your room, but for heaven's sake let's get out of the hall before Felicity hears us!"

Yancy's lips thinned in annoyance, but he dutifully followed Emma as she swept into his room, motioning the laboring waiter to follow.

The couple stood by silently as the waiter unloaded his tray onto the bureau and took his leave. Yancy frowned at the platters spread before them and muttered, "This certainly isn't how I imagined this evening was going to go."

"I'm sorry, Yancy." Emma sighed. "I didn't mean to throw you out of my room, but I didn't want to embarrass Felicity."

He summoned a resigned smile. "Well, as long as this food is here, why don't we eat while you tell me what's happened?"

She nodded and uncovered the platters, filling a plate with venison, mashed potatoes, and creamed onions, and handed it to Yancy.

"Aren't you going to eat?" Yancy asked irritably. "We haven't had a meal together in days and I thought you'd enjoy something special."

"I know, and it was very sweet of you," she replied, "but I'm so upset I just can't think about food right now. You go ahead, though. I'll just have a glass of this wine." Uncorking the bottle, Emma filled two glasses and headed for the settee where Yancy sat, precariously balancing his plate on his knees.

"Okay, Em," he said as he took a large bite of meat, "suppose you tell me what's going on. I know it has something to do with Felicity, but why are *you* so upset? You look like you've just lost your last friend."

"Well, I haven't," she said despondently, "but I deserve to. Felicity's whole life is ruined and it's my fault!"

His fork paused in midair. "Your fault? What in blazes are you talking about? Quit pacing and come over here. I want you to tell me exactly what's happened."

She obeyed, sitting down on the settee. "I don't even know where to start," she groaned.

"How about the beginning?" Yancy suggested dryly. "Tell me what's wrong with Felicity."

"Do you remember when Felicity came to visit me in January?" Emma asked.

"Vaguely. Why?"

"Well, she came to ask for my help. You see, she's gonna have Jake McCullough's baby and she wanted to stay with me until the train started runnin' so she could leave town."

"What?" Yancy exclaimed in disbelief. "Felicity's pregnant? Why, that low-down bastard . . . and he has the nerve to say that I'm no good? He ought to be horsewhipped! And I think I'm the one who's going to do it!"

Emma arched a brow at his vehement outburst. "Before you go off to avenge our little friend, you better know that she wasn't exactly unwillin'. Felicity's in love with Jake, and if you lay a hand on him, she'll come after you tooth and nail."

"I don't care who she *thinks* she's in love with," he growled. "That bastard seduced her, didn't he?"

"Calm down, Yancy!" Emma implored. "You've got this whole thing wrong. Just be quiet a minute and let me explain."

"Okay, but this better be good," he warned, "or I swear that bastard's going to know the end of my whip."

Emma explained everything that had transpired between Jake and Felicity, from their night spent at the Grand Hotel to Felicity's sudden and distressing appearance at Emma's door that afternoon.

His meal forgotten, Yancy swallowed the last of his wine as she finished her tale. "You mean the wedding is off, just like that?"

"Yeah, and it's all my fault. If I hadn't opened my big mouth, Felicity would've had time to tell Jake about the baby. Now he thinks she was tryin' to hide it from him."

"They're both acting like a couple of jackasses," Yancy said. "But, Em, you're not to blame. It was only natural for you to assume that Felicity had told Jake about the baby."

She looked unconvinced, but said, "Maybe you're right, sugar, but I still feel awful. Anyway, what do you think we should do to help Felicity?"

"Do?" he shrugged. "God, I don't know. What can we do? Give her a place to stay until the train starts running again, then send her on her way. That's what she wants, isn't it?"

She shot him a look of exasperation. "Yancy Parnell! You haven't listened to a word I've said! That's what she *thinks* she wants. But I keep tryin' to tell you, she's *in love* with Jake."

"Well, the first thing you should do," he advised, "is stay clean out of this mess and let them figure it out themselves. They're the only ones who can solve their differences. Besides, unless they work things out, I think Felicity's decision to leave is a good one. She can't stay here in Silverton with a bastard baby.

Why, the old biddies in this town would make mincemeat of her—and Felicity isn't the type who could stand that. Besides, once we're gone, she's not going to have any real friends here, so why would she stay?''

"But, Yancy," Emma protested, "she ain't got nothin' to go back to. No family, no home. What's she gonna do?''

He pulled her into his embrace, gently pressing her head against his chest and stroking her hair. "I don't know," he admitted. "But everything will work out. You'll see. Hell, if worse comes to worst, we'll take her to New Orleans with us and help her get set up in a little house down there." Suddenly realizing the soundness of his suggestion, he exclaimed, "Say, Em, that's not such a bad idea! It's not like she's penniless. That mine of hers and Jake's is making a little money despite the bad luck they've had.''

Emma suddenly sat up. "Oh, my God, Yancy, that reminds me! I have a message for you from Jake.''

He threw her a wary glance. "Message? What message?''

"Oh, Yancy, I'm sorry, I should've told you this before. I've just been so upset about Felicity that I plum forgot till now.''

"For God's sake, Emma, what is it?" Yancy demanded.

"Jake told me to tell you that the next time you try to kill him, you should come and meet him like a man. Yancy, what in tarnation did he mean?''

Although she was convinced that he was innocent of any wrongdoing, she was greatly relieved to see the look of complete shock that washed across Yancy's face. His surprise, however, quickly transformed itself into anger.

"How could you forget to tell me something like that?" he shouted. "Jesus, Emma! What's wrong with you?''

Ignoring his outburst, Emma reached for his hand and clutched it to her breast. "I told Jake he must be wrong, that you wouldn't try to murder anybody, but he wouldn't listen. He said you've been tryin' to buy the Silver Lady off him *and* his pa for months and that since they both refused to sell, you must've gotten impatient. Is that true, Yancy? Have you been tryin' to buy his mine?"

"Sure, I tried to buy his mine," Yancy admitted. "It butts up to the Dead Horse and I figured I'd get a higher price when I want to sell if I owned the rights to the whole slope."

Emma knew little about the mining business but Yancy's explanation sounded logical. Still, a question nagged at the back of her mind and she approached it in her usual direct manner. "If all you did was offer to buy his mine, why does he suspect you?"

Yancy grappled desperately for a plausible answer. As far as he knew, Jake had no knowledge that he was involved in the accidents at the Silver Lady, but Emma's question was disconcerting anyway. Finally, he lifted a shoulder in a careless shrug and answered evasively, "Jake McCullough is a hotheaded fool, Emma. You've seen how he's treated Felicity. Maybe he figured that I wanted his mine bad enough to kill him for it. You and I both know that isn't true, but he's enough of a jackass to think it."

He silently prayed that she wouldn't doubt his explanation or ask too many questions. He hated lying to her, but he knew that if she was aware he'd masterminded the accidents at the Silver Lady, she'd never leave Silverton with him. Emma had a sense of integrity unequaled by anyone he had ever known and she'd never tolerate his duplicity.

Remembering his last meeting with Jed Croft, Yancy had a sinking feeling that he knew exactly who had tried to murder McCullough. Jed must have gotten impatient and decided to take matters into his own hands. Yancy's angry expression reflected this new, grim possibility.

Emma saw the fury in his face and gasped, "Yancy, whatever are you thinkin' about? Do you know somethin' about this attempt on Jake's life?"

Cursing the momentary lapse of his poker face, Yancy relaxed his features and assumed a bland smile. "No, Em, I don't know anything. It just makes me mad as hell to be accused of doing something I had no part in."

She smiled and leaned back against Yancy's chest again. "I understand why you're mad, but please don't do anythin' to rile Jake. I don't want anythin' to happen to you, and I'm afraid he's spoilin' for a fight."

"I won't," he quietly assured her. "You can count on nothing happening to me, honey."

She sighed with relief and reluctantly stood up. "I suppose I should get back to Felicity," she said, regretfully.

Yancy also rose and pulled her against his lean body, pressing her hips against his seductively. "Don't go, baby," he whispered. "Stay with me tonight. Felicity needs to be alone and I need you here."

A shudder of anticipation ran through Emma and she quickly cast aside her guilt at abandoning Felicity. Lifting her gaze to Yancy's smoldering eyes, she parted trembling lips in anticipation of his kiss. His mouth met hers in a devouring caress that caused her to moan and move closer, her desire quickly building to a feverish pitch.

Releasing her, he gazed into her limpid eyes and chuckled rakishly. "May I take that for a yes, sweet woman?"

Without a word, she pulled him toward his big bed and drew back the covers.

The next morning dawned bright and clear, but the beauty of the day was lost on Felicity. For more than an hour she had sat at Emma's little table, staring forlornly out the window. Emma had returned very early to bathe and dress, asking Felicity if she wanted to accompany her to Gunderson's store. But having just suffered through her habitual bout of morning nausea, Felicity had glumly shaken her head and declined the invitation.

Now she wished she had gone. What was she going to do with herself all day? Up at the cabin, her days had been filled with an endless parade of chores. But here in Emma's small room, there was very little to occupy her. She knew that if she didn't get up and do something, her mind would stray to Jake, and those thoughts would only worsen the anguish she was already feeling.

With an air of purpose, she pushed herself out of the chair and began searching for a cleaning rag. Determined not to give into depression, she vigorously attacked the dusty knickknacks scattered throughout the room, thinking wryly that housekeeping was obviously not Emma's strong suit.

She had barely begun her task, however, when a knock sounded at the door. Knowing Emma wouldn't knock, and remembering her warning about the possibility of opening the door to a drunken customer, Felicity called out warily, "Who's there?"

"Yancy," came the immediate reply. "May I come in and talk to you for a minute, Felicity?" She slumped in disappointment, realizing that she'd hoped it was Jake on the other side of the portal. Silently deriding herself for the foolish notion, she opened the door and ushered Yancy into the room with a cheerful, if somewhat strained, smile.

Yancy bent down and placed a brotherly kiss on her cheek, taking her completely by surprise. "How are you doing, honey?" He grinned at her flustered expression. "You know, Felicity, I think even if you live to be a hundred, you'll still be a modest little convent girl."

"I can't help it," she protested, laughing. "It's handsome rogues like you that always catch me off guard."

Yancy took her elbow, leading her over to the settee. "Maybe you'd like me to teach you how to put on a poker face."

She nodded eagerly. "Oh, would you?"

His shoulders trembled with mirth as he shook his head. "No! I like you just the way you are. Besides, you women already have too many little tricks to use on us men. Why should I give you more ammunition?"

As always, Felicity found herself enjoying their light banter. "Yancy, you're a devil, but I'm glad you came to see me. I've been moping around all morning and in two minutes, you've got me laughing. From that first, awful day when I arrived in Silverton, you and Emma have taken care of me. I don't know how I could ever repay either one of you."

Yancy was embarrassed by her heartfelt remarks. Compliments had been a rare commodity in his life and he'd never quite learned how to accept them gracefully. "I don't know, Felicity, there's just something about you that brings out the white knight in me. Now, come sit down," he said, sobering, "there's a couple of important things I need to discuss with you."

Her mood greatly improved, she sank down on the settee, daintily crossing her legs and settling her hands over one knee. "What do you want to talk about, Yancy?" she asked earnestly.

Suddenly unsure of how to proceed, he swallowed and cleared his throat, casting about for a tactful way to broach the delicate subject. "Felicity, I don't want to embarrass you, but Emma told me about your . . . your circumstances."

She caught her breath, wishing the floor would swallow her up. She knew Yancy was a friend, but he was, after all, also a man. A lady just did *not* discuss such a personal topic with a member of the opposite sex, especially when the lady was in as awkward a situation as she was.

"Please," Yancy coaxed, "don't be embarrassed. You have no reason to feel ashamed, especially with Emma and me. We both care very much about you. I think you know that."

She nodded, but couldn't bring herself to look him in the eye. She stared at the dwindling embers in the fireplace and listened intently as he continued. "You aren't the first girl to fall in love with the wrong man, Felicity, and there's no reason for you to punish yourself for the rest of your life. God knows, life is too short for that!"

Felicity threw him a fleeting smile.

"Anyway," he went on, "Emma and I have been talking, and—well, we want to help you any way we can. That's why we thought you might like to go to New Orleans with us. It would be a damn shame, er, sorry, a *crying* shame for you to go back to Philadelphia where you'd be all alone. With all of us in the same place, you'd know you have friends who care about you and your baby."

Felicity stared at him in astonished gratitude. "Oh, Yancy!" she exclaimed. "That's so generous of you! But I'd never dream of imposing on you and Emma like that."

"Nonsense!" He waved aside her protest. "New Orleans will be new and strange to Emma and she'll be much more comfortable with a friend in town. Anyway, you wouldn't be imposing on us. We'd help you set up housekeeping in a little place of your own. You'd have your privacy and we'd have ours."

"It sounds very tempting," she confessed. "I'll give it some serious thought."

"Good." Yancy beamed. "And while you're thinking about that, think about this as well. I'd like to buy your share of the Silver Lady. Just name a price that you consider fair."

"Oh, Yancy, I don't know! I mean, well, I had thought about selling my share, but you know how

Jake feels about you! What kind of partnership could you two possibly have?''

''Not a friendly one, I admit, but I'll be down in New Orleans most of the time anyway. And our partnership wouldn't last long if everything works out the way I have it planned. Eventually, I'm looking to offer Jake a reasonable deal to let him purchase my share of the Silver Lady along with my Dead Horse mine. It backs up to the Silver Lady, Felicity, and it's only good business sense to join the two.'' A twinge of guilt rippled through him at how easily the half-truths were slipping off his tongue, but he forged on. ''Well, Miss Howard, what do you say?''

''I know Jake can't afford to buy both your mine and the other half of the Silver Lady just now,'' Felicity warned. ''You could be tying your money up for a long time, and won't you need everything you have to get established in New Orleans?''

''Yes, eventually,'' Yancy agreed. ''But I'll have money from the sale of the Last Chance, too. That will get us by for the time being, plenty long enough for Jake to raise the money he needs to buy me out.'' Again, Yancy's guilt surfaced. He hated being less than truthful with this trusting girl, but how could he let a fortune slip through his fingers when it was so close at hand? He and Emma could live like royalty if he could swing this deal. Besides, he comforted himself, Felicity needed money *now*. And finally, even if he *wanted* to back out of the swindle, he couldn't. He and Jed Croft were already in up to their necks with the plan to gain control of the Silver Lady. If Jed was behind the attempt on McCullough's life—and Yancy was convinced he was—then the foreman wouldn't be above implicating him as well. No, Yancy told himself, he'd gotten himself into this quagmire, and he'd have to see it through. Once McCullough hit that silver lode, Yancy knew he'd never sell the Silver Lady. Besides, its value would be so high that nobody would be able to afford it. He had to consummate this deal now.

"Well," Felicity demurred, "your offer sounds reasonable enough, but I have to think about it. It seems only fair that I offer to sell my share to Jake first, don't you think?"

"Fair?" barked Yancy. "You're worried about fair? Has Jake been fair with you, Felicity? I'd say McCullough has taken you for just about everything he could get from you . . . including your innocence. The way I see it, you don't owe that bastard a damn thing!"

Felicity hung her head, unable to face the indignation in Yancy's voice. Although her mind reasoned that what he was saying was true, in her heart she knew she couldn't betray Jake. He was the father of her child and, despite everything, she loved him.

Still, it did make sense to sell her half of the Silver Lady to someone. Felicity knew she should try to sever all ties with Jake. Why torture herself with prolonging their relationship? But sell to Yancy? She knew Jake would never forgive her for placing half his mine into the hands of a man he considered his enemy. But if Jake couldn't afford to buy her out, who else would? The chilling incidents that had taken place the previous fall had given the Silver Lady a bad reputation with the miners in town, and Felicity doubted that anyone would come forward with a decent offer for her. Who, besides Yancy, would be willing to take a chance on what seemed to be a jinxed operation? Suddenly, her options seemed to be more limited than she had first considered.

With new resolve, she turned to him and said, "You're right, Yancy. Selling my half of the mine before I leave Silverton seems like the only sensible thing to do. But you must allow me a few days to think over your offer. I have to be positive in my own mind that this is what I want. I promise you though, that while I'm making up my mind, I'll also do some concrete figuring and come up with what I believe is a fair price."

Encouraged by her promise, Yancy stood and drew her up with him. "Thank you, Felicity. That's all I ask. I want to be totally fair with you, too. Of course you can have a few days to make up your mind. That's only good business."

Walking to the door, Yancy paused and studied Felicity closely. "You're a wonderful woman, Felicity," he said in a quiet voice. "Never, ever forget that."

Before Felicity could reply, he was gone.

A week passed quietly. Felicity spent her days sewing baby clothes and trying to make some rational decisions on how to reconstruct the shambles of her life.

Earlier in the week, she'd had an experience that affected her more than any business decision ever could. She had, for the first time, felt the tiny movements of her baby, and that gentle fluttering had suddenly brought the full reality of her predicament home to her. She was too far advanced in her pregnancy to safely leave Silverton and make the arduous journey to either Philadelphia or New Orleans. She still hadn't decided whether she was going to return to Pennsylvania or join Yancy and Emma in Louisiana, but, regardless of the destination she chose, she knew she was going nowhere until after the baby's birth in August. She only hoped that the ensuing months would pass quickly and that Jake would continue to leave her alone. So far, she had neither seen nor heard from him, and although she missed him desperately, she knew it was better this way.

Emma was concerned about Felicity's silence and lack of interest in her surroundings. She repeatedly encouraged Felicity to join her and Yancy for dinner at the hotel but Felicity stubbornly refused, preferring to eat her meals alone in Emma's room.

It was a Wednesday morning in mid-March. Felicity sat in her wrapper at the little table by the window, mechanically nibbling a roll left over from the previous night's meal. When a knock came at the door, she looked up with trepidation, hoping it wasn't Yancy wanting to hear her decision about the mine. "Who is it?" she called.

"It's Jake, Felicity. I have to talk to you."

Her heart leaped into her throat and her mouth suddenly felt dry as cotton. "Go away, please. I don't want to see you."

"Felicity, please let me in." His voice was louder. "I need to talk to you. It's important."

She crossed the room and stood close to the door. "No, Jake." She hoped he couldn't hear the trembling in her voice. "There isn't anything for us to talk about. Just go away."

"Damn it, Felicity, if you don't open this door right now, I'm gonna kick it in!"

She released a tremulous sigh and slowly pulled the door open. Her surprise at Jake's appearance was evident. He was dressed in the same dark suit he had worn for his birthday dinner. His boots were polished to a high sheen and he held his good hat in his hand.

Striding into the room, he looked her up and down matter-of-factly and said, "Get dressed. There's a meetin' we have to go to. Put on that green dress of yours and hurry. We're late already."

She threw him a withering look. "I have no intention of going anywhere with you. I can't imagine what meeting could possibly be taking place that would involve me. If it's something to do with the mine, I am no longer interested. I have decided to sell my share of the Silver Lady to Yancy Parnell."

Jake smiled coolly. "You haven't sold out to Parnell yet, have you?" She shook her head. "Well then, I guess you're still my business partner. Somethin's come up that needs our attention and we both have to see to it. Now, quit arguin' and get dressed. I told you, we're already late."

In a voice laced with exasperation, she asked, "Just how do you expect me to dress with you in the room?"

He chuckled. "Well, it wouldn't be the first time I've seen you without your clothes, but if it will make you get movin', I'll wait in the hall. Just hurry up."

Before she could utter another protest, he left, slamming the door behind him. She heard his body hit the wall outside as he leaned against it.

Never in her life had Felicity moved so quickly. She knew she should refuse to accompany Jake anywhere, should stay as far away from him as possible, but she was so overjoyed to see him that she couldn't dress fast enough. Even if it was just a legal meeting at Mr. Ford's office, it would give her a chance to be near him. She had spent the past week trying to convince herself that she was over him and didn't care if she ever saw him again. But the moment he swept into her room, filling it with his huge presence, all her anger and resentment had flown. She loved him, and even though she knew there was no future for them, she would seize whatever opportunities she could to be with him.

She was brushing her hair, trying to decide whether she should take time to pin it up, when he knocked again. "For God's sake, Felicity," he bellowed, "let's go! You *must* be ready by now."

She flung the hairbrush onto the dresser and paused one last moment to pin the cameo brooch he had given her for Christmas to the high collar of her dress. Then, grabbing her reticule and shawl, she opened the door and stepped into the hall.

Jake's eyes were immediately drawn to the brooch. He smiled but said nothing except, "You look just right. I'm glad you left your hair down."

Felicity threw him a bewildered glance and was

about to ask him why he cared how she looked when he grabbed her hand, pulling her toward the staircase and saying, "Come on. We ain't got time to stand here and chat."

She dug her heels in and wrenched her hand out of his grasp. "Jake, I want to know where we're going and what the rush is. I'm not taking another step until you tell me what this is all about."

He slammed his hat on his head and threw her a look of sheer exasperation. "Please, Felicity, just come with me. I'll explain everythin' to you on the way there. We really don't have time to stand here and discuss this. It's a meetin' we have to go to and like I keep tellin' you, we're late. For once in your life, don't argue, just come on."

She sighed in resignation. "Oh, all right," she said. "But as soon as we get in the wagon, I expect a complete explanation."

"Yeah, you'll get it," he responded with a grin. Taking her hand again, he quickly ushered her down the staircase and out the front door. Seizing her by the waist, he tossed her up onto the wagon seat, then ran around the back of the conveyance and jumped up next to her. He grabbed the reins and flicked them hard over the horses' backs, causing the team to take off with a bone-jarring jolt.

She grabbed the seat on either side of her and held on for dear life as they flew down Greene Street and rounded the corner onto Tenth. As they pulled up in front of St. Patrick's, Jake hauled back on the reins and brought the wagon to a shuddering halt.

As if they'd just completed a leisurely Sunday drive, he turned to her and, in a nonchalant tone, said, "Here we are."

Felicity was by now truly angry. "How dare you, Jake McCullough? You force your way into my room, demand that I get dressed and go with you to God knows where, then throw me in this wagon and scare me to death with one of your daredevil driving demonstrations. Then you calmly pull up in front of my church and say, 'Here we are'? Well, I don't know what your important meeting is, but I want no part of it. I'm going back to Emma's.''

As she turned to jump down from the wagon seat, he gently grasped her arm. ''No, you're not goin' back to Emma's. Not yet. You want an explanation? Okay, I'll give it to you. When I said we're here, I meant we're here. You're gonna get out of this wagon, walk into this church, and marry me. Right now. Today. There ain't gonna be any of our discussions, no negotiations, no arguments. I love you, you're totin' my baby around inside you, and you're gonna marry me now.''

She stared at him so long that he finally lowered his eyes. ''Please, Felicity,'' he said quietly, ''please marry me. I want you to be my wife. I want you to come back up to the cabin and live with me for the rest of my life. I want to have this baby and about twenty more. I love you so much, honey, you just gotta say yes. I almost went crazy this last week without you. I even missed you yellin' at me for eatin' too much and gettin' your clean floor dirty. Please, Felicity. I don't ever want to be without you again.''

When she still remained silent, he sighed deeply and tried once more. ''Look, sweetheart, I'm sorry if I was too rough with you this mornin'. I was just so damn scared that you'd say you didn't want to marry me that I figured I better not give you the chance to think about it. I didn't mean to make you mad. I just want you so bad that I guess I went a little crazy. But you gotta believe me, Felicity. I want to marry you more than I've ever wanted anythin' in my whole life.''

The silence lengthened and lengthened until he shook his head and stared down at the reins he still held. ''Guess your not answerin' means no, huh?''

Suddenly a dam broke loose inside her. She launched herself across the wagon seat into his arms and burst into tears. She almost unseated him as she crawled across his lap in her impatience to kiss him. As he struggled to regain his balance and control the suddenly nervous team, Felicity buried her hands in his hair, pulled his head toward her, and rained kisses all over his face, laughing and sobbing. "I love you, Jake McCullough, and if you still want me after everything that's happened, then, yes, I'll marry you right this minute!"

"*Want* you?" Jake shouted. "*Want you?*" With a look of pure joy, he dropped the horses' reins, and, wrapping his arms around her shoulders to hold her on his lap, kissed her until her head swam.

The front door of the church opened and the couple was startled apart by a discreet "Ahem." Turning sheepishly toward Father Thomas, Felicity and Jake tried desperately to right their clothes and gather the shreds of their dignity. The priest smiled benignly. "Good morning, Miss Howard, Mr. McCullough." Nodding to Jake, he continued with a smile, "I see that Miss Howard has agreed to the marriage. I think, by the look of things, it would be best if we proceed immediately."

Felicity turned crimson with embarrassment but Jake laughed heartily and said, "I think you're right, Father. The sooner the better." He leaped down and swung her off the wagon seat, meeting her reproving glare with a wide grin. "Come along, my dear. We have a weddin' to attend."

A half hour later, Felicity Anne Howard became Mrs. Jacob Joseph McCullough. Although her wedding was attended only by two strangers called in to be witnesses, she knew there was never a happier bride. She stared up at Jake as he solemnly repeated his wedding vows and felt as if her heart would burst. He had done all this for her. He had come into town, met with the priest, arranged for the ceremony, dressed in his best clothes, and claimed his bride in an unforgettable manner. Felicity thought this had to be the most beautiful, romantic wedding she had ever attended . . . and it was hers. This devastatingly handsome man standing next to her was her husband. Hers to love for the rest of her life. Her happiness was complete. She had a husband, a home, and a baby on the way. She raised her eyes heavenward and, as the priest blessed their union, silently thanked God for giving her more than she had ever dreamed possible.

Chapter 21

❝**H**ey, Parnell, wait up! I gotta talk to you.❞
Heading toward his office, Yancy pulled up short. He looked over his shoulder to see Jed Croft shouldering his way through the crowd in the saloon. With a silent groan, Yancy pasted on a smile and stepped forward to greet his unwelcome guest. He'd known that Croft was bound to turn up and that he must confront the man concerning Jake McCullough's allegations. Still, he dreaded this confrontation. He was belatedly realizing that he'd misjudged Croft from the beginning. The man was insane with greed and would obviously stop at nothing in his quest for wealth.

He gave Jed's back a friendly slap. "Just the man I want to see," his voice boomed enthusiastically. "Come on back to my office." Croft grinned and let Yancy lead him away from the noisy din of the saloon and down the dim hallway to his office.

As the door closed, Jed seated himself in front of Yancy's desk and extracted a long cigar from his vest pocket. "Care for a smoke?" he offered.

"No." Yancy suddenly became terse. Leaning on the edge of his desk, he eyed Croft speculatively. "Glad you finally made it into town, Jed. Something's come up that I want to discuss with you."

Croft lit his cigar, then blew out the match and

tossed it carelessly to the floor. "Oh, yeah? What's that, boss?"

Yancy dropped his congenial facade. "For starters, how about your attempt to blow Jake Mc-Cullough to smithereens? And don't bother telling me you weren't behind it."

Croft gazed at Yancy, trying to gauge the man's mood, but Yancy's face remained enigmatic. Deciding to call Parnell's bluff, Croft took an unconcerned draw on his cigar, and exhaled with a smug grin. "Nope. I won't tell you that. Reckon it would be a waste of time since you seem to have things all figured out."

Yancy's voice was steely as he replied, "What I want to know is, why did you do it? I thought I made it perfectly clear that there was to be no violence. Christ, man! Are you trying to get us both strung up?"

"Damn it, Parnell, I just figured it was about time somebody did somethin'. You weren't gettin' no place with that Howard bitch. I was tryin' to do us both a favor. With McCullough out of the way, the woman would be easy pickin's. Too bad I didn't succeed with him, but no harm done. The way I heard it, they ain't found no evidence to point a finger at me or anybody else. I was real careful 'bout that. Ain't no way old 'Judge Lynch' is givin' me one of his 'justice will be served' sentences." He guffawed at his own joke. All the miners knew that a "just" sentence from their circuit judge meant one thing: hanging.

Yancy pushed away from the desk and paced furiously in front of Croft's chair. "You think there's no harm done? You damn fool, you've ruined everything! Even if we succeed in bankrupting Mc-Cullough with more accidents, he'll never sell out to me now. He came in here last week and told Emma that he thinks I tried to blow him away. The man's not stupid, for Christ's sake!"

"Emma? Who's that?" asked Croft.

"Roxie Wilson. Her real name is Emma, but never mind that. The point is, McCullough's getting too close to the truth to suit me."

Out in the hall, Emma stood frozen, her hand poised to knock on Yancy's office door. She was no eavesdropper, but she couldn't help but listen after she'd overheard the angry voices mentioning her name. Her face paled as the portent of the conversation hit her. Unable to tear herself away, Emma listened in horror as each damning word pounded into her reeling brain.

"You mean that redheaded whore knows about our plans?" shouted Croft in angry disbelief. "That's not good, Parnell, not good at all. What are you gonna do to keep her quiet?"

"Shut your filthy mouth!" Yancy exploded. "Don't let me ever hear you call her a whore again or I'll kill you with my bare hands. She's my woman and I'll handle her my way, understand?" Jed nodded, effectively silenced by Yancy's threats. Satisfied, Yancy continued, "Emma doesn't know anything except that I tried to buy McCullough out." Yancy stopped his pacing and nailed Croft with a furious glare. "Why couldn't you have been a little more patient? Damn it, man, I have Felicity Howard all but talked into selling me her share of the mine. As much as McCullough hates me, I know he'd have sold out rather than be partners with me. But you can be damn sure he'll never give me the satisfaction of owning his half now. Your stupidity took care of that."

Jed was at last beginning to understand how his actions had ruined Yancy's plan. "All right, all right, maybe I was a little too quick on the draw, but, damn it, Parnell, you can't blame me for gettin' impatient. This business has been goin' on for a year or better. Hell, at the rate you was goin', we'd be too old to spend the money by the time we got our hands on that lode."

"Yeah, well, better late than never," Yancy

snapped. "Letting me handle it might take a little longer, but at least I'll secure half ownership in the mine. After your stupid move, that's all we're likely to ever get."

"How can you be so sure you got that Howard bitch's half sewed up?"

Jed Croft suddenly found himself yanked out of his chair as Yancy's fist wrapped itself into the front of his shirt. Parnell's face was so close Croft could feel his breath hiss against his cheek.

"I'm sick to death of you calling the women in this town by your dirty names," Yancy snarled. "Miss Howard happens to be a lady of quality and if I hear one more of your derogatory slurs against her or Emma Wilson, I'm going to rearrange your ugly face so even your own mother won't know you." Yancy shoved Croft back into the chair and rubbed his hands on his pants in disgust.

It took Jed a moment to regain enough breath to speak. Looking at Yancy closely, he asked, "What's come over you lately, Parnell? You're actin' like one of them prissy Eastern tenderfoots."

Yancy pointed a rigid finger at Croft and sneered, "Just watch your mouth, friend. I meant what I said, so don't underestimate me. I assure you, I'm far from being a 'prissy Eastern tenderfoot'."

Wood scraped wood as Jed pushed out of his chair. "Okay, Parnell, take it easy. If you say *Miss* Howard is gonna sell out to you, I believe you. I'll just wait till I get word from you before I try anythin' more at the Silver Lady." Chuckling mirthlessly, he added, "It really don't matter none at this point. It'll be a long time before McCullough gets that mine dug out from the explosion. He ain't gonna find that vein anytime soon. I still wish that bastard would've got killed though. It would've saved us a whole lotta time and trouble."

"Maybe, maybe not," replied Yancy doubtfully. "At any rate, I'm glad you failed. I've done a lot of bad things in my life, but murder isn't one of them. I'm not about to start now."

Jed shrugged indifferently and turned toward the door. "Just remember, Parnell, there comes a time when a man's gotta do what a man's gotta do."

Hearing sounds of Jed Croft's impending departure, Emma hiked up her skirts and raced down the hall. She dashed out of sight just as the door opened, then waited until Croft's footsteps receded down the hall before marching back to Yancy's office for what she was sure would be a bitter confrontation.

Not bothering to knock, she burst into the room, shaking with rage and pain. The flimsy wall shuddered as the door slammed shut on the sounds of gaiety that rolled down the hall from the saloon. Fists resting on her hips, her chest heaved with emotion as she impaled the bewildered man on the other side of the desk with a livid glare.

"Emma—" Yancy's voice was wary. "—what's wrong?"

"How could you?" she shrieked. "You lied to me about everythin'!" Shock and guilt washed across his face as she nodded. "Oh, yes, I know it all now. I was comin' in here to ask you about lunch when I heard you and that weasel partner of yours arguin'. I don't usually eavesdrop, but I'm sure glad I did, otherwise, I'd still be playin' the unsuspectin' fool. Jake was right about you all along, wasn't he, Yancy? You *were* behind those accidents at his mine, and if he'd been killed in that explosion, it would've been your fault."

Yancy walked around the desk, his arms outstretched beseechingly. "Emma, honey, believe me, I never wanted it to go that far. I only wanted the Silver Lady so we could live in style." She dodged his embrace, slapping his hands away. Yancy stepped back and dropped his arms. "You've got to listen to me, sugar," he pleaded. "This was my chance to really make it big. Emma, there's people in New Orleans, old friends and relatives, who I needed to prove something to. I had to show them that they were wrong about me, that I could be *somebody!* Then, when I fell in love with you, it became even more important to me to succeed. You and me, Emma, we've had it hard. I just wanted to make the rest of our lives as comfortable as possible. I'd give you the world if I could, baby.''

Her expression was unrelenting. ''And you didn't care who you hurt in the process, did you? You were willin' to destroy Felicity, the only real friend I've ever had. And, I might remind you, an innocent girl who put her trust in you. Well, I won't let you get away with this!'' Emma spun around and jerked the door open, throwing him a look of anguish over her shoulder. ''Don't you ever try to excuse your actions by sayin' you did it for me. We're through.''

The door slammed behind her, its reverberation covering the sound of her fleeing footsteps.

Yancy felt as if he'd been shot. He couldn't let it end, not like this. The much-abused door was again flung open, slamming into the wall with such force that it swung back and closed on its own.

Tearing up the stairs, Yancy caught up with Emma just as she reached her door. He grabbed her upper arm and whirled her around to face him. ''Emma, you can't mean what you just said, not after all we've shared. You love me, I know you do.''

''No, Yancy, I loved the man I *thought* you were. Now let me go. We've said all there is to say.''

He averted his gaze from her stony countenance and noticed several men curiously poking their heads out of the girls' rooms lining the hallway. Cursing, he pushed Emma's door open and hurried her through it. Closing the door behind him, he entreated, ''Look, you know how fond of Felicity I am. I'd never do anything to hurt her. What's wrong with me buying her share of the mine? She doesn't want anything more to do with McCullough and she can use the money!''

Jerking herself free of his grip, Emma asked incredulously, "What's wrong with it? I'll tell you what's wrong with it. You're cheatin' her out of a fortune, and your slimy partner almost killed Jake!"

"But he didn't," Yancy reminded her quietly.

"That don't change nothin'!" Tears welled up in Emma's eyes but she blinked them back. "Get out, Yancy. Get out of my room and never come back. I meant what I said. It's over. I don't want nothin' more to do with you." She turned her back on him and hid her face in her hands.

Yancy gently grasped Emma's shoulders. He nuzzled the soft hair at her temple and implored, "Don't cry, honey. I'll do anything you ask, only please don't leave me. No amount of money is worth that."

She slowly turned within his embrace and gazed at him with searching eyes. "Do you mean that, Yancy? Really mean that?"

"I've never meant anything more in my life," Yancy answered honestly. "You're more important to me than all the silver in the world, Em."

"Then you'll give up this whole scheme? You'll forget about tryin' to rob Felicity and Jake of the Silver Lady?"

Yancy took a deep breath and nodded decisively. "Yes. I'll send for Croft and tell him the whole thing is off. I promise you, Emma Wilson, if you want this stopped, it's stopped." He pulled her closer, placing a gentle kiss on her forehead. Yancy knew his promise was easier made than kept, but he shoved the disturbing thought aside and asked anxiously, "Now, girl, will you stay with me?"

She encircled his neck with her arms and urged his head down. She pressed her lips to his before breathlessly giving him her reply. "Oh, yes, Yancy. Yes! If you love me enough to give up everythin' you've worked for, then I'm yours."

He chuckled roguishly, cupping her buttocks and pulling her hips against his own. "I'm not giving up *everything*, baby. I may go back to New Orleans shy of a fortune, but there's one treasure I'll never leave behind.'' He feathered kisses across her cheek, stopping a breath away from her trembling mouth. ''As long as I have you, I'll always be the richest man alive.''

Emma thought she'd never heard anything so romantic and she melted into his arms, sighing, ''Yancy, I love you so much. Never let me go.''

Yancy needed no more encouragement, and, swinging Emma up into his arms, he headed for the bed, murmuring, ''Never, love. You can count on that.''

While Yancy was pursuing a lusty morning of pleasure with his love, Jake McCullough was pulling his wagon up to the Grand Hotel with much the same entertainment in mind for himself and his new bride.

''Why are we stopping here?'' asked Felicity as he reined in the horses. ''I thought we'd pick up my things at Emma's and head back to the cabin.''

''Nope, not today.'' Jake laughed as he jumped down from his seat and rounded the wagon to assist her. ''Haven't you ever heard of a honeymoon, Mrs. McCullough?'' Before reaching up for her, he paused thoughtfully and commented, ''Hmmm . . . Mrs. McCullough. That's got a real sexy ring to it. I like the idea of you belongin' to me and no one else.''

Felicity hadn't stopped smiling since they'd left the church, and her grin widened at his words. She gripped his shoulders as he lifted her down. For a long moment, he just stood there, holding her close and staring down at her. She recognized the flame glowing in his hazel eyes and giggled nervously as several people walked by, looking askance at their unseemly public display. ''Jake, people are staring at us,'' she whispered. ''Don't you think we should go inside?''

''What? Oh! Well, to hell with 'em. What do I care? You're my wife, after all.'' In spite of his bravado, his eyes scanned their surroundings and saw the truth of her words. Tucking her arm in his, he whisked her into the hotel away from the gawking passersby.

Felicity smiled to herself as she hurried to keep up with her husband's long-legged strides. Mrs. Mc-Cullough, she thought happily, I'm really Mrs. McCullough!

As they approached the desk, she recognized the clerk as the same man who had checked them in on their last, momentous visit. He smiled at them and said congenially, " 'Mornin', Jake. Miss Howard."

Before she could open her mouth to correct him, Jake said, "We need a room, Henry."

The desk clerk raised his eyebrows and asked, "*One* room, Jake?"

"Yeah, one's all we'll need," Felicity looked at Jake imploringly, wondering why he didn't say something to clarify their new relationship to the smirking man.

The clerk swiveled the register book around and handed Jake a pen, never taking his eyes off Felicity's flaming face. Jake signed the book in his bold scrawl and turned it back toward the leering man.

As he glanced down at the signature, Henry's eyes bulged and his face turned crimson. "Mr. and *Mrs.* Jake McCullough?"

"Yup." Jake grinned. "That's what it says, don't it?"

"Well, er, yes," the clerk stammered. "I guess this means congratulations are in order, aren't they? You sure did keep this a secret, Jake!"

Jake just kept grinning as he pulled Felicity closer to him.

"Oh, Mr. Fellows," she said in a syrupy-sweet voice, "I wonder if you would do us a favor?"

"Why, sure, Miss, uh, Mrs. McCullough. What can I do for you?"

"Well," she purred, "since Jake and I want everyone in Silverton to know our happy news as soon as possible, I'd really appreciate it if you'd tell your sister about our marriage at your first opportunity."

Jake looked at her curiously, not understanding the devilish smile that tugged at the corner of her mouth. Turning his attention back to the desk clerk, he was further confused as the flustered man fumbled through a box of keys, finally spilling the entire contents on the floor.

Several moments passed as Henry frantically gathered the keys. Finally, he stood up and, looking somewhere over Felicity's shoulder, mumbled, "Ah, yes, Mrs. McCullough, I'll do that."

"Thank you so much, Mr. Fellows." She smiled. "I *knew* I could count on you."

With as much dignity as he could muster, Henry looked at Jake and said, "Any bags?"

"Nope." Jake winked. "We ain't gonna need any clothes."

Henry turned a deeper shade of scarlet, but didn't acknowledge Jake's risqué comment. "Then, if you'll follow me . . ."

"That won't be necessary." Jake laughed, reaching forward and plucking the room key out of the clerk's hand. "We can find our own way."

With one last meaningful smile, he whirled Felicity away from the desk and hurried toward the staircase, whispering, "I don't know what was goin' on back there between you two, but you're gonna tell me, ain't you?"

She flashed him an impish smile and nodded. "Sometime . . ."

Halfway up the staircase, she came to an abrupt halt and said, "Oh, Jake, before we go to the room, I have to run over to the Last Chance and tell Emma our news!"

"What?" he asked in disbelief. "Are you crazy, Felicity? This ain't no time for you to go visitin'. It can wait. Now come on, let's get up these stairs!"

"But, Jake!" Felicity protested stubbornly. "She'll

be worried! She doesn't even know where I am, and besides, I want her to know!''

He spun and shouted down toward the lobby, ''Hey, Henry! When you tell your sister about us, ask her if she'll run over to the Last Chance and tell Emma Wilson, will you? It'll save me a trip, and Mrs. McCullough and I got some things we gotta do upstairs.''

Without another word, he grabbed Felicity's hand and continued galloping up the staircase, leaving everyone in the lobby gaping at them in shock.

They finally reached their room, and as Jake put the key in the lock, he glanced at Felicity, astonished to find her glaring at him. ''How could you embarrass me that way?'' she demanded. ''Why, now everyone in town knows what we're planning to do in this room and it's only eleven o'clock in the morning! What will they think?''

He turned and grabbed her, kissing her hard. ''I don't care.'' He grinned. ''I just knew I couldn't wait another minute to get you up here and make love to you. I was about ready to rip your clothes off on that staircase.''

Sweeping her up in his brawny arms, he kicked open the door and swept through it. Without putting her down, he nuzzled her neck and said, ''You ain't mad at me, are you, Mrs. McCullough?''

''No.'' She giggled. ''I'm not mad . . .''

''Good.'' He lowered his lips to hers. The sensation of Felicity's body pressed against him ignited a fire in his loins and his caressing kiss quickly intensified into raw hunger. Without removing his lips from hers, he walked to the bed, sliding her down his body as he set her on her feet. His hands shook as they moved to the high neck of her dress, unfastening the first button. She reached up to assist him, but he caught her fingers in his own and softly entreated, ''Let me.''

A tingling warmth shot through her as he slowly freed each button, and a familiar, earthy ache unfurled in the tips of her breasts and spread like warm honey to the center of her womanhood.

Jake edged the dress from her shoulders and pushed the long sleeves down her arms. "Mmmm, nice," he breathed. "No corset."

She couldn't help but smile. "It doesn't fit anymore," she murmured shyly.

Her quiet statement gave him pause and his eyes glued themselves to her waistline. He'd been in such emotional turmoil for the past week that he hadn't given their coming child much thought. But now, the wonder of the life they had created together left him awestruck. He gently laid his hand on the slight bulge of Felicity's stomach and said, "You're still so tiny, no one would ever guess that you're . . ." His head jerked up and he pinned her with his gaze. "Are you sure it's all right if we . . . I mean, we won't hurt the baby, will we?"

With a reassuring smile, she shook her head. "No, my darling, we won't hurt the baby."

He breathed a sigh of relief. For his baby's sake, he'd have kept his hands off his wife even on this special day, but he had to admit, he was damn glad he didn't have to. "Good," he breathed. "Good . . ." His mouth again took possession of hers as his fingers loosened the ribbon at the top of her chemise. Felicity caught her breath as the filmy material took the same path as the bodice of her dress.

Jake moaned as her passion-swollen breasts were revealed. The soft globes beckoned him and he eagerly filled his hands, cupping and kneading the warm flesh while his thumbs circled and teased the aroused nipples. A soft, rapturous sound escaped her as he bent his head, tasting each pink tip.

She buried her hands in his chestnut hair, reveling in the erotic havoc his twirling tongue was wreaking on her. She groaned as he abandoned her nipples and dropped to his knees. "Jake, please, don't stop!" she begged.

"Shhh, baby." His voice was hoarse and breathless with the effort it was costing him to restrain his raging desire. "I want to see all of you, sweetheart." He reached up and tugged her dress down over her hips until it lay in a heap at her feet. Unbuttoning her petticoat, he hastily disposed of it, along with her gaping chemise. The only remaining impediments to her nudity were her drawers, stockings, and garters. With mounting impatience, he yanked the ribbon at the top of her drawers and curled his fingers around the waistband, hastily adding them to the growing pile at her feet. He kissed the delicate curve of her slender calves as he removed her garters and peeled the stockings down her legs and off her feet. Felicity took a step sideways, kicking the discarded clothing out of the way.

Still on his knees, Jake slid his thumbs caressingly up the inside of her legs, making chills spiral to the very center of her being and forcing her to grab his shoulders to steady herself.

He rocked back and sat on his heels as his eyes traveled the entire length of her gleaming, naked body. Panting as if he had run a great distance, he quietly commanded her to part her thighs.

Her eyes closed in an amorous trance, Felicity obeyed. The moisture of her desire glistened in the soft, curling hair between her thighs, exciting him till his entire body trembled with anticipation. She stood totally still, her head thrown back, her lips parted as she waited for his touch. Her knees nearly buckled when she felt not his fingers, but his tongue plunge into her hot, wet core.

Overwhelmed, she took a hasty step backward. But Jake was not to be denied. He gripped her buttocks and gently ordered her to stand still. With wonder, Felicity glanced down into his passion-glazed eyes as he rasped, "I've dreamed about doing this." Again his tongue delved into her creamy depths, causing her to quiver in reaction. Withdrawing again, Jake continued, "Before we leave this hotel, I plan to taste every inch of you. I'm goin' to make love to you till tomorrow mornin', Mrs. McCullough. Today, you're finally *mine*."

She tossed her head back in unabashed surrender as his provocative words ended and his tongue again began seducing her most intimate spot. Time and time again, he brought her to the brink of climax, only to retreat by kissing and nuzzling the inside of her thighs. Finally, she could take no more and, writhing and shuddering, she begged him for release. Only then did he grant her surcease, his moist, warm tongue delving deep to send her over the precipice of pleasure.

She slowly returned to reality and opened her eyes as he stood up and encircled her in his muscular embrace. Her arms wrapped around his neck and she met him in a scorching kiss. She could taste herself on his lips.

She clung to his big body, trying desperately to get closer. A feral growl emerged from somewhere deep in Jake's throat as he backed her to the edge of the bed and gently laid her down on the soft mattress. It wasn't until he straightened up again that Felicity realized he was still fully dressed.

His eyes never leaving hers, he pulled his coat off and tossed it onto a chair. A smile of promise beguiled and teased her as he slowly began unbuttoning his shirt.

"Did you know I once stood outside your window and watched you undress to take a bath?" he asked, running his tongue suggestively over his lips. She could only shake her head as more and more of his massive, furred chest was revealed. How she longed to run her fingers through that mat of curls!

Even as she willed them not to, Jake's hands paused in the middle of his chest. "Let's see, when was that? August, I think. Long before we ever . . . well, anyway, it was *then* that I first realized how gorgeous your body is. I know I should have moved on and left you to your privacy, but I couldn't take my eyes off you." Her fascinated gaze was anchored on his every movement as his fingers began to again work the buttons on his shirt. She was far too interested in his disrobing to feel shocked or dismayed by his confession.

"I watched you take off your dress." He was now leisurely tugging his shirt out of his trousers, tempting her to leap off the bed and rip it off him.

"I must say, I was damn excited when I saw those luscious, beautiful breasts of yours. You'd kept them well-hidden under those ugly binders and it was one hell of a sexy surprise." He saw passion glaze her eyes as he casually removed his shirt and tossed it on top of his coat. Unbuckling his belt, he lazily slid it out, loop by loop, watching her rapt gaze follow the belt to the floor.

"The real clincher, though," Jake continued in a languid voice, "was the bath itself." His hands meandered down the front of his trousers, hesitating for an eternity after each button was released.

Felicity's breathing grew ragged as she stared at the straining bulge beneath the material. She was having difficulty concentrating on Jake's words. What was he saying? Something about her bath?

"I nearly jumped through the window at the sight of that water runnin' between your breasts, down your belly, and into that soft little nest between your legs."

His trousers were finally completely unbuttoned. He bent over and removed his boots, then straightened up and grasped the waistband of both the trousers and his underclothes. He inched them slowly down the long, tightly corded muscles of his abdomen, again leaning over to remove his socks. Felicity never noticed where these last items of clothing landed because as he stood up, his manhood sprang free: huge, rigid, and throbbing.

"You see, sweetheart," he continued huskily, well aware of her interest, "I wanted to do then what I'm goin' to do now." Jake slid onto the bed and

gathered Felicity into his arms, lying on top of her
and rubbing his scorching shaft against the inside
of her thigh.

Felicity went up in flames. Throwing her arms
around him as his hot body melted against hers, she
captured his mouth in a fiery kiss. Her nipples
pressed into his chest and she undulated her hips
against his. As their tongues entwined, she realized
with delight that this man belonged to her as she
belonged to him. She was free to enjoy him with no
guilt to haunt her later.

Emboldened by these liberating thoughts, she
reached down and took him in her hand, feathering
caresses along his hot, satiny length. As always, she
marveled at his heat and size, astonished that she
was capable of accepting all of him. She gently
pushed him onto his back, allowing herself uninhibited access to his body. Following the trail of chest
hair as it tapered to a thin line down his belly, she
kissed and nibbled a moist path to his pulsing erection. Jake gasped as her lips closed over the tip of
his manhood, his hips arching off the bed as he cried
out in blind ecstasy.

Even more stimulated by the pleasure she knew
she was bestowing, she lifted herself over his body
and straddled him, facing his feet. Slowly, seductively, her tongue stroked and tasted his demanding, arching member.

Nearly mindless with lust, he reached around her
and teased her sensitive bud, further igniting her
desire. His sensual touch caused her to swallow him
more deeply and he was forced to disengage himself, knowing he was rapidly losing his battle for
control.

Jake urged Felicity onto her hands and knees and,
leaning over her, gently entered her woman's sheath
from behind. As he thrust in and out, Felicity forgot
her initial shock at this new, passionate assault and
cried out at the sheer eroticism of their position. At
the brink of that most vulnerable moment, he

reached around and fondled her breasts, increasing the tempo of his searing thrusts. Sanity fled as she surrendered to rapture's embrace. Her body clenched around Jake's pulsating force, hurtling them both beyond reality and into the euphoric world of fulfillment.

Much later, after languishing drowsily in the splendor of their lovemaking, Jake raised himself on one elbow and gazed down at his exhausted bride. Returning his loving scrutiny, Felicity reached up and caressed his cheek, playing with the chestnut curls at his temple. "How did you talk Father Thomas into marrying us so quickly?" she murmured. "You're not even Catholic."

He smiled and lazily twirled a finger around her nipple. "It was easy," he drawled. "I just told him the truth. You'd already told him you were in the family way, so I confessed I was responsible and he agreed that we needed to get married real quick." She turned a bright shade of red as she wondered what the priest must think of them. "He was concerned about me not bein' Catholic," Jake continued, "but I promised to convert before the baby was born and that seemed to settle everythin'."

"Jake!" she exclaimed. "You'd become Catholic for me?"

"Felicity, if there's one thing you should know about me by now, it's that I keep my word. Besides, for you, I'd go native and be a heathen!"

She sighed in sheer contentment as his finger continued its provocative massage. "Mr. McCullough," she sighed, "you've made me a very happy lady."

At these words, he finally asked the question that had been nagging at him all during the previous, torturous week. "Are you really happy, sweetheart? About the baby, I mean. I've been worried how you're gonna feel about the gossip that's sure to spread around town when he comes so quick after our weddin'. We're gonna have to face the fact that everybody in Silverton's gonna know we weren't married when we . . . made him.''

Felicity raked her husband with a seductive glance and purred, ''All the women in this town have to do is look at you and they'll understand why I couldn't resist your advances.''

He grinned with pleasure. ''You think I'm that sexy, huh?''

''Yes,'' she murmured, squirming against him as he dipped his head to tease at her nipple. ''And I have a feeling you're going to show me how sexy you can be right now, aren't you?''

His only response was a moan of assent as he moved on top of her, letting her feel his rapidly swelling arousal.

Lifting his head, he gazed deep into her luminous eyes and whispered, ''I'm sorry for all the pain I caused you. I know I acted like a horse's ass and I'm gonna spend the rest of my life makin' it up to you.''

''You made everything up to me the moment you walked into Emma's room this morning,'' she assured him. ''But say it again.''

''Say what again?'' he asked.

''You devil, you know very well what I mean.'' she giggled.

Crouching above her, he nuzzled the soft underside of her breast, breathing in her intoxicating, feminine scent. ''You mean, how much I love the smell of you?''

She played along with his game, softly replying, ''No, not that.''

His mouth moved back up to the pink crest of her breast where he lingered for a time. ''You mean, how much I love the taste of you?''

Her breath coming in quick, short gasps, she stammered, ''No, not . . . not that. You *know* what I mean.''

His chuckle was resonant with pure animal lust as he rubbed his throbbing erection against her. ''You

mean, how much I love to feel myself inside you?''
he whispered hoarsely.

''*Jake!* You know what I need!'' she cried as her
hips bucked upward.

''Oh, yes, little girl,'' he growled, ''I might not
always understand what you *mean*, but I always understand what you *need!*''

She cried out as he lifted her hips and thrust into
her with a frenzied rhythm that soon stoked their
mutual fires into a singular, raging inferno. As he
moved above her writhing body, his warm breath
fanned her temple and he whispered, ''I love you,
Felicity McCullough. I'll love you till I die.''

Chapter 22

Yancy sighed with satisfaction as he set a stack
of papers into his desk drawer. Ben Ford had
found a buyer for the Last Chance and there remained only a few financial loose ends to tie up before he and Emma could leave for New Orleans. The
only other issue still to be resolved was the fulfillment of his promise to her. He had yet to break off
his partnership with Jed Croft.

Although he'd sent a message to Jed to meet with
him shortly after his argument with Emma, a paralyzing blizzard had laid siege to Silverton and hadn't
let up for three days. Even when the weather finally
cleared, the mountain trails were impassable. Those
miners who'd been trapped in town during the
storm had passed the time emptying every bottle of
liquor in the city. Yancy's supplies were dangerously low; in fact, the whiskey was completely gone
and the beer barrels were draining fast. None of the
town's citizens dared to think what the wild bunch
of miners would do when the liquor ran out.

Even as people assured each other that this must
be the last storm of the winter, another blizzard del-
uged them. Liquor, food, and good humor disappeared and spurts of violence erupted in the town's
saloons and brothels, forcing honest folks to hide
behind locked doors and pray for sunshine. Finally,
the second storm abated and a warm spell set in.

Yancy, along with the rest of Silverton's residents, heartily cheered the opening of the passes as the bored and restless miners headed back up the mountain. The snow melted quickly under the bright April sun, turning the streets into muddy quagmires, but no one complained. At least the town was peaceful again.

Yancy sent another messenger to Jed's cabin, hoping that his perfidious foreman would now put in an appearance. He wanted to be done with the hated man and anxiously awaited his arrival.

As if his thoughts had conjured Jed up, the door opened and Croft strode into his office. Having no delusions where his partner was concerned, Yancy eyed his gun where it hung in its holster on the hat tree across the office. He surreptitiously patted his breast pocket, reassuring himself that his small Hammond Bull Dog pistol was tucked inside. Though he would have preferred having his larger Peacemaker strapped to his side, he felt relatively safe with the small pistol close at hand.

"Mornin', Parnell," Jed said shortly. "Got your message yesterday. You got some news for me?" He slumped into a chair across from Yancy's desk and eyed the gambler expectantly.

"Yeah, Croft, I've got news," Yancy replied, "but you're not going to like it." As Croft's eyes narrowed, Yancy plunged on. "The deal's off, Jed."

Croft leaned forward and growled, "What the hell do you mean, the deal's off?"

"I mean it's off," Yancy reiterated. "Felicity Howard has married McCullough, so that's the end of it. We'll never get the mine now. We made a good stab at it but it just didn't work out. These things happen."

"Why, you dirty, no-good, yellow bastard!" Croft exploded, jumping to his feet. "I knew you'd chicken out. Well, I ain't gonna let you. You're not callin' this deal off. You've kept me hoppin' for a

year now, runnin' here, runnin' there, doin' your
dirty work. I aim to get what's comin' to me."

"You've been well-paid for your time, Jed," Yancy
responded. "You should have plenty of money
stashed away by now to stake your own claim."

"It ain't enough!" Jed shouted. "What you paid
me ain't nothin' compared to what I stand to make
when we get our hands on McCullough's mine."

"Well, I'm afraid it's going to have to be enough,"
Yancy snarled. "Face it, Jed, it's over."

With a lightning-swift movement, Jed reached into his holster and pulled out his gun. Yancy's face
drained of color at the sight of the long barrel aimed
straight at his heart. "Croft," he said softly, "don't
be a fool."

"It's you that's the fool, Parnell," Jed sneered.
"You always thought you controlled this deal, didn't
you? You slimy river rat, you never controlled
nothin'! It's always been me. You think you're so
smart, so superior, but it's always been me!" Jed
laughed and waved the gun in Yancy's face. "It was
me that killed old man McCullough." At the look of
shock on Yancy's face, Croft nodded vehemently.
"Yeah, me! You didn't know that, did you, smart
boy?"

Yancy shook his head as icy fear clutched at him.
Seeing his expression, Jed laughed mirthlessly.
"Killin' Joe McCullough was just the first step in my
plan. The second step was to find a sucker stupid
enough to pay me to do what I was gonna do anyway. That's where you came in, Parnell. You was
never nothin' more than my backer. You was just
too stupid to know it. Now, I'll have it all, and by
the end of the day, neither you or Jake McCullough
will be around to stop me."

As if in slow motion, Yancy watched Jed lower the
barrel of the gun directly at his heart. Diving under
his desk, Yancy made a grab for the pistol inside his
coat. But Croft's gun exploded and a searing pain

erupted in Yancy's chest before he ever touched his weapon.

Not waiting to see if his shot was fatal, Jed yanked open the door and ran down the hall toward the back of the saloon.

Lying beneath his desk, Yancy reached up and felt the burning hole above his heart. His hand came away wet and sticky with his own blood, and as the door crashed open, admitting what looked like half the population of Silverton, his vision blurred and he passed out.

When he again regained consciousness, he was still lying on the floor, but his head was cradled in Emma's lap and Dr. Brown was gently kneading the skin around his wound. As if from a long way off, Yancy heard the doctor say, "He'll be fine, Mrs. Wilson, it's just a flesh wound. The bullet went clear through his shoulder and no vitals were damaged." Dr. Brown looked up and called to no one in particular, "A couple of you men help me get him to his room so I can tend him."

"No, wait," Yancy groaned feebly.

"Yancy," cried Emma, tears streaming down her face, "don't try to talk, sugar. We're gonna get you upstairs and take care of you proper like."

"No, Emma," Yancy gasped, "you have to . . . warn Mc . . . Jake. Croft's going to . . . to kill him."

"Yancy, I'm not leavin' you," Emma protested.

"You have to. If Croft kills Jake . . . it'll be my fault."

"But, Yancy," Emma wailed, "what can I do? I don't even know where to find Jake!"

"The mine, Emma," Yancy whispered. "Go to the mine . . . warn him."

He closed his eyes again and she looked at the doctor with panic-filled eyes.

"He's going to be all right," Dr. Brown assured her. "He's weak from losing so much blood, but he'll be up and around in a week or so. He's in no real danger."

As Emma got reluctantly to her feet, Dr. Brown added, "Mrs. Wilson, it's none of my business, but I think you should get the sheriff if you're going up to Jake McCullough's mine. It could be dangerous and you should have a man with you."

Emma was suddenly galvanized into action. She nodded at Dr. Brown's suggestion and raced toward the door, halting momentarily as she heard Yancy wheeze, "Emma! Take my gun!"

With a desperate glance at the wounded man, she grabbed his gun and holster, strapping it around her waist as she ran through the saloon and out into the street. She raced down the boardwalk to the sheriff's office and pounded furiously on the locked door.

"If you're lookin' for the sheriff, he ain't there," drawled a voice from behind her. Emma swung around to see an old miner sitting in a chair next to the door.

"Where is he?" she shouted in desperation. "I need him!"

"Went over to Howardsville today," the man replied, lazily spitting a stream of tobacco juice into the street.

"Then you come!" She grabbed the old man's shirt and tugged, but he pulled back and indignantly slapped her hands away.

"Quit that! I ain't no deputy and I ain't goin' nowhere with you, girlie. Now, get! Whatever trouble you got ain't no problem of mine."

Frantic, she wheeled around and spied a man untying his horse from the railing in front of the sheriff's office. "Hey, mister!" she cried. "I need your horse!"

The man looked up in surprise, asking, "You talkin' to me, Red?"

"Yes," Emma said, "give me your horse, please!"

"Are you loco, girl? Why would I give you my horse?"

Emma darted off the boardwalk, shoved the man

out of the way, and, with a flurry of skirts and petticoats, threw herself onto the steed's back. "Because I *need* it, that's why!" Giving the startled
animal a sharp slap with the reins, Emma flew down
the street, leaving the dumbstruck cowboy gaping
after her and the old miner guffawing.

Emma's heart outpaced the thundering hooves of
her stolen mount as she raced up the rough mountain road. Although she prayed that she'd get to Jake
in time, she knew the chances were slim. Croft had
too much of a head start on her. Still, if Jed thought
Yancy was dead and that no one else knew his plans,
he probably was in no hurry. With renewed hope,
Emma whipped the horse again, tearing heedlessly
up the treacherous path.

Jake and Corny were standing near the mouth of
the mine when an apparition of flying red hair, calico skirts, and long slim legs came dashing up the
road toward them. His eyes widening in surprise,
Corny crossed himself and muttered, "God in
heaven, what's that?"

Jake raised a hand to shade his eyes. "Appears to
be a woman, and she's in one hell of a hurry." As
the horse drew nearer, Jake exclaimed, "Why, it's
Roxie—Emma—Wilson from the Last Chance! What
do you suppose put a burr under her saddle?"

"Don't know," Corny responded, "but I think
we're about to find out."

Emma skidded to a halt and slid to the ground,
nearly falling into Jake's arms. "Thank God, I'm in
time, Jake!"

A bolt of apprehension shot through him as he
noticed her wild expression. Taking her by the
shoulders, he gave her a quick shake. "What is it,
Emma? Has somethin' happened to Felicity?"

Now that she knew he was unharmed, she paused
a second to catch her breath. Seeing his fear escalating with each passing moment, she finally gasped,
"No, it's not Felicity. It's Jed Croft."

"Jed Croft?" Jake asked in confusion. "Who's Jed Croft?"

"Isn't he the foreman at the Dead Horse mine?" interjected Corny.

"Yes," Emma replied, "and he's on his way up here to kill Jake."

"Me!" Jake exclaimed. "What for? I don't even know the man."

"There's no time to explain," Emma panted. "Jed Croft shot Yancy a little while ago and told him he was gonna kill you next. He's after your mine. He's the one who tried to kill you in January."

"But why did he shoot Parnell if I'm the man he wants?"

"Yancy owns the Dead Horse, Jake," she explained. "He and Jed were behind your accidents. They wanted to drive you out of business so they could have your mine. But when Yancy found out Jed tried to kill you, he told Jed the deal was off. Only now it looks like Jed isn't willin' to give up."

"Did this man say he was coming up here, then?" asked Corny.

"Yes, that's what Yancy said."

"How did you beat him here?" Jake questioned.

"I really don't know." Emma shrugged. "I know he had a good head start on me because I stopped at the sheriff's office. But I didn't even see him on the trail. He probably thinks Yancy's dead and he's just takin' his time . . . layin' some kind of trap for you."

Jake shook his head doubtfully. "I don't like it. There's only one trail up here and if you didn't see him, he must be waitin' to get me somewhere else." Suddenly his body stiffened and he shouted, "Jesus Christ, the cabin!" He took off at a dead run, throwing himself onto his horse. "Corny," he ordered, "watch things here. I'm goin' home!" Then he was gone, spurring his horse unmercifully down the mountain pass.

Emma quickly mounted her exhausted steed and

charged after him, shouting, "Jake, wait up! What's wrong?"

"Felicity!" he called over his shoulder. "She's alone at the cabin and she's in no condition to defend herself if Croft shows up."

"Do you think that's where he went?" she called in alarm.

"I think that's exactly where he went," he called back, "and I think the man's made a fatal mistake."

Emma kicked her flagging mount harder, desperately hoping that Jake McCullough was wrong.

Felicity sat contentedly rocking in the new chair Jake's men had given her as a wedding gift. They had come in a group to present it to her, shyly telling her they had built it for the new baby. After turning several shades of red, Felicity had aimed an accusing glare at her husband. He had grinned guiltily but defended himself by saying that he was damn proud and hadn't been able to resist telling his men that he was going to be a father. Seeing only respect and goodwill on the miners' faces, she had relented and forgiven her bragging husband.

The heavenly aroma of bread baking tempted her to have a snack before Jake came home for his noon meal. In the past month, her figure had blossomed, along with her appetite. Only that morning, he had teased her unmercifully, saying that her appetite was beginning to rival his own. At her outraged protest, he had given her a quick kiss and assured her that he *liked* robust women. She had punched him playfully, asserting that it was his fault she was "robust" and swearing that she would never have another baby.

He had leered at her and made several lewd comments about how much she'd be missing if she stuck to that vow. Their teasing had led to a passionate interlude on the rug in front of the fireplace and caused Jake to arrive at the mine an hour later than expected.

She smiled now, thinking about those intimate moments and all the others they had recently shared. The month since her marriage had been the happiest of her life. Jake treated her like a fragile flower, spoiling her shamelessly. Although she insisted he needn't pamper her, she enjoyed every moment of his loving attention.

Her knitting needles clacked industriously as she worked on a tiny blue sweater. Jake frequently warned her that she was making a mistake by sewing all the baby's clothes in boy's colors, but she knew better. Her husband deserved a son as his firstborn and she was confident she would present him with one.

When she heard the back door open, she called without turning around, "You're home early, sweetheart. The roast isn't quite ready." She dropped her knitting into a small basket and rose from the chair, asking, "Is Boozer with you? I haven't seen . . ." She froze as she turned and saw, not her husband, but a complete stranger. She ordered herself to stay calm but her voice, nonetheless, trembled as she asked, "Who are you? What do you want? If it's food you need, take it, but please go."

The man's ugly face twisted into an evil smile. "Now, ain't that generous of you, Mrs. McCullough? Too bad I ain't got time to eat. It smells right tantalizin' in here." Raising a gun, the stranger strode toward her.

"Just tell me what you want," Felicity whispered. "I'll give you anything I have, only please, don't hurt me."

Croft shoved her back into her chair and put the cold barrel of his gun to her head. She squeezed both eyes shut and gripped the arms of the chair, trying desperately to keep a clear head and think of what to do. Jed grabbed one of her breasts with his free hand and pinched the nipple through her dress. Her eyes flew open with a small cry, making him laugh. "Mmmm, you sure got a set on you," he remarked crudely. "Too bad I ain't got time to try you out now, but I got another use for you first. Maybe afterwards, you and me can really get acquainted. You ain't much of a looker, but there must be somethin' about you that made McCullough fall for you. Maybe it was these." He gave her breast another painful squeeze. Outraged, Felicity flung him a look of fury. His smile evaporated. "Okay, bitch, get out of that chair and do what you're told. I already killed one of your old boyfriends this mornin', so if you want to live a while longer, you better follow orders. Understand?"

She nodded and slowly stood up. With a rough shove, he propelled her toward the front door. "Let's go. We're gonna pay a visit to that new husband of yours."

Felicity was so terrified she could hardly walk. Stumbling, she nearly fell as Jed pushed her out the door. She caught herself with one hand while wrapping the other one protectively around her stomach. "Please," she begged, "I'll go anywhere you want me to, but don't push me. You'll hurt my baby."

Her pitiful plea only made him laugh again. "So McCullough's put one in ya already, has he? Well now, guess he likes you better than even I thought. That's good. That's real good. Men who care about their women are always more willin' to be reasonable."

They walked into the lean-to and Croft again held his gun on Felicity as he ordered her to saddle a horse. As she moved to do his bidding, she wondered again where Boozer was. Although she knew the big dog was harmless, his very size and presence might be intimidating enough to scare Croft off.

As she fidgeted with the saddle's straps, Jed shoved the gun into her ribs. "Quit dallyin', woman. The sooner I finish my business with your man, the sooner you and I can have a party."

She shuddered. It was obvious this madman meant to kill Jake and it followed that if he did, he wouldn't let her live either. Her only hope was that something would happen before they got to the mine—something that would allow her to escape in time to warn Jake.

Chapter 23

Tying their horses in a copse of trees by the road, Jake and Emma stealthily approached the cabin. The cabin door was open and Jake crouched behind a large boulder, pulling Emma down beside him. He cursed under his breath as he saw Jed Croft shove Felicity toward the lean-to. There was no way that he could get a shot off from this vantage point without endangering Felicity. His whole body shook with rage when he saw Croft grab Felicity's bottom and order her to mount the horse. Fearful that Jake's fury would erupt and endanger them all, Emma laid her hand on his arm and whispered, "Calm down, Jake. We gotta think of a plan."

He drew several deep breaths. "You're right, Emma. Now is no time for me to lose my head. Get your gun ready. I'm gonna move in and I may need you to cover me if somethin' goes wrong."

"Oh, Jake," Emma protested, "I can't shoot! I brought this gun along 'cause Yancy told me to, but I've never used one before!"

His eyes never leaving Felicity, Jake whispered, "Then let's hope you won't have to try to really hit anythin'. Just stay hidden and fire a couple of rounds into the air if things start goin' wrong. Jed won't know who I've got with me and the bluff might at least scare him a little."

She nodded, worry and fear contorting her face.

Felicity's life might depend on her actions in the next few minutes and she felt hopelessly ill-equipped to offer any real assistance. As she watched Jake slip away from the concealing protection of the large rock, Emma Roxanne Wilson squeezed her eyes shut and, for the first time in years, started praying.

Hoping that Jake really would show up early for lunch, Felicity dawdled, playing for time. But when she felt Jed Croft's dirty hand grab her, she instantly bolted upward into the saddle to escape his defiling touch. Croft held her horse's reins in the same hand that held his gun as he turned away to catch his own horse's bridle.

Realizing this might be his only opportunity, Jake stepped into the clearing. "Croft! Hold it right there."

Croft spotted Jake out of the corner of his eye just as Jake entered the clearing. Swinging Felicity's horse around, Jed ducked behind it, pointing his gun up at her. "That's far enough, McCullough," he shouted. "I got my gun on your woman. One more step and she'd dead. Now, drop it." With Croft using Felicity as cover, Jake was forced to comply. Cursing his luck, he threw his gun down and stood by helplessly while Jed forced Felicity to dismount.

Tears welled up in Felicity's eyes as she clumsily obeyed. She'd been sure that if Jake showed up in time, he'd be able to stop Croft's plans, but now it looked like all was lost. As soon as her feet touched the ground, Croft whipped his free arm around her thick waist and hauled her back against his chest, pressing the barrel of his gun to her head.

"Right accomodatin' of you to show up, McCullough," Jed shouted. "Saves me the trip up to the mine. Now, you go get a piece of paper and a pen. You're gonna sign over the Silver Lady to me."

"Like hell I am," Jake shouted back.

"You'll do as I tell you or I'll shoot your little wife's head clean off. And, if you think I'm bluffin', you better think again. I already killed your pa and Parnell, so one more don't make much difference.

On hearing Croft's unexpected confession, Jake's body stiffened and he swayed slightly. Croft saw his stricken expression and laughed out loud. "Hell, McCullough, you're disappointin' me. I thought you was smart enough to figure it out. Who'd you think killed your old man? That lily-livered gambler? No chance. If I'd left things up to him, he'd have took forever just tryin' to bankrupt old Joe with those two-bit accidents he had me settin' up. Well, I ain't got that kinda patience so I just hurried things up a little and knocked the old man off." Again his evil laugh rang out. "You see, Parnell was the stupid one, not me. I planned all along to get rid of him as soon as I was finished with him. Seems his luck just ran bone-dry this mornin'."

"Jake," Felicity cried, "don't sign anything! He'll kill us both anyway."

"Shut up, bitch," Croft snarled. "One more word outta you and I'll kick you right in that fat belly of yours." Turning his attention back to Jake, Jed shouted, "Now listen, McCullough, and listen good. You write out that deed and I'll let your woman go."

She wanted to scream to Jake that there was no way Croft would let her live, but she dared not jeopardize her baby. There was always the remote chance that Jake could yet, somehow, overcome Croft.

"Just walk over here, real nice and slow, McCullough," Jed ordered. "Me and your whore is gonna follow you into the cabin, so don't get no fancy ideas. My gun will be pointed at her head the whole time."

Jake felt his face mottle with rage at Croft's insulting remarks, but he reluctantly edged closer to the cabin. "You'll never get away with this, Croft. I'll see to it."

"The only thing you're gonna see is me havin' your woman while you're bleedin' to death!" Jed sneered.

Jake gritted his teeth against the almost insurmountable urge to lunge at the man and beat him to death. Instead, he groped desperately for some way to disarm Jed without hurting Felicity.

Just as Jake was about to step up on the porch, Boozer suddenly came tearing around the corner, barking a loud greeting. The big, friendly dog bounded over to Felicity and Jed, and, with his usual exuberance, leaped up, his huge front paws landing on Croft's shoulders and knocking the startled man off balance. The gun flew out of Jed's hand and landed on the ground as he wildly waved his arms in an effort to regain his footing.

Feeling the sudden release of Croft's arm from around her waist, Felicity ducked away from him, her elbow landing an unintentional but solid jab in Jed's stomach.

Croft doubled over from this new assault, and Jake, seeing his chance, catapulted himself across the short distance, landing on top of the stumbling man. The two men rolled over and over in the mud and dirt, each struggling to keep the other from reaching the gun.

Two shots rang out as Emma darted into the clearing, bravely brandishing her weapon as she made a valiant attempt to get a clear shot at Jed. But the men's bodies were hopelessly entangled and she was afraid her ill-trained aim might hit Jake. All at once, a flailing arm grabbed for and ensnared Croft's gun. Neither woman could determine which man had possession of the weapon as it was held between the grappling opponents. Frustrated by their inability to help Jake, Felicity and Emma watched the struggle in horrified anticipation.

Then came the shot. A simultaneous scream erupted from the women as Jake and Jed Croft slumped lifelessly over each other.

"Jake!" Felicity shrieked, running to him. Dropping onto her knees, she rolled him over, staring at his inert body. "Jake, oh, no! *Jake!*"

Jake blinked the sting of sulfur from his eyes and gently lifted Felicity's head from where it lay buried against his chest. Pushing himself into a sitting position, he gathered her close and entreated hoarsely, "Felicity, don't cry, baby. It's okay, sweetheart. I'm all right."

His tender words gradually filtered through her numbed senses. She opened her eyes and said in a dazed voice, "You're not shot? Oh, Jake, I thought I'd lost you!" Collapsing against him, she sobbed with shock and relief.

He ran his hand soothingly over her long hair, but she pulled away, needing to assure herself that he was truly unhurt. Spying the powder-burn spot on his shirt, she gasped and hastily unfastened it to examine his chest. Finding no wound, she choked on another sob and lunged back into his arms.

With a cursory glance at Croft's body, Jake verified that the man was dead. Then he looked at Emma over Felicity's shoulder and motioned with his head toward the cabin. Stooping, he picked up his wife, strode through the door that Emma held open, and headed straight for the bedroom.

He laid Felicity on the bed and sat down next to her, murmuring soft reassurances. Gradually, her sobbing stopped and she propped herself against the pillows, smiling at him tremulously. "I'm all right now."

"Are you sure, honey? He didn't hurt you, did he?"

"No." She shook her head. "Just scared me. But I'm fine, now that I know you're all right. Oh, Jake, for a moment, I thought he'd killed you!"

"For a moment, I thought he had too." He smiled and glanced down at his ruined shirt, marveling that he was still alive. "When the gun went off, I felt the powder burnin' and I thought I'd been hit. It took me a couple seconds to realize I wasn't. I guess I was just stunned. But when I opened my eyes and saw you, it was like being given a second chance at life."

She held her arms out and he eased into them, lifting her up and across his lap. "Oh, baby, I was so afraid for you," he breathed. "When I saw that slimy bastard put his hands on you, I knew he was a dead man."

Emma bustled into the room and handed Felicity a glass of water. "Here, drink this, honey. I had one myself in the kitchen and it made me feel a whole lot better."

Felicity accepted the glass, pausing for a moment to study the water's pale amber color.

"Well, don't just sit there starin' at it," Emma admonished, "drink it! It'll put some color back in your cheeks."

Felicity looked at her friend dubiously but tilted the glass to her lips and took a small swallow.

Jake threw Emma a look of gratitude, knowing that the dram of whiskey that had obviously been added was probably exactly what his wife needed.

As she drained the glass, he chuckled and plucked it from her fingers, setting it on the nightstand. "I want you to stay put in this bed for the rest of the day. I don't want to take any chances with you or the baby."

"But, Jake," she protested, "I'm fine, really I am."

"Just the same, you'll do as I say."

"All right, if it makes you happy, then I'll stay in bed." She threw Emma a look that clearly said she was acquiescing only to appease her anxious husband.

Jake gave her a quick kiss and rose from the bed. "I'm gonna go take care of Croft's body," he announced grimly. "Emma, if you'll stay here until I bring Corny back to sit with Felicity, I'll see you back to town."

"Oh, no, you don't!" Felicity retorted. "You're

not leaving me behind. I want to go with you. I can ride in the wagon.''

He threw an annoyed frown at his stubborn bride. ''I thought we just settled that. You're gonna stay in bed the rest of the day!''

''But, Jake, I'm perfectly all right, and fetching Corny is totally unnecessary.''

Emma rolled her eyes skyward and, deciding to let Felicity's husband handle this one, beat a hasty retreat for the kitchen. She smiled as through the closed bedroom door she heard the rugged miner's next words.

''I don't want any more arguments, Felicity. You're stayin' right here and that's final! You're still white as a ghost and I'm gettin' Corny to stay with you 'cause he'll know what to do if somethin' happens. Jesus, honey, women have lost babies over a lot less than what you've been through today. You're my wife and I aim to keep you around for a few years, so you just lay back and behave. If you don't care about yourself, then think about my baby.'' Then, in a softer tone, ''Felicity, what would I do if somethin' happened to you? Life wouldn't be worth livin' if I didn't have you, so please, make your husband happy and stay in that bed.''

Hearing Jake's voice trail off, Emma sighed, thinking that Felicity was one of the luckiest women in the world. Who'd have dreamed that Jake McCullough, the man every girl in Silverton wanted and no one could snare, would ever be heard shouting his love for a prim little girl from a Philadelphia convent?

The mere thought made Emma giggle, and she wished she could tell the girls at the saloon what she'd overheard. They'd be green with envy!

Felicity, meanwhile, knew she'd lost her battle. Sighing in surrender, she asked, ''You promise you'll be back by suppertime?''

Jake's face broke into a wide grin and he leaned down and kissed the end of his wife's nose. ''I promise.'' Opening the door, he turned back and added, "Just make sure you're still in bed when I get back.''

"Why, Jake McCullough.'' She smiled mischievously. "You better be careful what you say. Emma's going to think you want to keep me in bed all the time.''

His eyes raked her lecherously. "You know somethin', sweetheart? She'd be right!''

An hour later, Jake returned with Corny, then set out for town leading Jed Croft's horse with the body slung over it. He and Emma were halfway down the pass when he glanced over at her and asked solicitously, "Are you all right, Emma? You seem awful quiet.''

"I'm okay, Jake. I'm just worried about what will happen to Yancy now. You see, we planned to leave Silverton soon, but now . . . Jake, I want you to understand exactly what Yancy's part in this mess was. Maybe then you won't judge him too harshly. I admit that Yancy was involved in a plot with Jed Croft to bankrupt you. Yancy wanted the Silver Lady real bad and he set up those accidents to force you out of business so he could buy the mine cheap. But, about a month ago, I overheard a conversation between him and Jed where Jed told him he'd tried to murder you. Yancy was furious, Jake. He really didn't have any part in that.''

Jake nodded slowly, weighing Emma's words. "What I don't understand is why either one of them bothered to go to so much trouble to get my mine. The Silver Lady makes a little money, but it sure isn't the richest claim in the area. It can't hold a candle to the Silver Lake or the Aspen or the North Star.''

"Not yet, it can't,'' she responded.

"What do you mean by that?''

"Jake, you were in Europe when Yancy first arrived in Silverton and won the Last Chance. Then, right after he won the saloon, a miner lost the Dead Horse to him. You probably heard about that. Everyone in town was laughin' about it."

"Yeah, I heard." He chuckled. "The Dead Horse has been a joke around here for years. But what's that got to do with the Silver Lady?"

"Even though Yancy found out later that the Dead Horse is nearly worthless, he kept Jed Croft and one or two other miners in the hope of strikin' a new vein. Well, they found one all right, but the Dead Horse only contained a trickle. The real lode dumped into your claim."

His eyes widened at this incredible revelation. "Are you sure, Emma?"

"From what Yancy tells me, Jed was a pretty good miner, and, according to him, your whole side of the mountain is loaded with huge amounts of silver. Your father just started diggin' in the wrong place."

Jake kept silent as they rode on, mulling over everything Emma had just told him. The Dead Horse claim, which had originally been filed years ago, had quite a story behind it. The man who first owned it had been looking for gold. He found very little of that, and what there was had to be separated from silver and other minerals, a costly and tedious process. Not only that, but at the time, the only smelting plant was in Durango, and since there wasn't any railroad yet, freighters had to be paid to haul the ore by mule and wagon, another big expense. The first owner had neither the patience nor the financial backing to make the mine pay, for even the amount of gold and silver combined was minimal. So the Dead Horse became a joke, passed from one gambling miner to another, always a newcomer who hadn't heard about it yet. Those who were unlucky enough to win it usually had too much pride to admit they'd been duped, and simply held onto it until they could pass it on to the next unsuspecting fool.

"Let me get this straight, Emma. You're tellin' me that I'm about to tunnel into a mother lode?"

"Yup, that's about the size of it."

He looked thoughtfully out over the mountains, letting her miraculous disclosure sink in. "Well, I'll be damned," he murmured. Then he suddenly let out a whoop of sheer joy. "Whooee! Wait till I tell Felicity! God*damn* it, Emma, we're gonna be *rich!* Now I can build that girl a *real* house and buy her everythin' she ever wanted. She'll never regret havin' to leave Philadelphia and live out here in the middle of nowhere."

"Why, Jake!" Emma exclaimed. "Have you been worried that Felicity misses Philadelphia? Has she ever said that?"

He shook his head. "No, she's never said it, but the thought has crossed my mind. She's such a *lady*, Emma. So delicate and proper. And here she is, livin' in a little cabin in the woods, married to a big brute like me. You know, I don't hold my fork right, and I tromp into her clean house with my dirty boots on, and I swear, and—well, I just sometimes worry that she misses the city and all those *gentlemen* she could have married."

Emma impulsively leaned across her saddle and put her hand on his arm. "Trust me—" She smiled. "—you don't have a thing to worry about. Felicity doesn't give a damn if you have dirt on your boots."

Withdrawing her hand, she straightened in her saddle and looked at him searchingly. "Knowin' how you and Felicity love each other, I'm hopin' you can understand that it's the same with Yancy and me. You gotta believe me when I say that Yancy isn't capable of murder. He's not really a bad person, Jake. He's just a man who's had some tough breaks and he wanted to prove to himself and his family that he could make somethin' out of himself. I admit he went about it all wrong, but it's because he's basically a good man that his scheme failed. He didn't have it in him to fight down and dirty."

She paused, trying to gauge his reaction to her words. "I guess what I want to know is whether or not you plan on turnin' him over to the sheriff? I hope you'll keep in mind that it was Yancy who really saved your lives today. If he'd kept his mouth shut, you'd both be dead and out of his way for good. It would have been the perfect opportunity for him to take over your mine, but he still tried to stop Jed from killin' you.''

Jake remained silent, pondering her words. Although she hadn't succeeded in endearing Yancy Parnell to him, he reasoned that she was right about one thing. The gambler had saved their lives. When next he glanced over at her forlorn face, his tone was almost sympathetic. ''Emma, I don't rightly know what to say to you. I can't make you any promises, but I'll talk to Parnell before I see the sheriff.''

Encouraged, she smiled her gratitude. ''Thanks, Jake. I know after what Yancy has put you through, forgiveness is a lot to expect, but, you see, I have to ask. I love him and I don't want to lose him. Women like me don't often get the opportunity to start over, but with Yancy, I'll have that chance and I want it more than anythin' in the world.''

As if seeing her for the first time, Jake gazed at Emma and solemnly nodded his understanding.

True to his word, after dropping Croft's body off at the undertaker's, Jake accompanied Emma to the Last Chance. They found Yancy propped up in his bed sipping a beer that Rena had fetched for him. The saloon girl threw a haughty glare in Jake's direction and quickly departed, leaving them alone with Yancy.

''Emma, are you all right?'' Yancy inquired anxiously. He held out his hand and she took a seat on the bed next to him. Jake grabbed a straight chair, turned it around, and swung a leg over the seat, crossing his arms and resting them on the chair back.

''I'm fine, sugar,'' Emma assured him. ''How about you?''

''Doc says I got off easy. Guess I took that dive

under the desk just in time because Jed's a deadeye shot." For the first time since they'd entered the room, Yancy looked directly at Jake. "I see Emma got to you in time," he said. "I was afraid that Croft might have too much of a head start on her."

"He did have a head start on me," she told him, "and I wasted more time tryin' to find the sheriff. I finally gave up and jumped on the nearest horse, but I lost a lot of time."

Yancy looked confused. "Then how did you beat Croft up to the mine?"

"Croft never came to the mine," Jake interposed. "When Roxie—er, sorry, Emma found me, we realized that since Croft still hadn't arrived, he must have gone to my cabin instead. Felicity was alone so we headed out there real quick. It was a good thing we did because, sure enough, he was there. He was holdin' Felicity hostage against my signin' the Silver Lady over to him."

Jake and Emma finished telling Yancy what had taken place and how Boozer had turned out to be the real hero.

"I've never been so scared in my life." Emma shuddered. "I hope I'm never involved in a shoot-out again!" Her words were so heartfelt that both men burst out laughing.

"Is Felicity all right?" asked Yancy.

"Yes," Emma affirmed, "but me and Jake were mighty worried there for a while, what with her condition and all. Croft wasn't exactly bein' gentle with her."

"Well, thank God she's okay," Yancy said, and, after pausing a moment, added, "And I'm glad you weren't hurt either, McCullough. I never meant for anyone to come to harm." He swung his gaze toward Emma. "Honey, would you mind leaving Jake and me alone for a while? There's something we need to talk about privately. It won't take long."

A look of understanding passed between the couple and Emma nodded. "Don't be too long, Yancy.

You're still lookin' mighty pale and you need to rest.'' Smoothing his covers, she brushed his forehead with a kiss, silently reminding him that no matter what transpired, she loved him. Yancy smiled up at her and gave her fingers a gentle squeeze.

As soon as she closed the door behind her, Yancy's smile faded. "I suppose you know what I want to discuss with you, McCullough. You don't owe me any favors after what I've done to you these past months, but I hope you'll at least listen to what I have to say.''

"I wouldn't exactly say I don't owe you *any* favors, Parnell. Your warnin' did save Felicity's life and for that, I thank you.''

"You may want to hold back on thanking me,'' Yancy responded. "I'm probably hanging myself by telling you this, but I feel it's something you deserve to know. Before Croft shot me, he told me he was responsible for your father's death.''

Jake nodded. "I know. He bragged about it to me when he was holdin' a gun to Felicity's head.'' Yancy grimaced at the picture created by Jake's words. "I also know,'' Jake continued, "that you had no part in my pa's murder. Croft admitted that the killin' was his idea.''

"So you don't blame me?'' Yancy asked quietly.

"To tell you the truth, Parnell, so many things have happened so fast today that I haven't had a whole lot of time to think about where the blame lies. I guess you're partly responsible since it was your dirty plan to get my mine. But I owe you for today, so let's just call it square.''

Yancy stared at Jake in stunned surprise. He and McCullough had clashed from the first time they'd met and he'd been sure that Jake would have him charged as an accessory to Joe's murder. The fact that the man seemed to have no intention of doing so was almost incomprehensible.

His mouth dry as cotton, Yancy tried to reach the beer next to his bed, but it was just out of his reach.

Jake leaned over in his chair, picked up the glass, and handed it to the wounded man.

"Thanks." Yancy took a deep swallow and set the glass down. Meeting Jake's gaze, he said, "I'd like to repay you for the damage those accidents cost you. Not only because I owe it to you, but because I'm very fond of Felicity and I feel like I've betrayed her. I've often felt like her older brother, and, heaven knows, she needed one when she arrived in this godforsaken place."

Jake nodded his agreement, silently acknowledging his own part in making Felicity's life miserable when she first arrived in Silverton.

"So," Yancy continued, "in return for your goodwill, I'm going to deed the Dead Horse over to you. It probably doesn't seem like much of a gift, and I'll be the first to admit the Dead Horse, by itself, is almost worthless. But in one respect, it's worth a great deal. Unless Croft was being overzealous in describing his handiwork, it's going to take you months to dig out those caved-in tunnels."

"True enough," Jake confirmed. "We haven't finished shorin' up the left tunnel yet, let alone start diggin' out the right one."

"That's what makes the Dead Horse so valuable right now." Yancy smiled. "I'm sure Emma filled you in on the vein we found." Jake nodded, beginning to understand what Yancy was getting at. Acknowledging Jake's nod, Yancy continued, "Digging from inside the Dead Horse, you'll reach your vein a lot sooner. You were pretty close to finding it before Croft caved in the left tunnel."

"Are you sure about the silver bein' there?" Jake questioned. "Emma said Croft had a lot of experience, but did you get a second opinion?"

Yancy chuckled. "I may be a gambler by trade, McCullough, but I'm not fool enough to stake my fortune on Jed Croft's word. I brought in a top-notch surveyor and a mining engineer from Denver and paid them plenty to keep their mouths shut. They confirmed Croft's findings. The silver is there in your mine and the quickest way to it is through the Dead Horse. I hope that deeding the mine to you will make up for some of the harm I've done. Emma and I want to start a new life in New Orleans, but neither one of us would be happy if I didn't do something to make things right with you and Felicity.''

Jake regarded the gambler with an inscrutable expression. Yancy's nervousness increased as a new fear arose. Maybe McCullough had interpreted his offer as a bribe and was again considering turning him over to the sheriff. Yancy didn't think that anything could be proved against him, but a trial would force him to remain in Silverton, greatly hampering his and Emma's plans. He held his breath when Jake finally stood, and a profound sense of relief washed over him as the big miner held out his hand and grinned. Yancy took Jake's proffered hand firmly within his own.

''I accept your offer, Parnell,'' Jake said, ''and I thank you for it. And don't worry, I don't plan on pressin' charges.'' His grin widened and, with a sly wink, he added, ''Hell, if I turned you in now, Felicity would probably have me sleepin' with those damn chickens again!''

Chapter 24

Felicity finished the last of the breakfast dishes and threw the towel onto the counter with a weary grimace. In a gesture that had become almost habitual, she rubbed at the nagging ache in the small of her back. It was June now—eight months down and one more to go. The very thought of another whole month of lugging herself around in this condition made her groan. She looked down at her huge stomach with disbelief, wondering, as she always did, how anyone's body could expand so much.

Hearing the industrious clamor of hammers and saws, she waddled over to the front window and gazed out at her husband's new project. She smiled as she watched Jake hammering diligently, working alongside several carpenters brought in from Denver.

A new house, not just a bigger cabin, but a huge, two-story house was gradually taking shape in the clearing. She felt an overwhelming sense of pride as she surveyed the scene. At first, Jake had mistakenly assumed that she'd prefer living in Silverton, and although it would have meant a long, tedious trip to the mine every day, he had been determined to make the trek for her sake. It was only after weeks of discussion that she had finally persuaded him that she truly preferred the seclusion of their mountain home to the noisy confusion of Silverton.

She shook her head in wonder. What had happened to that cold, horribly rude miner she'd met on her first day in town? Now, that same man couldn't seem to do enough for her. Marriage and impending fatherhood had radically changed Jake McCullough, and as her body bloomed in the wake of his passion, so did her happiness blossom in the warmth of his love. She knew her comfort was one reason he had the carpenters working so frantically to complete the new house. Although the architect had been appalled, stating firmly that the task could never be completed in time, Jake had insisted that the house be finished by the time the baby was born. Knowing well her husband's stubbornness and dogged determination, she had no doubt the house would be ready.

As she continued to look out the window, she saw Jake walking toward the cabin, his hammer still in his hand. She smiled and waved before hurrying over to open the door. "Taking a break so soon?" she teased.

He grinned and tossed the hammer on the table, then pulled her as close as her huge girth would allow. "You looked so cute standin' there in the window, I thought I'd come in and see how you're doin'."

She grinned and playfully pushed him away. "I don't believe you for a minute, Jake McCullough! It would take something a lot more important than you thinking I'm cute to drag you away from that house!"

"Well, you're wrong," he stated. "I saw you standin' there, and couldn't resist comin' in to give you a kiss. Isn't that all right?"

"More than all right," she cooed in a sultry voice.

As he lowered his lips to hers, he growled, "And don't make none of them sexy sounds with that voice of yours. You're gonna drive me crazy, teasin' me when you know I can't touch you for months."

Felicity couldn't understand how Jake could possibly desire her when she was so fat and clumsy, but a thrill raced through her knowing that he did. As their slow, languorous kiss ended, she smiled up at him and said, "All right, I'll be good. Now, you better get back to work if you're going to get that house finished before your son makes his appearance."

"Actually," he confessed, "I can't work on it any more today. We're shippin' another load of silver out and I need to go up to the Silver Lady and oversee the loadin'. I wish you could ride with me, sweetheart. You wouldn't believe what they're takin' out of that mine every day. It's some sight."

"I wish I could see it too." She sighed. "But as big as you say this strike is, I'm sure there'll be plenty of time for me to visit after the baby's born." She shook her head. "I still can hardly believe how rich we are! It's so exciting, but it scares me too. I worry that we'll get greedy and forget what's really important in life. Promise me, Jake, that no matter how much money we have, we'll always stay just the way we are now. I want a simple, quiet life, living in our new home, raising our children, and loving each other."

He smiled tenderly and brushed his lips against her temple. "You don't ever need to worry about that changin', Felicity. I'd give up all the silver in the world if havin' it meant losin' you. You're the real treasure, baby. The money we get from the mine just lets me wrap my treasure up in prettier paper."

She sighed and laid her head on his shoulder. "Oh, Jake," she breathed, "I think you're just about the most romantic man in the whole world."

He chuckled. "I bet you didn't think that a year ago."

"No." She giggled. "But a lot of things have changed in that year."

Eyeing her bulging middle, he teased, "Yeah, they sure have!"

"Oh, you're terrible!" She laughed. "Get out of

here and go up to your mine before you embarrass me more than you already have. The things you say, Jake McCullough, I swear, you'd make the angels blush!''

''Oh, lady,'' he chortled, ''you just wait till you have this baby. I'm gonna throw you on that big bed and do a lot more than make you blush!''

''Right,'' she enjoined boldly, ''and before you know it, I'll look just like this again!''

''Yup,'' he agreed happily, ''and again, and again, and again. That's a big house I'm buildin' out there and I plan to fill it up with babies. And think how much fun we'll have fillin' it!''

At her shriek of laughter, he slammed his hat on his head and started toward the door. ''See you later, sweetheart,'' he called. At the threshold he suddenly stopped short and turned toward her again, a huge grin wreathing his face. ''Looks like I'm not goin' to the mine after all,'' he said, chuckling. At her look of confusion, he crooked a finger and said, ''Come here and see. We got company!''

She rushed to the door and her face lit up with a surprised, delighted smile as she saw Emma and Yancy getting out of a wagon. She was even more surprised when another man descended from the wagon, wearing a somber suit and carrying a Bible.

Seeing Felicity standing in the doorway, Emma lifted her skirts and ran to her friend, embracing her warmly. ''Gee, I've missed you, sweetie!'' Emma exclaimed. ''Just look at you, girl. Why, a body would think you was havin' twins!''

As Felicity rolled her eyes and groaned, Yancy joined them, along with the stranger who was obviously a preacher. ''Did you tell them yet, Em?'' he asked.

Emma smiled up at Yancy, her cheeks flushed with excitement and happiness. Still holding onto Felicity's hands, she gave them a quick squeeze. ''Oh, honey, it's so excitin'! Yancy and me are gettin' married!''

"Oh, Emma, I'm so happy for you!" Felicity cried. "When's the big day?"

Emma laughed delightedly and answered, "Why, honey, the big day is today!" At Felicity's look of astonishment, she laughed again and explained, "You see, honey, I decided that I just *had* to have you stand up for me—and seein' as how you couldn't come to us, we came to you."

"Oh, Emma!" she moaned. "I mean, it's wonderful, but I wasn't expecting . . . that is . . ."

"Now, don't you worry about a thing, sugar. I knew you weren't up to any fuss in your condition. The reason I didn't let you know in advance was because I didn't want you tirin' yourself out! You don't have to do a thing. I had the hotel fix us a regular feast and we've got it right here with us in the back of the wagon." With a broad gesture in the wagon's general direction, she pulled Felicity down the porch steps. "My dress is here too. We'll just have the men put the food in the oven to warm it while you and me go in your bedroom and get ourselves prettied up for the ceremony. You see—" She smiled widely. "—everythin's arranged. All we have to do is enjoy ourselves. Oh, by the way, this here is Reverend James. He's gonna say the words over Yancy and me."

Emma paused to take a breath and Felicity took quick advantage of the momentary silence to introduce Jake and herself to the smiling preacher.

Then, with her head still reeling from this unexpected turn of events, she allowed Emma to steer her back toward the cabin. "My, but your new house is comin' right along, ain't it?" Emma chattered. "Imagine, buildin' a palace like that way up in these mountains. You and Jake have caused quite a stir in Silverton, let me tell you." She paused a moment and yelled over her shoulder to where Yancy stood visiting with Jake by the wagon. "Yancy, bring my clothes in here, will you? Then you and Jake stick that food in the oven so it'll be ready after the ceremony." Rapping out her orders like a drillmaster, she continued on into the cabin and headed for the bedroom.

"It's hard for me to believe the way you've domesticated that independent gambler of yours," Felicity commented. She sat down on the edge of the bed and dubiously studied the pegs that held her clothes, wondering what on earth she was going to wear.

Emma quickly disrobed, tossing her dress across the bed. "It wasn't hard, honey." She smiled. "Whatever Yancy Parnell appears to be, he was raised a gentleman and he treats me like a lady." Felicity couldn't help but smile at the faraway look in Emma's eyes. Over the months, the brassy red had faded from her hair to be replaced by a natural, lustrous auburn color. Felicity thought Emma was far more attractive than the flamboyant Roxie had ever been.

Yancy tapped on the door with the toe of his boot and called, "If you ladies are still decent, I'll bring in these clothes."

"I'm not, but Felicity still is, so come on in," Emma responded.

Felicity grinned, surprised to discover that she felt no shock in Emma's allowing Yancy into the room when she was undressed. I've changed, she thought with amusement, really changed. All those rigid rules of proper conduct somehow seemed unimportant out here in the wilds. Westerners were more inclined to adapt society's long-held standards of appropriate behavior to suit their more relaxed and practical approach to life.

"Where do you want this stuff?" Yancy asked, peering around the stack of boxes he carried.

"Just set 'em on the bed, sugar, and we'll take care of the rest," Emma responded with a distracted wave of her hand. Yancy set his armload down and hurried out, closing the door behind him.

Felicity rose and walked over to where her meager

wardrobe hung. "I'm afraid I don't have anything
very appropriate for a wedding, Emma. I've let all
the pleats out of my skirts to get them to fit and
they're about as attractive as tents. Even the blouses
I made have gotten too small. I'm going to look terrible!"

"Never you mind, honey," Emma assured her.
"This ain't no fancy church wedding. Besides, I
brought you a couple of little things that will fancy
you up some." Picking up a small box from the bed,
Emma opened it and held up a delicate pink cro-
cheted collar. "Here, put this on over your blouse."

"Oh, Emma, it's lovely, but you shouldn't
have . . ."

"None of that now," Emma admonished. "I want
you to have it." Felicity eagerly removed her worn
dress as Emma retrieved a pink satin ribbon from
the package and held it up for her inspection. "For
your hair," she said with a wink.

After an hour of primping, the two young women
were satisfied they looked their best and left the
bedroom to seek out their men.

Yancy, Jake, and the preacher were sitting on the
porch, deep in conversation when the women approached.

"Well, what do you think?" Emma asked hopefully.

All three men stood up to admire the ladies in
their finery. Jake and Felicity exchanged an amused
glance as they noted Yancy's startled reaction to his
bride. Emma was stunning in her elegant wedding
gown. The cream-colored silk hugged her shapely
hips and was drawn up in the back into a small,
ruffled bustle. Its high, stand-up collar and the cuffs
on the long, snug sleeves were edged with delicate
blue lace that matched the color of her eyes.

When Yancy finally attempted to verbalize his
feelings, his voice was thick and rough. He took Emma's hand and stepped closer to her. "I'm the luckiest man on earth to have such a beautiful woman

consent to be my wife.'' Emma smiled at his compliment and a rosy blush painted her cheeks.

Reverend James cleared his throat. ''Where would you like the nuptials to be performed, sir?''

Yancy gave himself a mental shake and turned his attention to the preacher. ''Ah, well . . .'' He looked around and then said, ''How about if you just stand here on the porch and the rest of us step down in front of you?''

''I think that will do very nicely,'' replied the reverend with a smile. ''Shall we begin, then?''

Yancy looked at Emma and she nodded her approval. The couple took their places in front of the preacher with Jake and Felicity flanking them.

A cool mountain breeze lifted tendrils of Felicity's hair as the preacher began the ceremony. She lifted her eyes to find Jake staring at her and realized that he, too, was remembering their own wedding and the vows they'd made that day. Her heart swelled as Jake's unwavering gaze reaffirmed his love and his commitment to those promises.

A few minutes later, the simple ceremony was completed and Emma Roxanne Wilson was pronounced Mrs. Yancy Parnell. After much kissing, hugging, and back-slapping, the small party reentered the cabin. The women tied aprons over their dresses and headed for the kitchen, chatting happily as they set the food on the table.

''When are you and Yancy leaving for New Orleans, Emma?''

''We leave tomorrow,'' Emma answered.

Felicity threw her friend a stricken look. ''What? So soon?''

''We planned to be gone long before now, sweetie. The only thing that held us up this long was the saloon. It didn't sell as fast as we thought it would and we needed the money to buy a place in New Orleans.''

''I guess I just never wanted to think about your actually leaving here.'' Felicity sighed, then suddenly launched herself into Emma's arms. "Oh, Emma! Do you have to go? I'm going to miss you so much! Who am I going to talk to when you're gone?"

Emma's eyes grew moist despite her earlier resolve not to cry when she had to part from her friend. She gave Felicity a fierce hug, saying, "I know how you feel, 'cause I feel the same way. It's kinda funny, you and me. Who'd have ever thought we'd become friends, but look at us now. If anyone had told me, that day in Durango, that I'd become best friends with a little ex-nun from Philadelphia, and then get married to a handsome Southern gentleman, why, I'd have laughed them right off that train! But just look what happened. I've become respectable, and you . . . well, Felicity, you've become a woman." Emma chuckled. "Lord, but you were a prissy, straightlaced little thing, and just as ignorant about life as a babe. I'd never seen *anyone* blush as much as you did!"

Felicity smiled at Emma's recollections. "I guess we did make quite a pair, didn't we?" Tears welled up in both women's eyes as they again embraced.

Jake sat on the settee, watching the heartrending scene in the kitchen. Knowing the room was soon going to be awash with tears, he exclaimed loudly, "Dinner about ready, Felicity? I'm starvin' to death!"

"You're *always* starving to death," Felicity responded, "but, yes, the food is on the table."

As the five people enjoyed their small feast, the conversation turned to Yancy's plans. When Jake asked him what he was going to do in New Orleans, Yancy replied, "I've been setting some money aside, and with that and the proceeds from the Last Chance, I figure I'll have enough to buy a small place outside the city. I grew up around horses and I've always dreamed of starting a breeding farm. Thought I might grow a little sugarcane, too. Emma and I have decided we don't want to live in the city.

We both want a little place where we can raise horses and, hopefully, bring up a couple of kids.''

"Sounds good to me," Jake agreed. "Land's always a safe investment. Felicity and I plan on stashin' most of our silver profits away. Even the richest mine gets played out and I think it's smart to keep our eyes open for other opportunities.''

The conversation gradually turned from mining to politics, and Reverend James joined in, surprising them all. "Did you hear the council is talking about sending for Bat Masterson to clean things up in town? They hope he can do something about all the violence on Blair Street. Why, just last week alone, there were four shoot-outs. A terrible thing, just terrible!''

Yancy frowned. "I've heard talk about that, but I don't know if Masterson is the right man for the job. I'll admit he's been successful down in Trinidad, but I hear he's gambled himself into debt and out of friends. As partial as Bat is to cards, I doubt he'd do much about the saloons on Blair. Besides, the miners need someplace to blow off a little steam.''

Well aware that Yancy had owned the Last Chance, Reverend James shrugged and held his tongue. It was the man's wedding day and everyone was entitled to an opinion, even if it wasn't the right one.

Felicity was quick to fill in the awkward silence, asking hopefully, "Emma, are you sure you and Yancy couldn't delay your departure just one more month? I do so want you to be here when the baby comes.''

"I wish we could, Felicity." Emma sighed remorsefully. "But we've waited too long as it is. Yancy's lawyer in New Orleans has several properties that he wants us to look at before someone else buys them.''

"I understand," said Felicity forlornly. "I just hate to see you leave. I miss you both already.''

Jake reached over and laid his hand on hers. "You

and Emma can write each other, and maybe we can go for a visit when the baby is old enough to travel."

"Oh, yes!" Emma beamed. "That's a wonderful idea! You can see our new house, I can spoil that baby and, Felicity, you and I can spend some of Jake's money at those wonderful New Orleans shops!"

Felicity's face lit up with anticipation. "Oh, Jake, could we really?"

"The trip? Yes. The spendin' spree, we'll discuss later." Everyone laughed as Felicity's eyes narrowed.

"It would be so much fun, Jake!" Felicity pleaded. "Except for my trip from Philadelphia, I've never really traveled anywhere. And I was so nervous on the trip out here that even when the train did make a stopover, I never left the depot. The only sights I saw were through the train windows."

"Well, you're in for a treat when you visit New Orleans," Yancy assured her. "It's the most unique city in the country. It's part French, part Spanish, and part American, all rolled into one. It has a little something to please even the most jaded of travelers."

The conversation rolled along from one topic to another until finally the men returned to the porch for a smoke while the women cleared the dishes away. It was late afternoon when Yancy and Emma finally rose to leave.

After a long, tearful farewell, Yancy was finally forced to drag Emma from Felicity's embrace and propel her toward the wagon. Jake stood on the porch with his arm around Felicity's shoulders as they both waved at their departing friends. When the wagon was finally out of sight, he looked at his wife's exhausted face, bent down, and, with a grunt, picked her up.

"Jake," she protested, "put me down! I'm so big and heavy, you shouldn't try to carry me. You'll hurt your back!"

Ignoring her protest, he strode purposefully into the cabin. ''You're as pale as milk, baby. I'm afraid you did too much today and I'm personally gonna put you to bed.''

Boozer pranced up from out of nowhere, following them into the house. ''Now where do you suppose he's been all day?'' Felicity asked as Jake set her gently on the bed.

He smiled down at the faithful dog. ''I think maybe he's found a lady friend. Pete found a half-starved mutt on his last foray into Silverton to see the Widow Harris. The bighearted fool took the scroungy thing home, fed it, and even gave it a bath. Turns out the dog's female and, well, need I say more?''

She giggled. ''Cleaned up and filled out pretty good, did she?''

''Uh huh, turned out to be a real looker.'' Bending down and spreading his big hand over the swell of Felicity's stomach, he whispered mischievously, ''And if Boozer and his lady are anythin' like us, I bet there'll be some puppies around here pretty soon.'' Noting her reaction, he burst into a loud guffaw. ''God, but I love the way you blush!''

Chapter 25

Everything is just beautiful, thought Felicity proudly as she stood gazing about her new bedroom. The big bed was positioned against the middle of one wall with a luxurious new quilt lying over the top of it. Flanking each side of the bed were new Eastlake bedside tables in rich, burnished walnut. On another wall, between two large windows, were matching armoires, and next to the door sat a small bureau. The new furniture had been a surprise for her birthday and had just arrived from Denver two days before.

The windows were still bare of curtains and there was no rug on the floor, but Jake had promised that as soon as she was up to traveling, they'd take the train to Denver and order all that was needed to make their new home comfortable.

The baby's room was not yet finished, but it wouldn't be needed for the first few months anyway. Jake had spent many evenings making an intricately carved cradle which now stood at the foot of their bed and would remain there until the child needed more space. By that time, Felicity hoped to have his room finished and ready for him.

A door slammed downstairs and she walked into the hall to find Jake already halfway up the staircase. "How are you feelin', sweetheart?"

She smiled down at her husband. He had shed

his shirt and wore only his dusty Levi's and his boots. His chest was streaked with dirt and sweat and his hair hung damply over his forehead. Nevertheless she still thought he was the most handsome man she'd ever seen. "I'm fine, Jake. In fact, I feel better today than I have for weeks."

"Oh," he said, his voice laced with disappointment. "Guess today won't be the day then, huh?"

She chuckled and shrugged her shoulders. "It doesn't look like it."

He climbed the rest of the way up the stairs, took her arm, and steadied her as they descended. "It's probably just as well that it won't be today," he commented. "I need to finish shinglin' the roof."

They walked through the sparsely furnished house and into the kitchen just as the back door opened, admitting a freckle-faced, rosy-cheeked girl carrying a basket of eggs.

" 'Morning, Miss Felicity, Mr. Jake. You know, Mr. Jake, you were right about those hens. They're just plain mean!" The russet-haired girl set her basket on the counter and held out a bleeding hand for his inspection.

Jake shook his head. "The only person those hens ever took to was Felicity, so don't take it personal, Ellen."

Felicity watched the girl fondly and wondered what she ever would have done this past month without her. Ellen had unexpectedly appeared at the Silver Lady at the beginning of July, taking her brother, Corny, completely by surprise. While Corny was delighted to see her, he'd been saddened to hear that their father had died, leaving his sixteen-year-old sister alone in England. The enterprising girl had scraped together a little money by selling their small cottage, and had taken a ship for America to join her brother. It had been a long and arduous journey, but she'd finally found Corny. Because he lived with the other miners in the line shack, Corny didn't have the slightest notion of what he was going to do with the young girl and had asked for Jake's advice.

Jake had immediately taken Ellen home. Felicity had kissed and hugged him to the point of embarrassment, so delighted was she to have another woman in the house. In no time at all, she and Ellen were fast friends and Ellen was more than happy to do the chores Felicity could no longer manage.

"Well," sighed Jake. "I guess I better get back to work on that roof. I'll see you ladies later." He stood up and gave Felicity a quick kiss before walking out the back door.

"You're so lucky to have a big, handsome man like that love you so much," Ellen said dreamily.

Felicity grinned. "Yes, I'm a very lucky woman," she agreed, "but remind me to tell you someday about how Jake and I first met."

Ellen laughed. "I've heard bits and pieces from Corny, but I'd love to hear your version of the story."

"It's quite a tale." Felicity grinned.

It was mid-afternoon when Felicity was awakened from her nap by a sharp, cramping pain. Despite Jake's constant hammering on the roof, she'd fallen asleep, but now, as the pain eased, she realized that she didn't feel nearly as well as she had that morning. Thinking that she might feel better if she got up, she struggled to her feet. As she slowly pushed herself off the edge of the bed, a gush of liquid flooded down her legs. For a moment she just stood staring at the floor in stunned surprise, but finally realized her time had come. Carefully, she walked into the hall and called down the stairs to Ellen.

Although Felicity's voice was calm, Ellen recognized the slight tone of urgency. She hurried up the stairs to find Felicity leaning weakly against the wall. Seeing her soaked dress, the girl immediately sized up the situation, and, wrapping an arm about Felicity's waist, she urged her back into the bedroom

and helped her into a chair. "I'll go get Mr. Jake,"
she said, giving Felicity's arm a reassuring pat.

She turned to leave, but was brought up short when
Felicity reached out and grabbed her skirt. "No, wait.
Help me get undressed and let's clean this mess up
first. As nervous as Jake has been, he'll probably faint
dead away if he sees me like this. I've only had one
pain, so I'm sure we have plenty of time."

A few moments later, Ellen had Felicity in a fresh
nightgown and back in bed. She cleaned up the floor,
rising from her knees just as Felicity gasped with the
force of another contraction. "Now can I get Mr.
Jake?" Ellen asked anxiously. Felicity nodded her head
and the young girl shot out of the room.

Ellen found him bent over a bucket of water,
washing his face. "Mr. Jake!" she cried. "It's time!
You'd better come now!"

He grabbed his shirt and took off at a run, leaving
Ellen far behind as he raced toward the house. He
yanked the back door open, bellowing Felicity's
name, and by the time Ellen reached the kitchen, he
was already pounding up the stairs three at a time.

Ellen entered the master bedroom to find the big
miner standing beside the bed, staring anxiously at
his wife. "Okay, Felicity," he gasped, trying hard
to keep the panic out of his voice, "just be calm,
sweetheart. I'll send somebody for Doc Brown right
away. Maybe I should get Corny too, just in case we
run out of time. Yeah, that's a great idea. I'll send
somebody to get both of them. There's no need to
panic, Felicity. I've got everythin' under control."

He was halfway to the door when Felicity calmly
said, "Jake, come here, please."

His look of desperation as he whirled around was
so comical that Felicity started to laugh.

Turning toward Ellen, who was also smiling
broadly, he barked, "Jesus, girl, don't just stand
there! Do somethin' to help her. She's hysterical
from the pain!"

Ellen was immediately contrite. "Is there any-

thing I can do for you, ma'am?'' she asked solicitously.

Felicity sobered and threw Jake a quelling look.
''No, honey, I'm fine,'' she assured her. ''Now,
Jake, I don't want you bothering Corny. There's no
need to drag him down here. But will you please go
fetch Dr. Brown right now?''

He shook his head adamantly. ''I'm not leavin'
you at a time like this. I'll send one of the workmen
for him.''

Felicity knew she *would* be hysterical if her husband continued to hover over her like a nervous cat.
''Jake, I want *you* to go. You'll make better time and
you can't do anything here anyway. Ellen will stay
with me and I'll be fine. Just go. Please!''

As much as he hated to admit it, he knew Felicity
was right. ''Okay, I'll go, but I'm still sendin' one
of the carpenters up to the mine for Corny. That
way, if somethin' happens before I get back, at least
someone will be here who knows what to do.''

''But, Mr. Jake, Corny doesn't know anything
about babies,'' Ellen protested. Seeing Felicity's
quick negative gesture, the girl winced, wishing she
could call the words back.

''Well, he better damn well hope I get back here
in time, then!'' Jake shouted.

Felicity's hands flew to her stomach as another
contraction speared through her. ''Damn it, Jake!
Quit yelling and get . . . going!'' This last was uttered through gritted teeth. White-faced and completely nonplussed by Felicity's curse, he nodded
and bolted out of the room, his heavy boots barely
hitting the stairs.

He made the trip into Silverton in record time.
Jake even saddled the doctor's horse while the dig-
nified gentleman gathered up his medical supplies
and bag. As they tore off, hell-bent, down the street,
Dr. Brown shook his head and muttered, ''God save
me from first-time fathers . . .''

Despite Felicity's protests, Jake had sent one of

the carpenters to the mine to fetch Corny. The Englishman now sat in the corner of the bedroom perspiring more heavily than the woman in the bed. Felicity's pains were coming in such rapid succession that even she was beginning to worry that Corny would have to deliver her baby.

When Jake finally burst into the bedroom dragging a disheveled and winded Dr. Brown behind him, three very relieved faces turned to greet them. Felicity, in the grip of a contraction, said nothing as the doctor tried to hustle the two men out of the room. Corny was more than happy to leave, but Jake stubbornly seated himself on a chair next to the bed and refused to budge.

"All right, then, young man, you can stay," the doctor relented, "but don't you go fainting on me, because I'm going to have my hands full here." Jake glowered at this insult to his masculinity, but the doctor ignored him and began giving Ellen instructions on how she could assist him.

An hour later, Jake stood near Felicity's head as she gripped his hand and struggled mightily to bring their child into the world. "Come on, now, Mrs. McCullough," the doctor encouraged, "just one more good push. Ah, here we come. Good Lord, look at the head of hair on this child!"

Felicity sank back in exhaustion as the baby erupted in a lusty wail. "Congratulations, Jake." The doctor smiled. "You have a big, strapping son!"

Jake looked over at Felicity, grinning hugely. "Well, Doc, I ain't surprised. This little lady here has been promisin' me a son for months and I never doubted her for a minute!"

Kneeling down next to the bed, Jake placed a light kiss on Felicity's flushed cheek and whispered, "Thank you, sweetheart. You've made me happier than you could ever know."

It was nearly midnight and the house was quiet. Jake and Felicity were cuddled intimately in their big bed as she nursed their baby. Long moments passed in serene silence until finally, Felicity said quietly, "I know we've never really discussed names, but I thought it would be nice to name him after your father."

A slow smile spread across Jake's tired features. "I think Pa would have liked that, darlin'. We'll call him Joseph McCullough."

"Joseph *Jacob* McCullough," she corrected.

"Joseph Jacob McCullough." He tested the sound of it. "I like it." With deep pride in his voice, he continued, "Someday, he'll walk down the street and people will say, "That's J. J. McCullough, the silver king." He smiled and nodded firmly. "Yup, J. J. McCullough. It's a fine name, Felicity."

Just then, J. J. McCullough opened his eyes and stared solemnly at his father. "He's gonna have your eyes," Jake predicted. "They're kind of blue right now, but I can see some green in them. I'm glad, Felicity. I've always loved your eyes." He leaned over and touched his lips to hers, then placed a soft kiss on his son's head. "Did I thank you for the son, Mrs. McCullough?" he whispered. At her slight nod, he smiled and said, "Right now, I must be the proudest man alive."

Transferring the baby to her other breast, she chuckled. "J.J. may have my eyes, but he's definitely got your appetite." She guided the small, greedy mouth to her nipple as Jake watched in fascinated awe.

"Sweetheart?" he murmured.

"Hmmm?" Her emerald gaze lifted from the baby to her husband and her heart caught in her throat at the love she saw revealed in his eyes.

A tiny glimmer of moisture clouded his vision as Jake's gaze encompassed his family. Bending close to his wife's ear, he breathed, "I love you, Felicity McCullough. No matter how much treasure we get out of that mine, I'll never be richer than I am tonight."

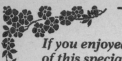

*If you enjoyed this book, take advantage
of this special offer. Subscribe now and . . .*

GET A *FREE*
HISTORICAL ROMANCE
——— NO OBLIGATION(a $3.95 value) ———

Each month the editors of True Value will select the four best historical romance novels from America's leading publishers. Preview them in your home Free for 10 days. And we'll send you a FREE book as our introductory gift. No obligation. If for any reason you decide not to keep them, just return them and owe nothing. But if you like them you'll pay *just* $3.50 each and save at least $.45 each off the cover price. (Your savings are a minimum of $1.80 a month.) There is no shipping and handling or other hidden charges. There are no minimum number of books to buy and you may cancel at any time.

send in the coupon below